It Happened in Minnesota

Tony Bridwell

Singing River Publications
Ely, MN

Published by:
Singing River Publications, Inc.
P. O. Box 72
Ely, MN, 55731 USA
www.singingriverpublications.com

Printed and bound in Canada

Permissions:

"Why is a Ranger" by Finny Lager originally printed in *Happy Depression On The Iron Range*, by H. E. Lager, D.D.S. Virginia, MN: Range Printing Company, 1979 and reprinted by permission of the author's son, J. Victor Lager, Virginia, Minnesota.

Obituary of Col. William Colvill originally printed in the *Pioneer Press* June 14, 1905, and reprinted by permission of the *Pioneer Press*, St. Paul, Minnesota.

Cover photograph, *Indian in a canoe, Pelican Lake*, reprinted by permission of *Minnesota Historical Society*, St. Paul, Minnesota

ISBN: 0-9759953-0-8

1. Minnesota History; 2. Historical Fiction; 3. Finnish Immigration;
4. Lumbering; 5. Iron Mining; 6. Fur Trade Era

TABLE OF CONTENTS

- INTRODUCTION -

It has been said that the history of Minnesota could only have happened in Minnesota—that is, the mix of resources and the way people have used them could not have occurred anywhere else but in America's thirty-second state.

Nature has been exceptionally generous to Minnesota. Its heritage of lakes and waterways, rolling plains and fertile soil, vast reaches of forest and bountiful mineral deposits extends back to cataclysmic upheavals at the dawn of creation. And as billions of years are measured, it was only yesterday that the bedrock upon which modern Minnesota stands was further reshaped by the grinding of gigantic masses of glacial ice.

The human story of the state began somewhere around 20,000 years ago. Big game hunters, the first arrivals, were followed by untold successions of primitives, who adapted to, rather than altered their wilderness environment. Prehistoric burial mounds and other artifacts depict peoples who survived through scores of generations by hunting, fishing and harvesting wild rice.

Schoolbook history about the coming of the Pilgrims clouds the fact that European explorers were probing North American wilderness long before the landing of the *Mayflower* in 1620. More than a century earlier Ponce de Leon had explored the coast of Florida, while to the north, a few years later, Jacques Cartier sailed into the St. Lawrence River. Others followed, and what is now Quebec was a thriving center of trade more than a decade before the landing at Plymouth Rock. From that post, the St. Lawrence became a gateway to a new French Empire as explorers, missionaries and fur traders ranged as far west as Wisconsin and the Mississippi Valley.

For two centuries leading up to the early 1800s, the region was a theater for fiercely contested claims upon it by France, Spain and England. The Old World's drive for profits from the fur trade was sharp and bitter. It was only after years of border dispute that the territory that was to include the future state of Minnesota emerged as an entity under United States control.

In years to follow, as Minnesota achieved territorial status and then Statehood, it was to become a beacon of hope for masses of immigrants, who braved harsh challenges of the unknown with dreams of a life better than they had known.

Also attracted were a new crop of entrepreneurs, their coffers bulging from Civil War profits, eager to exploit natural resources of the young state. For these moguls of capital, Minnesota was to become an arena where competitive enterprise vital to the growth of the nation went hand-in-hand with reckless despoilment of natural resources.

As observed by geologist J. Merle Harris, "It was as though the forces of nature had said to Man: Long ages have been spent investing in your inheritance. It is given to you to use as you will—wisely or foolishly. Scatter your cities, farms and mines along the rivers, on the plains, among the hills. You are ready now to make history."

The challenge has been to provide an appealing but bona fide account about that history and its forebears—the men and women who have carved out of wilderness a place like none other in the American experience. It simply isn't possible to spend three years digging into the facts of such a history without piling up an enormous debt of gratitude to so many others who have provided the spadework. Those to whom I owe the most are listed in the bibliographical supplement that follows this tale. Among them, however, I must single out William Watts Folwell and Theodore C. Blegen, whose authoritative histories of Minnesota supply much of the factual framework for this novel.

Special tribute is due the Minnesota Historical Society in St. Paul and to the Iron Range Resource Center near Chisholm, whose staffs and facilities were unendingly helpful. My thanks also to the public libraries in Rochester, Duluth and Virginia, whose people so graciously made available their resources. And I would be remiss not to mention Sara Samuelson, who so kindly allowed me to browse among the memorabilia tucked away in her library at Buhl, Minnesota.

It is a pleasure also to tip my hat to good friends Elizabeth Ritman, David Leonard, Sam Saran and Dan Wefler, whose many thoughtful suggestions helped bring a sense of order to the hodge-podge of my first draft. Thanks also to Richard Ranta, Iron Ranger turned academic dean, who during moonlit quests for the elusive walleye taught me much about the lore and ways of growing up on Lake Vermilion.

I offer a standing vote of appreciation to the publishing and production team under whose guiding hands 350 pages of raw copy were turned into the book you read today. To Christine Moroni of Singing River Publications, to editor *extraordinaire* Betty Vos, to Chuck Morello and the layout and production management team of IRIS Enterprises go my heartfelt thanks. Like alchemists of old they have toiled to turn base metal into something finer. My thanks also to marketing director Barb Dimich.

I received a great deal of generous help from friends and former colleagues at Mayo Medical Center. The design of the book jacket is the work of Carol Purcell of that Center's Publishing Services. I am grateful to Carol and her colleague Jon Bedsted for the time and many suggestions they have so kindly contributed to this effort.

Such success as may attend this first effort at a novel will be largely because of the places and people mentioned above.

Should there be errors or other shortcomings, only I am at fault.

Finally, I dedicate this book to my wife and best friend Lorraine, to whom I owe more than I can say.

Tony Bridwell
Rochester, Minnesota
April, 2005

- HISTORICAL NOTES -

This novel about America's North Star State conforms to historical fact as closely as I could determine. Most of its central figures lived and were leaders in their time. However, in weaving a narrative path through centuries of discovery, conflict and settlement, I have drawn upon imaginary recollections of fictional people whose make-believe diaries and memoirs will, I hope, bring fresh life to events and persons long gone. Where fictitious characters meet and interact with real ones, every effort has been made to create places, events and dialogue that are representative of what is known to have happened. Similarly, in the few instances where I have graced historical characters with thoughts or words, such detail rests on the records that have come down to us regarding their motivations and behavior.

For example, it is a fact that Zebulon Pike in 1805 led a U.S. Army expedition up the Mississippi River to help lay claim to the new American acquisitions. The scenario of Pike's arriving at a fur post flying the Union Jack and insisting that it be taken down was doubtless repeated many times over, and it is just as likely that the British flag was often run back up the pole after Pike and his troops had departed. Clearly Pike never stopped at the fictional fur post described in Chapter 24, nor did he have any such interaction with its fictional supervisor Louis St. Onge; but the incident thus described is offered as true in general about the events of that era.

End notes are given for chapters that draw on specific

historical sources beyond the work of Folwell and Blegen, and a more complete bibliography organized by topic is provided for readers interested in pursuing further study.

Here is a list of characters, both real and imaginary, to be met in pages to follow:

Minnesota Woman's skeleton was uncovered in 1931. As determined by state geologist Albert Jenks, her remains are perhaps the oldest ever discovered in North America. The fictional account of her fate is told to help depict the way of early Minnesota inhabitants for whom no written record exists. Similarly, the legend of Little Thunder's last charge as related by the fictional Gideon Thurlowe has been created as a possible explanation of what became of the Woodland Indian culture.

Pierre Radisson, Sieur de Groseilliers, Father Louis Hennepin and Sieur du Luth were early explorers of what was to become Minnesota. Much that we know of Sioux and Chippewa ways in the 17th century comes from their recorded observations.

Father Jean de Laittre is a fictional character whose journal reflects the travails of Jesuit missionaries in their zeal to carry the word of the Lord into the wilderness west of the Great Lakes.

The Battle of Sandy Lake was fought around 1768. Its narration by the fictional Lt. Byron Leslie is pieced together from Sioux and Chippewa oral history.

Col. Josiah Snelling was the builder of the fort named in his honor. Lawrence Talliaferro was for many years the Indian agent at that fort. Col. Zachary Taylor, later to be elected America's twelfth president, commanded Fort Snelling in 1828.

Henry Hastings Sibley, his brother-in-law Franklin Steele and Alexander Ramsey were 19th century contemporaries whose leadership was critical during the years of Minnesota's transition from wilderness outpost to statehood.

Joe Rolette of Pembina was a colorful fur trader, ox-cart trailblazer and Territorial politician whose herein-described shenanigans are said to have kept St. Paul as the state capital. James McGill, his fictional contemporary, was created to describe ox-cart days and events at the Old Crossing Treaty.

Fictional, too, is Kilbourne St. Onge, whose narratives are introduced to describe the era when trade in furs was Minnesota's first great industry.

Charles E. Flandrau was a justice of the state supreme court who, as a volunteer, led the defense against the Sioux attack on New Ulm. His account of that battle is excerpted from his *History of Minnesota.*

Col. William Colvill and other commanding officers cited in the telling of First Minnesota's actions during the Civil War were real people. Sgt. Charles Porter Weldon was not. But the First's wartime experiences described in his diary are based on documented history of that regiment and a personal statement by Colonel Colvill.

Ignatius Donnelly, author, orator and populist, was at once "The Stormy Petrel of Minnesota Politics" and champion of the rights of farmers and common folk.

Norwegian-born Knute Nelson was successively a soldier in the Civil War, lawyer, Congressman, Governor and five times U.S. Senator from Minnesota. The account of his rejection of Jim Hill's recommendation for State Commissioner of Railroads is based on fact.

James J. Hill was a railroad builder with uncommon vision of the future place of transportation in the economic life of the nation. Called "The Empire Builder" because of the importance of his railroads in the settlement and growth of the Northwest, he was likely America's most able railroad executive. His story as told by the fictional Toby Christianson is a true-to-life account of Hill's career and achievements.

With credit to sources cited elsewhere, the telling of the Great Hinckley Fire is accurate. Those named for heroic response in the face of flaming peril were real people.

With respect to the chapters on the discovery and development of Minnesota's iron ranges: George Stuntz, George Stone, Charlemagne Tower, Henry Oliver, the Merritt Brothers, Frank Hibbing, Archic Chisholm, Edmund Longyear, Cuyler Adams, the Rev. Frederick Gates, and tycoons like John D.

Rockefeller and Andrew Carnegie all existed and were part of the emerging saga of the Vermilion, Mesabi and Cuyuna Ranges. However, Henry Eschweiler and Pete Trobaugh, whose "recollections" recreate this epical phase of Minnesota history, are fictitious.

So too, is Anders Korvala, the "Black Finn," whose memoirs depict the harsh lives and strife of early 20th century iron miners. However, Elizabeth Gurley Flynn, the radical unionist, was a real person, as were most of the other protagonists cited in this account of labor-management struggles on the Iron Range.

Should there be a doubt, there is neither a Chippewa Junior College nor a Harwell College. Nor do any of the people mentioned in connection with these fictional places exist.

‡‡ ‡‡ ‡‡ ‡‡ ‡‡

Jim Makki, whose research notes and classroom lectures help piece together a history wrought over vast sections of time, is of course fictional. Sadly, so too are all members of his family as depicted through five generations—sadly, because I have grown fond of them. There is, however, a tiny slice of paradise on Lake Vermilion known as Forgy's Point. We miss it greatly.

- 1 -

A CALL FROM HARWELL COLLEGE

Spring, 1972

Only someone who has worn the patched-at-the-elbows jacket of an underpaid junior college instructor can appreciate my excitement over a surprise phone call that afternoon in early May.

"Hello," came a cultivated, slightly New England way of speaking. "This is Judson Leonard."

I almost gasped. Judson Leonard! Quintessential scholar ... author of *The Triumph of Federalism* ... winner of a Pulitzer Prize. Outside it was overcast and drab. But here in the cluttered cubicle that passed for my office, it was like the sun had broken through.

Here I was at age 28, an untenured member of the history department at a two-year college in Northern Minnesota. And calling me was the celebrated scholar and history chairman at patrician Harwell College. Even on the phone I could hardly keep from tugging at my forelock.

With its strong faculty, stiff entrance requirements and picture book campus, Harwell stands in the front rank of America's private liberal arts colleges. To even mention it in the same sentence as Chippewa Junior College, where I toiled, would be like hitching up a Derby winner to Old Dobbin.

Professor Leonard told me he had come across a monograph I had written my first summer at Chippewa and almost forgotten. It was a light-hearted account of pioneering days in Northern Minnesota. Our local newspaper had run it as a Fourth of July supplement. Its breezy presentation of somewhat scholarly matters had apparently caught the attention of my caller.

"Doctor Makki," he asked, "would you be able to squeeze in a visit to us sometime in the next month? We have an idea I think might interest you."

"Well, of course," I replied, trying to sound cool and controlled. "Just let me check my calendar."

Leonard probably knew my schedule wasn't all that backed up. But he was tactful enough to suggest several dates he hoped might work out.

So it was, a few days later, that driving toward Minnesota's southeast corner I gaped at magnificent bluffs towering above the Mississippi River. Near Lake City I turned inland and up a long curving rise overlooking mist-shrouded Lake Pepin.

In order to look the place over, I had started out long hours before dawn. The sun was rising east of the river just as I tooled my vintage Ford pickup onto the Harwell campus. I took it as a hopeful omen.

After an hour or so poking around Gothic halls of stone, I walked into Professor Leonard's office exactly on time. His secretary smiled a friendly hello and promptly led me into an oak-paneled study where the great man sat over coffee chatting with an associate.

A tall, silver-haired man with a floppy bow tie and the slight stoop of an academic, Judson Leonard rose with a smile of welcome. His shorter, mildly rumpled colleague turned out to be Walton Alexander, whose excellent history of 17th century Northwest exploration I had almost memorized as an undergraduate.

Sensing my nervousness, Leonard quickly put me at ease.

"Jim, if I may call you that, I'd be pleased if you'd call me Jud. As for Walt, he's here for reasons of parental pride. He's the one who showed me your work on North Country pioneering."

Pausing only to let me nod to his colleague, Leonard got down to business. "You're from Minnesota?" he asked.

"Yes Sir, born and raised an Iron Ranger."

"And you took your doctorate at the University in Duluth?"

I nodded, unsure whether I was being slighted. His next remark assured me I was not.

"You had a great teacher there in Thor Lund."

"He was my advisor."

"You were lucky. Thor is probably the best man around in immigration."

"That was my field."

"I'm delighted to hear it. Walt, why don't you tell this young man what we have in mind?"

Alexander turned to me with an easy smile. "Jim, I expect you'll agree that the History of Minnesota is pretty well documented. Following after giants like Folwell and Blegan there isn't much more to do in that direction."

"Not to mention your own work on the explorers," I couldn't resist. "It was like a bible for me in college."

He grinned. "Some might take exception. But thanks anyway."

Walt took time to sip his coffee. "By its nature the stuff of history is detail. But the recital of facts so exciting to the scholar can be sheer drudgery for the student."

"Exactly," I agreed. "That's the bane of our calling."

Walt nodded. "Now here in Minnesota, we've got a great story to tell. But it gets bogged down in a mire of boundary lines, treaties, dates, legislative acts and the like. In scrabbling around the archives we tend to forget it's not documents but people that make history."

"And that," Jud broke in, "is what's so refreshing about your monograph. It relates solid history through the actions of people and it was fun to read."

Pushing himself up, Jud apologized for butting in. "I'm going to have to leave you in Walt's good hands for a while. But before I go I want to emphasize what he's saying. Because of the talent and enormous energy of scholars like William Watts Folwell, Minnesota history rests on a solid base of fact. The problem is that even the most readable, like Ted Blegan, dug so hard for evidence, they got bogged. As you pointed out, I expect it's a fault of our calling." He paused. "Go on with your story, Walt. I'll see you at lunch." With that and a cheery wave he was out the door.

"Where was I?" Walt asked.

"Talking about my article," I prompted, hoping to move things along. So far lunch was the only offer I'd had.

"Ah yes," he resumed. "Bear with me, I'm almost done. The point is we're a one-of-a-kind state with a story that ought to sparkle. Instead it's told mainly in dry texts overloaded with footnotes. What's worse, except for a too brief exposure in the primary grades it's pretty well overlooked by our school systems."

He paused. "Wouldn't surprise me if tomorrow's kids grow up thinking Minnesota was discovered by Paul Bunyan."

"Or maybe Bronko Nagurski." I grinned.

Walt shook his head. "Kind of sad, isn't it? Jud and I stew about our kids growing up without a sense of their Minnesota heritage. But we didn't know what to do about it till I stumbled on your monograph."

I gripped the arms of my chair. Now we were getting to it. "It struck a tone," Walt continued, " a tone we think might be carried over into a survey course. It can't be a required subject. But if it can be made interesting the word will get around in a hurry."

I hesitated. Maybe we wouldn't be going to lunch after all. "I wouldn't want to come here just to run a course on Minnesota anecdotes."

Walt took this in stride. "If we thought that, Jim, we

wouldn't want you. We're simply hoping to put a focus on human beings and their doings rather than on lifeless documents, treaty boundaries and the like."

He paused and looked at me with a quizzical glance. "You gotta admit it could be a hell of a story."

And an even better cast, I was thinking. Sioux and Chippewa warriors, French trailblazers, missionaries, fur traders and voyageurs, immigrants who broke the rich prairie crust, lumberjacks, iron miners and exploiters. Some had come to settle the land, others to plunder it.

"Amen to that," I nodded. "But there's a problem at the start."

"You mean that couple billion years before the first humans showed up?"

"It's time so immense I wish we could just leave it to the rock hounds. But it's too essential to ignore."

"You can't get around it," Walt agreed. "Take away what Nature gave us over all those eons and the record of what humans did here would be entirely different. The trick is to make that point without getting trapped in a geological maze."

"Even after humans arrived it's a pretty blank slate," I said. "All we have till the Europeans got here are artifacts, legends and a patchwork of guesses."

"Maybe the place to start is up in Otter Tail County," Walt suggested. "That's where they found a skeleton of a young girl about ten feet down in the silt of a glacial lake."

"I'd forgotten that. But you're right—that shows there've been people here since the end of the Ice Age."

Walt smiled. "It's a fascinating story no matter where you start." He paused. "Are you interested?"

I stared at the floor. This was the kind of blood, sweat and tears history I ached to teach. Still, I didn't want to look too eager.

"Well, I'm flattered and excited. But I have to ask, where does this lead?"

"Jud will get down to specifics at lunch. But I can tell

you we want to add this course as a regular elective. We even hope it might serve as a model for other schools. After we get that established there'll be other teaching assignments probably taking advantage of your work in immigration."

Walt shrugged. "Who knows, maybe there'll even be a book by the newest member of our history department."

A few minutes later we adjourned to the faculty club. And it was there, over a Rueben sandwich, that Judson Leonard made me an offer I accepted on the spot.

Even while driving back the next morning, I was half afraid I'd wake up and find this was a dream. Out of the blue had come an appointment at a distinguished college to do the kind of teaching I always longed for. Starting in September, I would be a lecturer in history at almost twice my present salary.

The timing was perfect. I'd be able to wrap up my spring quarter at Chippewa while at the same time getting to work on my new course at Harwell.

It was going to be an interesting summer.

- 2 -

ABOUT GLACIERS AND HUMANS

Back at Chippewa Junior College, Dean Paul Bullard was not known for cheery reception of unwelcome news. Accordingly his warm response to word of my impending departure was an agreeable surprise.

"No question, this is a grand opportunity to do something important and I expect you'll do very well."

Bolstered by his encouragement, I confessed to being in a bind about how to begin. "Prehistoric times aren't exactly my long suit."

Bullard considered this and said, "You should talk to old Ernie Van Velsor. Even in his 80s he still spends his summers in the field rooting about for artifacts."

Ernest Van Velsor, Professor of Earth Sciences *emeritus*, was the grand old man of Chippewa Junior College. When I tracked him down the next afternoon in the stacks of the library, he greeted me with a twinkle in his eye. "What's this I hear about you jumping ship?"

When I told him my problem, he suggested we walk over to his bungalow, a block off campus. "At my age, it helps to prime the old brain cells with something liquid."

While Ernie fussed with drinks, I looked around his den. Like the house, it was small and cozy. Books were everywhere, crammed into shelves and spilling over an old-fashioned library table onto the floor, where a few with bookmarks were piled up by his chair. Elsewhere scattered about the room were samples of his calling—spear points, stone cooking vessels and the like.

Handing me a scotch and water, Ernie pointed to a marble-like cylinder about six inches high, holding down a stack of old journals.

"Know what that is?"

"Beats me—some kind of projectile maybe?"

Ernie grinned. "I never thought of it that way. Actually it's a section of petrified mammoth dung, probably a million years old."

"That," he said after a sip of his sherry, "may seem ancient. But the fact is Minnesota's story goes back way before that mastodon paused to placate his bowels. For your purpose I think it should be enough to make the point that Minnesota's mineral wealth began when the earth was a brand new planet, billions of years ago."

He paused. "Even Einstein might stumble over numbers like that. We're a people used to measuring time in units of days, months and years. It's not easy even for people like me, who've spent our lives poking around the strata of ages, to grasp the notion of billions of years."

I shook my head. "If it's hard for you, think what it is for me. My kind of history barely covers two centuries. Not to mention my students. Their idea of eternity is the time till Spring break."

"It's a problem," Ernie agreed. "Once I thought it might help to put it in terms of how many lifetimes would add up to a billion years, if everyone lived to be a hundred. Ten million, in case you're curious. But even that was too much. Besides, with new means of calculation, we now know that the earth has been around not two or three, but maybe four or five billion years."

"So on that awesome scale, I suppose it's like yesterday that the first human came along?"

Ernie shrugged. "If you mean modern man, it's more like

a few minutes ago. The latest 'Out-of-Africa' assumption is that *homo sapiens* originated on that continent and began to scatter around the planet fifty or sixty thousand years ago."

"When do you think they got here?"

"There's not a lot of archaeological evidence. But there's general agreement the first humans crossed the ice bridge to this continent some time before the glaciers left. They came as hunters and as they moved into what was to be known as North America, they discovered a land rich in big game."

"That would have been fifteen or twenty thousand years ago?"

"We'll talk about that—but first," he glanced at my empty glass, "let me sweeten that up."

With drinks reconstructed, Ernie got right back on track. "The Ice Age was the last hurrah of Prehistoric times. It started about a million years ago when a spread of ice a mile thick moved down from Canada to eventually cover most of northern America."

"Just one great sheet of ice?"

"Not really. The glaciers weren't a continuous mass. They were separated by warm interglacial periods. In all there were four of them over a million years. The last one was only ten thousand years ago."

Ernie looked up with a wry smile. "Kinda makes you wonder."

"You mean there's more on the way?"

"Well, I don't think you have to rush out and buy a hot water bottle. But the answer very likely is yes."

"As is happens," he continued, "Minnesota's tremendous resources of iron, granite and other minerals were embedded billions of years before the Ice Age. But the glaciers drastically redid the landscape, gouging out the lakebeds and watersheds, hills and valleys we know today. That's why southern Minnesota is so fertile and the northland so barren. As those great masses of ice ground their way down from Canada, they scraped up the soil of the north and dropped it off later in the south."

"Was there life here before the Ice Age?"

"Seems like it. Bones and tusks of large mammals have been found in pre-glacial gravel pits."

"But no humans?"

"So far as we can tell, no race of humans originated in the Americas. The fossil record indicates that the development of human like creatures into modern man occurred over several million years and took place overseas."

"You're saying they didn't get here 'til after the Ice?"

"That's a stickler. Fact is, the whole question of when man came to North America is up for grabs. Once we were pretty sure it was about twenty thousand years ago by way of the old land bridge between Asia and Alaska. But now there's some who think it was much earlier."

Ernie saw my puzzlement and grinned. "Confusing, ain't it? What you have to realize is that prehistoric means just that. Nothing is written down. Geologists scraping at strata and archaeologists picking over bones get fascinating glimpses. But in the end they can only offer careful guesses."

"So what's your best guess about when the first humans showed up here?"

"Probably some time during the most recent comings and goings of ice. No one knows for sure. But it's pretty certain the first humans arrived in Minnesota about the time the glaciers left—say twenty to twenty-five thousand years ago."

He scratched his head. "The best evidence of human habitation here before the Ice Age is a skeleton of a young girl found in 1931 near Pelican Rapids. Ironically, it was first known as *Minnesota Man*."

"Oops! That wouldn't wash today."

"Didn't yesterday, neither. Seems trifling to quibble over the sex of a heap of bones. But anyway they corrected it quite a while back."

Ernie surveyed me over the rim of his glass. "As it turns out the young lady is a problem child."

"How so?"

"Well, they found her underneath the bed of an extinct glacier lake. The question is, did she get there by herself or did someone bury her there?"

"Does it matter?"

"You bet it does. If the skeleton is as old as the glacial deposits where it was found, it could go back twenty-five thousand years or more. But a burial could have occurred thousands of years later." Ernie set down his glass. "It's a riddle, with so far no answer. But one way or another that young lady is the oldest Minnesotan we know about. Maybe that's where your history should start."

- 3 -

CLASS NOTES
MINNESOTA HISTORY COURSE

Re: "Miss Minnesota, The First."

Crucial
Question — How did a human skeleton wind up ten feet under glacial deposits near Pelican Rapids?

Facts — As the ice melted during the northward retreats of the glaciers, temporary lakes were formed, which have long since drained away.
— One of these was "Glacial Lake Pelican." Sometime after drying up, its site was covered by "Glacial Lake Agassiz," formed during the final meltdown. Drainage to the north blocked by the huge barrier of the retreating glacier—hence the water backed up to form the largest glacial lake on the continent. Once Lake Agassiz covered the entire Red River Valley, parts of North Dakota and extended north almost to Hudson Bay.

Guesses A) Minnesota Woman drowned in extinct Glacial Lake Pelican. Bones could be 10,000 or more years old.

— B) She was buried later, perhaps even after Lake Agassiz had drained away, 6,000 years or less.

<u>Evidence</u> — Radiocarbon dating inconclusive.

— Finding of skeleton 10 feet under old lake surface supports (A).

— Shell pendant found nearby supports (B) — ornaments like that not known as early as 10,000 BC, but individual burial ground unlikely in that mound-building era.

<u>Probability</u> — Paleoindian period, ca. 20,000 BC to 6,000 BC. Sheer speculation to assert exact time. It is likely that first Minnesotans arrived ca. 20,000 BC just after retreating glaciers opened up new hunting grounds for mammoths, moose, bisons, giant beaver, etc.

Paleoindian <u>Tradition</u> — Small nomadic tribes who roamed the land from end of Ice Age to ca. 6,000 BC. They came to hunt large game ... lived in temporary shelters ... moved with the seasons ... prairies in the summer, sheltered woodlands in winter.

— Men hunted, fished, harvested wild rice, fashioned fish traps, chipped out flint tools and projectile points. No evidence they knew about archery. Main weapons for big game were spear throwing devices and clubs.

— Women tended babies, cooked, scraped animal hides, gathered nuts and berries, carried water, collected firewood, processed pemmican and wild rice.

Paleoindian
Perspective — Single-minded focus on existence differed from the animals they hunted in little more than their perception of the needs of tomorrow. They had no concept of growing food for the future. But they sun-dried and stored food for the winter ahead.

Hard to believe that in the millions of years of man's evolutionary development no human being ever set foot here until ca. 20,000 years ago. What did these Minnesota primitives make of their lot—the grueling meagerness of their short existence? Did they have a sense of a world beyond the few square miles in which they roamed? Was their vocabulary limited to basic needs? Did they converse; have humor or notions of things not of this world? No way to know. All we can say about these first Minnesotans is what we can guess from the shape of their bones, their stone tools and weapons. Need to apply imagination to bridge the few known facts.

Possibly it went something like this supplement I will hand out.

‡‡ ‡‡ ‡‡ ‡‡ ‡‡

Western Minnesota, ca. 15,000 BC.

THE GIRL AND THE GREAT WHITE PTARMIGAN

Sleep came fitfully to the girl lying on the floor of the tepee she shared with eight members of her clan. Her name was Singing Bird and she was young and very short. Like the others, she lay fully dressed, huddled under a bearskin that served as both blanket and robe. The fire rocks at the center of the tepee no longer radiated heat. In the darkness the cold was penetrating.

Finally after a night of restless dozing, she saw signs of a new day. Pulling the bearskin over her shoulders, she crawled stiff and numb through a flap out onto hard, snow-dusted ground. In the grayness before sunrise, she made out the shapes of three other tepees pitched nearby.

The girl walked to the bank of a frozen creek running past their encampment. Finding a break in the ice, she knelt to drink and splash water on her face. Across the creek, spruce trees starkly outlined against the pre-dawn skies were an unfamiliar sight. They had come to this place only yesterday, after long, hot days of moving about the prairie as the sources of food changed.

It had gone well. Big game roaming the grasslands had been plentiful. Using patterns of stalking handed down through the ages, the men had twice managed to creep close to browsing herds of mammoth. Helped by the extra punch of their spear-throwing devices, they had both times brought down several of the great beasts before the rest of the herd had charged away. The hide of these shaggy monsters, like those of the deer and bison they had also slain, were as welcome for their warmth as was the meat for food.

Once killed, these animals were totally consumed. Bones were worked into scrapers, fishhooks and needles. Rawhide was cut to make binding; hooves were converted to glue and antlers into points for weapons.

The hunters had returned to camp bearing great hunks of crudely butchered carcass for cooking over the roasting pit.

What was not eaten immediately had been given to the women, who with slate knives cut the flesh into strips for sun drying and preserving for the ever-returning winter.

In summer, the women had wandered in woodlands, picking berries, acorns, wild cherries and plums. Other times they had combed the shores of lakes and streams for shellfish.

As the days of sunlight shortened, the band had packed up their tepees and moved on, this time in quest of the wild rice grain they called "good berry." Because wild rice was an important staple, a sparse crop foreshadowed times of hunger during the harsh northern winters. This year the crop had been good.

From the shore where they had pitched their tepees, the rice looked like a prairie of waving grass. Behind them from the woods the men had dragged a felled tree trunk, which they hacked and gouged into a clumsy dugout canoe.

Once on the water, a man standing in back poled the craft into the thickets of rice. In front of him sat two men, working from opposite sides, who used tapered sticks to bend the plants over the edge of the boat and then with sticks in their other hand tapped the rice into the boat. By day's end, weighted by a heaping mound of green rice, the lumbering craft rode low in the water. Ashore, the grain was spread out on sheets of birch bark for drying in the sun.

After several days, the women poured the rice into a scooped out hole lined with deerskin. Then tromping down on the rice they performed a curious jig to remove the husks before storing for the winter months ahead. For days Singing Bird and others had stomped on the grain. The soles of her feet still prickled from bristles while the skin of her fingers was callused from hours of gripping a hard rock, battering away to make pemmican from sun-dried flesh.

On a morning when the first frost touched the ground the clan had made ready to depart. After striking their tepees, they wrapped them around the long support poles. Then with one man shouldering each end, they moved out followed by the women and children carrying leather sacks full of rice, pemmican and dried fish. Behind, the only sign of their presence were the blackened stones of the fire pit and the abandoned dugout canoe.

Passing over a rise and out of sight of the lake, they did not look back. It could not have occurred to them that they had been the first of a long line to follow, or that descendents far removed would one-day pole this lake gathering rice from graceful birch bark canoes and parching their harvest in large iron kettles.

And now, after a march of many days, they had come to a sheltered woodland; a place where signs of abundant game bore promise of welcome change from their diet of preserved pemmican. Here they would stay out the winter. Tepees were set up, this time with earth and moss anchored at the base to help keep out draft and blowing snow.

Now, as first light crept in from the east, the girl wandered into the forest looking for windfall wood to rekindle the fire. Abruptly she was startled by the drumbeat of a white ptarmigan, the largest one she'd ever seen. What a thing it would be if a girl were to come back to camp with a bird this size! What would her foolish, teasing brothers say to that?

All thoughts of gathering wood forgotten, the girl picked up a stone and ran deeper into the forest. Ahead she saw again the flash of white wings. Jumping from rock to rock, she pursued it across the narrow stream and with sturdy legs pumping ran deeper into the woods. But now there was no bird in sight, and shortly the girl stopped to catch her breath.

As she looked around it came to her that having rushed blindly into the forest, she might have a problem finding her way out. Now, with overcast sky and not even a shadow to guide her, she had quite lost her bearings. Starting back the way she thought she had come, she soon realized something was wrong. Where was the creek she had hurried across? Quickly she started in another direction, only to realize after a number of steps that she was lost. There was no stream in sight or hearing and nothing here looked familiar.

I must stop and listen, she thought. Soon they will miss

me. When I hear them call, I'll go in that direction. But there were no calls, not even an answering cry when she herself shouted.

Starting now to feel the chill, the girl realized that to stay warm she had to keep moving. But which way to go and how to keep a straight line? Often, sitting with the women, she had heard old men boast of finding their way by sun or stars. But here in gray gloom there were neither.

An answer, when it came, was a stroke of exceptional reasoning. First marking her present location by a particular tree, she would sight on another further along. Once there, she would line up the starting point with this tree and one ahead. Using this way to keep in a straight line, she felt she must eventually come to a creek or a stream that would lead her back to safety.

And so, marking tree after tree, sometimes a boulder or another forest object, she continued until dusk began to settle. Only then did the girl realize she had to shelter down for the night.

Stopping, she found a small depression, which she filled with moss and pine needle scrapings from the forest floor. Wrapping her bear robe around her, she burrowed in, thirsty, hungry and frightened. Just before falling asleep she thought she heard the drumming of the white ptarmigan.

Again and again during the long darkness she woke whimpering from cold and fear. Sometime before dawn fever entered her body. Instead of cold she began to feel hot. Pushing her way out of the makeshift bedding she found herself wet with sweat. Hardly aware of where she was, she knew only that she must find water.

Daybreak at last found her stumbling through a thicket, hair tangled, face scratched and burning up. Seeking to ease her hunger the girl bit into a spruce cone only to gag and spit it out. Now her craving for water was even greater.

And then she heard it, a low booming summons from the ptarmigan. "Keep coming," it called. "I'll take you to water."

"Wait for me, please wait," she cried.

"Hurry," came the answer.

Trying to run faster the girl stumbled and hit her head on the root of a giant spruce. It was several minutes before she pushed herself up, forehead bruised, pine needles clinging to her face. And then through tears of pain she saw it, the great white ptarmigan, looming at the edge of a clearing. Tail fanning, red wattle gleaming above its eyes, it beckoned, "Come, follow me."

But when she got there the bird had moved away and what she thought had been a clearing turned out to be a small, ice-covered lake. Sobbing, the girl stumbled forward, hearing out there the sound of the ptarmigan, its great wings drumming. And then the ice gave way dropping the girl into waters of shocking cold. Screaming, she clung to the jagged edge of the hole.

"Do not fear," the ptarmigan sang. And then as Singing Bird slowly released her grip, "One day you will rise again and people will know about you forever."

It was upon hearing these words that the girl let go. She and the ptarmigan were soon out of sight.

‡‡ ‡‡ ‡‡ ‡‡ ‡‡

NEWSPAPER ITEM
June 16, 1931

> Pelican Rapids—What may be the New World's oldest human remains have been uncovered here by a road working crew. According to a University of Minnesota archaeologist, the bones, discovered in clay under an extinct glacial lake, are those of a teen-age girl.
>
> Dr. Albert E. Jenks, noting that the lake in that place had dried up more than 10,000 years ago and that the skeleton was covered by soil laid down centuries before that, believes the girl died there by drowning.
>
> If true, the discovery is one of the most important of all North American archaeological findings.

- 4 -

RAMBLING JOURNEY

Late June, 1972

Exams were over at Chippewa Junior College, the kids were gone and so shortly was I. Since I hadn't put much of a dent on the local social scene, most of my good-byes had to do with faculty.

The exception was Eulie, the auburn-haired temptress who presided over the cash register at "Herbie's Idle Hour Café." My overtures toward this attractive young lady had been notable only for their lack of success. But now she surprised me by saying she was sorry we hadn't got to know each other better.

"We've still got time," I sallied, perhaps a tad eagerly.

Laughing, she shook her head, "Sorry Jim, I don't think I want to get acquainted all that quick." Happily, she softened the turn-down by leaning across the counter with a hug and a kiss. "That's so you won't forget me."

Stammering my thanks, I retreated to the cheers of Herbie's regulars. I wouldn't forget Eulie, at least for a while.

Although I didn't need to be at Harwell College until September, I intended to get there long before that. I had a lot to finish on my course outline and looked forward to using its library. But first I wanted to visit the site at Pelican Rapids where they had found the skeleton of Minnesota Woman. After that I planned to swing back north for a Fourth of July break at our cabin on Lake Vermilion.

So it was on a morning as June wound down that I piled my clothes and a couple boxes of books into my vintage Ford pickup. After a final hug from Bertha, my landlady and substitute mom for the past two years, I set out on a rambling journey across Minnesota.

As it turned out, the trip itself was more instructive than my inquiry into Minnesota Woman. Sticking mainly to back roads, I worked my way west over miles of Upper Minnesota country I had never seen before: places like Cass, Hubbard and Otter Tail counties, Leech Lake Indian Reservation and just to the north Lake Winnibigoshish, better known as "Big Winnie," fabled home of lunker walleye.

At Itasca State Park, I hopped across the narrow creek hailed as the true source of the Mississippi. Old Henry Schoolcraft's avowals in this regard have more or less held up. But it seemed pretty dinky to me.

Last stop for the day was at Fergus Falls where I polished off a man-sized steak at Mabel Murphy's Restaurant before crawling under the sheets at the Super 8 Motel.

In the morning an obliging archivist at the Otter Tail Historical Society let me browse through their file on Minnesota Woman. There wasn't much I didn't already know. The finding had been accidental by a road crew working at the site. After the blade of their bulldozer turned up bones from ten feet deep in the ground, the crew began digging by hand and shortly unearthed a human skull. State archeologist Albert Jenks was summoned to the scene and took possession of the bones. Following careful study, he reported the skeleton to be that of a type human dating perhaps to the late glacial period.

A marker a few miles north of Pelican Rapids commemorated the discovery of the first Miss Minnesota. There was no other local recognition of this historical finding. Instead, the community had elected to beam its tourism spotlight upon a nearby park, where the attraction was a statue billed as "The World's Largest Pelican."

Except for getting acquainted with parts of Minnesota I had not previously known, I had come a long way for not very much. That was about to change. With a couple days to spare, I decided to return by way of the Red River Valley, a main route, so to speak, of the receding Ice Age.

Driving north from Pelican Rapids I came shortly to a cluster of glistening lakes scattered like beads from a broken necklace. This was the Detroit Lakes area with its hundreds of excellent walleye lakes. *Detroit* is a French word for inlet and legend has it that the area was named by a French missionary, who having long ago chanced upon the scene, is supposed to have exclaimed, "What a beautiful Detroit!" One is left to guess who was present to record these words.

After lunch at a local diner, I headed west on U.S. 10. Almost before I realized it, the universe of pine forests and sparkling waters was behind me. Gradually the land had flattened out and I was on the edge of the Red River Valley. To the west billowing seas of wheat and other crops stretched as far as I could see.

Except for occasional intrusion of a hamlet or grain elevator, the table-like panorama stayed pretty much the same as I drove for hours through the heart of one of Earth's most fertile depressions. At Moorhead astride Minnesota's western border, I turned north to follow the Red River on its sluggish course toward Canada.

The rich loams of western Minnesota are a legacy of Lake Agassiz, a prehistoric sea formed by glacial melt as the last great slab of ice retreated to the north. Named for Jean Louis Agassiz, a Swiss-American geologist who had studied its origins, Lake Agassiz was five times larger than Lake Superior. Long ago it had covered northwestern Minnesota as well as an even larger section of North Dakota. In all it was the largest body of fresh water ever to exist on the North American continent.

During more than fifty centuries the receding glaciers

poured a rich mixture of silt into Lake Agassiz. When finally seven or eight thousand years ago the lake dried up, it left behind the wonderful sweep of soil that according to the claims of its first settlers "would grow almost anything."

In the late 19th century, with its wheat fields stretching along Minnesota's western border all the way to Canada, the Red River Valley was famed as "The Nation's Bread Basket." Although its farmers planted other crops, wheat was the mainstay until soil exhaustion led to crop rotation and increased diversification. Today on these prairies once dotted with pioneer sod houses, wheat has yielded to other cash crops such as sugar beets and soybeans. And the Red River Valley, with a farming mix that also includes corn, oats, potatoes and livestock, remains a world leader in agriculture.

Traffic was sparse as I continued through the heat of mid-afternoon. Of the ten or so crossroad villages along U.S. 75, Halstad, with a population of 600, was by far the largest. To my left, the river was never far away, its turgid flow brightened by reflected sunlight.

Shortly after passing through a hamlet curiously named Climax, the highway veered away from the river. And a few minutes later, I drove into Crookston astride the Red Lake River. Along with being the county seat of Polk County, Crookston is home for a coordinate campus of the University of Minnesota. Richie Erickson, who holds forth there as a math instructor, is a friend from college days.

I gave him a ring and the next morning we got together for breakfast at the Northland Inn. Richie had been a pretty good weight man back at UMD. And seeing him now, arms straining at the sleeves of his sport shirt, he still looked able to heave a shot-put across the river running just below our dining room.

Over scrambled eggs and hash browns, I told him about going to Harwell and my spur-of-the-moment decision to ramble for a few days in these parts of Minnesota. As I stoked jam on a last piece of toast, Richie suggested I give up on Route 75.

"There's nothing further up you haven't already seen.

Just more of the same all the way to Canada."

"You got a better idea?"

"Well, you're the history buff. And it's not far from here that old Alexander Ramsey pulled off one of his big land grabs."

I slapped my forehead. "Of course! The Old Crossing Treaty, the one that squared off our northwest corner."

"Yeah. It's just a hop, skip and jump over on 57, a mile or so past Huot. There's a park there with a statue of a Chippewa brave."

"You say it's real close?"

"Not more than twenty minutes away. But before you go you ought to stop by our historical museum. They're sure to have something on that Treaty."

By way of thanking Richie for good advice, I tried to grab the check. But he was too quick. "My treat. You catch the tip."

As we shook hands outside Richie had a parting shot.

"Ever hear from Christie White?"

"Nah," I winced. Just hearing her name summoned a sharp pang for what I sometimes still thought might have been. "You know she married Buddy Cosgrove?"

"Yeah. Well that's the breaks. I remember you were always soft on her. And he's a copper plated S.O.B."

"No argument there. But he's the S.O.B. she wanted."

"Well, drive careful ol' buddy. If you really want to get off the beaten path head up to Thief River Falls. Then cut over to the Red Lake Indian Reservation. From there it's a straight shot up a gravel road to Warroad."

"Kinda bumpy, isn't it?"

"Not too bad. And a heck of a lot more interesting than another hundred miles of sugar beets."

Richie's suggestion to visit the historical museum was a ten-strike. The curator gave me a copy of a hand-written manuscript, which unexpected windfall was by itself enough to justify the trip. It was an eyewitness account of a time before railroads when Minnesota's flourishing fur trade relied for transportation on crude, two-wheeled carts drawn by oxen.

- 5 -

THE RECALLINGS OF AN OLD OXCART DRIVER

James Bruce McGill,* whose reminiscence follows, was a child of the Red River Valley. Living always in Pembina at the top of the United States, he was in his early teens when Minnesota came into the Union. Pembina, on the west side of the Red River, missed by the width of that stream being a part of Minnesota. Instead it went to territory that later became part of North Dakota.

Interrupted only by a short hitch with the Union Army, McGill made a dozen oxcart runs from northern fur posts to St. Paul. When that colorful era ended in the 1870s, he went to work for the St. Paul, Minneapolis and Manitoba Railroad, where he worked his way up to be station master at St. Vincent, across the river from Pembina.

James McGill never married and died at 74, a Civil War veteran who lived long enough to see the end of World War I. He is buried in Pembina.

The manuscript that follows is a vivid personal remembrance of an all but forgotten chapter of Minnesota history. Considering that McGill's schooling ended when he was ten, it is

---

* Fictional character and narrative created to describe Minnesota's ox-cart days and events at the Old Crossing Treaty.

easy to overlook occasional lapses in grammar or spelling.

Pembina, N.D.—1908

How I come to be from Pembina is because of my grampa, Andrew Duncan McGill, a Scotch crofter, who come west to help start a farm colony in what's now Manitoba. When that colony failed in the 1820s, Grampa and his son, who later became my Pa, come to Pembina.

Grampa and my Pa scratched out a living growing oats and barley. After a few years Grampa took ill and died and left my 13-year-old Pa on his own. However, because Grampa had taught him how to write and do ciphers, Pa soon got a job clerking at the Pembina post of the American Fur Company.

That was when the Company was still owned by John Jacob Astor, the richest man in America, who never set foot in Pembina. Astor pulled out of the fur business not long after and the Company was taken over by new owners. Like Astor, they run it from New York City but they put Henry Hastings Sibley in charge of all the posts in our territory.

Mr. Sibley run things from around Fort Snelling. But one time when I was still pretty little he come to Pembina by horseback to talk with traders and hunters who kept the post supplied with furs and buffalo meat. I recolleck there was a big to-do and Pa carried me on his shoulders to shake hands with the great man.

By then Joe Rolette, the famous trader and politicker, was in charge of the post at Pembina. But Pa had worked his way up to be chief storekeeper and he run things all the time Joe was off hunting or politicking.

Pa was almost 30 before he married the daughter of a fur hunter, who was half Chippewa. I came along in 1846 but I lost my Ma a few years later when she and my new borned sister died abirthing.

Three years later Pa married her sister, who gone to the Jesuit mission school at Pembina. She was a good woman, real gentle. She died of smallpox when I was about ten. But not before she gave me all the book learning I ever got.

In spite of us missing her so much, things was pretty good for me and Pa. We had our own quarters in the post. I learnt to cook and help with chores. In the fall we went hunting and sumtimes fishing. I was 12 or 13 when I brought down my first buck. Then one terrible winter afternoon it all ended.

Pa had trubbel before with a Chippewa hunter called "Black Dog," who run up a big credit on the company books but never delivered any furs in return. On this day Black Dog come in asking for goods but with still no pelts or nothing to trade. When Pa refused him more credit, the Chippewa turned as if to go. But then he suddenly whirled around and stabbed my father in the throat.

While Pa was on the floor choking in his own blood, Black Dog scooped up a handful of tobacco and fled. I screamed and run to Pa just in time to hear his last bloody gurgle.

It didn't do Pa any good but hunters from the post tracked Black Dog down a few hours later and hung him on the spot. That was in 1860 and I was 14 years old.

Joe Rolette got back from the Territorial legislature a while after we buried Pa. In return for my work as chore boy, he let me have a room and board at the post. For a few months I hauled water, cut wood, slopped pigs, cooked or did whatever else was wanting around the place. But early in June as Joe was getting ready for the Spring oxcart run to St. Paul, he took me in hand as a wagon driver.

Sum years before I was born, Mr. Sibley sent Joe to Pembina to set up a freight line to St. Paul. In short order Joe put together a string of ox carts, the first of hundreds of Red River trains that followed. It was Joe who trail blazed the Pembina root to Crow Wing and then along the Mississippi to St. Paul. For 40 years up to the coming of the railroad, ox cart trains trundled over the prairie, across rivers and through woods back and forth between St. Paul and the new settlements in the Red River valley.

Going southeast they creaked under loads of furs, buffalo robes and smoked pemmican. Coming back they carried stoves, axes, plowshares, hammers and nails, pots and pans, bolts of cloth, rifles, gun powder, tobacco and just about everything else from blocks of salt to barrels of whisky.

Red River carts was pulled by oxen hitched up like horses. For proteckshun and to help each other in fording rivers, they mostly traveled in trains, sumtimes 2 or 3 hundred. With prosesshuns that long, the screech of their ungreased wooden wheels was a terrible racket. Old timers in St. Paul swore they could hear a Red River train coming half a day before they could see it.

With crossing rivers, breakdowns and all, 15 miles in a 10-hour day was pretty good. Sumtimes when the going was speshul hard, it was a lot less. I recolleck that first trip with Joe took mostly 6 weeks to cover the 400 miles to St. Paul. We left early in June and got there when July was half over.

At night after eating, we sat around our campfires before turning in. If it rained we crawled under the wagons but mostly we slept out under the light of 1,000 stars.

Sumtimes Joe and a few hunters went looking for buffalo or deer. After a week or more of chewing on pemmican it was a welcom change when they came back with fresh meat.

Just about everything on that run was new to me. What I recolleck mostly was night times around a fire listening to the men joshing and telling storys. And when it came to spinning yarns, nobody could beat Joe.

I dout in all the Red River valley there was anybody more famous than Trader Joe Rolette. He was a rough and tumbel, hard working, hard drinking French Canadian, a frontier man and a politicker who could skin a bear just as easy as he could speechify at the Territorial Legislature.

Joe was tougher than a boiled owl and always ready for direct action. But he was also fun loving and a great one for playing jokes and telling whoppers. There's a lot of storys made up about Joe, how he could rassel a buffalo or guzzel a gallon of red eye at a setting, and like that. But the ones that are true are even better, like his way of chasing rival traders out of the country.

They still tell about how he got Governor Sibley elected by 240 votes by sending along 316 Pembina votes for Sibley and none for Ramsey. As Joe told it, he held up delivering the returns till he knew how many votes the Democrats needed. When he heard it was close he decided on a clean sweep.

During the 1850s Joe was elected four times to the Territorial Legislature. He probly wooda kept getting elected if Minnesota didn't become a state. When that happened in 1851, the Territorial Legislature went out of business. Besides, when they layed out the west boundary for the new state, Pembina was on the wrong side of the Red River. Instead of being in Minnesota we was part of the Dakota Territory.

In winter Joe hitched up dogs and went by sled to attend the legislature sesshuns in St. Paul. There come a time just before Minnesota became a state when a greedy Territorial governor, by the name of Gorman, hatched up a real estate scheme to get the capitol moved to the new town of St. Peter.

As I tell this more than 50 years later, Joe is still talked about as the man who saved the day for St. Paul. What he did, after the legislature voted for St. Peter, was to simply run off with the official copy of the bill. Joe holed up for a week, playing poker and drinking whisky with cronies till the Legislature ended. And the capitol stayed in St. Paul.

*The Minnesota Club in St. Paul is where politickers offen get together after a working day at the capitol. Nowadays, when you walk in, the first thing you see is a big likeness of Joe Rolette with a plack telling how he took the bill and run.**

Well we finally got to St. Paul on that first trip and I never seen such a bussel. Company clerks buzzed around like flies on

---

* In his *History of Minnesota*, Judge Charles Flandrau was later to comment that Rolette vetoed the bill "In a way not known to parliamentary law. He put it in his pocket and disappeared."

a cookie, sorters threw furs into different heaps and onto big scales, roustabouts lugged packs of furs into sheds along the wharf and hawkers swarmed around the ox cart drivers, shouting out their wares.

From St. Paul, the Company sent the furs down river to St. Louis, then by railroad to New York for shipping across the ocean to Europe. It's kinda funny to think about some rich lady in England or France with a fur around her neck that started out in a beaver pond in northern Minnesota.

Once a train of ox carts got to St. Paul, it took a cuppel weeks for Joe and other traders to transack their business, bargaining for their skins and robes and loading up with trade goods to carry back. For us drivers this was a good time to rest, fatten our oxen and test the town's attrackshuns.

St. Paul in them days was a raw boomtown. Joe told us it was once called "Pig's Eye Landing," after a one-eyed crook who sold rotgut in a tavern along side the river. Since then more respecktable settlers had changed it to St. Paul, which was the name of a little log cabin church, built there by a missionary.

Being just a ways down river from St. Anthony's Falls, it was the last good landing place for steamboats coming up the Mississippi. When I first saw it, side-wheelers with tall smokestacks were jam-packed against each other on its crowded levee.

Away from the river, horse drawn carriages and freight wagons left a trail of manure and dust stirred up from the summer-baked clay of its main street. Lumberjacks walked side-by-side to immigrants jabbering all sorts of strange talk. Ox cart drivers in worn buckskins rubbed shoulders with mill hands, street venders, pickpockets and Indians with red blankets.

Steamboat traffic and the need for more wharf space pushed Pig's Eye away from the river. His new saloon down town was a good place to start for anyone thinking about what the preacher calls transgreshuns. But gullible lads with money in their pocket and befuddled by hard drink were easy marks for painted women and slick talking sharpies.

One of these was my friend Charlie, who late one night

stumbled back to our boarding house with a lump on his head and separated from his wallet. Lucky for Charlie, Joe Rolette, wise in the ways of St. Paul seducements, had turned us greenhorns loose with only part of our wages.

In August, when we left for Pembina, it was still hot. But by the time we got back the leaves were falling and the nights were chilly. Ever since I was littel, I stood with Valley folks cheering as the ox carts came home loaded with trade goods. This time it was different and I couldn't help tingel with pride as I guided old Plod Foot through the lines of people and into the stockade.

- 6 -

THE OLD CROSSING TREATY

Needless to say my visit to the Crookston museum was an unexpected and most welcome boon. I had gone there hoping only to learn something more about the little known treaty that opened the way for a flood of immigration into the rich farm lands of the Red River Valley. I had not guessed I might also find an eye witness account to the days when that region was still unsettled frontier traveled mainly by fur traders and ox carts. Neither did I anticipate the wealth of information provided by James McGill's description of the eventful treaty of 1863.

Minnesota today is literally a patchwork made up of giant tracts of land ceded by Chippewa and Sioux by means of a series of 19th century treaties. Of these, the best known are the treaties of 1837 that turned over the large triangle between the St. Croix and Mississippi Rivers, and the 1851 treaties whereby the Sioux gave up virtually the lower half of what was to become Minnesota.

For some reason history has skipped rather lightly over the eight other treaties that helped make up our thirty-second state. "The Old Crossing Treaty," which secured safe passage to the lush valley that came to be known as "The Breadbasket of the World," is a case in point.

Here follows James McGill's second manuscript that

added so greatly to my understanding of the proceedings that gave Minnesota its northwest boundary. Given the nature of those and similar proceedings, it is perhaps not inappropriate to begin with the caustic observation of a 19th century cynic quoted by Meridel LeSueur in *North Star Country*:

> "Barrel of 32 gal., bushel of rank black twist chewing tobacco, 3 or 4 of bad whiskey or quantity of raw alcohol—fill in with river water. Let it stand awhile and serve."
>
> —Old Recipe For Dealing With Indians

McGILL MANUSCRIPT, CONTINUED

Joe Rolette took me in after Pa's murder and I was beholden. But he had too much on his mind for me to ever think of him as a second father. Besides he was off sumwhere most of the time and outside of a few how do you do's, I dout we said a dozen words during the next 2 years. So I was surprised one day when he asked me to come along with him and a few traders to a powwow with a group of Chippewa chiefs. That was late in the summer of 1863 and I was 17 years old.

Sitting around our campfire the first night out, Joe told us the meeting was to parley for a safer way through the northern part of the Pembina trail. There was a couple roots for Red River traffick. The carts from up in Canada usually stayed west of the river down to where they could follow the Minnesota River over to Fort Snelling. That way steered clear of trubbel with the Indians but it took more time.

The root we went crossed the Red River the first day. Then it meandered south and east to Crow Wing. From there we went along side the big river to St. Paul. Where we sometimes ran into trubbel was from hostile bands during the first leg. You never knew when they might come raiding for provisions or otherwise obstruck traffick through their lands. Now finally the U.S. government sent Senator Ramsey out to buy a strip of Chippewa land through which the ox carts could pass safely.

On both sides of the Red Lake River where the powwow took place, the banks were deep rutted from years of ox cart crossings. When we got there we set up on the north side of the river. There must have been 1000 Indians camped in the clearing on the other side. There wasnt any other whites there yet, so we were a little nervous about the shouting and other noises going on across the river that first night.

Ramsey got there the next day with a escort of mounted soldiers and leading a train of 90 supply wagons, mules, horses and a drove of beef cattle. The troops barely got off their saddles before Ramsey set them to work putting up corrals for the livestock. Next he had them ereckt a council area with sawed-off logs in a half circle for the chiefs to sit on.

One of the traders whispered to me that Ramsey knew the value of show. "He wants those chiefs to feel important." It was for sure Ramsey knew how to deal with Indians. Twelve years before he pracktily stole a huge parcel of land at Traverse des Sioux. Now he was setting the stage for another grand powwow.

Things got started the next day with the firing of a cannon. Down from their tepees came a passel of chiefs and braves wearing brite feathers and decked out with furs and deerskin leggings. The chiefs of each band wore speshul colors.

Tables nearby were heaped with colored blankets and bolts of cloth, looking glasses and other goods and trinkets to give away after the treaty was signed. The Indian agent who had been sent out from Washington to help negoshiate, believed the matter would be setteled quick. But Ramsey told Joe it was for sure going to take longer.

Once the chiefs were perched on their stools, the most important in the front row, Ramsey told them about the goverment's offer. He said the terms were fair and they should take time to talk it over.

Just then a big very hansome chief stood up. His name was "Tall Tree" or something like that. "My Brothers," he shouted, "Listen to me! What I tell you is truth." He waited while Ramsey's translater spoke it in English.

"Brothers" he said again. "We know that those who come from where the sun rises are like a great white cloud. Soon it will cover all of our land and we will have it no more. But if this land where our fathers are buried is to go, we must be sure the white man will pay for it fairly. Those who come to us with their terms must now wait until we agree about ours."

If Ramsey was mad he managed to hide it. "Tall Tree speaks with wise words," he said. "It is right that the Chiefs take time to consider what has been offered. But remember, the Great White Father has been very generous. If you parley too long, he may change his mind."

Joe Rolette winked at us. "He's telling them they better take it cuz the whites are coming even if they don't sign."

After waiting to let that sink in, Ramsey switched to cajolery. "But come my friends we must selebrate this wonderful occashun. Tonight we will have a great feast in your honor."

That was the start of a softening up time that began with strong drink and plenty of it, followed by great slabs of beef, lots of other vittels and more strong drink. Each day and night the chiefs would gorge with food and whisky. And the next morning, still half drunk, would gather in shaky council.

During the days while the chiefs was trying to sort things out, younger braves carried on with games, races, gambling and the like. One day a Chippewa pack from the Pembina branch gave a challenge to a band from Red Lakes for a game of lacrosse. This was a wild affair with a 100 or more braves on each side hitting each other, shoving and whooping. Using a stick with a leather pocket at one end, the idea was to scoop up a small ball and run with it or throw it toward the other band's boundary line.

One side was painted blue to tell which was which. They started in the middle of a field that was maybe a half-mile long. If one of the braves managed to get the ball in his scoop, the other pack would chase him down, slashing at him with their sticks and howling like wolves. The game went back and forth lasting for hours, till the blue team finally forced the ball over the other's boundary line. The losers had to settle with a bundle of robes or whatever was bet.

Other times they would gamble on a horse race or a bow and arrow shooting contest. This went on for days. When they wernt playing games or betting, they were dancing, eating or drinking. With whisky and vittels provided by the government, the roystering went on till dawn. In our tents across the river we'd hear the drums beating and the shouting. Sometimes shots got fired. Over in our tents we'd get a littel nervus.

When the sun came up it looked like the morning after a battel. But the human reckage stroon all over the field wasent dead, just dead drunk.

On October 2, 1863, after 2 rawcus weeks of cheap gifts, food and whisky, the chiefs caved in. This time when Ramsey summoned them they went along like a flock of sheep. The few changes agreed on were mostly face saving.

For the promise of cash and some reserved land, Chippewa chiefs were ready to sign away their rights to land stretching across both sides of the Red River. * *But not before a last objeckshun from Tall Tree. "Fathers," he said, "Your coming and taking our land makes me very sad. You say the Great White Father is paying us a great deal for this country. I do not think so. Soon you will have the land and the money will go to the traders who cheat us."*

Ramsey answered sharply. He told them that white settlers and their steamboats and railroads were coming. This was going to happen one way or another, Ramsey said. And the Great White Father had offered those generus terms because of frendship.

After that the chiefs some of them still half drunk came up to put wobbly marks on a paper they couldn't read anyhow. Then presents were handed out, the chiefs got a medal to hang around their necks and more whisky was drunk. Ramsey after some more

---

* Nearly ten million acres.

flowery words left the same day with his party. So did we. But the Indians stayed around a few days maybe starting to realize what they had given away.

It wasent till years later that I figgered out that I had seen a great moment in Minnesota history. What come to be known as "The Old Crossing Treaty" was followed by a rush of settlers and farmers who turned the Red River Valley into the biggest field of wheat in the whole world.

‡‡ ‡‡ ‡‡ ‡‡ ‡‡

The site of the Old Crossing Treaty is now a pleasant wayside park. Standing there where moccasins had trod, I could almost hear the shouts of young braves flailing at each other with lacrosse sticks, see in mind's eye the chiefs in their colorful regalia. At river's edge I looked for ancient ruts and imagined carts being half floated across, the bellow of oxen and the urgings of drivers hip-deep in water. Before leaving I looked across the meadow where young Jim McGill had camped. His eyewitness accounts were the surprise bonus of my spur-of-the-moment odyssey into Western Minnesota. I felt like saluting.

- 7 -

WAY UP NORTH

Back on the road, I followed the Red Lake River up to Thief River Falls. This is where the river bends like an elbow in its meandering course west from Red Lake. Shaped like an hourglass, Red Lake is the largest body of water entirely within the state. Lake of the Woods is larger but more than half its waters lie up north in Canada.

At a lunch counter in town, I asked the waitress how Thief River got its name. Her answer as she plunked down my coffee was right to the point: “Damned if I know!”

It was then the old timer next to me jumped in. “There’s some say it’s an Indian word that got mixed up somehow. But others allow it was named for a thievin’ Sioux, who used to rob settlers passin’ by. Take your pick, boy. Ain’t nobody gonna prove you wrong.”

Thus enlightened, I got back in my pickup and drove east on County 1 toward the sprawling Red Lake Reservation. From there I drove north on the secondary road bordering Beltrami State Park, named like so many other place in Minnesota after an early explorer. Giacomo Constantino Beltrami was an intrepid Italian who in 1823, after a solo trek into northern wilderness, claimed to have found the source of the Mississippi. To give him his due, he thought he had. But what he discovered is at a distance from the big river's real source and runs in a different direction.

I've always enjoyed reading about this flamboyant figure who rode across the Minnesota scene like a knight out of the pages of a novel by Miguel de Cervantes. Driving so close to where he had so magnificently failed, I could not help but bring to mind his almost comic-opera antics in quest of his personal Holy Grail.

In late spring of 1823, Beltrami arrived at the fort then known as St. Anthony aboard the *Virginia*, in its history-making first steamboat trip up the Mississippi from St. Louis. From there he hitched up with an Army unit going north to more accurately survey the border between the U.S. and Canada. At Pembina, a few miles from Canada, lured by dreams of glory, he split away from the survey party to go in search of the birthplace of the "King of Waters." Accompanied only by several Chippewa canoe men, Beltrami set off to the southeast following the course of the Red Lake River. Picture, if you will, the spectacle of a foppishly garbed gentleman wanderer, shielded from the elements by a red silk parasol, being paddled in stately splendor through the reeds and swamps of what he called "Bloody River."

He progressed reasonably well in that manner for several days. But after a chance encounter with a small band of Sioux, Beltrami was abruptly deserted by his Chippewa companions—up the creek, so to speak, with a paddle he did not know how to use. Give the man credit; he rose to the challenge. Dragging the canoe by one hand, clutching his umbrella in the other, and up to his hips in water, the intrepid Italian struggled on alone. Soaked to the skin and fighting off clouds of mosquitoes Beltrami somehow persevered for three days before coming across a Chippewa he talked into guiding him to a small lake about twelve miles north of present day Bemidji.

Convinced that here was the source not only of the Mississippi but also of the "Bloody River," he named the place "Lake Julia" to honor the memory of a former lady friend.

Ecstatic in belief of his great discovery, he was later to

write: "Oh! What were the thoughts that passed through my mind at this most happy and brilliant moment of my life! The shades of Marco Polo, of Columbus, of Americus Vespucius, of the Cabots, of the Zenos, and various others appeared present, and joyfully assisting at this high and solemn ceremony, and congratulating themselves on one of their countrymen having, by new and successful researches, brought back to the world the inestimable services which they had conferred on it by their own peculiar discoveries ..." (Severin, *Explorers of the Mississippi*).

Beltrami struggled back to civilization to proclaim how at one stroke he had discovered the fountain head for two great rivers. By year's end, still with no doubts, he published a book extolling his adventures and great discovery.

Alas, the world was not impressed. The book did not sell well. Neither did his claims hold up under the scrutiny of scholarly critics. Not long afterwards he returned to Europe, his stab at fame clouded in ignominy. Although never accepted as valid, his writings along with his flamboyant personality added a dash of color to the history of Minnesota explorations. It seems only fair that the county embracing the lake he believed to be the fount of the Father of Waters has long since been named in his honor, even though it lies many miles northwest of the true source later identified by Schoolcraft.

Daylight was down to an orange haze when I checked into a rustic motel on the outskirts of Warroad. Although the customs entry into Canada was barely five minutes away, the inn keeper told me I could go 35 miles further north and still be in Minnesota. "But," he said, "You'd have to swim or go by boat."

The reason for this geographic oddity, as I dimly recalled, is because of a curious glitch by 19th century surveyors attempting to fix the boundary between the U.S. and Canada. Unable to agree on a straight line from the mouth of the Rainy River to the 49th parallel that sets the border the rest of the way west, they compromised on a projection into Lake of the Woods known as the Northwest Angle. The result is a 130 square mile plot of America separated from the rest of the country by Canada and waters of Lake of the Woods.

Warroad, the only U.S. port on Lake of the Woods, was founded by the American Fur Company in 1820. It is at the end of a trail once used as a route to do battle between Chippewa and Sioux. Indians called it "Dark and Bloody End of Trail." Eighteenth century French traders changed that to "Chemin de Guerre," which less lyrically translates to the Americanized "Warroad."

Lake of the Woods, the celebrated fishing mecca we share with Canada, is the largest body of water left over from glacial Lake Agassiz. With 65,000 miles of shoreline and thousands of charted islands, it extends from Warroad more than 80 miles north to Kenora. As a Vermilion laker practically born with fish pole in hand, I yearned to wet a line in the big lake's fabled walleye waters. But with the sands running out on a two-day trip that had somehow stretched into four, there simply wasn't time.

The first leg of my drive the next morning was down a corridor of wildflowers that crown the top of Minnesota. Scattered among them were patches of soft pink lady slippers, which reign as our state flower. Kind of a surprise to find them out in the open, since they mainly bloom under the umbrella of a pine forest.

An hour or so along Highway 11, I came to Baudette, in its heyday a saw-milling capital of the northwoods. In the dry summer of 1910, Baudette and its twin village of Spooner were wiped out by fire. Spooner never came back but Baudette rose from its ashes and is now a farming and tourist center.

On a whim I crossed Baudette's toll-free bridge into Canada. After a short Customs check I continued east on the Ontario side of Rainy River. Curiously the roads on either side are number 11s. Since both are bordered by immense spruce forests, the only noticeable difference was that for the next 70 miles the river was on my right instead of to the left.

Arriving at Fort Frances around noon, I crossed the bridge only to discover it had been easier to exit Minnesota than to get back in. The U.S. customs agent who checked me at the border was what Harry Truman once called a four-ulcer man on a two-ulcer job. Although I like to think of myself as an upright sort, this bellicose guardian of our northern border seemed determined to prove otherwise.

"Why did you go into Canada?"

"Uh, no special reason, just a spur-of-the-moment thing."

I don't think he believed me. With a look to imply suspicion he started a five-minute search that began with my glove compartment. Then he poked under the seats, rooted through my duffel bag, peered under the hood and even stooped down to probe under the chassis. When red-faced from exertion or frustration, he stood up to freeze me with an icy glare, I could almost see him thinking, "There's no way this guy went into Canada just for the scenery."

When finally he snapped that I could go, I fought off the urge to tell him to try Preparation H. Instead I smiled sweetly and even resisted telling him to have a nice day.

My impromptu detour into Canada had caused me to bypass the old Indian burying ground at Grand Mound. But I'd already seen that years before during a high school field trip. Of the burial grounds that once peppered the Upper Midwest, only a fraction remain. Of these, Grand Mound on the south bank of the Rainy River is the largest. Even after the erosion of centuries, it stands 40 feet high and covers an area the size of a football field.

Long before the coming of the Sioux and Chippewa, this region was home to a native people about whom very little is known. At the edge of Smokey Bear Forest, Grand Mound is believed to have been used for a thousand years up to around 800 A.D. by a woodland people whose life style archaeologists have labeled "The Laurel Culture."

Much of what is surmised about the Laurel Indians comes from artifacts and skeletal remains found near Grand Mound. Occupying forests in what is now Koochiching County, the Laurels are believed to be ancestors to tribes that were recorded by French explorers in the 1600s. But in pre-history it is hard to do more than speculate about linkages between and among tribes and their many branches.

In International Falls, I wolfed a “Big Mac” before going over to the historical museum in Municipal Park. Among its memorabilia are letters, old-time photos and tools used during the 19th century logging boom.

Also in the park, and very aptly, given the Falls’ reputation as “Icebox of the Nation,” is a 22-foot tall thermometer. Casey Stengel, the old manager of the Yankees, is supposed to have said, “you don’t have to tell me about the cold in Kansas City, I was born there all my life.” Maybe so. But if you’re looking for real chill, the place to start is Northern Minnesota, where in winter the air is so cold you could almost cut ice cubes out of it. By early December we can usually drive our trucks across lakes, and going into an unheated cabin is like stepping into a deep freezer. Hours later when the place is warmed up you still have to shake out folded blankets to get rid of secreted pockets of chill. And no matter what you hear about tough batteries, you better have the engine hooked up to a heater, or you can count on needing a jump start. As I recall, that big Falls thermometer has more than once registered a low of minus fifty, and that’s not counting wind chill!

But for kids, a greater attraction is the giant statue of “Smokey the Bear.” Gazing at its enormous bulk, I wondered if the statue might have been modeled with Bronko Nagurski, the Falls’ bigger-than-life hero in mind. I vaguely remembered a trip to I-Falls with my Dad, when I was very young. Coming over from Canada we stopped for gas at the station owned by the legendary fullback. At the time, the “Bronk” was old and hobbled by arthritis. Now that I think of it, the big guy looked more like Bullwinkle the Moose than Smokey the Bear.

Finally, after a 750-mile loop around central and northern Minnesota, I arrived back on the Mesabi—home on the Range, so to speak. And then on to Buhl, the mining town where I was born and raised. Driving down Wanless St. past my old high school, I wondered if my picture still collected dust in the gloomy trophy case just off the main entry. Eleven years before—it seemed an eon—I had won the state high hurdle championship. My time hadn't threatened any records, but for Buhl it was a first.

Our home on Woodbridge Avenue was a two-story wooden frame house with the roof pitched high to shed the snows of northern winters. Finished with white clapboard and looking much like its neighbors, it had been built by my grandfather in 1925. Grampa Eino Makki was now gone from this world. Literally worn out from seeing his family through the harsh years of Depression on the Range, he survived just long enough to cash a single pension check.

Nobody was home to greet the returning son. Mom and Dad had left earlier for our cabin on Lake Vermilion. I decided to get a good night's sleep in my old bedroom before traveling up to the lake. Meantime I used the rest of the afternoon chasing down a manuscript at the library.

Owing to my Finnish-American heritage, I had literally been nurtured on lore from the old country as handed down from my great-grandparents and kept alive in the memories of their off-spring and other close kin. Now it occurred to me that the written account of Great-Grampa Reino's migration and early years in America might be a useful supplement to my Minnesota history course.

Although she was not familiar with the manuscript in question, the librarian very kindly turned me loose in their archive room. There, after considerable rummaging, I turned up a tattered folder labeled Makki, Reino—1939. In it I found a dog-eared but legible copy of his story as told a half century after coming to America. Miss Ranta, the librarian who remembered me from my high school days, obligingly ran off a copy of the full interview.

- 8 -

REINO MAKKI COMES TO AMERICA

Reino Makki's story started out on a small farm near Vaala in the Finnish province of Oulu. Born there in 1872, Reino was third of the four children of Timo and Lona Maki. In Finland "Maki," like "Smith" in England, is a very common name. Minnesota's Iron Range literally abounds with hundreds of Makis. But ours is the only one spelled with two k's. According to Grampa Eino, that's the way the immigration office wrote it when his Dad got off the boat in New York. It's been spelled that way ever since.

Much has been made of the movement of hordes of immigrants who during the past hundred and more years came to America from countries all over Europe. Millions came, and given all the reasons why, it's only surprising millions more did not.

Some who left were fleeing famine or grinding poverty. Others came to escape military conscription or to break away from social fetters that bound them to an existence of serfdom. As the saying went, "The Promised Land beckoned … the upper class sneered … and the oppressed left."

The push factor most common to immigrants was poverty. The 19th century population explosion in Europe had outstripped agricultural and industrial capacity. There were more farmers than land and more workers than jobs. With almost no chance to acquire land of his own, the best a young man could look forward to was a lifetime of peasantry. This at a time when America, hungry for farmers, was offering free land and when shipping lines eager to fill steerage holds were trumpeting New World job opportunities.

Lured by such siren calls, masses of young people decided to try for a new and infinitely better life across the ocean. Between 1880 and 1920 occurred the greatest population transfer in history as twenty-five million immigrants came into America.

One of them was my great-grandfather, who at age 17 came all by himself. As a number two son, Reino Makki had no hope of being a landowner in Finland. That was likely his main reason for leaving. However, as he later explained it, "I just got fed up with being pushed around."

Here follows my great-grandfather's account of how after pulling up stakes in Finland, he came to settle in Northern Minnesota.

Interview of Reino Makki*
On occasion of his fiftieth year in America
Interviewed by WPA Historian Matti Hanula
Buhl, Minnesota, 1939

What I remember most about that time back in Finland, was that I already had two strikes on me the day I was born. One was my father. The other was my brother Auro, who was the oldest son and never let me forget it.

My sister Joanna, who was ten years older, took care of me when I was little. But she got out of there just as fast as she could, getting a job as a housemaid in Oulu, when she was 16. Then she got married and after that we didn't hear much from her.

My baby sister Hilda was three years younger than me

---

* Like all the Makki characters, Reino Makki is fictional, as is this interview.

and a happy smiling girl. When I left the only ones I missed were Hilda and my poor Mother, who was worn out from working 15 hours a day.

I don't think my father wanted to be mean. But life is hard in that place. He never went to school and couldn't read. All he ever knew his whole life was work. He got up while it was dark and except for eating, kept working till it was dark again. He never saw it different for his kids. There was always something to do. He got me started when I was about six hauling water and feeding the pigs. By the time I was ten, I was working in the field with him and Auro. There was a koulu a few miles away but we never went there. Ma could read some but other than opening the Bible a few minutes on Sundays, she was too busy all the time to try and teach us.*

After I got to America I went to school for grown-ups to learn English. It's kind of funny that I can still speak Finnish pretty well but I can't read it. But I can read American even if I don't speak it so good.

It was awful hard work on the farm, never a day off even in winter. Everything we did was by hand, reaping, threshing, pulling stumps or cutting wood, which we did a lot getting ready for snow and cold. When winter came there were blizzards just like here in Minnesota. The winds would howl, sometimes for two or three days and the snow would pile up in drifts around our tupa which was what we called our house.

Our three cows had to be milked twice a day. Sometimes in winter I had to shovel through snow out to the barn. At night I milked those cows by just feeling with my freezing hands. If it was still snowing when I was done, I had to shovel my way back.

After supper there was nothing to do but go to bed. Mother usually stayed up mending socks or whatever she had to do. There was always something.

Late Saturday afternoons I carried pails of water up to fill a barrel in our sauna. Just before supper I stoked up the brick

---

* Interviewer's note: Koulu is Finnish for school.

firehouse with birch logs. In an hour or so the stones on top got so hot they'd be singing. Before bed we'd go in, first Mother and Hilda, then Father, Auro and me. We'd throw a dipper of water on the stones and the steam would hit us like a wall of fire. But it felt good to sit there and sweat out the aches of all that farm work. Then we'd switch each other with bundles of cedar twigs and last scrub with soap and then dump pails of cold water on each other. I think that was the only times Auro ever did anything for me.

I didn't mind the work. But it seemed like I couldn't never get things right for my Father. He was always asking me why I did something this way or that way. And he never said thanks or anything nice. When I was little, he once in a while gave me a licking for doing something bad. He'd grab the back of my shirt and whale at my behind with a barrel stave. It hurt but I probably had it coming. Years later I had once in while to spank my own sons but instead of a stave I used a razor strap.

What I really hated was Auro lording it over me. He'd call me names and say someday when he owned the farm he'd hitch me beside our ox to pull the plow, and things like that. He was always shoving me around and sometimes he hit me. Mother didn't like it neither. But what could she do all worn out from work and half scared of both Father and Auro.

But what Auro forgot to reckon was that I was growing older and all that hard work was making me strong. By the time I was 17, I was just as big as him and maybe stronger. Then one morning we was out in the field haying when Auro stepped on a rake that came up and hit him in the ear. When I laughed, he took a wild swing at me. And for the first time I swung back and hit him in the nose which started to bleed. He was so flabbergasted he just stood there holding his nose and looking foolish. So I hit him again and knocked him down.

Then my father came charging at me and I grabbed him and pushed him down into a pile of hay. "You get out of here!" he hollered. "Don't worry, I'm going," I shouted back.

Then I went up to our tupa and told Mother I was going.

She said my father didn't really mean for me to leave. But I didn't care, I was going. She gave me a few coins she had and some bread and cheese. I hugged her and kissed Hilda and left with just the clothes on my back.

That afternoon I walked to Vaala, a little village 12 miles away. I spent the next two weeks with my mother's brother, Uncle Heikki Makela, who owned a blacksmith shop in Vaala. Uncle Heikki and my father didn't like each other very much. A couple times they argued and almost came to blows over the way my father was so mean to my mother.

So when I told Uncle Heikki what happened, he said I was best to get away. He was right, not just because of my father. Someday Auro would own the farm and I'd have to leave anyway because I wouldn't work for him even if he wanted me to stay. But wherever I went I'd still be just a farmhand for somebody else.

Uncle Heikki was a good man and I could have stayed there and learned the blacksmith trade. But one day he read me a letter from his brother Anders, who had gone to America a long time ago and had a good job as a carpenter in Chicago. Up to then Vaala was as far as I had been and all I knew about America was it was someplace across the ocean. But the letter from Anders made it sound so good I wanted to go there too.

If it wasn't for Uncle Heikki I never would have made it. He told me what I had to do and said when I got there I should go see Uncle Anders in Chicago. He gave me 500 markaa which he said I would need to get there. I told him I didn't know when I could pay him back. But he said, "You're a good boy, the son of my dear sister. This is a gift from me."*

Uncle Heikki arranged with a boatman he knew for me to work the first part of my trip helping load and unload freight. His name was Kutsi or something like that. We left Vaala early one morning and it took all day to go 70 miles down to Oulu. The next morning, after I helped Kutsi unload the boat, he took me to

---

* About one hundred dollars.

where the ship would leave for Helsinki where I had to go next.

The boat for that day was already gone so I slept that night under a freight shed. The next morning it was there and I went aboard. The cost was ten markaa. On this part of the trip there were about twelve of us like me going to America. They were all young and off farms in the Oulu Province. One of them could read. His name was Esco and he told us we were going to Helsinki to get the boat that would take us to England.

Coming to America, I remember the boat and train rides. But I'm not sure of just where we went. That's because I couldn't read and never heard of most of those places anyway. All I knew was I was going to Chicago somewhere in America and Uncle Heikki had given me a note that told where Uncle Anders lived.

It took two days to sail to Helsinki. But all I remember about that place is the docks were bigger than the ones at Oulu. Two days later we went aboard the boat that would take us to England. This time there were a lot more Finlanders coming with us. We were packed in on the bottom deck with suitcases and wicker baskets. But all I had was a few things in a rucksack that I used for a pillow.

Getting to England took three days and it wasn't long before most of us got seasick. That was an awful bad feeling but at least I wasn't hungry which was a good thing since I had run out of bread and cheese.

When we got to England even Esco didn't know what to do next. But finally one of the others found out how to get to the railroad station. From there we went across England to Liverpool. That took about a day but all I remember about it was looking out the window at how green every thing was.

In Liverpool I bought a couple of big sausages and some cheese and bread, which I hoped was enough before we got to America. The steerage fare was 75 markaa which left me with about half the money Uncle Heikki had given me. Our ship was a Red Star liner and it took 12 days to cross the ocean. Besides Finlanders, there were a lot of people along from other places,

Germans, Swedes and Irish. They looked pretty much like us but they talked different. The Irish were always singing and it was fun to listen even if we didn't know the words.

Half way across I used up my food and had to spend too many markaa to buy some more from the steward. I would have had to spend more except for a nice Finnish lady who a couple times gave me some bread and cheese. Her husband didn't look very happy about it.

When finally we came to New York the first thing we saw was a big statue of a lady with a torch. It had just been put up a few years earlier.

We landed at a place called "Castle Garden." First we had a medical checkup, then a man in uniform asked me something I couldn't understand. But I showed him the note with my name and that I was going to Chicago. He wrote something down and let me pass. In those days we didn't need passports. So that was all I needed to walk out the door into America. Since about half the other Finlanders who had come with us were going to Chicago I went along with them. First we changed our markaa for American money. After that it was a long train ride all night and most of the next day to when we came into an old tunnel-like train station.

It was there in that giant train place in Chicago that I said goodbye to Esco and the others that had been with us since Oulu. Esco was going on to see a brother in Milwaukee and I never saw him or any of the others again. As Esco walked off he turned and waved and just like that I was a 17-year-old Finland farm boy on my own, and I didn't know where to turn. All I had was piece of paper saying where Uncle Anders lived but where was it and how was I going to get there?

In all my life since, I don't think I ever felt so all alone and lost. Finally, I went up to one of the ticket windows and showed my note to the man inside. But whatever he said, I couldn't understand. So then he called a policeman who looked at my note and then took me outside and hollered to a horse cart driver. I don't know what he told him but it must have been to take me to my Uncle's house. Then the policeman made me dig into my pocket for some change. He picked out a couple of coins and gave them to the driver. Then he pointed for me to get in and off we went.

Sitting there while the cart jounced along dodging around horse trolleys, other people and stray dogs, I was scared for a lot of reasons. Were we going to the right place, would my uncle be home and if he was would he take me in? Just about when I was ready to jump out and run the driver stopped and pointed to a small wooden frame house. So I picked up my rucksack and got out. Then I walked up the stoop and knocked on the door.

After a minute a man answered. And I said, "Hello, Uncle Anders. I'm Reino Makki. Do you remember me? First, he looked at me in wonder. Then he threw his arms around me and said, "Come in, boy. Welcome to Chicago."

As soon as Uncle Anders got settled in Chicago, he had sent for his wife Sophie and their two children. When I got there, he could speak pretty good American and was boss carpenter for a big construction company. That night in his house was spent mostly with Aunt Sophie filling my supper plate and me filling them in with goings on back in Vaala. They were as hungry for news about kinfolk as I was for Aunt Sophie's dumplings. The kids were nice but it was plain they didn't know what to make of a cousin they had never heard of and couldn't speak American.

That night for the first time in my life, I slept on a soft mattress with a feather pillow. By the time I woke up Uncle Anders was gone to work and the kids to school. All our talk the night before had been about Finland. But it was America that interested me, and I wanted to start seeing it at once. When Aunt Sophie asked me what I would like to do, I said, "See Chicago."

So after breakfast she took me to a place where there was a train of cars with no horses attached. When we got on, a bell sounded and the train jerked and started to move. Aunt Sophie told me it was pulled by a cable car. It took us downtown where I saw a building ten stories high which Aunt Sophie told me was called a "Skyscraper." Chicago in those days was putting up buildings everywhere and there was a lot of jobs for workers with skills like carpenters or bricklayers.

That night Uncle Anders asked me what I could do. And I said, "All I know is how to farm and work hard." I said I would like someday to own my own farm. And he told me there was two things I had to do. One was to earn some money and the other was to learn to talk American.

Uncle Anders took me on as an apprentice carpenter at eight dollars a week which would have been more than forty markaa back in Finland. He also loaned me the money to buy work clothes and shoes. I paid him back a dollar a week.

After a few days I moved into a boarding house run by a Finlander and his wife. That cost me four dollars a week. But after I got Anders paid back, I was able to save a couple dollars a week. It wasn't long before I got pretty good at the work and Uncle Anders raised me up to ten dollars which was almost as much as his best men were making. Almost every week we worked all day Saturday and sometimes even Sunday, and the company would pay extra.

After two years I had saved almost $400 and was able to speak a little American.

Coming over on the boat I had heard about how the U.S. was giving free farms of 160 acres to anybody who could build a house, grow things on the land and live there for five years. But I also heard all the land was taken up by Swedes and Norskis who got here earlier. Then, one night at the boarding house someone read in a Finnish newspaper that there was still more land up in northern Minnesota. The next day after work I told Uncle Anders I was going up to Minnesota.

He warned me that he had heard the only land left was cutover land left behind by the loggers who had chopped down the pine forests. He said I was a good worker and if I stayed there, someday I'd be a boss carpenter like him. But I couldn't stop thinking about getting land of my own. And two weeks later I got on a train to Duluth. But first I gave Uncle Anders ten dollars and asked him to mail it to Uncle Heikki to buy something nice for Mom and Hilda.

In Duluth I learned that the free land to be had was up around the iron mining area of the Vermilion Range. So I rode the Duluth and Iron Range Railroad up to Tower which by then was the biggest place around north of Duluth. Now that the railroad connected with Two Harbors and Duluth, mining and lumbering was big business up there. But after looking around for a couple of weeks I saw Uncle Anders was right about farmland.

All there was, was what the loggers had left behind with pine stumps everywhere and big boulders and lots of small rocks. Talking to other Finlanders trying to scrape out a living there, they told me that the soil that once grew pine trees wasn't very good for growing potatoes or corn.

The boarding house where I was staying was run by a widow whose husband had gotten buried under a ton of rock and mud when the wall of an underground mining chamber gave way. Staying there besides me were eight or nine other Finlanders, most of them not much older than me. For three dollars a week we could sleep there two or three to a bed, and get the kind of meals a miner needs in order to swing a pick ten hours a day.

After a hard day underground, these miners turned in early. But sometimes after supper they'd sit around a little while and talk. One night one of them told me about some other Finns who had quit mining and gone a few miles south where the land was better for farming.

"You should go there and look for the best land left," he told me. "It's free. And even if it's not very good you can buy some cows and raise hay."

So with my rucksack and lugging my toolbox on my shoulder, I hiked down the old Indian trail to where after ten or twelve miles, I came to the valley of the Embarrass River. Here was country like back home along the Oulujoki. After looking around for a few days and talking with other Finn homesteaders, I staked out land that fronted on the river, a few miles north of the railroad station. There's a post office and a cooperative store there now. But then there was just the railroad station.

The loggers had been through and cut down the big pine, so that the land looked like a forest of stumps. There was lots of rocks, some swampy spots and a rise with cedar trees too small for the loggers to bother with. That was in June 1891. Except for my toolbox, it was the first thing I ever owned. I was proud of it. But in order to keep it, I had to build on the land and get something growing before five years was up.

It was early summer and I felt there was time to get started on a aitta or something before winter. In Tower, I loaded up with a saw, axes and sharpening stones, a tarpaulin, blankets, ropes, a peavey pole and some beans and cook pots. A wagon driver rode me and the supplies down to my land. It took nearly all day and I had to give him five dollars.*

I put up the tarpaulin for a shelter and piled up some stones for a fireplace. Then I decided to start with the sauna cause once I got it framed in, I could sleep in it. For the rest of the summer and fall I cut and stripped the bark off cedar trees. After skidding them down to near the river, I used my adz for dressing and grooving the logs for the walls. Then I fitted them together and stuffed moss and mud into the cracks.

*For the roof I used birch bark weighed down with poles like we did back home. The firebox came up from Duluth on the train and was left off at the railroad station. It was a barrel-like contraption with a door. I put firebrick around it and on top I put a layer of stones I dug out of the riverbank. This was a Finlander savasauna with a small hole in the wall to let out the smoke. By the time it was done, halla** was on the ground and I was sleeping inside of it.*

Having the sauna was a good start but before I'd be able to start farming I needed an ox to plow and pull stumps. I also needed some cows to start the herd and other things like a scythe and some seeds. Things like that were going to cost maybe $300 and the only way I could get that was to go to work.

---

* aitta is Finnish for small wooden shed

** halla is Finnish for early frost.

There were jobs to be had in the Tower mines or up north in the woods. Both paid about $2.00 a day but I figured to save more money lumbering since room and board went with that work. So in October I went up to the woods near Tower where I worked as a chopper and barker. First we'd chop the trees down. Then we'd slash the bark off one side so they'd skid along easier. I didn't have any trouble learning how, cause this was what I'd been doing all summer building the sauna.

In the woods we worked all day while it was light. At night we'd come in stompin' cold and there'd be tables full of pork and beans, biscuits, gravy, meat and potatoes. I never ate so good since.

There were about 80 of us in the crew. After supper we'd sit around smoking our pipes or gabbing for a bit before lights out. The racket of 80 men snoring was almost as loud as a sawmill. It went on till the bull cook, a half-witted old fellow who did camp chores, rousted us awake banging on an iron skillet. After stoking up with pancakes, hash and fried cakes, we'd head off for the woods before it was half light and wouldn't come back till dark.

Along about April the ice melted and the logs wouldn't skid. So cutting was stopped till things froze up again. Except for what I spent in the camp store, I had saved everything I earned. After five months working in the woods I had more than $200 and was ready to start farming.

- 9 -

FOURTH OF JULY ON LAKE VERMILION

They say childhood's most cherished memories are of the house in which one grew up and gathered for holidays with family. For sure every room in our old house in Buhl has meaning for me. But even more precious are memories from our family cabin on Lake Vermilion. Built by my grandfather, it now belongs to my Dad and his brother.

Following a system of log construction handed down through unknown generations, Grampa Eino Makki had fashioned its walls and beams from hand-hewn pine fitted by tongue and groove and secured by wooden pegs. Inside, the place is divided into kitchen, large front room and two bedrooms beneath a loft where kids fall asleep listening to the chatter of grownups down below. I close my eyes and hear again the gossip of women sipping coffee, the pot simmering on the ancient, wood-fired range.

Out on the porch, a kerosene lamp casts its flickering nimbus over the men smoking and talking. Let me anywhere smell pipe tobacco and I'm instantly transported back to that screened-in porch as Grampa Eino along with Dad, my Uncle Ty and assorted in-laws relive old times on the Iron Range.

Across the lake on a summer evening echoes the haunting warble of a loon. Some say it signals the start of a minnow run. Others claim it's simply a loon checking in with its mate. Either way it's a call that once heard is never forgotten.

Here on Lake Vermilion I have trolled for walleye in May, picked berries in July, set nets for whitefish in October and skied across frozen waters on starlit January nights. Grampa Eino long ago taught me how to repair docks, split and stack firewood and weave a cedar fan for the sauna. From Dad I learned to read evening skies and find my way home day or night from anywhere on the lake or the forest around it. In short, by the time I was ten, I could do what any other kid growing up on a northern lake could do.

Vermilion has been called the most beautiful lake in Minnesota, though how this was established out of thousands to be considered, I cannot say. But I question if anyone gazing upon its waters shimmering under skies of purest blue could deny its special charm. Running east to west for almost 30 miles, the lake twists beneath ancient rock bluffs, through narrow channels and across wide and sometimes turbulent bays. From its russet, iron-tinged waters rise islands large and small. And everywhere along its forested shoreline are craggy points, inlets and secluded coves.

Beyond scenic appeal, Vermilion also enjoys considerable historical fame. There is, of course, the Indian and fur-trading lore it shares with other northern lakes. More than that is its considerable significance in the development of Minnesota's iron mining industry.

In the 1880s, nearly a decade before the opening of the giant Mesabi Range where I grew up, underground mines at Vermilion's eastern shore were producing large quantities of ore. By the time they were closed in 1963, the mines at Tower and Soudan were the deepest in Minnesota, with shafts going down nearly a half a mile.

There being no roads along the north shore of Lake Vermilion, our cabin at Forgy's Point was accessible only by boat from a landing on the south side of the lake. In winter, we simply drove across thickly frozen ice and parked in front of our boathouse.

The air outside, except for the sweet pungency of birch smoke, is crystal clear. The stars are brilliant and cold, the silence so utter you can almost hear it. At water's edge the sauna is outlined against moonlit snow. Built of interlocking grooved pine logs and lined with cedar slats, it had endured the rigor of fifty northern winters.

From Buhl it was a forty-minute drive to our landing at Lake Vermilion. As I pulled up Dad waved to me from the dock. He looked the same as always, except even at my ripe old age of 28, I still hadn't got used to him looking up at me instead of looking down. I was taller by maybe four inches but he was wider through the chest and shoulders, a strong-looking man with wide blue eyes and steel gray hair. At age 53 he looked fit enough to try out for his old football team at Buhl High.

John Makki wasn't one for hugging his sons but now he put a hand on my shoulder. "You're lookin' kinda skinny."

"Don't worry, Mom's cooking'll take care of that in a hurry."

"Yeah," he grinned. "She'll wanta put ten pounds on you at the same time's she's tryin' a get ten offa me. It don't seem fair."

Crossing the lake in our old Alumacraft, Dad asked me how long I'd be able to stay.

"Probably four days. I have to leave right after the Fourth."

"That quick?"

"I wish it could be more. But school starts in a couple of months and I've still got to finish up my course outline."

Dad nodded. "Well, get ready for a big weekend. Looks like the whole gang'll be here. Dick's coming up tomorrow and so are Ty, Aunt Evie and your cousins. Near as I can tell everybody else in the bay'll be here for the weekend."

Along with our cabin, which is the second oldest, there are six others tucked along the shore of our bay. This stretch is called Forgy's Point after the man who first built there after

World War One. Mickey Forgy was gone before I was born but he's well remembered by old timers around Lake Vermilion. They say he was quite the character.

Almost any gathering of Makkis puts a strain on sleeping arrangements. Mom and Dad take one of the bedrooms, Uncle Ty and Aunt Evie the other. Cousin Elna, her husband and two kids sleep in the loft. And my brother Dick and I, along with our cousins Emil and Paul, bed down on cots on the porch. When once in a while the whole clan shows up, we open up the bunkhouse out back.

Even though we think of the cabin as belonging to all of us, its actual title is shared by Dad and his brother Ty. Some day this might lead to an inheritance problem but for now we don't think about that. What we do is take turns. The men come up for walleye opener and deer season. Uncle Ty and his family come for a month during the summer. And we all try to get here for long weekends like the Fourth and Labor Day.

Dad and Mom live the closest and take care of the place, cutting the grass, tending to whatever needs fixing, opening up in Spring and shutting down in late Fall. Considering that when the whole gang is here we have to stand in line for everything from the sauna to the biffy, we get along pretty well.

Except for supper, meals are catch can. My first morning there was no exception. Mom put out biscuits and gravy for whoever showed up, which turned out to be me, Dad, cousin Elna and her kids. The others trickled in later and put together whatever they wanted. Lunch is pretty much the same. But for supper we all cram around the big table in the dining room.

Although all the women help out, one of them is in charge every night. Big favorites are the cabbage rolls Aunt Evie calls "galompkies," and Mom's pastys, the Cornish meat and potato pies that miners used to carry in their lunch pails. Served piping hot and smothered in gravy, pastys are a special Iron Range treat.

The Fourth is a big affair in our little bay. Things get started with what we grandly bill as the Forgy's Point Yacht Club Invitational. If there actually was such a club, any connection with the sea going jumble we called a regatta would have besmirched its fair name.

The first thing a stranger might note is that no two boats in this ragtag flotilla are the same. The nine or ten craft inching up to the starting line might include an eight-foot pram, a 60-year-old restored wooden Star, a scow, a catamaran and once even a canoe with a sail.

Prerace ritual requires their motley crews and loyal supporters to get jump-started with a "splice of the mainbrace." The potation, known as "Dock Walloper," is said to have been invented by the estimable Mickey Forgy to celebrate the building of his first dock. Its ingredients are closely guarded secrets which are changed every year at the whim of the maker. The one constant is rum and plenty of it with the effect that the event becomes more a test of sobriety than a race.

The eagerly fought for trophy is an old-fashioned thunder mug, gilded and inscribed with the names of past winners. Competition for this poor man's version of the America's Cup is, to put it mildly, intense. There have even been allegations, though never proven, about one shifty skipper, who obsessed by dreams of conquest, secretly contrived to sail sober.

It must also be told that skullduggery is the rule rather than the exception. There was the time, for example, when the pre-race favorite couldn't figure out why his finely trimmed Buccaneer wallowed so badly at the start. That was until he discovered that a rope lashed to his keel was dragging a twenty-pound anchor.

Early in the history of the race the front-runner tipped over just a few yards short of the finish line. Kicking furiously, the skipper pushed his capsized craft over the line a split second ahead of his closest pursuer. Despite loud cries of protest, the victory was upheld.

A memorable episode was the time a noted loser cleverly resorted to a golf umbrella in hopes of squeezing out an extra iota of propulsion. Alas, this laudable scheme was undone by a gust of wind that transformed the hapless bumbershoot into a colorful display of shreds.

Although I had tried several tricks including the sewing of an extra two feet on our mainsail, what promised to be my most successful touch of chicanery was the time I covertly rigged a homemade jib. Sneaking it aboard hours before the race I unfurled it shortly after the starting gun, only to discover that the extra tension was more than my boat could handle. Instead of added thrust it pulled the bow under water while elevating the stern. The effect was not unlike a U-Boat in the first throes of a crash dive. While I tugged at the disruptive canvas other crews went by with hoots of derision. By the time I got it down the mast was bent and we were getting a great view of the race from a hundred yards astern.

The course is a four-mile loop out of our bay, around Center Island and back. The only quarter given is for little boats like a pram or a sailfish, whose skippers get a ten-minute head-start. After that the shotgun sounds, followed by five minutes of pandemonium and shouted invective that continues even as faster boats pull away.

This year, the race went to the swift, as my wily cousin Emil ran away from the fleet in a secretly borrowed E-Scow. Ten minutes later my brother Dick and I came across as a respectable third. By then after an hour on the water, we were darn near sober.

- 10 -

ENTER CHRISTABEL WHITE

After the sailboat shenanigans the company adjourned to a post race bash hosted by the Fogartys at the other end of the bay. By the time I got there the party was in full swing with people spilling out onto the verandah. There were at least sixty there in various stages of partying, gabbing, laughing, munching hot-dogs or nursing drinks.

Pouring myself a beer from a keg buried in ice, I looked across to the happy company, some old friends or neighbors, others new to me. There'd been a lot of departures since Fourth of July blasts I remembered as a kid. Old timers like Doc Pederson, Pop McCall and my Grandfather Eino had gone to their reward. Others had moved away, replaced by newcomers I hadn't yet met.

Happily, I saw big Ernie Olshefski talking to somebody I couldn't quite see out on the porch. Ernie and I shared more than a few secrets, including the long ago Saturday night back in Buhl that we scaled the steeple of the First Lutheran Church and made off with the bellclapper. Our regret was not seeing the face of the warden, who the next morning tugged at the bell rope to summon the faithful. A couple nights later, chastened by congregational outrage, we took once more to the heights to restore the clapper to its rightful position.

Grinning at the memory, I started toward Ernie only to stop in my tracks. It couldn't be but it was! It was Christie he was talking to—Christabel White, the girl I had yearned for since she wore ribbons in her pigtails. There never was a prettier girl in grammar school, Buhl High or college. I could still see her walking to class, her pleated skirt, white collar above a plaid sweater, bobby sox and loafers. For me, through all those years, Christie had been the unattainable, the smoky beauty with grace and style to her movements and a smile that spread down to her dimples.

There had been other girls, of course. It wasn't like I sat around in sackcloth and ashes. But somehow it had always come back to Christie. A glimpse of her anywhere, in class or passing in the hallway, was enchantment. Christabel White—even her name had sounded like poetry. I used to say it to myself just to hear it.

But some things are not meant to be. At Buhl High she had fallen for Buddy Cosgrove, our All-State fullback. And that's the way it stayed through college and right up to the altar. You'd think I would have gotten over it, particularly since mine wasn't the heartbreak of a busted romance. What I was doing was mooning over something I never had, which is kind of like a double negative. Only in this case it didn't make a positive. As far as Christie was concerned Buddy Cosgrove was a one-way street.

Now suddenly there she was, a perfection of raven hair and creamy complexion. Just looking at her I felt the way you do when an old song triggers a bittersweet memory. Six years and I hadn't gotten over anything. By comparison, my hankering for Eulie, the cashier back in Babbitt, was like a taste for warm beer instead of champagne. The date Eulie and I never had was just that. But seeing Christie even now seemed a lifetime lost.

Her smile when she saw me beamed across the room. "Jim!" She came toward me with arms extended. "We were just talking about you. How long has it been?"

Way too long," I said, holding her for a moment. If she

didn't remember the last time, I wasn't going to remind her.

Back at Buhl High all those years ago, I had a lot of fun going out for track and football. Running and the hurdles were my favorites. But I also had a knack for catching a football which got me the job at right end. So after our games on Saturday, I was a regular at the football parties, where Buddy, who was usually the hero of the game, was the main attraction.

I myself wasn't a great fan of his, and not just because of his lock on Christie. Maybe it was his swaggering confidence. He just seemed too full of himself. Obviously he was fond of Christie. But I wondered if it was because she was an adornment to his ego rather than for her as a person.

There's no question mine was a minority opinion. At parties kids flocked around him. The big shouldered extrovert was as quick with the suds as he was hitting the line. He loved to sing and most always before the night was over, there would be Buddy, red-faced, one arm around Christie and the other waving a beer stein, leading a chorus of *Clementine*, or some other drinking song.

Once when it went beyond boisterous to bawdy, Christie retired to the sidelines. And it was there, sitting on somebody's hallway steps, that we talked about our plans after high school. We were both headed for the University at Duluth, I on an academic scholarship, Christie, because that's where Buddy was headed as the star recruit for the football team.

For him, life at UMD was more of the same. He hit the books just often enough to get by and went on to have his number retired as the only Bulldog ever named All-Conference four years in a row. For me, it worked out different.

Football at Buhl had been fun. Here it was business. Things like class work, time in the library and other activities tended to get buried under the obsessive go-go of college football. It was a grind that went on all year, the weight room, the running, spring practice, two-a-day fall practice, the intensity of the regular season. The coaches weren't happy if you spent more time on homework than your playbook.

It took me about half my freshman season to realize four years of that was not a commitment I wanted to make. Finally, after a restless night, I told the Coach I was giving it up. He must have thought I was angling for something.

"What's the problem? You're getting playing time. Next year you'll probably be a starter and I'll get you a full ride."

"Sorry, Coach. I've already got a scholarship. But I have to hit the books harder if I'm going to keep it."

Coach threw up his hands like he didn't understand. But good old Buddy figured he did. He cornered me as I was clearing out my locker.

"O.K. Chicken," he rasped. "Now I know why I never liked you. You're yellow."

"Get stuffed, Buddy! You don't like me because I don't like you. And the reason I'm quitting is so I won't wind up on dumb street like you."

As he came charging at me, I was saved by Ernie Olshefski who jumped between us. After looking at Ernie, who was even bigger and every bit as tough, Buddy backed off. "Get lost, quitter!" he snarled.

Sad to say, Ernie flunked out in the middle of his sophomore year. Besides being my best friend, he was the rock of the offensive line. Buddy'd been running off his tackle since high school. Some said he was never the same runner after Ernie left.

Meanwhile it wasn't till my junior year that I felt comfortable enough with my studies to think about sports. That spring I went out for track and broke a few tapes as a quarter miler and hurdler. And finally during the last semester of my senior year, I wound up sitting next to Christie White in a medieval history class.

Sitting by her side for three months, drinking in her perfume, her smile and unassuming grace, so full of her and yet so hopelessly unable to speak of this, was almost more than I could bear. And then one day, almost without thinking, I blurted out an invitation to come with me for a dorm picnic the following Sunday. The words were barely out of my mouth before I tried to choke them off, not because I was worried about good old Buddy but because there was no dorm picnic on tap.

The whole thing was absurd, a mindless, off-the-wall impulse. When everybody knew she was Buddy's girl, why in the world did I imagine she would say yes to me?

Christie and I had been schoolmates since first grade. Now, she looked at me as though seeing me for the first time. "I don't think Buddy would like that."

"Well, that's his problem, isn't it?"

Instead of answering, Christie stared at me slightly puzzled. Then wonderful to tell, her face lit up with a smile that had been magic for me since sixth grade. "I'd like that very much."

Talk about words to live by. I must have got to my next class by floating on air. It wasn't till I began to worry about how to explain about the picnic that I came back to earth.

Two days later, on a motorcycle borrowed from my roommate, I picked her up at the Lake Superior residence hall. It was late spring and the scent of lilacs was in the air. For all the years since, the perfume of their flowering has been enough to set me off in almost haunting memory of that day with Christie.

I remember her grin of agreeable conspiracy as I stumbled over a lame excuse about the other kids having to study. And I can still see her look of disbelief when she spotted the bike.

"Do you know what you're doing on that thing?"

"I know one end from the other. Here, put this on." I handed her a safety helmet that didn't quite fit but on her was awful cute.

Looking more than a little dubious, she followed my instructions and saddled the machine behind me, arms around my waist.

"All set?"

"I just hope you are."

And off we went, over Skyline Drive to Mesaba Avenue, where coasting down the long hill Christie hung on even more tightly—which was all right with me. Finally, after we leveled out on Lake Street, she began to relax.

At Harbor's edge the Aerial Lift Bridge was up and traffic stopped. Parking the bike, we walked up close just as an ocean freighter, the *Kapitona A. Lucka*, blasted its big horn and came gliding through. Christie waved and what seemed like the whole crew waved back, gesturing and shouting strange words that Christie took to be friendly greetings.

Moments later the bridge came down and we crossed over onto Minnesota Point, a curious finger of land that sticks out into the lake to form a natural breakwater for Duluth Harbor. Whizzing along Minnesota Avenue, we passed a community of quaint little houses lining either side of the road as it stretched south toward the point.

Nowadays, the tip of the island is a well-groomed park and recreation area. Back then, it was less developed with only a rustic road and a scattering of picnic tables. At the point, facing across a half mile of water, we could have boated over to Wisconsin in five minutes—a trip that by our motorcycle would have taken an hour.

Finding a spot where the grass had been mowed, I parked the bike and spread the blanket I had jammed into one of the saddlebags. From the other, I fished out a bottle of wine and some ham and cheese sandwiches.

While I fiddled with the corkscrew, Christie wondered how I'd found this place.

"Uh, a friend of mine told me about it," not wanting to tell her the "friend," who had indeed been friendly, was a very pretty secretary who worked in the Dean's office.

Later, with the sandwiches gone, I dug once more into the saddlebag for my surprise, a red kite which I assembled and hitched to a big ball of string. Then, while Christie held it up, I took off running. As she let go, the kite took off and was soon way up and out over the water. As we sat on the blanket drinking wine and taking turns holding the string, the kite bobbed and weaved far out over the harbor.

Finally, with the wine gone, Christie turned to me, "Should we let it go?"

When I nodded, she threw up her hands and the kite took off in a wobbling, gradual descent before disappearing into the trees along the Wisconsin shoreline.

Counting a final stop for a beer in the taproom at Fitger's, it was dark when I delivered Christie back to her dorm. Turning to me with a kiss on my cheek, she said, " Today was the most fun I ever had here."

It was after that I knew I'd love her forever.

The next day Buddy chased me down. "Listen, creep, if you ever even look at Christie again, I'll turn you into a platter of hash."

"You know what Buddy? I think I'll leave that up to Christie."

If we hadn't been in the middle of the Quad, I think he would have popped me. Instead, he just glared and said, "I ain't gonna tell you again." Then he stalked off.

The next day I waited for Christie after class. When she saw me, she hesitated and then walked up.

"Jim, you're somebody special and I've always liked you. But Buddy is the guy I'm going to marry. So," she paused, "it's best I don't see you any more."

With a sad little smile she turned away. And I grasped that something was over and something begun. Whatever I would do after college it would be without the wistful hope of a future with Christabel White.

Shortly after graduation, I got an invitation to their wedding. It was a big affair at the Chapel on the Lake. Not surprisingly, I didn't go. That was July of 1965 and two weeks later I was in the Army.

In the end, Buddy's hoped for career as a pro-footballer didn't pan out. The Vikes cut him halfway through training camp. After that, he and Christie moved to Duluth, where Buddy worked for a car agency. Over the years I had often wondered about Christie but that was the last I had heard of her.

And suddenly there she was, holding my hands and saying, "You're just as handsome as ever."

"Hey Christie," I blurted, "You're stealing my lines."

In her case it was true. Christabel Cosgrove nee White was even more stunning than I remembered, skin creamy, raven hair glossy, ebony eyes set wide apart, high cheekbones curving down to a full soft mouth. At 28, the girl I'd adored since grade school was altogether a striking presence in beauty and ladylike grace. Almost overwhelmed, I didn't even notice when Ernie slipped away.

It turned out she had come up from Duluth as a weekend guest of Ellie and Ken Reimers, who had a cabin on an island across our bay. Ellie had been her roommate and best friend in college. Buddy, it seemed, was in Detroit on business. Monkey business, I suspected from the way she said it.

"Can I get you a drink?"

"Not just now. But I'd like some fresh air."

So we wandered outside and since she'd never been there, I led her down the shoreline path to our place. The rest of the family was at the party, so sitting on the porch steps, we had the place to ourselves.

Her smile as she turned to me was only half teasing. "You didn't come to our wedding."

"C'mon Christie!" I was a little nettled. "You know darn well why I didn't come."

"I suppose I do. But I'd still like to hear it from you."

We are a curious people, we Finnish Americans, when it comes to talking about emotions. I looked at her, not at all sure I wanted to tell about a love she hadn't accepted. "Do you really want me to rake over those old coals?"

Her eyes troubled as she stared directly into mine. "Only if they're still warm."

I sighed. "Christie, if you have to know, if I'd come to see you marry somebody else, it would have been like looking on while my heart was being chopped out. Even if I knew it was hopeless, I just wasn't up to the pain of seeing you walk down the aisle with Buddy."

Her hand on my wrist was soft, "And now?"

"Do I still feel that way? I don't know, Christie. It doesn't hurt so much as it used to. But seeing you now," I paused. "Yeah, I guess I do. Does that bother you?"

"Bother me?" She breathed softly. "No Jim, it doesn't bother me."

Then she began to cry and I didn't know what else to do but put my arms around her. Holding her close, her tears wetting my face, I was confused but happier than I could ever remember. It was maybe the most tender moment of my life, even if I didn't know what was going on.

After a while she sat up and wiped at her eyes with a hankie. "I think now I'd like that drink."

So I went into the cabin and made one for both of us. When I came back Christie had gone down to the dock and was staring out at the lake. She looked at me with a half smile as I handed her the drink. "I suppose I'm acting like a darn fool."

I shook my head not knowing what to say, or even think.

Christie sipped her drink and then set it down. "Jim, dear kind Jim. You were part of all my years of growing up, the kid who used to carry my books, the friendly face in class."

"Part of the scenery you mean, like the lamp post on the corner," I kidded her.

That brought a smile. "Not like that, you idiot. More like the brother I never had. I used to hear the girls talk about you and when you ran those hurdles, you were the most graceful boy in school."

She shook her head. "But by then I was completely wrapped up in Buddy. He was so big and popular, so sure of himself."

"Yeah," I said dryly. "I seem to recall."

Ignoring that, Christie went on. "When Buddy came along I never really thought about anybody else until the time you asked me out on that picnic."

She reached for my hand. "I have to think about how to say this. You see when you asked, I thought you were kidding. Everybody knew I was Buddy's girl. But there you were, the boy

I knew all my life asking me for a date. And after a minute when I saw you were serious, I thought 'why not?' Buddy doesn't own me yet."

"You probably knew there wasn't really a picnic."

At that Christie laughed outright. "I did when you showed up with that silly motorcycle. But once I got over being scared it was so much fun that day. You were so different than Buddy. Just as sure of yourself but in a quiet way. I guess you knew Buddy didn't like you. He told me you were scared of football. But when you asked me to go with you, I knew you weren't afraid of him or anything else."

"So then you told me to take a hike."

She looked at me, her wide eyes direct in their gaze, "I guess I did. But what else could I do? I mean, Buddy was real upset."

She was quiet for a moment. "In the excitement of graduation and planning the wedding, I managed not to think too much about you. But when you didn't show up it hurt. I don't know what I expected but somehow I wondered if I'd made a mistake."

"Aw Geez, Christie!" It was almost a moan. "I don't know what to say."

"What is there to say? Except I guess I owe it to you to say I've got a soft spot for you. But I'm married to Buddy."

What she said was direct and honest. Still there was a sense of something unsaid.

She squeezed my hand, "We'd better get back before people start thinking the worst."

So we walked back to the party and a short while later she went with Ellie and Ken Reimers back to their cabin across the bay.

As I drove to Harwell College the next day, remembrance of Christie clung to me like the haunting trace of her perfume. But whatever I longed for my brain was telling me to forget. Christie had let her guard down for a moment but the reality was she was married and planned to stay that way.

Lake Vermilion, Christie, growing up in Buhl—all essential parts of who I was. The miles down to Harwell flowed by in hours of bittersweet memory.

- 11 -

HARWELL COLLEGE

Down at Harwell, I spent the rest of the summer toodling between my room at the faculty club and the campus library. Towering over Lake Pepin like a Greek acropolis, Harwell is unique for having been founded on a site where at the time no road or structure of any kind existed. As the story goes, Bishop Lyman Harwell had come down from St. Paul to meet with members of his flock in Lake City. His purpose was to establish for posterity a place of learning where young men of stout faith could prepare for ministerial calling in environs free from urban corruption.

Curiously for the times, he decreed that the College should also admit young women of high moral standing. Possibly this was with foresight that future propagators of the faith would need helpmeets, wherever in the wilderness their calling might beckon.

Legend has it that on a crisp September morn, Bishop Harwell led a small company of laity across open fields overlooking the mighty river below. Then, according to Elephalet Partridge, a Lake City merchant present on the occasion, "Just as the sun rose above the vapors of Lake Pepin, Bishop Harwell walked away from the group. Suddenly he stopped and in his quick, decisive manner thrust his staff into the ground, 'Here gentlemen, here is the spot for the College.' And on that spot it was placed."

That was in 1871, and five years were to pass before the College opened its doors to admit the first class of twelve men and two young ladies. Meanwhile Bishop Harwell and members of his fold had put their shoulders to the wheel, not only in the raising of funds but also in the erecting of its first buildings. Trinity Hall, a dormitory, and "Old College," with three classrooms and faculty offices took their place near a small chapel, standing, according to Elder Partridge, exactly where the Bishop had planted his staff. For several years, until the raising of a woman's dormitory, female students resided in rooms in Lake City.

The original buildings, faced with native stone, now look across an elm-shaded quadrangle. Though still in use, they are dwarfed by the great campus of classrooms, labs, dorms, library, administrative buildings and athletic facilities that have grown up around them.

Although Harwell has maintained traditional ties with the order of its founder, it is no longer thought of as a Church college. This is largely to do with the vision of its second president, the Rev. William Potter Knotts. While mindful of the parochial concerns of his calling, he was also able to foretell the needs of a burgeoning region for people trained for entry into other professions, as well as for leadership in the business world.

During the years in which Doctor Knotts recruited faculty and broadened curriculum, he was able to draw on the wise counsel of his friend, William Watts Folwell, President of the recently established University of Minnesota. Though Bishop Harwell was never in wholehearted accord with the new direction toward worldly affairs, it is to his credit that he continued for all of his years to rally financial support for the College which bore his name. Nearly all of the campus buildings erected during its early years bear names of wealthy Twin Cities parishioners whose deep pockets had been plucked by the artful fingers of the good Bishop. In those days it was said that Knotts was the

College's leading scholar while the Bishop was its chief extractor.

Today, owing largely to their legacy, Harwell is a well-endowed private college with a faculty teaching in just about every discipline that can be accommodated under the banner of liberal arts. Its student body of 3,000 men and women come from all over the United States and 50 foreign countries. However, it was upon the thousand or so in-state students that I pinned my hopes for enrollment in a course about Minnesota history.

In that regard, I was pleased to note that the catalog for the academic year 1972-73 listed a three credit course, entitled, "History 240—Only in Minnesota," James R. Makki, Ph.D.

With just two months to get ready, I repaired to twin-spired MacNaughton Library, where the first order of business was to fill out my course outline. Starting with an overview of material to be covered, I wanted to include some of the distinctions that set Minnesota apart from all other states in America.

- 12 -

NOTES FOR COURSE INTRODUCTION

History 240-J. R. Makki

Welcome to 1st class to take this course. Also my 1st time to teach it. So join them in hoping for the best.

Every state has at least something unique to boast about. But it is a premise of this course that Minnesota has more than most. Like the mythical giant Paul Bunyan, it's bigger than life.

Nature has been exceptionally lavish to Minnesota. Vast forests, fertile plains, sparkling lakes, mighty rivers and three giant iron ranges—one of which, "Mesabi," was for years the world's largest iron deposit ... Ore from that one range helped build 20th century America—and defend it in two World Wars.

Cavalcade of characters: Ice Age primitives, early Indians, later Chippewa and Sioux, European explorers, missionaries, voyageurs, fur traders, soldiers, pioneer settlers, statesmen, immigrants, magnates of industry, medical leaders, lumberjacks and iron miners.

Minnesota became a territory in 1849. At that time its western border reached all the way to the Missouri River. Clipped off at Red River when Minnesota became a state in 1858.

Today's boundaries: Canada in north, Iowa in south,

Lake Superior and Wisconsin in the east and Dakotas in the west.

We won't worry too much about dates, treaties and boundaries but above dates and rough boundaries strike me as likely to bob up on a quiz.

Name of state probably from Sioux word sounding like *Mnishota.* Note: English spelling from sound of Indian words is pretty much guess work. Mnishota is supposed to be Sioux for "cloudy waters," or more lyrically, "sky tinted waters."

Nicknames: 10,000 Lakes—Probably another 4 or 5,000 but "Land Of Almost 15,000 Lakes" would look awkward on our license plates.

Also called "North Star State"—because for a century before Alaska came in Minnesota was northern most state in the union.

Minnesota lumber industry at peak in mid-19th century. Forests of white pine believed endless ... great rafts of lumber floated down Mississippi and other state rivers before coming of RRs. Lumber cut and milled in Minn. forests built houses and factories in Chicago, St. Louis, Kansas City, Des Moines, Twin Cities and throughout America's expanding heartland.

Wheat and flour industries also burgeon here in late 1800s ... Rich soil ... inventions like the McCormick Reaper and emerging network of RRs push Minn. to world leadership in wheat growing ... Red River Valley becomes "Breadbasket of the World."

Flour mills ... powered by Falls of St. Anthony ... new methods of processing ... propel Minneapolis into flour milling leadership ... by end of century 24 mills operating around the Falls ... names like Washburn, Crosby and Pillsbury known all over the world.

Great distinction to be number one in anything. Here in Minn. we've been four times a world leader: lumbering, wheat growing, flour milling and iron ore mining ... not to mention leadership in the fur trade, Minnesota's 1st great industry.

Natural resources basic to our history ... tough to rank them in importance ... e.g. Between iron ore deposits or our great rivers which more vital to Minn. development?

During 4 centuries Minn. waterways have provided a network of routes for exploration and commerce. Three of continent's longest rivers—Mississippi, Minnesota and Red River of the North start in this state.

Mississippi is principal river of U.S. ... starts in Minn ... runs 2,400 miles ... touches on 10 states ... tributaries such as Missouri and Ohio connect with at least that many more.

Laurentian Divide in northeast Minn. one of few places in world rivers drain in 3 directions. Saying: a raindrop falling there could wind up in one of 3 oceans. Rivers north of Divide drain to Hudson Bay and eventually Arctic Ocean. Streams south of that hilly ridge drain into the Mississippi and on to the Gulf of Mexico ... The St. Louis and other rivers that drain into Superior go via the Great Lakes and St. Lawrence to the Atlantic. It's been suggested that Minnesota be called the "Mother of Three Seas."

These are some of the distinctions that interwoven with our human history set Minnesota apart from anywhere else in the world. A geologist has pointed out that Minnesota's history could have been enacted only in Minnesota. That's the gist of 1st session.

Mineral resources that set state apart had origin billions of years ago. Reading assignments will touch on some of the cataclysmic events during eons before humans arrived. That's all there's time for in a 16-week course. For more, refer them to a geology course.

It's pretty well agreed there was animal life here before, or at least between the comings and goings of glaciers. 1st humans didn't show up to near the end, or just after the Ice Age. In future meetings we'll talk about some of the successions of prehistoric peoples who occupied the land before recorded history.

Ask if questions:

- 13 -

HOW THE MAKKIS CAME TO BUHL

At our department meeting September 15, Jud Leonard said he'd be happy if twenty kids signed up for my new course. As it turned out, twice that many showed up a few days later for my first lecture. And we were even more tickled when four more checked in late for the second session. One of them told me he'd heard this was a fun course.

"A fun course?" I had to think about that. Sure, it ought to be interesting. That was the whole idea. But it also needed to be meaningful. I wanted to give these kids a feel for what had been exacted in raw human effort to give them the place they had grown up taking for granted.

With that in mind I headed back to the library to try and beef up my notes for the next few sessions on prehistoric peoples in Minnesota. At least that was my intention. But sitting there at my study desk, I couldn't seem to get started. For some reason Christie White popped into mind. And once she got there she stirred up a lot of memories about growing up in Buhl.

How the Makkis came to settle in that once busy mining town came about after my great-grandfather Reino got tired of trying to coax a living out of the stingiest soil in Minnesota. As he was to tell it in his WPA interview, the only good thing about farming around Embarrass was that all his neighbors were Finns.

One of the first to arrive had been Kalle Saarinen, who in 1880 walked up from Duluth with his family in tow.

The Saarinens had emigrated from the province of Vaasa and had landed in Minnesota by way of the Great Lakes. In Duluth, Kalle worked in a sawmill for several years before walking up the Vermilion trail to stake a claim near Embarrass. With the help of his wife, five sons and two daughters, he had cleared a dozen acres and was well established in dairy farming by the time my great-grandfather Reino came in 1891.

As neighbors only a few miles apart, Kalle had been helpful in suggesting how to get started during Reino's first year on his claim. But in the second year, as summer waned, Kalle asked a pointed question. "Who's going to look after your place when you go up north to work in the woods?"

Reino had already been stewing over that problem and had decided to ask Arvo Salmi, whose land bordered on his, if one of his sons would tend to his cows in return for keeping the milk.

When Reino explained this, old Kalle said, "I got a better idea. You need a woman and my oldest daughter Hilma needs a man. Marry her and she'll take care of your place in the winter, help you in the summer and give you sons to help you even more."

Reino was flustered. He'd seen Hilma only once and recalled her as an unsmiling, rather shy girl, who seemed older than her 20 years. At the time she was working in Duluth as a housemaid.

"I hadn't really thought about taking a wife just yet," Reino stammered.

"It's time you did. You can't handle that farm all by yourself and Hilma's just the one for you."

"But what if she doesn't want to?"

"That don't matter. She's the oldest and it's her time. What's more," Kalle extolled, "she goes to night school in Duluth and knows how to talk English. She can teach you and your children."

This may have been the clincher. For in fact Hilma and Reino were married in October 1892. Three weeks later he left to work in the woods north of Tower. And in July, after his return, Hilma presented him with the first of three sons and a daughter.

The boys, Kalle, Heikki and the youngest, Eino, who was to become my grandfather, were introduced to farm chores early. Along with lugging water to fill the copper boilers on the stove, collecting eggs, slopping pigs, gathering berries and stacking wood, all three boys and their sister Johanna could milk cows by the time they were six. But they were still too young for the backbreaking work of plowing, scything and pulling stumps.

Hilma helped with the heavy work whenever she could between bearing children, cooking, patching pants and boiling and beating clothes on the scrub board. Like Reino, she knew little rest from dawn to dusk.

That was how it was when Reino began to reflect on their lot. For eight years, long enough to get clear title to his land grant, Reino had hacked at rocky soil, pulled stumps, grown meager crops for the kitchen and hay for the cattle. He had done it—become a landowner in America. Compared to the five and ten acre plots he remembered back in Finland, his holding was enormous. But most of it was still stump land good only for hay. It had taken him eight wearying years to clear about four acres, just enough to eke an existence out of the grudging soil.

With help from Hilma's brothers, he had built their tupa, or main cabin, on a rise facing down toward the river. Connected underground behind the cabin was a root cellar for storing the potatoes, squash, beets and other vegetables needed to get them through the winter.

Modest as these holdings were, they were his. Besides that, he was free. But what kind of freedom was it to be a slave to his own land? For the bare three months between the killing frosts of spring and fall, he worked "dark to dark," grubbing at ungenerous soil. In winter, it was ten hours a day stripping and axing in the woods.

So here they were, a family of six living in a one-room cabin, lit by the feeble light of coal oil lamps. At night, the boys climbed a ladder to the loft to sleep on sacks filled with hay. Reino and Hilma made their bed behind a curtain in the corner while Johanna slept on a pallet by the kitchen stove.

On the same kind of land, his father-in-law had 20 acres under cultivation, a large herd of dairy cows and a two-story framed farm home. But Kalle Saarinen had the unpaid help of five husky sons.

Reino Makki had come to America hoping for a better way than he had known on that farm back in Oulu. Maybe this was the best he could do. But he had a want to do something for Hilma and the children, to give them somehow more than a life of drudgery and bare survival.

These were not easy thoughts for Reino to give voice to. His conversation with Hilma, normally sparse, was conducted in two languages. Hilma had pretty good English but Reino's was just passable. By themselves Hilma was willing to talk Finnish. But in front of the children she spoke only English. "These children are American," she insisted. "And that's the way they have to talk."

Reino agreed but he was more concerned about their schooling. Hilma had tried to teach them things youngsters should know. But now they were ready for more and the nearest schoolhouse was eight miles away at Embarrass Junction.

Most of the men who emigrated from Europe came looking for work. Those without a special skill had to take what they could get. In cities like Duluth they dug ditches or worked on docks. In the country they hired out as farm hands. But Reino did have a skill and he could talk English. Years before in Chicago, he had turned away from carpentry in order to live on his own land and make thing grow. Now he began to wonder if he had done the right thing. To Reino's deliberate way of thinking, notions of change came slowly. And it was only after many nights of brooding that he decided, almost with pain, to try a way of life more beneficial to his family. Money was one object. But more important were his hopes for his children. He wanted them to have the schooling he never had and to know more in life than pulling stumps and grubbing at stubborn soil.

In 1897, with iron mining booming in northeast Minnesota, there was plenty of work for a skilled carpenter. Reino could have gone north to Tower, but work there in an underground mine meant toil by candlelight deep in the bowels of the earth. Instead, he decided to look into the open pit mining operations of the western Mesabi. After a short visit to check things out, he made up his mind. Over the pleas of his father-in-law, he sold his farm to Arvo Salmi for $400 cash.

In early summer, he loaded his family and a few of Hilma's household needs onto a farm wagon. And off they went, Reino leading his oxcart with Sophia, their best milk cow, trailing behind. After two days and nights they came to a cluster of mining sheds and rough cabins, which rude settlement on the shores of Longyear Lake was later to be named Chisholm. There Reino could have bought land fronting on the lake for three dollars an acre. But there was no school yet established, so the Makkis continued on a few miles to the boomtown of Hibbing.

What they found was a village of a thousand or more people surrounded by open pit mines and swarming with transient miners and lumberjacks. The place had more saloons than stores and a few dirt roads, some of them still with uncleared pine stumps. But there was also a Lutheran Church and best of all a village schoolhouse. Acting on a tip from a Finnish lumberjack, Reino located a tool shed left behind when the Swan River Lumber Company moved its lumber camp east of town. After buying it from the company for $50, Reino fixed it up enough for his family to move in.

By the time of the Makkis' arrival in 1897, Hibbing was just starting to blossom into the "Iron Ore Capital of the World." Its Hull-Rust-Mahoning open pit was the largest and richest iron ore deposit ever known. And as mining operations surged so did Hibbing's population. With each new wave of miners and shopkeepers, the demand for housing and other structures became more intense. For Reino the situation was perfect. He found work immediately, not in the mines but with a lumberyard that built houses. Before the summer was over he was promoted to crew boss at four dollars a day.

Hilma, despite her earlier qualms about leaving Embarrass, soon found herself happier than she could remember. In September, Kalle and Heikki, her two oldest, began walking a mile a day to school. And on Sundays she led her sometimes reluctant flock to worshipful services at Christ Memorial Church.

As the years passed and the children were able to take on more chores, Hilma's work burden eased. Reino, meanwhile, continued to work at building houses in Hibbing and in the newly incorporated village of Chisholm. In 1902, he and his crew did much of the framework for Chisholm's first schoolhouse.

Except for real busy times, Reino worked nine-hour shifts and half a day Saturday. This left time to further fix up and add to the tool shed he had converted into a home. In growing season, he and the boys planted potatoes, squash, cabbages and beets on the small plot they had cultivated out back.

No longer did Reino have to go into the woods for winter work in a logging camp. When the weather turned harsh, he and his crew found plenty of work indoors. And with Reino earning $25 or more a week, the Makkis found themselves in the unaccustomed position of being able to put something away for a rainy day.

As the new century arrived, my great-grand parents Reino and Hilma applied for American Citizenship. And it was while studying for such that Reino first learned what his children already knew about George Washington and the Declaration of Independence.

In 1900, Reino and Hilma, standing beside a dozen other immigrants in Hibbing's new city hall, proudly repeated oaths of allegiance to their new nation. In the same year, they joined the *Knights and Ladies of the Kaleva*, which order took its ritual from the Finnish national epic, the *Kalevala*. This, since neither had belonged to any of the other Finnish clubs, amounted to their first taste of socializing outside the family.

Meanwhile, their children were growing up and becoming Americanized in school. Kalle, the oldest and biggest, took up football and became a crushing tackle for Hibbing High School. In 1912, after playing every minute of his senior year, he was recruited by Coach Hank Williams to play at the University of Minnesota.

Two of Kalle's teammates were Clark Shaughnessy and Bernie Bierman, who later became Hall of Fame football coaches. In his junior year, when there was talk of making Walter Camp's All America team, Kalle wrecked a knee and dropped out of school. After that he went to work in the Northwoods, which was the start of a lifetime career in the lumber business.

It says something about opportunity in America that, unlike generations of their Finnish forebears yoked to the plow, not one of Reino's children chose farming as a way of life. In fact all four went off in different directions.

Heikki, after taking a commercial course in high school, got a job as a clerk-bookkeeper for the Sharon Ore Company with open pit operations near Buhl. He became the first ever of his clan to make a living sitting down.

Johanna went to the normal school at Duluth to prepare for her future as a math teacher at Roosevelt High School in the booming Iron Range town of Virginia. In that day, when most teachers were spinsters, Johanna became an exception. After 15 years of scrawling equations across blackboards, she married the chairman of the school's history department and quit teaching in order to raise two stepsons.

Eino, the baby of the family, while working as a lifeguard at a summer church camp, fell in love with Lake Vermilion. The next summer, after graduating from high school, he apprenticed himself to Kusti Heikkila, a crusty old world craftsman, who built cabins and boat houses at the Tower-Soudan end of the lake.

It may seem surprising that after 15 years in Hibbing, Reino and Hilma decided to leave. What happened was that the village was caught up in a dilemma. At the time of its original platting it was thought to be on the edge of ore deposits. Instead, it was later discovered to be right on top of them. When the Oliver Mining Company began buying up all the surface rights, the handwriting was on the wall. Sooner or later Hibbing was going to have to move.

In 1915, a company agent approached Reino with an offer either to move his home a mile south or to buy it outright. Against Hilma's wishes, Reino decided to sell. For one thing, he guessed correctly that someday the town would have to move again.

More important, he told Hilma, was that for the first time in their married life, they were free to do what they wanted. And what Reino wanted was to work by himself as a carpenter with more time to spend tending a garden and doing things for his family. Heikki, who worked near Buhl and boarded in that young village, had assured him there was land to be had as well as plenty of work for a skilled carpenter.

Finally, Reino told Hilma that in 23 years of marriage they had lived only in a log cabin and a converted tool shed. In Buhl, he promised he'd build her a real house just the way she wanted it.

So it was that after some weeks of persuasion, Hilma agreed and Reino sold their household and land for $800. Considering the wealth that lay below, it may seem he let it go cheaply. However, the Oliver Mining Company had long before bought up the mineral rights to all Hibbing land below the surface. By holding on Reino had nothing to gain.

In 1919, Hibbing and its homes, shops, schools and churches were moved one by one to a new site one mile to the south. By then Reino and Hilma were settled in the young town of Buhl. And that was where their grandchildren and, although they never were to know them, their great-grandchildren grew up.

- 14 -

TRANSCRIPT: HISTORY 240

"Preliterate Peoples In Minnesota"
J.R. Makki-Lecturer

"History," as we use the term, refers to written words about people and events from the past. From that perspective our history of Minnesota would begin with notes and memoirs of French trail blazers who opened the gates of the American interior. That was a few years before the Pilgrims struggled ashore at Cape Cod.

As early as 1618, one Etienne Brule, a delegate of Samuel Champlain, pushed his way as far west as Lake Superior. In short order he was followed by Radisson, du Luth, Hennepin and Nicollet, names that are the warp and woof of Minnesota's early history.

Because of the recordings of these pathfinders, we know something about the native peoples they first observed. What happened before their coming we know only through artifacts and speculation. As a result there is a tendency to regard the eras before the French as a kind of marking-of-time before the start of real history. The irony becomes obvious if you consider that the first whites arrived less than four centuries ago, while the Redman's sway over the land began ten or more thousand years earlier.

To help set the record straight someone has suggested that the story disclosed by artifacts is not prehistory but rather history told by other means. And that is what we'll be looking at for our next few meetings—history as passed on to us by preliterate peoples.

No one can say for sure when it began. But it is thought likely a few scattered hunting bands made their way here near the end of the Ice Age. The unearthing of Minnesota Woman's bones near Pelican Rapids in 1931 suggests the presence of Paleo or Primitive Indians as long ago as 15,000 B.C., or even earlier.

The hunting skills of wandering bands of Paleos had been developed over hundreds of generations going back to primitive forebears from other continents. Curiously, the bow and arrow so emblematic of the American Indian did not come along until around 800 A.D. But the Paleos had refined their spears or "atl atls" through use of a flexible throwing stick. Like slinging apples off a willow switch, the whip let them hurl a killing missile a hundred yards or more.

In the centuries following the great glacial thaw, vast evergreen forests came into being. Gradually, over thousands of years, Paleo hunters traded their nomadic ways for a more settled life that embraced crude efforts at hoeing and planting to augment their quest for big game.

What happened to these aborigines is unknown. Were they slaughtered or subjugated by an unknown invader? Or did they simply evolve as ancestors of Indian peoples to come? Although such questions remain unanswered, artifacts and oral legends handed down through generations indicate they were succeeded on the land around 8,000 years ago by the so-called Woodland Indians.

We won't dwell on it. But you should know that the Woodland culture has been divided into early, middle and late periods. The chronology has been arbitrarily assigned according to advances in tribal language, settlement, government, crop growing, cooking wares and ornaments.

Archaeological shards tell of the introduction of clay pottery as containers for food and water. Stone hoes fostered the working of soil for vegetables. Trees were cleared for garden plots by burning or hacking with crude axes.

Systems of governance varied from tribe to tribe. But usually Woodland Indians lived, hunted and made war under a political structure that included separate chieftains for hunting, peace and war, as well as tribal councils and medicine men.

Medicine men or their counterparts—witch doctors, wizards, and sorcerers—seem to have been a fixture of all primitive societies. The American Indian medicine man had a place within the tribe equal to the chieftains. With his nostrums, rattles and incantations, he was a cross between healer and mystic. As intermediary with mysterious powers of the occult he had rituals for a successful hunt, a good crop or just about anything else vital to the welfare of his tribe.

Long before the arrival of Christian missionaries, Woodland Indians believed in a Supreme God who ruled from the sky. Along with this deity whose name has come down to us as "Manitou," they also paid homage to a host of lesser gods relating to such natural things as sun, moon, stars, rain, thunder and lightning.

Burial sites all over Minnesota attest to belief in life after death. Indian mounds have yielded countless types of offerings placed alongside the dead to sustain them during their journey to the sky world of the Great Spirit.

Although Woodland Indians—or, for that matter, Indian primitives in general—had no regular meal hours, eating was the core of their existence. They simply ate whenever they were hungry and food was on hand. What better way to celebrate a good hunt or bountiful crop than to eat. Revels of feasting, dancing and games were a welcome diversion from the rigors of survival.

While Woodland artifacts—chopping tools, decorated bowls, copper bracelets and the like—point to a way of life well adapted to forest surroundings, they do not tell us what became of these people. About that we can only speculate. Stories from earlier times handed down orally through the generations are unauthenticated but perhaps provide clues.

A part of this body of lore is the legend of Little Thunder, as told during the 1800s by fur trader Gideon Thurlowe, a self-taught speaker of the Dakota tongue. Having dredged this manuscript from deep recesses of our library, I pass it along with the caution that nowhere else in the Woodland oral tradition is there any mention of a Chief Little Thunder. There is also Thurlowe's reputation for never being one to let truth stand in the way of a good tale.

On the other hand, who is it that can vouch for the fate of Troy as sung by Homer 800 years after the event? Thurlowe dwelt with the Dakota for twenty years. His story, like the epics of Homer, bears the stamp of the plausible about the ways and possible fate of a vanished civilization.

- 15 -

SUPPLEMENT FOR LECTURE 2, HISTORY 240

LITTLE THUNDER'S LAST CHARGE

As recorded by Gideon Thurlowe*
Edited by J.R. Makki

Little Thunder was at home in the forest by the great water one day to be known as Rainy Lake. It was the land where he and his father before him had hunted and fished, and which he also knew from bloody raids on the hated tribes from the place where the sun rose.

Warfare was as much a part of this chieftain's life as the moccasins he wore. From the time when he was small he had sat near the campfire listening to the braves boast of daring deeds. With other young boys he had practiced shooting with bow and arrow and dreamed of the day when he too would lead a war party and become famous in battle.

Little Thunder's people fought to repel attacks and to protect or secure hunting grounds. They fought also to avenge

* Gideon Thurlowe is a fictitious character whose narrative offers a possible explanation of what became of the Woodland culture.

insults—had not Bear Paw, his own father, killed with a knife the father of war chief Porcupine, who had dared lay hands on one of his wives without first asking permission?

Now, as a chieftain in his own right, Little Thunder was a warrior celebrated for success in battle. Always in the thick of action, he had many times led raids to repel attackers or to steal supplies and weapons from rival tribes.

On this night he sat with the council of chieftains summoned to consider what to do about encroachments by the powerful tribe to the north. Long gone to the Great Spirit in the sky was his father, the brave chieftain Bear Paw. Facing him across the council circle was Porcupine, his black eyes glittering with hatred. Once they had been friends. But now Porcupine, ever burning to avenge the murder of his father, was Little Thunder's bitter enemy.

Loud in their cries for war against the encroachers were the followers of Chief Porcupine. But then suddenly Little Thunder took a stand before the council fire and silenced them with upraised arms.

"Hear me well," he cried loudly. "All you young braves so thirsty for blood. Listen to my words!"

"It is true that the intruders from the north seek to push us off land that was our fathers' home. Here, my brothers, is where we have broken the soil, celebrated bountiful harvests and come back from great hunts. Now our hold on this land is threatened by powerful invaders and we must choose.

"Drive them off, you cry. But words do not frighten strong enemies. They are many more than we. If we fight and do not win, our women will be raped and stolen. Our elders will be put to the knife. Our children will be butchered or taken as slaves. Our way of life will end.

"But there is another choice. In days past I have followed the great river that flows like a snake to where the sun goes down. There I have looked upon green forests and much game. All is there that we have here. That is our other choice. We can leave here and start again."

Now rose Porcupine snarling. "Is this a warrior chieftain who whimpers before us like an old squaw? Run away like rabbits at the sound of a moccasin. Is this what he tells us? Well I, for one, reject such counsel. If Little Thunder has no heart for battle let him stay back, and I will lead you."

On hearing this the young braves responded with warlike screams. Porcupine sat down, sneering at his adversary. And Little Thunder spoke again.

"So you choose war. Do you now choose Porcupine to lead you?"

Now there fell a silence. Despite Porcupine's bitter words, no one truly believed Little Thunder a coward. He was famed as a great warrior. Porcupine, for all his bluster, was not. The matter was settled when Snapping Turtle, ever fierce in combat, arose. "Little Thunder has spoken wisely. This may be a battle we cannot win. But if fight we must I will follow only him."

As others took up the cry, Little Thunder once more raised his hand for silence. "Very well. You have spoken and I shall lead you. But before that I go to seek a vision. When I have it, we will council again to make our plans."

Turning as though to leave, Little Thunder looked once more across the council fire. "Let us pray the Great Spirit will smile upon our efforts. For then Chief Porcupine, you and I can talk again about my heart for battle."

So saying, and carrying neither food nor drink, he walked into the shadows. Wading across the narrow stream by their village, he followed the path into the woods that brought him to the tribal burying ground. It was place he had come many times to tell of happenings as though the dead were still alive to listen.

Inside at the lowest level of the mound lay bones from the mists of creation, warriors and sachems known to him only through tales around the campfires. On tiers above these ancients were the remains of others well remembered by Little Thunder, first among them, his honored father, Bear Paw, the great warrior chieftain. Beside him lay Lame Buffalo, the famed leader of the hunt, who had taught him how to scoop out trout with his bare hands.

It was to the spirit of these departed warriors that he now spoke. "In times past I have brought you word of great hunts and success in battle. Now I come before you to plead. In life you were strong and wise. Surely some of your wisdom remains here in this mound. I call now for your counsel to save our tribe."

There was no answer. The only night sound was the far off cry of the wolf. Little Thunder shrugged. I am no Shaman, he thought. I have no magic to summon ghosts. If I am patient they will come. For have not those whose bones lie her, fought and bled for the tribe? I must stay here and wait.

So thinking, Little Thunder sat alone in a pit by the burial mound. Through the chill of the night he did not sleep and during the heat of the day he remained, slowly turning with the sun, facing it when it rose and when it set in the west. On the second night he fell into a dreamlike state and lived again the days of his tribe as he had heard it from the old story teller White Rabbit.

Once they had been hunters and wanderers moving always with the game and changing seasons. But then, many generations before, they had learned how to cultivate corn and squash. After that they had begun to settle in permanent villages where they erected log stockades and birch bark wigwams. They had become a part-hunting and part-farming people. The men still went on hunting parties but with crop-bearing fields, they no longer had to wander in constant quest of big game.

Now, in his dreamlike state, Little Thunder recalled the celebrations after a good harvest, the feasting and dancing, the games and gambling. Outside the stockade the men and boys challenged each other with footraces and spirited tug-of-war. But inside, enjoying the festivities even more, were the women from whose toil the crops had come. It was they who had hacked at the hard earth with hoes fashioned from the shoulder bones of a bison and who had planted the seeds by poking into the soil with pointed sticks. This was their day of triumph. He saw them now, shouting and laughing, wagering trinkets as they cast marked stones into a bowl trying for winning combinations.

It was early on the third morning that Little Thunder while dreaming of these things awoke with a start. He heard a voice saying, "Your father has returned. He is with you now between the Sky and the Earth. Go now, your appeal has been heard. You will find the answer in the first thing you see in your wigwam."

Weak and dizzy, Little Thunder crawled out of the vision pit and stumbled back down the path to camp. Entering his wigwam, he glanced at his lacrosse stick lying beside his sleeping robe. Lacrosse! Here was the guidance he had sought.

All along he had known he could not win in face-to-face battle against a force so much stronger. Their only hope was to somehow catch the enemy off guard. Now the answer had come. They must lure them with a game of lacrosse to be played for high stakes. Then while the rival braves flailed at each other for possession of the ball, Little Thunder would launch a surprise attack from the woods in back of the enemy camp.

That night, before the council, Little Thunder laid out his plan. Spotted Possum, their peace chieftain, would approach the intruders with the challenge of an intertribal lacrosse match. The game would be played the day after next on a clearing between their stockade and the enemy camp. Half a hundred braves to a side would contend for a hundred pouches of maize.

The next day just as the sun dipped below the tall pines to the west, Spotted Possum returned with word that the challenge had been accepted. So it was that much later that night Little Thunder departed with a handpicked company of ambushers. Silently and crouching low they worked their way in a wide half-circle around and behind the enemy camp. There they hid in underbrush while waiting the call to attack.

Meanwhile, at the time appointed for the game, players led by Porcupine came in single file out of the stockade, lacrosse sticks in hands and their bodies painted blue. Behind them came a procession of women and elders bearing pouches of maize. These they set down beside the pile earlier placed by their rivals.

Now umpires from the rival camps met in solemn discussion of rules. As agreed, there were no boundaries and after the initial face-off there would be no further restriction. The sole purpose was for one tribe, or the other, to try, by whatever means, to force the ball across one of the lines at opposing ends of the clearing.

No one will ever know which tribe might have won the maize. For barely had the struggle begun before Little Thunder and his horde burst into the enemy camp in murderous frenzy. Screaming, torching and killing everyone before them, they charged through the camp and out onto the clearing.

Meanwhile, on the field the blue painted warriors had reversed their lacrosse sticks and using their sharply pointed ends like spears, were thrusting at and maiming the shocked opponents. Caught in-between and with no plan of battle, the foe fled in disorder. And it was at this moment, as Little Thunder surveyed the carnage of his greatest victory, that treacherous Porcupine thrust a spear into his back to claim his long delayed vengeance.

With a screech of triumph Porcupine turned to rally the warriors around him. "Little Thunder has died in battle. Snapping Turtle is dead and I am your chieftain."

Of all the tribal leaders who had gone before, Porcupine's reign was to be the shortest. For that very night the enemy regrouped and descended on the village with blood lust. While his warriors tried vainly to protect their people, Porcupine fled, only to be captured and burnt alive by the enraged enemy.

On that awful night, the village of Little Thunder and his forebears ceased to exist. And in keeping with his direful warning, the only survivors were the women carried off as slaves.

- 16 -

SUPPLEMENT FOR LECTURES 3 TO 6

HISTORY 240
MINNESOTA INDIANS AND THE COMING OF THE FRENCH

The two Indian tribes of major importance in Minnesota were the Dakota and the Ojibway. For reasons not entirely clear, the Dakota are also known as Sioux, while Ojibway are often called Chippewa. According to some authorities, Sioux is a general name for a number of tribes speaking a similar language, while Dakota refers to an alliance of seven of these tribes.

The Ojibway-Chippewa pairing appears to be the result of the white man's garbled attempt to spell Ojibway as the Indians pronounced it. The Rev. Peter Jones, a converted Ojibway chief, who spent many years among them as a missionary, dismissed Chippewa as being a corruption of Ojibway; he spelled his tribal name "Ojebway."

For this course, in order to avoid the confusion of using them interchangeably, we'll stick with Sioux and Chippewa when discussing these two tribes so prominent in Minnesota history.

By the time of the Europeans' arrival, four tribes loosely allied as the Santee Sioux were clustered around the lakes of the upper Mississippi valley where wild rice was a main staple of their existence. It is believed they were there long before the coming of the French. But oral tradition about their origin is not very helpful.

Historian Doane Robinson reports conflicting claims by two old men of the same band. One of them solemnly related to him how the Sioux came from "the far-off land of the setting sun." The other just as gravely, spoke of their coming "from where the sun rises."

Artifacts provide clues but all that is definitely known is that when the first white men came into Minnesota, they found a large number of Sioux making their home by the shores of the sacred lake we now know as Mille Lacs. It was there, in 1679, that they were visited by Sieur du Luth and Father Hennepin.

Most of what we know about the Sioux at the dawn of Minnesota's written history comes through the recordings of 17th century explorers and missionaries. The question of who actually saw them first is but slightly clouded by the "discovery" in 1898 of the Kensington Runestone which purports to tell of an expedition by Norseman into what is now Minnesota, three centuries before the coming of the French. However, setting aside the Runestone claim as an amusing hoax, the first known Europeans to encounter Sioux were Pierre Radisson and his brother-in-law, Sieur des Groseilliers.

These daring men are said to be the first to sight the shores of what is now Minnesota during an epic canoe trip from Three Rivers on the St. Lawrence in 1659-60. It is not known whether they came upon Siouxian people on that trip. But they definitely did a year later, when once again braving hazards of uncharted wilderness, they canoed along the south shore of Superior to what is now Wisconsin and then by canoe and portage into the prairie lands of present day Minnesota.

There, believed to be near today's site of Mora, Radisson tells of convening a large assembly of Sioux for a great feast. Every indication is that Radisson and des Groseilliers journeyed together on several occasions including their 1661 voyage to the vicinity of southern and southwest Minnesota. However, it also seems clear that some of the information reported by Radisson is based on hearsay of journeys for which he was not present.

In spite of the doubt cast on whether Radisson was actually present for the occasion, his account offers a colorful description of Siouxian pageantry (Adams, *The Explorations of Pierre Esprit Radisson*). "They arrived with incredible pomp ... Most of the men, their faces were all over dabbed with several colors, their hair turned up like a crown and were cut very even, but rather so burned, for the fire is their scissors ...They grease themselves with very thick grease and mingle it in reddish earth ... with this stuff they get their hair to stand up. They are clothed with oriniak* and stag skins ... They had swords and knives of a foot and a half long, and hatchets very ingeniously done and clubs made of wood like back swords."

"Then the women, laden like unto so many mules ... unfolded their bundles and flung their skins whereof the tents are made, so that they had their houses less than half an hour."

In telling of the feasting that followed, Radisson offered the first known description of the harvesting of wild rice.

"We had there a kind of rice, much like our oats; it is grown in the water in three or four foot deep ... They have a particular way to gather up that grain: two takes a boat and two sticks by which they get the ear down and get the corn out of it; their boat being full they bring it to a fit place to dry it, and that is their food for the most part of winter ... For each man a handful of that they put in the pot; that swells so much it can suffice a man."

The above procedure bespeaks ways handed down through generations before Radisson. Except that the canoes are no longer birch bark, it has remained the same over centuries. Actually, it isn't rice at all, but the grain of a tall aquatic grass. As anyone who has ever gathered it knows, natural wild rice is easier to cook and better to the taste than so called "wild rice"

---

* Elk.

grown in commercial paddies.

Further on in what is now eastern Minnesota, the explorers came upon a large Sioux village.

"We wondered to find ourselves in a town where great cabins, most covered with skins ... They told us that there were seven thousand men ... These have as many wives as they can keep ... The people stay not there all year. They retire in the winter towards the wood of the North."

Some twenty years after Radisson, Sieur du Luth and Father Louis Hennepin came into the area. Their writings, in complement with those of Radisson, describe a settled culture of a kind that had been long on the land.

In 1679, Daniel Graysolon, Sieur du Luth, landed near the city which now bears his name. After parley with Sioux Indians camped nearby, du Luth pushed west nearly a hundred miles to a large Sioux settlement along the shores of Mille Lacs. He, along with French explorers, traders and missionaries to follow, opened the way for European expansion into Minnesota.

It should be noted that French and Spanish explorers in Florida had recorded encounters with Indians nearly two centuries earlier. It seems an irony of history that Ponce de Leon never got to test the staying powers of the fountain of youth. Fatally wounded by Calusa Indians, his bones had moldered in a grave 160 years before Sieur du Luth laid claim to Mille Lacs as a possession for Louis XIV. The fountain legend reminds us that Spaniards like de Leon, Balboa and DeSoto were blazing trails in America's south and west a century before French counterparts like Radisson and du Luth were even born.

In 1680, du Luth opened a new route into Minnesota via the St. Croix River to the Mississippi. There he rescued three white men who had been held by the Sioux as prisoners*. One of them was Father Louis Hennepin, a Recollect Friar, whose place in Minnesota history was secured the day he came across

---

* According to historian Francis Parkman, one of the men in du Luth's rescue party was named Pepin; hence perhaps the name of Lake Pepin.

the falls he said interrupted navigation of the river he called "Meschasipi." This waterfall, on the site where Minneapolis now stands, he named after St. Anthony of Padua, whom he had taken as his protector saint.

A lesser known fact about the good father is that he was very likely the first European to be treated to a Sioux style steam bath. Writing about his three months of captivity, Hennepin (*Description of Louisiana*) tells of his revival after an exhausting overland march. First, he was rubbed down and anointed with wildcat oil. And then one of the Sioux "made a small sweating cabin in which he made me enter with four Indians. This cabin he covered with buffalo skins and inside he put stones red hot ... When he me made sweat thus three times a week, I felt strong as ever."

Elsewhere in his journal, Hennepin tells of being fed by his captors, "who gave me beaver to eat, putting three first morsels in our mouths, according to the custom of their country, and blowing on the meat which was too hot, before putting the bark dish before us to let us eat as we liked."

Hennepin also describes the Indians' belief in the supernatural, citing their opinion that the turning of his compass was brought about by spirits. Although he made light of such superstitions, including their notion of a happy hunting ground, Hennepin as a preacher of salvation must have felt he was on fertile ground in his observation of their belief in what he termed "immortality of the soul."

"They give the dead their best apparel" and put into the grave "everything that belonged to him" for what he will need "when he is in the land of the dead or of souls."

Hennepin's book has been challenged for accuracy and self-glorification. Among the good father's earliest critics was 17th century explorer Sieur de la Salle,who in a letter back to France wrote, "...If you wish to confer with Father Louis Hennepin, Recollect ... you must know him a little, because he will not fail to exaggerate in all things. ...To me he has written as if he were about to be burned when he was not even in danger" (Neill, *History of the Minnesota Valley*).

Considerably less restrained is the judgment of Timothy Severin (*Explorers of the Mississippi Valley*). In a chapter entitled "The Mendacious Friar," he dismisses Hennepin as a "hoax" and "a liar with a plainly odious personality," whose writings, he charges, "were largely stolen from others." Calling them "top heavy with obvious inaccuracies, slander, flattery and boasts," Severin sums them up as "a tissue of lies thinly spread over a framework of truth."

Whatever the truth of Hennepin's claims or accuracy of his descriptions, it is indisputable that he did travel through Minnesota in 1680 and that his adventures did include the sighting and naming of St. Anthony's Falls. If for no other reason, his widely read book is important for its disclosures about the people and the wilderness west of the Great Lakes.

- 17 -

BLACK ROBES IN THE WILDERNESS

As French explorers and traders pressed the claims of Louis XIV further into Minnesota, others with more precise observations came on the scene. These were members of the Society of Jesus—Jesuit priests—who after long and rigorous training went forth to establish Catholicism in the New World. During the 17th and 18th centuries they penetrated deep into the wilderness to found a string of missionary stations across French-controlled America.

In his monumental account of the French and English struggle for dominance in North America, Francis Parkman said about the Jesuits: "Two objects inspired their zeal, 'the greater glory of God,' and the influence and credit of the Order of Jesus. If one motive had lost its power, the other had gained. The epoch of the saints and martyrs was passing away; and henceforth we find the Canadian Jesuit less and less an apostle, more and more an explorer, a man of science."

One who never faltered in his Christian zeal was Father Jean de Laittre*, a young Jesuit called in the late 17th century to carry word of the Lord into the wilderness west of the Great

---

* Although Father DeLaittre's story is fictional, it reflects accurately the travels and experiences of 17th century Jesuit missionaries in the North American wilderness.

Lakes. Born in Quebec in 1671, Father de Laittre was educated there at Jesuit College. Soon after his ordainment in 1694 he received orders to establish a mission on the St. Louis River a few miles upstream from present day Duluth. From this outpost of his Order, de Laittre went several times on expeditions where few white men had gone before.

In his quest to convert savage souls, the young priest was also a careful observer of the land and its people. If his journal and letters abound with spiritual purpose, they also reveal much about the way of the Sioux at the close of the 17th century.

Here follow excerpts from Father de Laittre's record of a remarkable odyssey into unknown wilds of what would one day become northern Minnesota.

‡‡ ‡‡ ‡‡ ‡‡ ‡‡

Dearest Father and Mother,

There being a small company of military surveyors at our mission this night, I hastily accept their offer to carry with them this renewed assurance of my devotion.

I go shortly on His work into the western wilderness. It will be a journey of several hundred leagues and it will be many months before I have opportunity to write again. In my absence the mission will be guided by Father LeFerve, about whom I have earlier written.

Reverend Father Garneau, my Superior, has accorded me the honor of carrying God's word into country where the name of His Son and our Savior is unknown. Although I confess some perturbation to go among savages known for hostility, I accept its assignment as a mark of His Holy and Divine Will.

Pray for me, dearest parents, that I shall conduct myself in manner worthy of His trust.

I close with the love and gratitude of your devoted son.

Jean de Laittre

June 24, 1696:

At a time when the armies of the Grand Monarque are under assault on every frontier of Europe, the expansion of French and Christian authority into the interior of North America escapes claims upon our notice. In little more than a lifetime since the founding of New France, expeditions have been pushed beyond the Great Lakes, and the far-reaching enterprise of the Society of Jesus has extended Christian salvation through the conversion of countless savage souls. Being now engaged in an expedition through a portion of this domain never before charted, I am accordingly endeavoring to make record of these wilderness lands and of the unlettered children of God who here abide.*

*On an overcast morning in the middle of June 1696, I embarked from the Mission in a company of six, traveling in two large canoes. With me were five Sioux, two of them "donees" along with three "engagees."** The St. Louis River we were about to ascend is here a league wide and of sluggish disposition. However, after a course of five leagues, it begins to narrow and rise between heightening banks. On the second day we came upon a series of falls, each rising more steeply as torrents of white water churned through the narrowing ravine and over enormous walls of rock. This tumultuous cascade proving impossible to navigate, we commenced the arduous portage along the rim of the rocky gorge.*

Up the treacherous and narrow path we floundered, each of us laden—canoes, dried meat, sacks of flour, axes, kettles and weapons. Clambering over fallen trees, stumbling on rocks, wading through bogs, besieged by mosquitoes, on and on we climbed until near dark when we stopped to encamp.

Throwing my burden down I sank exhausted to the ground gratefully leaving it to my companions to attend the camp chores.

---

* The attack upon Louis XIV by a circle of European enemies that led to his defeat in 1697.

** *Donees*—volunteers, most likely Dakota converts; *engagees*—hired hands.

Later after chewing on dried venison and hard biscuits I read by firelight from my breviary. The others sat silently, smoking their pipes as I completed my devotions. Then, covering myself with a robe, I lay down on the hard earth and knew no more till sunrise.

For three days we toiled up this desolate trail, coming at one time to a stretch where razor-like projections of slate cut into the soles of my shoes. These were rigors to be overcome only by immense physical effort and will of mind. By now we had gone beyond any prior knowledge of cartography. To go on where there was no certainty taxed fully my devotion to carry the word of God to Indian tribes of the interior.*

It was not until the fourth day that we were able to return our canoes to the water. Even then the passage was tedious owing to the swiftness of the current. When finally after seven days in which we had ascended upriver no more than 25 leagues, it was not without relief that we turned thither away from this tortuous river into a small tributary flowing from the west.

July 8:

Our hopes for respite after leaving the St. Louis proved fleeting. Except for the absence of current, the way if anything, was even more retarding. Where hitherto the swift flowing St. Louis had been clear of debris, here the narrow channel was choked with fallen timber and other impediments to progress.

It was in fashion most halting, working around, under and sometimes over obstacles, that we came at length to a savannah of tall aquatic rushes so thick as to conceal Moses and a legion of his followers. Within this density of rushes we had only our compass to keep us on course as we pushed our way along, less than half a paddle's length a stroke. It was only by seeking shallow water and wading up to our waists that we finally managed to push our canoes to open water.

There, we were much astonished to observe that the waters of our river had reversed their course and now flowed

* Today a part of Jay Cooke State Park.

west. And so at last, after the torments of miserable swamp and the harshness of exhausting portage, we came on the 12th day to a broad body of water, where after paddling for some distance, we espied a wreath of smoke that bespoke of human habitation.*

Hastening the cadence of our strokes we came shortly to a cove upon the shores of which stood a small collection of wigwams. Waiting on shore by several dugout canoes was a cluster of savages, their curiosity excited by our appearance and unexpected arrival. Men and boys, naked and splendidly formed, waded into the water to guide our canoes to shore. Behind them dogs barked and children and squaws laughed and shouted.

Standing apart from his people was a tall savage of stately bearing. When he extended a highly ornamented calumet toward me, I held out my hands in a gesture of friendship. In halting discourse, I explained we came in peace and that overcome by fatigue from our journey, wanted only to rest among them for a few days.

Aware of the imperative place of gift giving as an introductory token of good will, I removed from my habit a brightly colored string of rosary beads, which I placed around his neck. Upon seeing this, a murmur of approval arose from all who surrounded us.

Generosity as a virtue being highly prized among the Sioux, we were shortly feted as honored guests at a feast of friendship most welcome to us. It was only after I offered compliments about the meal that I learned its chief delicacy was stew of young puppy.

‡‡ ‡‡ ‡‡ ‡‡ ‡‡

After hearing that a much larger band of Sioux was encamped along a nearby river they called "Mesebebi," Father

---

* After leaving the St. Louis River, deLaittre's party had turned into a tributary now known as the East Savanna River. Its headwaters are separated from the headwaters of the West Savanna River by a continental divide. The western portion of the Savanna flows into what is today called the Big Sandy Lake and, in turn, into the Mississippi.

deLaittre determined to go there. To safeguard his passage, Village Chief Clear Waters sent along a warrior escort of four canoes.

However, before dipping further into the young priest's journal, it may be useful to dwell for a moment on the role of Jesuit missionaries in furthering French colonial expansion. Perhaps as revealing as what deLaittre said about this is what he did not say. Typical of other Jesuits at this time, he makes scant mention of civil authority, fur traders or the soul-saving endeavors of rival Catholic orders.

The reason, very simply, is that the Jesuit was too often as zealous for his Order as for his faith. Their purpose, as described by Francis Parkman, was to see the region grow as a "nation of converted and domesticated savages, docile as children, under the paternal and absolute rule of Jesuit fathers." In this vein they looked upon all other outside influences as obstacles to their mission.

Sieur de la Salle, who many times crossed swords with Jesuit hierarchy, once summed up the order in a sentence: "The Jesuits think everybody an enemy to religion who is an enemy to them."

The role of the Society of Jesus in 17th century North America is not easily demeaned. As recorders and chart makers, Jesuit missionaries shed light on then dark wilderness. And as zealous servants of Christianity, they embraced the hardships and perils of their calling with uncommon fortitude.

Much that we know of the new land and its people comes to us through the journals of missionaries like Father deLaittre. However, it is also true that the arrogance of their order was a source of continuing friction with civil and military authorities, fur traders and other religious sects.

To what extent 17th century preachments of any order planted deep Christian roots is questionable. Without constant attention from missionaries many wilderness Indians soon fell back into heathen ways. But there is no doubt that the Jesuits were among the first to introduce European customs that altered forever a culture formerly adapted to wilderness self-sufficiency

Now let us rejoin Father deLaittre, who after leaving the village of Chief Clear Waters was escorted to a larger Sioux encampment downstream on the Mississippi. Situated on a point where the big river is joined by a small tributary now believed to be Willow River, its rich meadows and abundant fish and game made an attractive summer place for this band of Sioux.

‡‡ ‡‡ ‡‡ ‡‡ ‡‡

THE JOURNAL OF FATHER deLAITTRE RESUMED

July 22, 1696:

In all God's realm, I know of nothing more serene than a wilderness dawn in mid-summer. Here on a point where a smaller branch enters upon the great river called 'Mesebebi,' the waters of this mighty stream flow majestically past, on a course known only to our Creator. Through shrouds of mist, the far shoreline emerges, whilst nearby, waters lap gently against dark forms of overturned canoes. Nowhere is there a sound.

I have risen early to walk down from the village of conical, fur-covered wigwams behind me. Curious, I reflect, to experience a moment so tranquil in this place where savagery is cultivated as a virtue. As before, in the village of Clear Water, I must confess to some misgiving as we had come upon this much larger band of the nation of the Sioux. A party so small as ours could easily have been overcome, robbed and put to unmerciful death. Such, however, had not been a part of Heavenly Design, for our reception here had been one I deemed most cordial.

Glancing often at me, their Chief, Running Elk, paid careful heed as one of my Indian escorts explained our presence. Then, pointing to me, the Chief extended his calumet, which after a few puffs I returned. Next, holding a small crucifix aloft, I stepped forward and placed it around his neck. Following this simple act of giving, the Chief spoke briefly to his people, before turning to me again.

In halting Sioux and aided by sign language, I conveyed to them that I had come in peace and hoped they would let me dwell with them for a while in order to learn of their customs. I told them that I brought word of a God different than any they had known, and of new ways of worship.

To this Running Elk responded somewhat as follows:

"My Father, our hearts are joyful that you have come here upon our ground. We rejoice that your great Chiefs are for keeping the peace. May it ever be so. You bring words about the white man's God. This night we celebrate your coming. Tomorrow we will listen."

Upon this word, an old man came forward and removed my shoes, thereon replacing them with a pair of beaded moccasins. Next, I was abruptly lifted onto a large animal robe and thus conveyed to the center of the village where what I adjudged to be the entire tribe had assembled.

An aged squaw laid before me an earthen bowl of meat and cornmeal soup kept heated by the placement therein of several fire heated stones, each the size of an egg. Three times she dipped small bits of a course bread into the soup before placing them on my tongue. Then I was given a spoon wrought from some kind of animal horn. Thereafter, accompanied by shouting and gestures of approval, my crew and I joined in sating our travel hungry appetites.

Would that the words of my calling be so well received. So far, however, a fortnight after our coming to this place, there is yet to be manifest serious interest in the apostolic canon of our Order. Once, after listening to my preachments, Hawk Wing, one of their elders, told me, "Your way of the lamb is not our way. From our Fathers and their Fathers, we have learned that it is better to die in battle than to live to be old."

August 21:

Although I do not despair, my days here so far have been occupied more as observer than missionary. Late summer being a time to build caches of meat and to provide new skins for lodges and robes, the men have been absorbed in preparing for a bison hunt. A day before leaving, Red Owl, the old tracker who led the hunt, invited me to go along. I can only imagine how we must have appeared, a long procession of breech-clad Indians, and bringing up the rear, a priest in black habit.

A league or so further back, there followed a second party composed of squaws. Although they readied camp at day's end, their main purpose for accompanying this expedition did not become evident until after the hunt.

Toward evening of the third day, Red Owl signaled a halt. Creeping up a slight rise, he sighted a small herd of buffalo. It being almost dusk, we withdrew and moved well away before making camp. After eating, the old hunter gathered his party around him. First, calling softly to the Great Spirit, he invoked success in running down and killing many buffalo. Then, using a stick, he scratched out on the ground a plan of envelopment calculated to encircle and surprise the herd.

An hour before dawn the party moved out to where once again Red Owl located our quarry. Then, following his scheme, the men and boys crept into positions surrounding the still resting herd. At first light, on signal from Red Owl, the hunters rushed forward to shoot arrows at the startled beasts as they bellowed and milled in all directions. With admiration akin to awe, I observed swift-running Sioux firing, restringing and firing again, all the while keeping pace with their panic-driven quarry.

On warning cry from Red Owl, I turned just as a massive bull charged through the circle of bowmen directly toward the rise where I stood. As I jumped away, the old Sioux hunter sent it crashing down with a single arrow through its enormous chest. No longer able to run with the younger braves, Red Owl retained the wondrous shooting skills of his youth. Now, as the great beast thrashed on the ground barely two rods from my person, the old hunter dispatched it with a blow from his war club.

Below us, the rising sun illuminated the sanguinary consequence of this well-planned ambuscade. Amid clusters of rejoicing hunters lay the ponderous forms of eight cows and four bulls, slain in less time than it has taken to commit this accounting to paper. Responsive to howls of triumph from the men, the women moved in quickly to begin skinning and butchering. A portion of one of the felled beasts was reserved for a period of feasting on raw slabs of meat, the liver being judged to be most excellent. The rest was laid out by the women for drying and transport back to their village.

Upon our return there began a round of continuous feasting. The Sioux on the warpath can go with little or no food for days at a time. But when a hunt is successful they devour without heed to any regular sequence of meals. So long as food is available they eat whenever they are hungry, which to my differently attuned appetite seems almost always. Ever before them is the spectre of harsh winters and days when food is short.

On the night of our return to the village, Red Owl pranced about the campfire, reliving with much emotion the details of his successful hunt. Although I was by then long abed, I was later informed that the old hunter had spoken of my presence on the hunt as being a talisman of good fortune.

Whether or not his gratuitous commendation impressed Chief Running Elk, I cannot say. However, the next day, following earlier denials, he granted my request to hold council with his people about the Holy Scriptures of Christianity.

With the help of my donee converts, I set up my portable altar in the center of a large clearing. Then, in the absence of a tocsin, the people were summoned by the unchristian pounding of a war drum. First came the council members in ceremonial garb befitting of their rank. Behind them, young braves, imposing of physique and with feathered head-dress, seated themselves in a half-circle before me. Further back were toothless elders and row upon row of modestly garbed squaws, some holding infants secured in a curious sort of cradle. Finally, I noted with disappointment, were the children, seated at the very back. These were the braves and squaws of the future, the ones I most wanted to reach.

With Joseph, my first and most trusted convert as

interpreter, I told them the story of our Lord Jesus Christ and the symbolic meaning of the crucifix. "My brethren," I concluded, "heed my words. The miracle of Jesus is proof that all who are baptized in his way shall one day pass through the gate to eternal life. As you learn more about our Blessed Savior and the sacred rituals of life and death, you will know the only certain escape from the fires of the evil pit beneath."

In closing, I raised my crucifix and sang Te Deum. *It seemed to me that this, their first exposure to Christian teaching, had been well received. However, when I ventured this opinion to Joseph, he replied with judgment less encouraging.*

In halting French, he cautioned me not to be deceived. "These people," he said in effect, "look upon your crucifix as a magic charm like the Shaman's rattle. They listen to your words about Jesus as they would an entertaining tale told around campfires at night."

Here Joseph looked around before speaking to me in lowered voice. "Father, you must be on guard against the wicked intentions of the Shaman, 'Twisted Foot.' He fears you as a rival for his claim to supernatural powers and scoffs at your words. I have seen the way he looks at you in hatred. While we are with these people you must not go anywhere alone."

If my spirits are dampened by Joseph's comments, my resolve is not. I am determined to continue my efforts to bring these heathen people into the embrace of our Lord. It is with this tribe I will remain for as long as it takes, or until convinced that further effort is to no avail.

As for Twisted Foot, I too have sensed the hostility of his malignant stare. In his incantations, rattling of gourds and bodily contortions, I see nothing but an evil mix of guile and duplicity. Beyond that I spare little thought for this false sorcerer. I harbour no yearning for martyrdom. * *However, should it come to that, I place myself in God's hands and am ready to offer Him the sacrifice of my life.*

---

* By the end of the 17th century at least five Jesuit missionaries had been murdered while in pursuit of their calling.

A day or so after that first meeting, Joseph came to my tent with what seemed Heaven-sent response to my prayers for help in winning the trust of these people. Yellow Feather, the young daughter of the Chief, had been stricken by fits of chills and trembling. Despite daylong ministration by Twisted Foot, her condition had worsened, until finally Running Elk had summoned me.

Hastening to his bark-enclosed hut, I found Twisted Foot in throes of frenzy, howling like a wild animal and banging on a drum. Below him, the little girl thrashed about on her pallet. Upon shouted command from the Chief, Twisted Foot came slowly out of his trance-like state. Then, after turning toward me with face contorted by malice, he stalked out of the hut.

Kneeling by the child, I construed her affliction to be some kind of ague, agitated I have no doubt, by the rantings of a false Shaman. The first thing being to bring her to a state of quiescence, I asked the chief to send from the hut all but himself and his squaw.

Next, I gave the child a gourd of water admixed with a tincture of a sleeping draught. Then, as she slowly stopped writhing, I wrapped her in a buffalo robe and sang softly a lullaby recalled from youth. Slowly, as she stared at me in childlike trust, her eyelids drooped and she was taken by sleep. Not daring to move, I held her thus until observing the evenness of her breathing. Arising, I instructed the squaw about warm nourishment after the child awoke. Then, after invoking God's blessing, I departed.

When late the next day, Yellow Feather awoke, she was free from torment. In a matter of days she was back playing games with her young friends. I had won the esteem of the Chief and the animus of his Shaman.

- 18 -

"... A PIOUS LIFE WELL SPENT"

Like most Indians, the Sioux of Running Elk's band believed that some men were given supernatural powers. Now, they perceived that the black-robed priest who had come to dwell among them was such a man. In days to follow, as Father deLaittre and Joseph went about the village communing with small groups, people listened carefully to their words about salvation.

As summer faded, autumn became the busy time of the year. Women gathered corn and using a sharp stick, dug out root vegetables like wild potatoes and onions. Old women and young girls went into the woods for berries and nuts. In camp they made pemmican, sun-dried buffalo meat packed in fat and flavored with pounded-in berries. This, with the vegetables and parched wild rice, they stored for approaching winter.

Young men worked in teams, hunting for buffalo and deer to assure adequate supplies of meat during the harsh months ahead. They also fished narrow streams in pairs, using seining nets fashioned out of animal skins punctured with holes.

All these things about the Sioux deLaittre observed and noted in his journal. Gradually too, as reflected in a missive to his Superior, his views on conversion began to change.

LETTER TO FATHER GARNEAU

October 21, 1696

Reverend Father, the Peace of our Lord Jesus Christ.

Winter beckons as I write these lines from this place where I have spent summer with the people of the Beef. It is situate on a point of the great river they call "Mesebebi," 35 leagues or so from our mission on the St. Louis River. For all of the wretched conditions surmounted during our passage here, it might as well be a hundred. At some future time, I hope to lay before you a detailed accounting of this wilderness region about which so little is known.*

Now, however, in hopes this missive may shortly be in your hands, I will dispatch two of my donees, Paul and Francis, to convey it to you in Quebec, where God willing, they may arrive before winter closure of navigation.

I must tell you Reverend Father, that my time with those who dwell here compels within me concern whether their full acceptance of our creed and rituals is possible. Here are a people groomed from childhood in the skills of survival in harsh wilderness; a people who believe in visions and guidance of dreams. In their pagan notion, immortality is the passage of the soul to a place where game is plentiful. In this "paradise" they will dwell eternally with a great spirit they call "Manitou." No one will ever be hungry and feasts, dancing and revelry will be continuous.

It is not only to Manitou that they make obeisance. They believe in and make offerings to a host of lesser gods they associate with all aspects of nature. These include sun, moon, rain, thunder and lightning deities along with hunting, fishing and even corn and tobacco spirits, all to be propitiated at various times.

I question, Reverend Father, whether large numbers of

* A reference to Sioux status as buffalo hunters

these unlettered children of God are likely to exchange such heathen beliefs for a way founded on a rock across a great ocean they have never seen. However, I take heart in their belief in life after death. If we can persuade them to accept our Lord Jesus as the way to salvation and eternal life, let that be the beginning. The catechism and rituals of our faith, I believe, must come only over time and with more mission schools.

I beseech you, Reverend Father, to consider my words not in tone of despair, but rather in vein of seeking more efficacious ways to reach the hearts of these benighted children of God. Owing to winter's approach and the distance that separates us, it will be many months before I receive word from you on these matters I have raised.

In the meantime, trusting to your accord, I will travel with this band to their winter camp, which I understand to be ten or fifteen leagues removed from this place. There, working with them more closely during enforced winter seclusion, I will hope to improve my facility in their language and with guidance from Our Heavenly Father, to bring converts under His care.

I take liberty to enclose with this letter a small list of necessities I hope may be sent here when Paul and Francis return in the Spring. Particularly important are the medical supplies requested, which perhaps more than any words of mine, will help further win the trust of these people.

I must tell you about their Medicine Man, a charlatan, who takes credit if a sick person recovers but has a ready excuse if otherwise. "The time had come that he should die," he will say, even if the patient is a child. I have been warned his jealousy may lead to violence against my person. Although I do not view this with light heart, I accept it as but another trial in the pursuit of God's work. Whatever the outcome, I leave it in His omnipotent hands.

Pray for me, Reverend Father, that through this mission I may favor the cause of our Lord and the purpose of our Order.

Your most humble servant in Jesus Christ,

J. deLaittre, Jesuit Missionary

‡‡ ‡‡ ‡‡ ‡‡ ‡‡

The foregoing, from archives in Quebec, was to be the young priest's last letter to Father Garneau. Shortly after he sent it, the first sprinkling of snow set the band in movement to its winter campsite. Tepees were pulled down and loaded along with deerskin bags of food, onto primitive vehicles known as a travois. These consisted of two trailing tepee poles connected by a skin platform. When packed, the rig was harnessed to and dragged along by a stout travois dog.

The trek to a sheltered woodland was north following the stream now believed to be Willow River. To select the campsite, a few old men went ahead the last day. When finally they were satisfied as to protection from winds and availability of water and firewood, they sat down. On arrival of the main procession, the camp was formed around them.

There, as winter arrived in full force, a different life style ensued. Locked in by snow and severe cold, the men stayed close to camp. This was a time for fashioning bows and arrows, snowshoes, axes and the like. Rarely did they venture far from camp. When they did, it was to cut and haul firewood or to hunt and set traps. Even then, unless food supplies ran low, they stayed close.

It was there during the long winter confinement that Father deLaittre began to win converts. Night after night, sometimes with twenty or more souls crowded together in an earthen lodge, he captured their imagination with narratives from the Old Testament. And after such tales about Moses, Samson and David and Goliath, he preached to them about the meaning of the New Testament and the Holy Trinity.

When sometime in mid-winter Chief Running Elk and his family came forward, a number of his tribe also hastened to accept the new religion. Among them were whole families, including children and even a sprinkling of elders, their heads white with the frost of many winters.

It was likely the happiest moment of the young priest's life when, standing inside a makeshift chapel, he received a procession of converts. First came Joseph holding aloft a wooden cross, followed by the Chief bearing a torch. Once underneath the birch bark roof of the chapel, a score or more of Indians knelt while Father deLaittre offered a prayer for their deliverance. Then, standing over them, he administered the sacrament of baptism.

In meetings that followed he instructed them in the rites of the Church. In addition to learning about prayer, confession and the sign of the Cross, the new communicants were given a small crucifix to wear and a rosary to count their prayers.

Instruction about the teachings of Jesus, especially the Sermon on the Mount, posed a dilemma for the young priest. How, he pondered, to reconcile its message of non-violence with the terrible penchant of Sioux braves for success in battle? Given on-going harassment from roving bands of Chippewa, any attempt to quell Siouxian spirit to retaliate could only be taken amiss.

The quarrel between these two powerful tribes was an old one, rising from Chippewa intrusion into the Minnesota domains of the Sioux. It was a conflict in which the Chippewa, provided with firearms by French fur traders, enjoyed a distinct advantage. It is ironic that warfare between these two tribes was detrimental to French efforts to extend its fur trade into the lake region of northern Minnesota.

An uneasy truce negotiated by Sieur du Luth in 1679 was often violated by flare-ups over some offense or other. The Sioux were proud and fierce warriors, quick to redress any affront, real or imagined.

Word that a Chippewa hunting party had slain deer less than a league from Running Elk's village rekindled Sioux resentment of their hereditary enemies. But what touched off their rage for revenge was word of the fate of two of their young braves who had followed the trespassers in order to give protest.

The Chippewa, after feigning contrition, suddenly sprang

on their accusers and carried them off as prisoners. A day later, a search party came upon the slain and brutally mutilated bodies of their tribal brothers.

When running Elk heard of this outrage, he vowed massive retaliation. Winter was not entirely over when he called his warriors together for a pre-battle feasting during which he explained his plan. Concerning that occasion and the action to follow, here are Father deLaittre's final journal entries.

‡‡ ‡‡ ‡‡ ‡‡ ‡‡

March 16, 1697:

The pines, crusted with nighttime frost, drooped in melancholy manner as we left camp this cold morning. My presence among the 20 braves who filed silently into the forest was not by choice.

Last night Running Elk summoned this band for a war feast in the large earthen structure that serves as their council house. Imagine a convoking of savages, faces painted in a rainbow array of colors, heads shaved excepting a tuft supporting feathers. I, invited by the Chief as a guest, sat in one of two lines of warriors facing each other with wooden bowls of food in between. Old women refilled bowls and stoked the fire pit, whilst through the haze of smoke slowly venting through a hole in the sod roof, younger squaws danced and chanted a mantra of praise for the warriors.

Finally, having done with feast and the women gone, Running Elk arose in full dress before the war party. "My brothers," he began, "Our enemies smile at us and talk of peace all the while whetting their knives for treacherous attack. They steal onto our hunting ground and by deceit murder our brothers. With the thunder weapons of the white man, they would take from us what is ours. They believe they have only to appear and like sheep before the wolf, we will run bleating into the wilderness."

"My brothers, we will teach them about Sioux warriors. It will be a lesson they will not soon forget."

Here he was interrupted by howls of approval. Then continuing and to my acute discomfort, he pictured a foray of blood-letting beyond Christian imagination. "We will strike them", he ended, "like a shrieking williwaw in the night. In its path no wigwam will stand, nor warrior, squaw or child be left alive."

Standing there, he thrust out his arms to silence the frenzied band. Abruptly and to my utter dismay, he turned to me. "Father Jean, will you now call upon our Lord Jesus to cast his blessing upon this raid?"

Shocked and all but speechless, I stammered an entreaty of safety for all of this party and a prayer that there might soon be peace among all Indian people. Even Joseph, my faithful friend and interpreter was unable to insert vigor into these forlorn words.

Sitting there like a bird of carrion perched on a dead branch was evil Twisted Foot, the jealous Shaman, of whom I have written before. Now, his baleful eyes blazing with malice, he pounced on my words.

"Great Chief, you have heard the whimperings of this so-called man of God. Is this the talisman that will help us in battle? I challenge him to come with us on this expedition. Let us see if his medicine has power in war."

Vengeful Twisted Foot had seized the moment to ensnare me in a trap of my own words. But what else could I have said? To seek benediction for a plan to utterly destroy one's trespassers was apostate to the teaching of Our Lord. To have agreed would have been a forsaking of His principles of mercy and forgiveness.

Though of lesser concern to me, there was also a secular consideration appertaining to French national interest. The Chippewa were a strong ally in the furtherance of colonial New France ambitions to extend its fur trade in North America.

Granting that His will permits, I must one day seek guidance from my superiors in the Order. For now, however, I had no recourse but to accept this malevolent challenge. To have declined would at a stroke undo my purpose to win Divine Grace for these savages.

So it was this dour morning, that with disconsolate heart, I trailed Running Elk's procession into the northern wilderness. All day, with scouts ahead and to our sides, the column moved silently through this dank and cheerless forest, traveling perhaps six leagues before making rude camp. We are allowed no fires and our meal, a few pieces of pemmican, is washed down with water.

I conclude this entry by the faint nimbus of light reflected from western skies.

March 18:

Camp is early astir with word of a Chippewa encampment four leagues removed. After two days of stumbling through forest and bog land, our scouts return to tell of a sighting. Sometime last night, War Hawk, the keenest of stalkers, had picked up the scent of wood smoke. Creeping to the edge of a clearing, he had observed a small encampment, which judging by the number of campfires, he took to be a place of a handful of families.

Now Running Elk bade us to retreat several leagues and set up a day camp for purpose of restoring strength with food and rest. Meanwhile, he went back with War Hawk for personal reconnaissance.

Now in late afternoon, Running Elk is back and we leave soon to march through the night in order to surround the village before dawn. The camp is a little larger than earlier described but Running Elk surmises that some of its braves are away on a hunting party.

I view the hours ahead with dread, not for my wretched person, but for the horror to ensue. So far as Running Elk is concerned, I might as well not be here. Neither he nor his warriors pay heed to my presence. Only faithful Joseph is solicitous, staying close and attending to my few needs. As for Twisted Foot, that creature of low instinct has quietly disappeared from the scene. One day out from our start he departed, telling the Chief he would go alone into the woods to make medicine for success in battle.

According to Joseph, who communes freely with the others in the party, it is the custom of this false Shaman to slink always from impending battle, only to emerge in aftermath claiming to have foreseen whatever had been its outcome.

Joseph told me also that in peacetime Running Elk would continue to follow the path of Jesus. For battle, however, he would address his supplications to Wolf, a Sioux protector of warriors. In the circumstance, I view this as at least a half victory for our Lord and Creator. And now as we go forth, I place myself in His infinite care.

‡‡ ‡‡ ‡‡ ‡‡ ‡‡

The following is a letter from Father Pierre Baptiste* in St. Ignace to the parents of Father deLaittre.

Mission St. Ignace

Monsieur and Madame,

I commit this letter and its tragic tidings to a company of voyageurs who shortly leave this mission bound for Quebec. It is with extreme sorrow that I now inform you of the death of your dear son and our esteemed brother, Jean deLaittre.

Three days ago there arrived at this place a ragged and half-starved Indian convert named Joseph. Almost incoherent after a harrowing six weeks during which time he traveled over water and through wilderness for more than 100 leagues, this servant of our blessed Lord has related to us the circumstances of Father deLaittre's death in manner I believe to be reliable. Incredibly, the hardships of his ordeal notwithstanding, he has brought with him your son's journal of his time amongst a tribe of savages in the territory of the Mesebebi River.

In each entry of this document we see the Grace of God

* Father Pierre Baptiste is also fictional

and are glad. For it bears witness to wilderness hardships borne nobly and of remarkable progress in the salvation of heathen souls.

Less than a year ago, when Father deLaittre went among this tribe of pagans, their worship was confined to a host of imaginary gods. During his time among them our brother awakened their Chief and some of his people to the one True and Living God.

As much for its record of a pious life well spent, as for its description of heathen existence in previously uncharted wilderness, the journal of Father deLaittre is a welcome addition to the annals of the Society of Jesus.

It is with dolorous heart that I must now turn to the circumstances of your dear son's final hours. As I piece it together from his journal and Joseph's account, Father deLaittre was coerced into going with members of his host tribe during a punitive raid against an enemy village. Though he had not wanted to be there, it was our brother's hope that his presence might serve to curb the warriors' spirit of vengeance. This was not to be.

On the morning of March 21, with his war party encircling the village of the Chippewa, the Chief waited till just before dawn. Then, upon his signal, the frenzied attackers stormed into the village with torches flaming and knives bared. Shrieking like fiends they ran in murderous assault, setting wigwams ablaze, stabbing and thrusting their blades into the bodies of their foe, many of them still struggling out of their sleeping robes.

As they laid waste on every side, some of the raiders displayed ferocity that even Joseph, a full-blooded Indian, had never imagined. It was seeing a warrior snatch up an infant and dash it against a tree that drove Father deLaittre to desperate act. Overcome by horror he ran to the infant's side. As he knelt there frantically seeking to succor, he did not see the child's crazed mother, who with partially torn scalp, rose from the ground and with the strength of hysteria smote our brother with a tomahawk. As he fell she struck him thrice more before herself being dispatched by Joseph. It is a fact I have gathered, that your son never suffered as his was an instant union with our blessed Maker.

A second fact is that his body was placed on a blanket and at the Chief's command transported many leagues back to their village. There, the earthly remains of our martyred brother were laid to rest in front of the little chapel he had caused to be erected. A cross, fashioned by the Chief himself, was planted deep in the ground to mark the grave of your blessed son.

My personal sorrow at reporting this tragic episode finds relief in the certainty that Father Jean deLaittre dwells now in the House of the Almighty. It is my earnest prayer that your own Christian grief may also be eased through certainty of his eternal grace.

Your most humble and obedient servant

P. Baptiste
Jesuit, Indian Missionary

- 19 -

THE BATTLE OF SANDY LAKE
CIRCA 1768

" ... The Sioux and Chippewa have been hated enemies so long as anything has been known of them. Their deadly war will continue so long as there lives a single warrior from either tribe."

—Byron Leslie*
2nd Lieutenant
1st Infantry Reg.'t.

Embedded in the conflict between colonial New France and England, as well as between and among tribes, the 18th century history of Minnesota Indians is complicated and murky. It is clear, however, that animosity between the Sioux and encroaching Chippewa continued to smolder and occasionally flare. The challenge to me as a teacher was to cull out from a maze of raids, failed treaties and shifting alliances something of the essence of the hostility innate between these two principal Minnesota tribes.

This turned out to be a purpose not easy to fulfill. And I

* 2nd Lt. Byron Leslie is a fictional character created to tell the story of the Battle of Sandy Lake

had about given up when deep in the bowels of Harwell Library I stumbled on a packet of documents relating to the U.S. First Infantry's time at old Fort Snelling. Second Lieutenant Byron Leslie, later a Colonel, was killed at the siege of Vera Cruz in 1847. His journals had come to rest in the Harwell archives, owing to some family connections. Though written long after the events in question, the journal offered a first hand account of the strangest and perhaps most decisive battle ever between Sioux and Chippewa.

The Battle of Sandy Lake, as it has been called, is in some ways the epitome of the 18th century circumstances that were changing the life of Minnesota Indians. It had begun with the earlier coming of French missionaries and traders who pushed into upper Minnesota—the former to save souls, the latter to corrupt them.

Their efforts, especially those of the traders, won lasting loyalty from the Chippewa. French traders were sent to live with and learn the customs of Chippewa people. They came bearing coveted goods, including firearms and ammunition. Theirs was to become an alliance of trade and mutual support that endured through a century of stormy conflict between French and British forces. In almost every battle during that long and bloody war, the Chippewa fought beside the French. Indeed, one band of the tribe traveled so far east as to stand against the British at the final decisive battle on the Plains of Abraham. Even after that French defeat, the Chippewa continued to view the English as their enemy.

The Sioux also had come to rely on barter with the French for all kinds of trade goods. But theirs was a relationship more of necessity than friendship. Proud Sioux warriors never forgot that it was French firearms first traded to the Chippewa that had given battle advantage to their ancient foe. When, as occasionally happened, trade with the French was cut off, the Sioux reacted with hostility. Such was likely the case in 1736 when a band of Sioux attacked a French expedition camped on an island in the Lake of the Woods. All twenty-one members of the French party were slaughtered and their goods stolen.

Eventually, the Sioux established trade with the British, with whom they sided during the American Revolution and later in the War of 1812. It was only after the establishment of Fort Snelling in 1819 that the Sioux finally acknowledged American authority.

Although both Sioux and Chippewa eventually came to accept the U.S. as their new white father, there was no let-up in their own intertribal warfare. The few decades of partial peace arranged by Sieur du Luth in the late 1600s had long since been shattered. At best it had been little more than a fragile truce to which not all members of either tribe had agreed. When, around 1730, it broke down completely, there followed more than a century of relentless warfare.

As told by missionary Peter Jones, himself an Ojibway chief, the Indian manner of battle was different from that of civilized nations:

> " ... They have no idea of meeting the enemy upon an open plain face-to-face. Their aim is to surprise the enemy by darting upon them in an unexpected moment, or in the dead of night. ...When they find them unprepared or asleep they creep in slowly and stealthily, like panthers in pursuit of their prey. When sufficiently near, they simultaneously raise the war whoop, and before the enemy awake or have time to defend themselves, the tomahawk is rattling over their heads. When a village, a wigwam, or a party of them is surprised, there is seldom any mercy shown to age or sex. All are doomed to feel the weight of the tomahawk and the deep incision of the bloody scalping knife. Such close battles ... seldom last long, not for more than a few minutes." (*History of the Ojebway Indians*)

After sweeping like a tornado through an unsuspecting village, the invaders, bearing scalps and sometimes dragging captives, were quick to escape back to their own country. It was a hit and run tactic that was usually but—as we're about to see—not always successful.

French efforts at peacekeeping aside, the better-armed Chippewa steadily pushed the Sioux away from their ancestral domains around the forests and lakes of the upper Mississippi Valley. Although out numbered and out gunned, the Sioux did not go meekly. Sometime around 1768, smarting over the loss of their hunting grounds and ricing lakes, they set out on a grand effort to win them back.

Curiously, the eyewitness account of the fighting that followed did not come to light until sixty years after those savage encounters. In summer of 1828, Lieutenant Byron Leslie of the First U.S. Regiment, was sent with a squad of infantry and two Sioux guides on a reconnaissance and timber-scouting expedition along the Rum River north of Fort Snelling. The following excerpt from his journal carries a description of the Battle of Sandy Lake, as told him by an aged Sioux warrior, who was likely its only still living survivor.

‡‡ ‡‡ ‡‡ ‡‡ ‡‡

24 August, 1828: Arrived back at the Fort last evening shortly before dark. All well, no one hurt, but very tired after 2 weeks struggling through the forest of the Rum River, all the while slapping at mosquitoes. After reporting to Col. Taylor, surprised to be asked to join him for dinner in his quarters. Also there was Mister Taliaferro, the Indian agent. Sherry and roast pork at the Commandant's house, a welcome change after two weeks of camp fare. Disappointed that the Colonel's wife and*

---

* Zachary Taylor, recently appointed commandant at Fort Snelling. Twenty years later "Old Rough and Ready" was elected twelfth President of the United States. Lawrence Taliaferro, from 1819 to 1839, was the U.S. Indian Agent at Fort Snelling. He is an important historical figure for his work with the Indians and his chronicles of frontier life during those years.

especially his oldest daughter Ann, the belle of the post, did not join us. But the rumor is she only has eyes for Bob Wood, our assistant surgeon.

Colonel Taylor, a sturdy man, ramrod straight with strong features and a prominent nose. While we talked, his sharp eyes looked deeply at mine, as though judging my every word. Although he is very much down to earth, I would not like to be on the wrong side of this man. Mister Taliaferrro quite different, courtly, somewhat haughty and visibly wearied after years of dealing with the foibles of Indians and unscrupulous traders.

Both men are concerned with peace, Agent Taliaferro to encourage it, Col. Taylor to enforce it. After dinner they pressed me about the mood of the savages we had encountered along the Rum River. I replied we had seen only Sioux, but if the hatred they expressed toward Chippewa is any measure, I could not see how these old enemies would ever make peace. To illustrate, I told them of bitterness still smoldering 60 years after a Sioux plan to seize back their old homeland was shattered by Chippewa ambush.

At an isolated camp a few miles north of where the Rum joins the Mississippi, I had come upon "Broken Face," a battle-scarred ancient, who of certainty must be the last person alive to have fought in that action. Though long of tooth and dim of eye, his recall of its details is acute and woeful. Here, as translated by my scout, Bear Claw, is the old warrior's account of that sanguinary affair.

"The land the Chippewa have stolen is where our fathers hunted. I do not know how long. No one who remembers is alive. It is the ground where I was born. The trees, the deer, the waters and rice all were ours. But then came the Chippewa, who wanted all the woods and lakes where we had hunted and fished. Their warriors were many and they had white man's guns. Sioux do not run. Our fathers fought like wounded bears. But arrows not good against bullets."

"Our white fathers preached to us of peace. And we try to do as they say. But what good peace talks when Chippewa do

not listen? They keep driving till finally we are here where hunting is poor and no rice."

"Not know how many winters ago. Broken Face very young brave when war chief Red Cloud make parley with other chiefs. Want our sacred land back. Many warriors come.** Chiefs make plan to surprise enemy from behind. We go up Mesebebi in many canoes. Carry canoes around enemy to place way upstream. Paddle long days. Leave big river and carry canoes. Finally come to big lake where waters flow back in Mesebebi. We rest and make war dance. Then we start back down big river. That day we surprise and kill two men hunting and at end of day find and kill small family."*

"On third day we attack little camp and kill them all. Broken Face get first scalp. When my friends see it is white they make jokes about me. But they not laugh next time when I show them scalp of young warrior."

*"Early next morning scout come back. He find big village.*** Chiefs make plan. Some attack by water in canoes. My party go to land and come in behind village. On way we capture party of young women picking berries."*

"At start everything good. Many of their braves away on war party. Those behind all drunk or old. But someone give warning. Squaws pour water on warriors, some they throw in lake. After that they able to stand and fight."

"We attack by water and from behind on land, killing many and burning their lodges. But enough of them stand so we cannot kill them all. Late in day we leave with many scalps and women prisoners, most were young. That night at camp downstream we danced and shouted. We had killed many Chippewa and would kill more as we went further down river. For my scalps I was given one of the women to keep as my squaw."

Here the old warrior broke off and began to sob. Turning away, he said only, "It did not come about as we had planned."

---

* 1768 (Warren, *History of the Ojibway People*).

** Four to five hundred (Warren, *ibid.*).

*** Semi-permanent camp at Sandy Lake.

After that he would talk no more and his son took up the story.

What happened was that the Chippewa warriors, who had earlier gone out on a hunting party, somehow got word of the attack on their village. Reasoning that the invaders would return by way of the Mississippi, they laid ambush at a point just below where the Crow Wing flows into the big river.

With cunning verging on the diabolical, they took concealment along high bluffs on the eastern shore. It was at a point where they knew a strong current from the merging Crow Wing would force the enemy canoes in close to their shore. Then they waited till alerted by a scout of the approaching canoes.

The result for the Sioux was catastrophic. Floating in a compact flotilla almost up to the bluffs, they were caught in a murderous hail of musketry and barbed arrows. Many were killed or wounded. Others drowned when their canoes tipped. A few of the captives, including the squaw given Broken Face, escaped and swam ashore.

So long as the Sioux stayed in range a rattle of musketry pursued them. The shattered remnants of the war party, some clinging to canoes, others swimming and a few who were untouched struggled ashore a few miles downstream. There they determined to go back for vengeance. But after two days of hand-to-hand fighting against the dug in and tenacious Chippewa, the Sioux were compelled to withdraw. Broken Face claimed to have killed two of the enemy but was clubbed in the face, which accounts for the stoved-in appearance of his right cheek.

There is a Sioux legend of a warrior brave, who prior to leaving on this star-crossed expedition, swore to his young wife that he would return. Days later as the young squaw waited by the river for the return of the overdue war party, she noticed a dark object floating toward her in the sluggish current. As an eddy brought it to her feet she screamed to recognize the dead body of her husband, an arrow sticking from his chest. That, as the legend goes, was the village's first indication of the defeat suffered by their braves after the battle of Sandy Lake.

Such was the tale I related at dinner last evening. Mister Taliaferro knew about the battle, though he had not heard of Broken Face. Although I have been told the Sioux are the most trustworthy and generous of all Indians, Taliaferro cautioned that we must always be alert for an abrupt outburst into savagery. Theirs, he said, was a deeply embedded instinct for violence.

‡‡ ‡‡ ‡‡ ‡‡ ‡‡

Although the Battle of Sandy Lake may have been decisive, hostilities between the two tribes continued for decades thereafter. In his book published nearly a century later, the Rev. Peter Jones lamented their unrelenting strife: "For many years past a wasting war on a small scale has been kept up between the Ojebways and Sioux...This originated in encroachments made by either nation upon the hunting grounds of the other. When any hunter was found trespassing, he was immediately killed and scalped. This called for revenge on the part of the relatives of the person killed, who would pursue the murderer until they had satisfied the calls of their friend's blood. This warfare is still kept up; it is both treacherous and cruel; every year they are thinning each other's numbers; and the author sincerely wishes that the British and American Governments would unite to put it down" (*History of the Ojebway Indians*).

Actually, the British and Americans, as the French before, tried very hard to put it down. But all efforts were without avail. Savagery on both sides continued, carried on by succeeding generations with hatreds instilled and nurtured from birth.

In 1805, after negotiating with the Sioux for the land on which Fort Snelling now stands, Lieut. Zebulon Pike recorded in his journal, "I addressed them (The Chiefs) in a speech … touching on many points, yet the principal ones were the Granting of Land at this place … and the making peace with the Chippeway's … They gave me the land required: … and promised me safe passport for myself and any Chiefs I might bring down; but spoke doubtfully relative to the peace." (*The Journals of Zebulon Montgomery Pike*).

As Pike worked his way further up the Mississippi, he sought wherever he met them to encourage Sioux and Chippewa to treat each other in friendship. However, despite his claims of successful mediation, the two tribes kept on fighting until at last the Sioux were ousted from Minnesota after the outbreak of 1862.

- 20 -

MY BUDDY SUE

With two lectures a week and long afternoons in the library, that first term at Harwell was literally flying by. The plan was for me to teach the Minnesota history course in both fall and spring terms. Meanwhile I was to develop a course on European immigration to add to my teaching load for next year.

Along with soaking up Minnesota lore, those hours in the library brought an unexpected bonus. And that was making friends with Sue Humboldt from Pipestone, Minnesota. Trim, with a scrubbed-clean look and a grin endearingly impish, she had an air of upbeat candor. I felt good and open with her from the start.

Despite Mom's stewing that I was going to wind up a "frumpy old bachelor," I had more than a passing interest in the fair sex. In the Army and before, I had dated often. And during graduate school I was very much involved with Josie Boltan, a scrumptious triage nurse for the University Health Services. Our affair lasted nearly a year and only broke off when it became clear I wasn't ready for the big step, while a doctor she worked with was.

But for Josie like the others before her, the magic was female attraction. This is not to discount Christie White, the girl, now married woman, who had lived in my dreams since about fifth grade. I had no problem imagining Christie as both lover and friend. Only the way it worked out, I never had a chance to be either.

With Sue Humboldt it was different. Although I was probably always a bit in love with her, ours was more like a brother-sister relationship of easy comfort with each other. What we had, even if we never spelled it out, was an understanding we'd be pals. I placed Sue up there with my old church-climbing buddy Ernie Olshefski. Except with Sue I could talk about things I wouldn't dream of opening up with Ernie.

Although I had chatted with her several times while she chased down books for me in the library, our friendship really began the night she sat next to me at a faculty meeting. As old Foster Partridge, Professor *emeritus*, maundered into a second hour of deadly reminisce, Sue whispered, "Nominations are in order for next year's speaker."

Biting my lips to stifle a giggle, I turned to Sue, "What do you say we blow this scene and go get a beer somewhere?"

"I know just the place," she grinned.

Happily we were back far enough to be able to slip out without waking up any of the comatose assembly seated nearby.

The place turned out to be The Chestnut Lodge, a laid back, old-style lounge halfway down the hill toward Lake City. Without piercing hard rock music, it was never to be an "in" place for students. Except for a handful of regulars at the bar, the place was nearly empty as we took over one of its vintage 1930s booths. In semi-darkness and with high mahogany backing between us and the next booth, it was perfect place to get acquainted.

Our talk flowed as easily as the Leinenkugels we sipped. And it turned out, we had a lot in common. Sue was two years younger but we both had memories of growing up in a small town. Pipestone, on the southwest edge of Minnesota, was bigger than Buhl, but not by much.

"Buhl has the finest water in America," I boasted.

"But we're the Pipestone Capital of the World," she

countered, laughing. "But I guess that says it all."

For both of us, college was our introduction to life beyond a small town. Sue had made it to the Twin Cities on a scholarship to the University. Her goal was to get back to some place like it.

"You don't like it here?"

"Sure I do. It's a great place if I want to grow old stamping books. There's just more opportunity in a big city."

Her dream, she said, was to get aboard a magazine staff in Chicago. Back in high school, a well-meaning counselor had steered her toward a career as a librarian. At the time she thought that was good advice. As an honors student at the U, she took a special course in library science along with working as a student in the library systems.

Somehow she also found the time to serve on the editorial staff of the *Minnesota Daily*. She loved that work and was good at it. Now her plan was to earn enough to keep herself going until she could latch on to an editorial job somewhere, hopefully Chicago. Meanwhile, she was shooting out resumes.

Listening, I began to see Sue's dream wasn't all that farfetched. Along with a flair for writing, she had a solid grasp on a vanished grammatical art called syntax.

"When do you think you'll be ready?"

"Probably next fall. Maybe sooner, if one of my resumes hits."

"What about marriage and family and all that sort of thing?"

I'd meant it as kind of a joke but when she turned away, I realized I'd struck a nerve. "I'm sorry, I had no right to ask that."

She pushed a strand of auburn hair back and then said with a sad little smile, "That's okay. Maybe we'll talk about it someday, but not just now."

That's how it began, and for the rest of the year we were more and more together—lunch at the faculty club, student plays and occasional long walks. It was after a Saturday of tromping around on the bluffs above the Mississippi that she told me the story.

Warming up by the fireside at the Chestnut Lodge, we were sipping brandy and soda. "You asked me about marriage," she challenged. "What about you?"

"A fair question, but I asked first."

She looked away. But then she turned to me with a questioning smile. "Are you sure you want to hear this?"

"I want to hear whatever you want to tell me."

Sue signed. "Well, I don't want to shock you. But I've already had a go at the marriage and family bit."

If she didn't want to shock me, I wondered what she thought would. Sitting there I could hardly believe my ears.

The guy had come on to her where she worked at Walters Library. A senior and a big fraternity man, he swept the little frosh from Pipestone off her feet. It turned out he was just fooling around while the heiress he planned to marry was spending a year at some school in Europe.

When Sue broke the news, Kevin—that was his name—tried to wriggle off the hook. He folded only after her Dad threatened the scandal of a lawsuit. What followed was an out-of-town, secret wedding. They never lived together, but this marriage-in-name-only made an honest woman of Sue. She dropped out of school for a year and the marriage was annulled after the baby was born.

Sue's folks had stood by her like a rock. They sent her back to school and told her they would take care of her son until she was ready to take over on her own. "That," she wound up, "will be as soon as I get settled in Chicago or wherever." And, it turned out, that was why she was gone so many weekends—visiting her family to be with her son Tim.

Sue wasn't sure whether Kevin's heiress ever found out about his straying. But she took what she called "poetic consolation" when she heard the girl had married someone else. Sue didn't know what had become of Kevin and she didn't want to find out.

And there she paused with a sad little smile. "So now what do you think about your friendly librarian?"

Impulsively I reached across the table and squeezed her hands. "I think she's a hell of a nice lady."

There were tears and a muffled sob as she squeezed back.

A week or so later over dinner at her apartment, I raised the question again. "What about love and marriage? Are you going to do penance the rest of your life?"

Sue took time to sip her wine. "There is a guy, a very nice guy named Dave. I knew him back in Pipestone. Now he's an accountant in Chicago and wants to marry me. He'll probably be my future if he's willing to wait a while. But first I want to make it on my own."

"Do you love this guy?"

"I suppose so. Who really knows what love is?"

"Let's skip the metaphysics. If you're thinking about a future with this Dave, you better grab him. In this day and age there's no reason you can't have him and a career too."

She looked at me but didn't answer. After a moment she smiled. "Now you've heard my story. When am I gonna hear yours?"

And so I told her about Christabel White: how I'd known her since kindergarten. Her Dad had been manager of the Grant Mine where my Dad and Uncle Ty once toiled with pick and mall. Now the mine was closed, her parents had moved away, and their old, gabled house on Jones Street stood vacant and going to seed.

Somehow once I started talking the details just spilled out: how I used to try to time it so as to be able to walk with her a few blocks on our way to school, my fantasy through high school and college, that someday I was going to sweep her off her feet, how the crush lived on even though my dreams began to break up the day Buddy Cosgrove transferred in from Grand Rapids at the start of our junior year.

His Dad had come to manage the local power plant. Buddy had already made his mark as a sophomore fullback for the Grand Rapids Indians in the tough Iron Range Conference. At Buhl he was a starter right away and voted All-State at the end of the season. I suppose he met Christie in class or maybe at a pep rally. Wherever, the attraction was immediate and Buddy and Christie were an item from then on.

"So that's pretty well it." I smiled at Sue. "Kinda crazy, huh, mooning over a teen-age dream who's married to someone else? I thought I was over it until seeing her at that party last summer. You probably think I don't have all my marbles."

The look Sue gave me was like a mother might give her kid with a skinned knee. "No, I don't think you're nuts. It's very touching, really. But where's it gonna end?"

"Wish I knew. I haven't been a hermit all this time, but so far nobody quite measures up to how I feel about Christie. I almost wish I hadn't seen her last July."

"What about that? Sounds like she was trying to tell you something."

I sighed. "You think I haven't thought about that? But what can I do? She's married."

Sue studied me for a moment. "But not very happily, it seems."

We finished the wine and I hugged her at the door. For us that night, maybe we'd both got over some kind of a hurdle.

- 21 -

BEACON IN THE WILDERNESS

On a whim I once asked the class to vote on what they considered Minnesota's most striking landmark. The bluffs towering over the Mississippi down by Dresbach got most of the votes. The rest were scattered around among places like the Capitol, Duluth Harbor and the like. My own vote goes to Fort Snelling and I was pleased to see several others thought so too. I had only seen the place once on a high school trip. But there was something about that old bastion of stone that made a deep impression. Perhaps it was the enigma of that mute sentinel of the past, standing guard over a frontier that has long ceased to exist. For a few short years, hardly more than a decade, its ramparts had bristled with musketry, cannon and mortar, weapons never to be fired in anger.

That is the paradox of Fort Snelling, this colossus of limestone astride the confluence of the Minnesota and Mississippi Rivers. Although never to be the scene of combat, its imposing battlements were the fountainhead for civilization throughout what was then the Northwestern Frontier. Indeed, so quickly did settlement follow its establishment that the fort was shortly left behind a frontier moving ever west. Though short-lived, its run had been crucial, marking as Theodore Blegen suggests, "The beginning of the modern, American period of Minnesota"

(Blegen, *Minnesota: A History of the State*). And in this sense it can certainly be argued that the raising in 1819 of the Stars and Stripes over that wilderness outpost was the most important single action in the history of what was to become America's thirty-second state.

Events leading up to the decision to establish the fort began in 1805, soon after Thomas Jefferson had bought nearly half the continent from the French. The young nation had discovered that it needed more than paper treaties to gain control of its new frontiers. Accordingly, Lieutenant Zebulon Pike had been dispatched to explore the region of the Upper Mississippi. His orders were to follow that river to its source and look for sites for military and trading posts.

In a journey of many months Pike and his 20 weary, half-frozen soldiers pressed north to Leech Lake which Pike took to be the source of the Mississippi. He was off by a whisker. But a far more important accomplishment was his earlier negotiation with the Sioux, by which the U.S. acquired the site on which Fort Snelling was later to stand.

In 1820, the fort as it began to rise on a bluff towering over the joining of two great rivers was the first real evidence of U.S. determination to extend authority over the vast wilderness of the upper Mississippi Valley. An immediate consequence of the fort's military occupation was the withdrawal to the north of the British fur posts still operating in the region. In years to follow, the fort was to emerge from frontier sentinel to beacon of civilization in the Northwest wilderness.

One of the reasons for building Fort Snelling was to curb the continuing warfare between Sioux and Chippewa. As Pierre Radisson had described it 160 years before, "this cruelle warre" seriously interfered with fur trade.

Another purpose was to provide an outpost of protection. Today as one stands by the old fort's ramparts overlooking a metropolitan skyline, it is hard to imagine that here, not all that long ago, was only wilderness. Once it was occupied by soldiers, the fort became a haven of safety under whose protective embrace

St. Paul and Minneapolis came shortly into being.

Along with trying to establish peace and order, Fort Snelling soon became a stimulus for smaller settlements that spread outward in a wide semicircle to places like New Ulm and Mankato on the Minnesota River and Hastings, Red Wing and St. Cloud on the Mississippi. On the heels of soldiers and fur traders came farmers and lumbermen. As Theodore Blegen put it, "One must interpret Fort Snelling in terms not of gun and sword, but of axe and plow" (Blegen, *ibid,*).

It fell to Colonel Josiah Snelling, who assumed command in 1820, to design and build the fort which bears his name. Snelling chose the present site and oversaw the fort's completion from log cutting on the Rum River to construction of its thick stone walls and towers and essential facilities to include barracks, mess halls, officers' quarters and parade grounds. Within its stout confines were established the first school, hospital, library and church in what is now Minnesota.

From its first days as a symbol of American authority to its later use as an Army induction center during 19th and 20th century wars, Fort Snelling was literally the rock on which Minnesota based its transition from Indian territory to thriving statehood. During those years a number of young officers who were to distinguish themselves in future battle saw service there. Of these, Zachary Taylor has already been mentioned. Another notable early visitor was Winfield Scott, later commanding General of the Army, who inspected the fort in 1824. In his report, Gen. Scott wrote, "I wish to suggest ... the propriety of calling this work Fort Snelling, as a just compliment to the meritorious officer under whom it has been erected" (Hansen, *Old Fort Snelling, 1819-1858*).

In 1866, General William T. Sherman came to inspect the fort after its Civil War service. He recommended to the War Department that the fort should be retained as an active Army post.

Perhaps the most celebrated individual to set foot on post ground was neither military person nor citizen. He was Dred

Scott, a slave, whose legal bid for freedom was the most famous case in the pre-Civil War controversy. In 1836, Dr. John Emerson, an Army surgeon from Missouri, a slave state, took Scott to Illinois and then to Fort Snelling. Two years later, they returned to Missouri where after Emerson's death, Scott became the center of a test case in which his freedom was sought on grounds of his earlier residence in Illinois, a free state. Although the Supreme Court ruled against Scott, the anti-slavery dissenting opinions served to heighten the controversy over slavery.

Fort Snelling's time as an active military post endured until just after its World War II service as a reception center. During that War, 300,000 men entered the Army there to be tested, inoculated and given their first lessons in military discipline. When, in 1946, the flag was lowered for the last time, the old fort's service as a military post came to end after 126 years.

- 22 -

MID TERM REVIEW

During the first eight weeks of the course we had surveyed billons of years against which awesome span the coming of man seemed about five minutes ago. Through unknown eons which preceded the sound of human voices, convulsive natural forces had created the resources and waterways that were to transform America's thirty-second state into a world leader in agriculture and industry.

The time clock is uncertain. But it is doubtful that man appeared in these parts until near the end of the receding glaciers, some 15 to 20,000 years ago. Sometime in the wake of the Ice Age, the region was invaded by scattered tribes of big game hunters. Gradually through the course of centuries, these primitives altered their nomadic ways into the more settled life of hunter-agrarians. Such were the native peoples first witnessed by European eyes during the mid-17th century.

French explorers and missionaries were shortly followed by traders and voyageurs from Quebec. Fur trading, the region's first important commerce, became the crux of a long and bitter struggle between France and England. Both nations recruited Indians to sack enemy villages and murder their inhabitants.

In this, the region that was to become Minnesota, warriors of the Chippewa fought for the French while those of the

Sioux came eventually to side with the English. The warfare, carried on for more than a century, ended only after English victories at Quebec and Montreal. In that regard, I had passed along to the students the little known fact that although British triumph on the "Plains of Abraham" resounds down the corridors of history with a ring of biblical grandeur, in fact the field of combat was a pasture granted in 1635 to one Abraham Martin and known thereafter as "Abraham's Plains." In all events, by terms of the peace treaty of 1763, Canada and French possessions east of the Mississippi were ceded to the English.

The French era of supremacy in North America had ended. But the stamp of their courageous explorers and missionaries remains indelible. Memory of pathfinders like Radisson, du Luth and Hennepin is kept alive in numerous place names in Minnesota. And French legacy is honored in our state seal which proclaims to be *L'Etoile du Nord.*

On the heels of victory the British were quick to hoist the Union Jack over trading posts abandoned by the French. And they clung to these posts even after America's throwing off of the British yoke and the subsequent Louisiana Purchase, which nearly doubled the size of U.S. holdings on this continent. Included in the 800,000 square miles of rich land bought from France was most of present day Minnesota.

Despite these expanded American territorial claims, British fur traders continued to conduct business from numerous posts in the Minnesota region. It was not until after the War of 1812 and the establishment of Fort Snelling that American authority over the region was enforced.

The foregoing was the main "stuff" of the first half of our course in Minnesota history. Upon grading mid-term exams, I was tickled to find out that the kids had been paying attention. Along with a cluster of As and Bs, no one had done worse than a "gentleman's C."

- 23 -

KING BEAVER

For 250 years trade with Indians for fur was the main business of the New World. Beaver, which provided weather resistant felt for tall, fancy hats, was the deluxe crop. But the bread and butter of the fur trade consisted of less expensive hides ranging from otter and fox through raccoon, muskrat, deer and later buffalo robes.

If a single person can be said to be the father of the North American fur trade, it would be Samuel de Champlain, the explorer honored as founder of the French Colonies in the New World. Starting in 1608 with a trading post he established at the future site of Quebec, Champlain aggressively forged a chain of forts and trading posts that in years to come were to multiply throughout the vast colonies of New France. By the time of his death on Christmas Day 1635, Quebec had become the center of a fur empire which at its height extended from Hudson Bay to New Orleans and westward to the Rockies.

European demand for North American furs was insatiable as first France, then England and finally the United States vied for control. However, by the time the U.S. wrested supremacy in the Minnesota region, the era of fur trade was beginning to wane. Changing styles and scarcity of beaver had started to put a damper on this first great commerce of the New World.

Its great run had begun with French Canadian *voyageurs*, bold and resilient men, able to stand up to the rigor and perils of long journeys into the northern wilderness. As beaver became scarce in the east they went ever further by paddle and portage deep into the Northwest. From Montreal, the so-called "birch brigades" stroked their frail craft up the Ottawa and other rivers, fighting rapids and boulders, then shooting down wild stretches of the French River before emerging into Georgian Bay. Next came Sault Ste. Marie and finally out onto the vast and often violent reaches of Lake Superior.

Hugging the shoreline, they came after many days to the lake's western end and the challenge of *Le Grand Portage*. Here, over a nine-mile by-pass of unnavigable waterfalls, they hand-carried their canoes and trade goods. With each *voyageur* shouldering two eighty-pound packs at a time, they didn't walk, they trotted—panting, fighting off and sometimes swallowing mosquitoes.

In order to allow room for trade goods, very few of these sturdy *couriers des bois* were much bigger than today's Triple Crown jockeys. Nevertheless these incredibly tough little men were the heart and soul of a canoe system of waterways extending deep in the continent. Paddling and singing, sweating over steamy portages, garbed with their colorful sashes and red toques, *les voyageurs* each summer moved hundreds of tons of trade goods to and fro between Montreal and the wilderness beyond Lake Superior.

Sadly, few of them survived into their forties, victims of rupture, disease, violent quarrel, exposure or drowning. Once the forests and lakes of the north rang with the spirited *chansons* of hard-paddling *voyageurs*. Now their voices echo only in imagination to remind us of one of the New World's most picturesque eras.

Over the passage of a century, Indian tribes in the Minnesota region had become dependent on the goods French traders brought in exchange for furs. But after 1763, the French were expelled from North America. The British moved in, spearheaded by the fiercely competing Hudson's Bay and North West Companies. English interests dominated the region's fur trade for nearly half a century.

It was only after the military occupation of Fort Snelling that the Union Jack was replaced by Old Glory over fur posts in the Minnesota region. Many of these posts were swallowed up by the giant American Fur Company, put together by a New York City tycoon who had begun his working life as a village butcher in Germany's Black Forest.

John Jacob Astor, who came to this country as a 20-year-old immigrant, was to become America's first multimillionaire. Three quarters of a century before the likes of Rockefeller or Carnegie, Astor had built the fortune that has left his family name synonymous with immense wealth. His may well have been a model borrowed by his contemporary Horatio Alger, in concocting one of his familiar "rags to riches" adventures. In this case however, the hero would not be without ethical blemish.

For it was as much by sharp or unscrupulous dealings as by shrewd management that Astor came to dominate American commerce for half a century following the Revolutionary War. One of his more notable shenanigans occurred in 1808 while Astor sought to extend his foreign trade to China. Scheming to get around an embargo forbidding American ships to trade with any overseas port, Astor came up with a ruse that has become legendary (Morrison, *The Oxford History of the American People*). His vessel, *Beaver,* was granted an exception when a person representing himself as "The Honorable Punqua Wingchong, a Chinese Mandarin," requested its use to carry him to China to settle his grandfather's estate. In reality the alleged Mandarin was a clerk in Astor's employ.

The sale of *Beaver's* jammed-to-the-gunnels cargo while the embargo was still in effect was a financial coup that put Astor in a position to charter the American Fur Company as a major rival to Canada's North West and Hudson's Bay Companies. After 1812 American Fur took over most of the trade in the Great Lakes region with headquarters on Mackinac Island.

Included among assets that reinforced Astor's business savvy was a keen perception of when and where to cut bait. In 1833, sensing that the fur trade was topping out, he left the field in order to concentrate on his enormous real estate holdings in Manhattan. In his final years this free enterprise Midas, who devoted a lifetime to amassing money, bemoaned that he hadn't been smart enough to buy up the whole *verdammte* island.

Not long after Astor sold out, the American Fur Company was reorganized under new management. One of its first acts was to send a 22-year-old man to supervise trading affairs in the vast Minnesota region. He was Henry Hastings Sibley, who more than anyone deserves to be remembered as "First Citizen of Minnesota."

Born in Detroit and for the times well-educated, young Sibley set up his trading center on the heights across from Fort Snelling. From this place called Mendota, he managed a region stretching to Pembina to the north and the Missouri River in the west. Scattered over that huge territory, Sibley's traders and post managers dealt mostly with Sioux, bargaining for beaver pelts, buffalo robes and other skins in exchange for blankets, guns, knives, tobacco, beads and flour.

Sibley's arrival in 1834 marked the beginning of a career in which he was to build an empire of furs, help create the Minnesota Territory, be a persuasive advocate for statehood, help write its constitution, be elected Minnesota's first governor, command an army to put down the Sioux uprising, help found a University and finally become an honored recorder of the young state's history.

We will look more closely at Henry Hastings Sibley in future class sessions. But for now let us hear from a fur trader friend of his, whose memories extend from boyhood companionship with Sibley through the final decades of what was Minnesota's first great industry.

- 24 -

STATEMENT OF KILBOURNE ST. ONGE

Maribel Hinman was a school teacher in St. Peter, MN, who spent many long hours in conversation with her uncle, Kilbourne St. Onge.* Deeply interested in history, in 1887 she compiled her notes on these conversations into an account of his life and experience which she labeled, "Statement of Kilbourne St. Onge."

My grandfather was a voyageur for the North West Fur Company. I have heard there is a simple wooden cross to mark the place where he drowned saving a companion. That would have been around 1765, along a wild stretch of rapids on the French River. Louis St. Onge was stern paddler in a trading canoe, who was thrown into the surging waters when the canoe smashed against a boulder. There he grabbed the floundering bowman and held him up long enough for another canoe to pull him in. But then my grandfather just disappeared into the swirling current. Someone said he was knocked out when his head hit a big rock.

At age 33, Louis St. Onge of Montreal had left behind a

* Maribel Hinman and Kilbourne St. Onge are fictional characters who provide an insider's view of the fur trade era and the world of Henry Hastings Sibley.

wife and the year-old son who was to become my father. How they got by after his death I do not know, though I have heard my grandmother took in washing for a detachment of British soldiers stationed there after the French left. I don't think my father ever knew what became of her. That's because around 1777, he marched off with the Redcoats and never saw her again. As a 13-year-old drummer boy, Joseph St. Onge went along as General Burgoyne marched down from Canada into New York. He was there beating the charge when the British won a big battle in which the rebel General Herkimer was killed.

Later, my father's company was sent west to support Chippewa raids on American settlements. The attacks planned by a British General were sent out from Detroit. During one of them, my father was shot in the leg. Although the ball went clean through, my father was left behind bleeding on the ground. Lucky for him, two Chippewa braves took pity and carried him a long ways back to their village where a medicine man took care of him. Although he had a slight limp the rest of his life, he slowly recovered.

And it was there, two years later that he met Colonel McKee, the British Indian agent at Detroit. McKee's job was to win the trust of the Indians and to stir up trouble for American settlers. The Chippewa respected him as the white man who helped them the most. He had come to the village where my father was, in order to mend fences with the Indians who had heard the rebels had beaten the British.

Nothing would change, he told them. It only seemed America had won. In time, he promised, the war would come again and the British and their red brothers would drive out the hated Yankees. Meanwhile, British posts would continue to provide trade goods in exchange for furs. He urged them to keep on with their raids and attacks against American settlements.

It was while McKee was there that he heard about a white boy living in the camp. He was quick to see the benefit of taking on a young assistant who knew Chippewa customs and could parlay with them in their own language. When McKee left the village, 15-year-old Joseph St. Onge went with him.

That was in 1780 when the Revolutionary War was supposed to be over. A peace treaty had been signed, but things were still pretty bitter. The British hung on to their posts in the Northwest. And the Indians, who mainly sided with them, kept up with their raids on American settlements.

My father began to learn the fur trade at a time when the frontier was a dangerous place. And it pretty much stayed that way for a long time. Like his father before him, Joseph St. Onge was working for the North West Company. But instead of being a voyageur, he was learning how to run a trading post.

*After a few years, I doubt he was 20 yet, my father was sent out from Detroit to open a new post in the Minnesota region. He picked a place on the Kettle River near where it runs into the St. Croix. This was Chippewa country and my father, knowing their ways and tongue, soon earned their trust. It was like he was one of them. However, despite the goodwill, the post he started did not do very well. So after a year he moved southwest to the Mississippi where he got permission from a Chippewa chieftain to build a log cabin post at a point of land where the Sauk runs into the big river.**

At that place the trade with Indians was much better. Twice a year my father led a string of canoes up the Mississippi and over the Savanna and St. Louis Rivers to Duluth. Going, the canoes were crammed with beaver furs, deer hides and the like. Coming back, they brought guns and knives, tobacco, blankets and all the kinds of other things the Chippewa wanted.

After a few years my father brought in a clerk to run things so that he could be free to roam the forest doing business with scattered Chippewa bands. He once in awhile even traded with Sioux. But that was risky because of the hatred between them and the Chippewa.

By then in his early 20s, Joseph St. Onge stood more than

---

* The first post was near present day Sandstone, and the second at what is now St. Cloud.

six feet and even with his slight limp, he moved nimbly over the tricky footing of a forest trail. Going over long portages he easily hefted his canoe and one or two packs up on his broad shoulders. In winter, he slogged along on snowshoes made by his Chippewa friends and sometimes dragged along a kind of sled, loaded with furs or goods for trade. Always in hand, no matter how heavy the packs, was his rifle, ready to bring down a partridge for supper, or meet a threat whether animal or human. Being a fur trader was a dangerous way to make a living. Along with the usual risks of storms or blizzards, bears and the like, there was always the chance of ambush by a thieving tribesman or even a jealous rival trader.

Partly because of knowing his way around in the woods and mainly because of getting along with the Chippewa, my father survived and began to make money. As the years went by he brought in more agents from the North West Company and set up a string of trading posts. But in all that time of building up his trade, my father kept pretty much to himself. It was a way that grew more fixed during his long days alone in the woods.

But then in 1805, two things happened that changed his way of life, and mine too, even if I wasn't born yet. The first was that after nearly forty years, Joseph St. Onge quit being a bachelor. I'll come to the second part in awhile. But it's the first part that had special consequence for me. The way it happened was that during a stop over at the village of Chippewa Chief War Cloud, he set eyes on the Chief's pretty daughter. Blue Flower was her name, though in later life she was called Iris.

The way my mother told it, they never spoke. But something passed between them when she helped serve supper that night. Whatever it was, Dad was smitten. The courtship, carried on entirely through the Chief, was short. Once War Cloud found out she was agreeable it became simply a matter of settling how much in trade goods Dad was willing to pay.

They were married the next day in a Chippewa ceremony. And two years later in Duluth, the marriage was sanctified by a Jesuit priest. A daughter, Inez, was born in 1806, but she died of typhoid fever before I came along in 1811. So who knows, if my father hadn't happened to visit the village of War Cloud when he did, I probably wouldn't be here to tell this story.

The other thing that happened to my father in 1805 was meeting up with Lieutenant Zebulon Pike, who was leading a U.S. Army expedition to explore the upper Mississippi. Pike and his men had been struggling through snowdrifts when, exhausted and famished, they came upon my father's Sauk River post flying its British colors. There, after being fed and rested for several days, Pike repaid my father's hospitality by ordering him to take down the British flag.

This was U.S. territory bought from the French, Pike told Dad, and the Americans intended to take full control of the area by building a chain of military forts throughout the northwest frontier. Pike and his travel weary squad were in no shape to run off dozens of British posts doing business in the region. But neither was my Dad in a position to defy 20 armed soldiers no matter how tuckered out. So he hauled down the flag.

Of course, it went back up after Pike left. But the young officer's warning set my father to thinking. It looked to him like he was sitting on a powder keg. If the Americans came with more soldiers, would the British run or fight? And what about the Chippewa and Sioux, who hated each other more than they feared losing their land to the Americans? Which way were they apt to turn?

My father stewed over these questions for over two years. He had done well with the North West Company, but now he guessed its days of trading on U.S. soil were numbered. Finally, in 1808, he decided to get out while the getting was good.

In May of that year he led a fleet of fur bearing canoes northeast from the Sauk Post. This time his wife was with him, and they skirted around the company outpost at Duluth. Instead, they paddled directly to the company's western headquarters at Fort William. There, after conducting his final accounting, he cut his ties with North West Fur.

Then as the fleet went back to Sauk River with trade

goods, my yet-to-be father and mother set off in the opposite direction. Paddling along the eastern shore of Superior they passed the old trading post at Sault Ste. Marie, following the canal around its rapids and then over the strait to Fort Machilimackinac. After resting there two days, they set out along the eastern shore of Lake Huron down to the St. Clair River leading to Detroit. Paddling 50 or 60 miles a day, they made the trip in about a week. The hardest part was crossing the open reaches of Saginaw Bay. Fearful of a sudden squall, they paddled all day and into the night before crossing back into sight of the eastern shoreline.

Detroit by 1808 was a busy center of U.S. fur trade. Not long before, it had been burnt to the ground. But now it had risen from its ashes and was the capital of the newly established Michigan Territory. And it was there my father built a log cabin and opened a shop to sell Indian goods, many of them fashioned by the skillful hand of Iris, his wife. So that's how I came to be born in Detroit.*

*As it happened, I arrived during a howling blizzard in February, 1811. By then the store run by my folks was doing very well. But a year later British General Isaac Brock captured Detroit, and my Dad, afraid of being hung as a traitor, took off for the woods. He stayed away for nearly a year until the town was recaptured by William Henry Harrison.***

When he came back, the first thing he did was take out American citizenship. After that he sold his shop and signed on with John Jacob Astor's American Fur Company as field manager for its Northern Michigan territory.

We continued to live in Detroit. Our log cabin, set back from our dirt road, was mostly a home for my Mother and me.

---

* After the fire of 1805 destroyed nearly all of Detroit's 200 buildings, the town was rebuilt to a plan drawn by Pierre L'Enfant, famed for his earlier design of Washington, D.C.

** Harrison pursued the British into Ontario, routing them at the Battle of Thames. The Shawnee Chief Tecumseh was killed in this battle, thus ending his insurrection against the United States.

Dad's job as agent for a string of trading posts kept him away for weeks at a time. Twice a year, he would go on a wilderness circuit that began with a canoe and portage up the Grand River to the post he had set up at Muskegon inlet off Lake Michigan. From there he went north up the Muskegon and Au Sable Rivers and finally along a web of lakes and rivers to the company's Mackinac Island headquarters at the crossroads of the Great Lakes.

Working his way along this route my father dealt with scattered bands of Chippewa as well as collecting furs and doing business at the six or seven posts he had set up, like at the junction of the rivers at what is now Lansing. Between traveling and settling accounts, he was sometimes away several months or more.

Unless he happened to run into somebody headed for Detroit, my mother wouldn't hear from him from the morning he left till he showed up again. But she kept busy by continuing to make and sell Indian craftwork. As she became more and more accepted in town she applied herself to church work and learning to read and better talk her adopted language. She never said it, but I know now she was determined to help her half-breed son learn what he needed to know in order to get along in white America.

In 1817 she enrolled me in Detroit's new teaching academy where I learned to write and do ciphers. And it was there I began a friendship with Henry Sibley that has lasted ever since.

- 25 -

WELCOME RECESS

At Harwell, where we were on a 16-week semester system, the fall term was to end with the final exams in mid-January. By then I planned to cover events leading from Minnesota's transition to statehood, its participation in the Civil War, and the booming aftermath that saw Minnesota emerge as a world leader in wheat growing, flour milling, lumbering and iron mining. But now after some 20 lectures we had come up to a five-day Thanksgiving break.

I had planned to use the time up in St. Paul digging into archives of the Minnesota Historical Society. I needed to know a lot more about Henry Sibley and Alexander Ramsey, and the Society housed large collections to record the life and deeds of both. Of particular interest to me were their parts in events leading up to Minnesota statehood.

However, that plan went up in smoke after a phone call from my mother that amounted to a matriarchal decree. "I'm not doing all this cooking just to feed your father's gang," she declared. "You haven't shown your face around here in a coon's age. So just hop in that truck of yours and get on up here."

After a few sputterings, I caved in when Mom agreed to let me leave early to spend a day doing research in Duluth. My first thought was to take my buddy Sue Humboldt with me. But she had already made plans to eat turkey with her family back in Pipestone before going on to Chicago to spend a weekend with her "real nice guy," Dave.

Now that I think about it, that Thanksgiving weekend would have turned out a lot different if Sue had gone with me up to Buhl. But I'm getting out in front of my story.

There were fifteen of us in all who showed up for turkey back in that little house on Woodbridge Avenue. It was a great family get-together made even better when Uncle Ty, who loved to reminisce, pushed back from his second helping of pumpkin pie and began talking about growing up in that house.

In 1930, when the Depression started to get serious, the Makki brothers ranged in age from my Dad who was ten, Ty nine, and Eino, Jr. eight. That was a tough time to grow up on the Iron Range. Old timers sometimes recall that period sort of wistfully. "Sure it was hard," they'll say. "But we shared what we had and were happier for it." Time seems to have covered those bleak days with a warming blanket of nostalgia. But the reality is that Depression on the Range was a time to be endured but never enjoyed.

With the mines working at less than half capacity, everything suffered. Men who wanted to work couldn't find any. People bought only what they needed to survive: food for the table, coal for the furnace and clothes or shoes only when absolutely necessary. Stores went out of business, banks in Virginia and Hibbing failed, and men, their faces blank with defeat, stood in breadlines.

Uncle Ty recalled walking to school with newspaper stuffed in his shoes to plug up the places where rain or snow came up through the soles. But bad as it was, the Makkis got by better than many. At one time during the worst of it, there were thirteen of them, young and old, living in the house on Woodbridge that Grampa Eino and his father had built in 1924.

The oldest were Great-Grampa Reino and his wife Hilma, who after a lifetime of hard work and frugality had set enough aside to tide them through retirement. In 1931, stooped and worn from years of pounding nails, Reino sold his house on Franz Street and moved in with Grampa Eino. For the rest of his days Reino, and later his widow, anted up five dollars a week for the family larder.

Grampa Eino added a few more dollars by taking on just about any work he could find. When not busy with hammer and nails, he often worked into darkness cutting railroad ties or firewood which he delivered split and neatly stacked for four dollars a cord.

In 1932, the cruelest year, the household was nearly doubled by the arrival of Great-Uncle Heikki and his family. First Heikki was laid off when the Sharon Ore Company closed its doors. Then after losing their home, Heikki, Aunt Sophia and four kids, Waino, Matti, Laurie and Bobbi, moved in with Grampa Eino, "Just temporarily." They stayed six years.

Uncle Ty got flustered when his wife asked, "What about living with those girls?" "Aw," he stammered, "All we did was trade a little information. Ain't that right, John?"

Dad grinned. "I doubt we learned anything they don't teach in second grade nowadays."

Then he changed the subject, recalling that Great-Uncle Heikki wasn't much with a hammer and saw, but he did know how to make things grow. And the garden plot he tended out back put a lot of cabbage and potatoes on the table.

Heikki also developed a mysterious sideline that let him every now and then toss a bonanza of forty or fifty dollars into the family kitty. The folks never talked about it, but the kids knew it had something to do with Prohibition and Heikki's occasional trips up to Canada. Once, when Ty asked where he was going, Heikki winked and said he was going to see a man about a dog. But when Ty asked his cousin, Waino, if he was getting a dog, Waino just looked blank.

My Dad recalled how the kids helped the men dig a root cellar out back to store the vegetables Uncle Heikki grew. "So we could count on cabbages and beets for nearly every supper all winter."

Listening, I realized that Iron Rangers, in those day, came awfully close to living off the land. There was always something—planting in the spring, fishing in the summer, gathering crops in the fall. In berry season, the women and kids went into the woods carrying pails and fighting off mosquitoes. Blueberries were a favorite along with wild cherries and raspberries for making jam.

In the fall, when the men went into the woods for deer, it was for sustenance, not for sport. They did their hunting at a stand back of the old cabin up at Lake Vermilion. And at night, they set nets out in the bay for whitefish.

Ty recalled going along in their old lapstrake rowboat as the men pulled in their nets, checking for a whitefish catch. Those bottom feeders sometimes measured a couple feet and were taken home for smoking. Sometimes, besides whitefish, their nets snagged a walleye or two which they were supposed to let go, but which usually wound up as a breakfast treat.

In summer the whole family would pile into Grampa Eino's old Ford truck for weekends or longer up at the cabin. Since there aren't any roads on the north side of the lake, Eino and Heikki took turns at the oars, shuttling the family by relays across a mile of open water to the cabin. With groceries and all it usually took at least three trips. It was only after World War II that the brothers could afford to chip in for a 10-HP Evinrude outboard. As a kid I remember when we went home, we'd chain the boat to a wooden dock and take the motor home with us. When we'd come again, we'd have to use a coffee can to bail out the rainwater.

That old boat was an all-purpose workhorse. The men used it to tow home cedar logs for dock repair and took it on moonlit nights to troll for walleye or northerns. During the day, the kids got to use it to explore nearby coves or for fishing. Talking about this, Ty and Dad broke us all up telling about their fish that got away. The boys had caught several northerns and a couple of bass when the old clothesline they were using as a stringer came loose. By the time they noticed it was gone, the fish were several hundred yards away and trying to swim in all directions. Pulling excitedly on the oars they couldn't understand why the boat seemed so sluggish until one of them remembered they'd forgotten to pull up the pail of rocks they were using for an anchor. They never did catch up with the fish.

Uncle Ty recalled that Grampa Eino had to wait for winter to haul lumber across the ice to build the cabin that has been the family center for the Makkis. Dad remembered going fishing with their Uncle Kalle during his one visit from far out west. He took the boys out for a night's fishing and pointed out constellations like Orion the Hunter (for years Dad thought it was an Irish hunter named O'Ryan). Kalle also told them how to locate the North Star at the end of the handle of the Little Dipper. "Get a fix on that bright star," Kalle said, "and you can always find your way home at night."

When Ty and Dad mentioned their kid brother, Eino, Jr., their talk was tinged with sadness. Young Eino had been an honor student and star of a strong Buhl High basketball team. In 1944, the year I was born, he graduated and immediately joined the Marine Corps. After boot training at Paris Island, he was sent to the Pacific where in the First Marine's last great battle, he was killed at Okinawa.

Dad was in the Army and Uncle Ty in the Navy during that War. But they didn't talk much about those days and almost never spoke about young Eino's death. What they did remember was his sunny smile and special moments from his life. Now, they talked about the time their forty-pound little brother hooked into a fifteen pound northern.

Eino—they always called him "Junior"—was five or six at the time. Dad and Ty were pulling at the oars while Junior was trolling out of the back of that old rowboat, hanging on to a bamboo pole and a wooden plug. When "Old Snaggle Tooth" hit, it nearly yanked the pole out of his hands. Junior shrieked but somehow held on. Without a reel, all he could do was keep towing as his brothers rowed toward shore, all the time hollering for him to keep the tip up. Finally they ran up to a flat rock where

Dad jumped out and horsed the thrashing beast up close enough for Ty to push it up onto the rock with an oar. After that, Ty claimed, "We held the fish up next to Junior and sure enough it was longer than he was."

Great-Grandfather Reino, the family patriarch, died a few years before I came along. Although I can nearly recite by memory his account of coming to America, my only image of him as a person comes from a faded snapshot of a white-haired, unsmiling oldster in a rumpled suit I expect was his Sunday best.

Dad and Uncle Ty, who grew up in the old man's presence, remember him as a stern man, gruff but not unkind, and with no sense of humor. His, I imagine, was a manner not uncommon to Finnish immigrants who came to Northern Minnesota toward the end of the 19th century. Many, like Great-Grampa Reino, were peasants, who came from farms near the Arctic Circle. They came at a time when most of the good land was taken up by masses of Germans, Swedes and Norwegians, who got there earlier.

Unlettered, knowing little of the world beyond their home province, and speaking a different language, their job qualifications were not much more than a strong back and a willingness to work. These were traits that suited them for the hard, dirty toil of quarries, ore pits and lumber camps of northern Minnesota. Stubborn as well as strong, they spent their days from dawn to dark with backbreaking labor. And as with cramped hands and twisted fingers they swung their picks, gripped axes or bucked saws, their thoughts went to simple wants: a plot of land, a cow, and a wife.

Great-Grampa Reino was one of the lucky ones to achieve such dreams. No doubt his skill as a carpenter along with a wife who spoke English eased his way. Thinking about this kinsman I never knew, words like *dour, reticent* and *obstinant* come to mind. I ask myself, if I had been in his shoes a century ago, would I have been much different? Interestingly, his son Eino, the glue that held the family together during the brutal 1930s, was.

- 26 -

GRAMPA EINO MAKKI
1898-1963

Years after his passing I close my eyes and see Grampa Eino, his face round like a cherub, merry blue eyes and gentle smile. I listen and hear his quiet voice, musical with its Finish intonation.

In other circumstances my grandfather might have been a teacher. He loved nothing more than to show a child how to pound a nail, weave a cedar fan for the sauna, listen for the call of a loon at dusk, or see the grandeur of a lily pad sparkling with morning dew. It may have been that his was a calling of art, unfulfilled. Without training, Grampa Eino had a natural flair for pen and ink re-creations of North Country scenes that seemed to just flow out of his fingers.

I was six or seven when I watched him sketch one of an old man and woman in a rowboat, disappearing into Lake Vermilion mist. Finished, he turned to me with a smile. "I better tear this up before Gramma sees me wasting time."

When I protested, he winked, "Here, you hide this for me. It'll be our secret."

That "secret" is still one of my dearest possessions. Just to look at it hanging in my den is to rekindle the magic of Autumn at Lake Vermilion.

Sitting around our living room after Thanksgiving dinner, Dad got out a bottle of port and began to talk about Grampa Eino. "I don't think we understood all the things he did to keep us going during those tough years."

Uncle Ty agreed. "We just took for granted what he wore himself out to give us. Mostly he was gone working or looking for work before we even got out of bed for school. And sometimes we were back in bed before he came home."

"But we knew he was there," Dad picked up. "Because we could smell the Sloan's liniment Mom was rubbing on his back. He'd maybe tell Mom he was hurting but he never told us."

"You want to know how tough it was up here," Ty jumped in. "Well, most of the kids we grew up with all got false choppers now. That's cause hardly anybody could afford to take care of 'em. The only reason John and I still got ours is because Dad somehow came up with the means to see a dentist whenever we got a toothache."

Uncle Ty thought for a minute before adding, "And it wasn't just us. With Heikki's brood, there was seven of us kids growing up here and we all got treated the same."

"It's kinda funny," Dad put in. "When our Dad was growing up, most young Finns up here quit school early to work in the mines or the woods. But probably because of Gramma Hilma, all their kids got through high school before going their different ways."

Grampa Eino, the last of Reino and Hilma's brood, chose his way even before he finished high school. In the summer of 1913, while working at a church camp on Lake Vermilion, he struck up acquaintance with a Finnish craftsman who built cabins and boathouses along the shores of the lake. The next year after finishing high school, Eino went to work as an apprentice to Kusti Heikkala.

Old Kusti didn't pay much, maybe a dollar a day, about half of what the miners were getting at that time. After a year of hard work and more responsibility, Eino had learned about everything Kusti had to teach. So when the old man refused to give him a raise, Eino picked up his toolbox and struck out on his own.

Those were years when times were pretty good and he quickly found work with a crew building big cabins and boathouses for rich people who came up from Duluth and the Twin Cities to summer at Lake Vermilion. Using skills of grooving, mortise and tenon handed down through generations of Finnish cabin builders, they turned pine and cedar logs into rambling structures stout enough to endure the harsh realities of northern winters. Among many of them still standing are impressive vacation homes of the Dayton and Hoerner families, rustic counterparts to the summer mansions erected along Atlantic bluffs by eastern moguls of that era.

In 1917, after America entered World War I, Eino and Heikki joined the Army. As it turned out they spent the War at Fort Snelling, Heikki as a reception clerk, Eino as a corporal in a maintenance platoon. In all their lives that was as far either brother ever got away from Buhl.

When the war was over, Eino went back to building lake cabins at Vermilion. There around 1921, he met Mickey Forgy, who had bought up the entire shoreline of a sheltered cove. Mickey was the first to build in that area just east of Wake-em-up Narrows.

Dad remembers Mickey Forgy as a kind of a jolly Uncle, who loved to tell stories and sometimes took the family for picnics on his big wooden powerboat. Seated at the Captain's perch he entertained his Finnish neighbors with a cheerful mix of off key Irish ballads and tales from his colorful past.

When Mickey found the cove in the early 1920s, the only way to get there was by railroad to Tower, at the east end of the lake, and by packet boat from there. Not wanting to be tied down by a fixed packet schedule, Mickey commissioned a 40-foot inboard cruiser of his own. Specially built at Two Harbors, it was hauled up north on the old D & M Railroad. In late fall he winched it ashore on a makeshift set of railroad tracks running up from the water. For years after Mickey's passing in the mid 1940s, the boat stayed perched on that spur as a landmark to guide fishermen headed for the hot walleye reef off Forgy's Point.

But back in 1921, when Mickey got ready to build his cabin, he'd heard about Eino's all-round skill in carpentry. Although most of the 23-year-old's work had been done at the Tower-Soudan end of the lake, he had also helped put up cabins further west in Niles and Frazer Bays. Word about Grampa Eino's craftsmanship had gotten around and Mickey, liking as he put it, "The cut of Eino's jib," hired him on the spot to do the finishing work for his cabin.

Impressed by his manner as well as by his work, Mickey took an immediate shine to young Eino Makki. As it happened neither Mickey nor, in those days, Grampa Eino were averse to strong spirits. And it shortly became a ritual after Saturday's work for Mickey to set out a bottle of what he called "squeezins," whereupon he and young Eino would pass a pleasant hour sipping and trading yarns.

When finally the work was done, Mickey, convinced that his young friend would be a good neighbor, made him the offer that was to add untold hours of happiness to generations of Makkis living or as yet unborn. By way of partial payment for his work, Forgy deeded him a 200-foot section of shoreline toward the west end of his cove. It was there, assisted by his father and brothers, that Eino built the cabin that has for so long been the core of Makki family life.

It was about that time that Great-Gramma Hilma, stewing about her youngest's bouts with the Demon Rum, put her maternal foot down hard. It wasn't that Eino was a habitual sot. He rarely drank during the week and never missed a day's work owing to a hangover.

But come Saturday night, Eino and his work crew headed for the nearest "speakeasy." This was how bachelor miners, lumberjacks and carpenters blew off steam after a week of toil. However, when Grampa Eino showed up a tad "overtrained" for the family's Sunday dinner, Hilma laid down the law to a point where Eino finally agreed to attend the next regular meeting of the *Pohjan Leimu* (Northern Flame), a Finnish version of Alcoholics Anonymous at Soudan. He'd been there before, even taken the pledge, only shortly to fall from grace. But this time he met Nestor Kekkonen, a fellow backslider of his own age. So well did the two hit it off that after three hours of testimony about the virtues of abstinence, Nestor was moved to invite Eino for a drink.

Accordingly, they adjourned to "Tarpaper Annie's," a blind pig that opened and reopened every month or so between Prohibition raids. On that particular night, after a payday at the Tower mine, Annie's was no place for a pacifist. Eino was never one to go looking for a fight, but neither was he known to back away should one show up. And it wasn't long after a few belts of Annie's homemade "Katonka" that just such a situation came to pass.

It happened when a burly miner who couldn't find room at the bar solved his problem by pushing Nestor off his stool. Nestor came up swinging only to catch a kick in the groin that sent him gagging to the floor. This left the field to Eino, who grabbed the offender and almost casually tossed him over the bar. But while reaching down to help his new friend, Eino was knocked flat by a blow from a bung starter delivered by no less a personage than Tarpaper Annie herself.

After that Eino only vaguely recalled being thrown out the door head first into a muddy alley out behind. Coming around after a bit, he found himself face down in the mud alongside the still retching Nestor. Although hardly in better shape, Eino managed to half carry his new friend home while the latter gasped out directions. When finally they got there, both of them collapsed on the front stoop.

Sometime later, Eino woke up to a rude jolt in his ribs. Groaning as much from Annie's bathtub distillations as from the knot on his head, Eino lifted his mud-covered face to gaze into the furious blue eyes of the most beautiful girl he had ever seen.

Ignoring Nestor snoring alongside, the unknown princess lit into Eino for leading her brother into such wayward plight. Finally, she ordered him off by threatening to sic the dog on him.

Eino stumbled away, not even sure where he was or how to get back to his lodging house. All he could think of was that somehow he had to see that lovely creature again.

Listening to my Dad tell about Eino's pining, I couldn't help wonder if maybe my longing for Christabel White (now Mrs. Buddy Cosgrove) wasn't a kind of thing that runs in the Makki family. I mean one look and Grampa Eino knew that Nestor Kekkonen's sister (her name was Lauri) was the girl for him. But unlike me, Eino didn't just sit back and pine.

A couple days later he tracked down Nestor, who after listening to Eino pour out his feelings, allowed he had some doubts. For one thing, Lauri was disgusted with both of them. For another, she already had any number of suitors, the most serious being the son of a well-to-do lumber mill owner.

He doubted it would help, Nester said, but it wouldn't hurt if Eino went to one of the Saturday night socials at the Lutheran Church hall. There'd be play acting, music making and probably some singing. He said Lauri and her girl friends went there most Saturday nights. It was a good place to make friends and meet boys.

"All they have to drink is fruit punch that tastes worse than Annie's Katonka. But if you go there, maybe you'll get a chance to talk to Lauri. Meantime, I'll try to put in a good word."

So Eino went and sure enough there was the lass who, after one bleary glance, had stolen his heart. As she sat there chatting with girl friends, Eino noticed a well-dressed but pudgy young man he took to be the sawmill scion standing in attendance beside her.

Even to Eino, the smitten, it looked hopeless. But he finally decided if he had to struggle through life without her, it wouldn't be because he didn't have the gumption to at least try.

Arming himself with a cup of something red and sweet from the punch bowl, he walked up to young Miss Lauri

Kekkonen. Handing it to her, he was prepared to duck if she threw it back. Instead, to his joy, she took it and smiled.

It turned out that Nestor had told his sister that rather than leading him astray, Eino had been his rescuer on that regrettable occasion of their first meeting. Nestor had also told his sister that Eino was hoping to talk to her at the Social. So his abrupt appearance wasn't exactly a surprise.

What Eino couldn't have guessed is how he looked in Lauri's eyes. In his clean work shirt, fresh shaved and blond hair slicked back, he was a sight different from the muddy heap she had shooed off her front stoop. Compared to the pale-faced, overweight dandy standing smugly beside her, Eino appeared like a clear-eyed, lean and tan breath of fresh air.

Ignoring those around her, my grandfather leaned down and declared his feelings. "What I want most in the world is to make you happy. If you will marry me, I will make you a good house and take care of you all of my life." And finally, he vowed, "I will never get drunk again!"

If Lauri had laughed at so startling a proposal, it would have ended right there. But this young lady was no giddy flirt. Something in Eino's straight forward declaration struck a chord never before touched by any of her other swains.

Nevertheless, if a young lady with Lauri's spunk was to fall in love with a carpenter, she would do it on her own terms. Standing up she looked directly into Eino's gentle eyes. "If we are to marry, you must court me in a proper manner. You can start by walking me home."

And that, in all simplicity, is how it began. Lauri married Eino in 1922 and my Dad was born a year later. Grampa built the house he had promised Lauri and it was there he saw the family through the harsh years of Depression.

Like everybody who loved that good old man, I was shocked at his passing in 1963. Literally worn out from his great effort for so many years, he just didn't wake up one morning. He had lived just long enough to collect one pension check.

Gramma Lauri, his partner for 48 devoted years, left us in

1970. She lies beside Eino at Lakeview Cemetery where nearby rest Eino, Jr., and my great-grandparents, Reino and Hilma Makki.

- 27 -

DULUTH AND CHRISTIE

Heading down Route 53 to Duluth after Thanksgiving, I thought about Uncle Ty's stories. Most of them belonged to family lore I'd heard before, but not the one about Grampa Eino's proposal. I could only wonder what might have happened if I had shown that kind of spunk with Christabel White.

All this time and it still hadn't chased away my thoughts about the girl with the jet-black hair to outline the lovely structure of her face. Almost with an ache, I remembered how she could make you go weak in the knees with just a smile. And her special look, a sort of unspoken intimacy over a shared understanding of something, like maybe somebody said something silly.

Childish, I told myself. Quit raking over dead coals. But it nagged at me as I came down that big hill into town. What if under the ashes something still smoldered? What would she say if I phoned?

"She'd say you were nuts," I answered myself. The hell with it. These thoughts about Christie were adolescent fancies played out in my mind alone. I'd come here to look for information about ore carriers and that was what I was going to do.

Driving along Sky Line Drive, I found a small motel looking out over the striking panorama of Duluth harbor. To me, this city rising from rocky bluffs above Lake Superior has magic attraction. Within its sweep of rugged grandeur, there seems almost to exist the spirit of strong men and women triumphant over lifetimes of harsh existence.

Named for the intrepid explorer who three centuries ago won the region for France, Duluth has long been the chief ore shipping port for America's blast furnaces. Today, the freighters that pass under its Aerial Lift Bridge carry taconite and grain to ports far across the seas.

After spending an afternoon at the downtown library, I got back to my room in time to catch the late autumn sunset dancing over the great harbor below. Standing there, my plight as a lonely bachelor abruptly struck like a sharp pain. I wanted someone beside me to share this moment. That someone was Christie. And there I was, almost without thinking, fumbling in the phone book for her number.

It was crazy, I realized while the phone was ringing. What was I going to say if Buddy answered? But just as I was about to hang up, there she was. I would have recognized that low, almost husky hello anywhere.

"Christie," I stammered, "It's Jim Makki. Can you talk?"

During the second or two of silence, I half expected to be cut off. But then she asked me where I was. When I told her she said, "I'll meet you in front in 20 minutes."

As I waited outside, she drove up almost to the minute in a blue Mustang. After that we went to Maxwell's, a rendezvous remembered from our days at UMD. Ten years ago we might have bumped into a friend. Now even the help didn't know us. Even so, heads turned as we walked in. And you can bet they weren't looking at me.

Christie, at age 28, would have stopped conversation anywhere—skin creamy and flawless, eyes like smoky agate, well spaced over a slightly turned up nose and lips full and generous. In a word, she was luscious.

As I held her seat, she looked up and smiled. "This is an occasion, and I want champagne."

When the waiter, after fussing over the ritual of testing and pouring, left us, Christie touched my glass lightly. "Dear old Jim. You wanted to talk."

Still bewildered by the miracle of her presence, I stuttered out something about the view from my window and how I wanted to share it with her. "Kinda silly, huh," I ended lamely.

Christie reached her fingers across the table and touched my hand. "No, it wasn't silly." And then softly, "I love you for doing it."

"I was all set to hang up if Buddy answered."

That drew a grin of conspiracy. "You timed it just right. Buddy's in Detroit on business."

Over a sandwich and the rest of the bubbly, I told her about our Thanksgiving in Buhl. Christie hadn't been back there since her parents moved away. She was curious about changes.

I told her about the new coat of paint on the water tower. "That's about it. Things don't happen all that fast in Buhl."

Christie laughed and then she pushed her glass aside. "Now I'd like to see that view of yours."

And that, thanks to Grampa Eino, is how it happened, a night with Christie that I had long since written off as hopeless. Later, as we clung to each other, I whispered my feelings. "I've had girl friends, Christie. But I never felt this way about anyone else. I want us to have a future."

As I said this, I felt her grow limp in my arms. When she didn't answer, I asked if I had said something wrong. And then I felt her warm tears on my face. "God knows, I love you Jim, but there's more to it than you know."

She stopped and then put her head on my chest. "Let's not talk about it now. Besides, we'll always have this to remember."

It was only as I walked her out to the car that I asked, "Where do we go from here?"

"I just don't know, Jim. Please give me time to think about it."

Then she put her arms around me. "But if you want to

know how I feel, you're my knight in shining armor, the only one who ever wanted me for me. I must have always loved you. I just didn't know it." And then with a kiss she was gone.

Back at Harwell that night, I fell asleep still feeling the softness of Christie in my arms. Someday I dared hope we'd be together at Harwell.

- 28 -

SIBLEY AND RAMSEY COME TO MINNESOTA

If Washington and Jefferson stand tallest among America's founding fathers, their counterparts in Minnesota would be Sibley and Ramsey. Like most hardheaded pioneer leaders, much that they sought to accomplish was for personal gain. Still, there is no denying the impact of their presence for more than five decades of Minnesota history. Had either of them not been here when they were, the boundaries of America's thirty-second state would likely be different than those we know today. That is, if in fact, we were a state at all.

Henry Hastings Sibley came to Mendota in 1834 to supervise the American Fur Company's trading interests for a vast area extending to the north and west. It was the start of a career in which he was to play a commanding political and military role during Minnesota's emergence from raw and sometimes hostile wilderness.

Alexander Ramsey arrived in 1849, after being appointed governor of the newly established Minnesota Territory. Like Sibley, he was well educated for the times, having studied law after several years as a student at Lafayette College in Pennsylvania.

Though destined to be political rivals, the two men, only a few years apart in age, were to become and remain close friends. Between them, they were to dominate Minnesota's political life for nearly thirty years.

Sibley was the prime mover during the Congressional battle to win territorial status for Minnesota. Thereafter, Ramsey, who had been active in Whig Party affairs, was appointed by President Zachary Taylor to be the new territory's first governor. So remote was frontier Minnesota at that time that Ramsey's wife, upon being told of the appointment, wasn't sure it was even in America.

As Territorial Governor, Ramsey found that his major goal was the drive to obtain Indian lands. He spent much of this time regulating Indian affairs. "Indian regulation," according to a cynical observer of that time, "meaning crowding them off the face of the earth so that aggressive white man can take his place." And it is a fact that during Ramsey's term from 1849 to 1853, treaties were made by which Chippewa and Sioux gave up lands which form more than half of present-day Minnesota.

In 1853, after two terms as Territorial Delegate to Congress, Sibley came home to tend to his fur empire while also helping organize Minnesota for statehood. Four years later, he presided over the State Democratic Party Convention that helped fashion a constitution as a required preliminary to winning admission to the Union.

Ramsey meanwhile had bolted the faltering Whig movement in order to affiliate with the new Republican Party. And in 1857, just prior to Minnesota's admission to the Union, these two old friends vied to become the first elected governor of the new state. After a wild and wooly campaign featuring charges of fraud by both sides, Sibley won by 240 votes out of more than 35,000 cast.

Following a contentious two years in office, Sibley stepped down. Then in 1859, it was Ramsey's turn as he easily defeated Democrat George Baker. This was the start of a dynasty that was to see him rule Minnesota's political fortunes for 16 years, first as Governor and then for two terms as U.S. Senator.

Frontier Minnesota in the early 19th century was no place

for wimps. Its men and women had to be tough. In a time of praise for self-made men, Ramsey and Sibley did not get what they sought by always being nice guys.

Of the two, Ramsey was probably the more callous, as witness his stiff bargaining during land cedings from Sioux and Chippewa. Sibley, on the other hand, is remembered as being reasonably fair in his fur trading with the Sioux. But when it came time to crush their rebellion in 1862, he was relentless in this purpose as well as to drive them forever away from their Minnesota homelands.

History seems to judge Ramsey as a man who, while accomplishing much for Minnesota, was at all times the calculating politician, a leader whose considerable abilities were flawed by willingness to bend principle to accord with private purpose.

Sibley is not quite so easy to characterize. The Rev. Nathaniel West, a close friend who was also his most favorable biographer, places him in the company of heroes from Greek mythology.

The biography was written while Sibley was still alive and one can almost picture the old General urging his admirer along through more than 500 pages of stilted encomium. Even so, setting aside flowery rhetoric, there is ample reason to call Henry Hastings Sibley a central figure in Minnesota history. As fur trader, frontier politician, advocate for territorial status, first governor of the state, commander of the forces that put down the Sioux rebellion, historian and early Regent of the University of Minnesota, Sibley was part and parcel of the most important things that happened during Minnesota's formative years as a state.

If there are reservations about his greatness, they relate to alleged hesitance in his service both as governor and military leader. But there is no denying Sibley's role during Minnesota's 19th century emergence from wilderness frontier to thriving statehood. When he came here in 1834, the principal means of travel were horseback and canoe. The white population was mainly soldiers, trappers and a few squatters clustered in the shadow of Fort Snelling. During Sibley's 57 years in Minnesota, the population statewide grew to more than a million and half, along with a network of river and railroad transportation to support its growth as a world center of industry and trade.

Archives of the Minnesota Historical Society house a large collection of Sibley materials. However, for all that has been said and written, we are left with little insight into his upbringing and early career. In a manuscript known as *The Unfinished Biography*, Sibley provides only a sketchy outline of his youth and early days in the fur trade. For instance, he writes almost boastfully of being a ringleader in boyhood mischief but gives no examples. In fact, the first 18 years of his life, to include classical and legal studies, are covered in less than a paragraph.

In closing, Sibley speaks chastely of rejecting the offer by a Sioux chieftain of the companionship of his pretty daughter. But nowhere does he mention the Sioux woman he took into his stone house at Mendota, and who bore him a daughter before he later sent both away.

If it is true the youth is father to the man, it is likely Sibley was more of a human and less of the paragon pictured by the doting divine, Nathaniel West. In order to bring him back to life as a flesh-and-blood mortal, I turn once more to the testimony of his old friend, Kilbourne St. Onge.

- 29 -

KILBOURNE ST. ONGE AND HENRY SIBLEY

Statement of Kilbourne St. Onge, continued:

One thing I'll always remember about growing up in Detroit was when Henry Sibley hit me in the eye with a snowball. That was when we were playing war in the schoolyard, and I couldn't see out of it. I was twelve or so, same as Henry. Too old to cry. But after one look at it the teacher sent me home and I didn't come back for a couple days.

Henry never said he was sorry but after that we got to be pretty good friends, though I don't think I ever got asked to his house, his Dad being a judge and all. There were five or six of us who got together after school almost every day. Except for me, the others were white. But that didn't seem to matter. It maybe helped that in wrestling and other sports, I was a little stronger than they were. And I could also run faster. Even so, Henry just sort of natural took charge and it seemed like he had us doing something different every day.

In the fall we sometimes got into mischief stealing apples and cherries from nearby backyards. One time a man caught us up in his cherry tree and hit us with a stick as we jumped down and tried to run away. That night Henry led us back to tip over his outhouse.

During summer vacation we went fishing and when we got older sometimes camping. In the fall we would go hunting for rabbits and partridge and all of us could shoot pretty good. But Henry was the best. I doubt I ever saw him miss.

One time we were skating on the Detroit River when Henry got too far out on the thin ice and fell through. I managed to pull him out but by the time he got home his pants was froze so stiff he could hardly walk. That was one time I got to see his father when he came to our house to tell me thanks.

Well, that kind of thing went on till we finished our schooling at the Academy and then I didn't see much of Henry for a while. He took to reading for the law while I went with my father to learn the fur trade. Dad was in charge of the Northern Michigan territory for the American Fur Company and right after school ended, he took me with him on a long trip through part of his territory.

It was while we were out there that Dad told me about his father, who was drowned while Dad was still a baby. Louis St. Onge was a French Canadian voyageur, who during his short life helped provide muscle for the fur trade. Unlike my father, Grandpere Louis was small and wiry like most of that breed. But each spring these tough little men moved hundreds of tons of trade goods into the north and west interior. In fall they came back to Montreal with canoes loaded with fur which had been brought to the meeting place at Grand Portage by "winter overs" from the Northwest.

Dad's only memory of his father was what he was told by his mother. As a boy he would sometimes talk to other voyageurs, who in winter hung around Montreal taverns spending hard-earned money like it was water. With beaded moccasins, silk sashes, and red toques, they boasted of carrying three or four heavy packets of trade goods over long portages and paddling all day for as much as 80 or 90 miles.

Years later when Dad got in the business, he made several trips with the old voyageurs, even though he was being trained to be a trader. He told me he was too big to be a voyageur because his long legs got all cramped up in a canoe.

It was a couple of years before I ran into Henry Sibley again. We were both nineteen and he was just back from a job he had up north near Sault Ste. Marie. He had quit studying law and wanted to get into something more adventurous.

Of course we're both old men now. But I've heard that Henry tells of getting a job with the American Fur Company. Well, that's true enough. But it was my Dad that got him the job. What happened was after I told Henry about me learning to be a fur trader, he said that was the kind of business he'd like to get in.

It took a while but Dad arranged it for both of us to go up to be clerks for American Fur at Mackinac Island. At that time, Henry was back working in Sault Ste. Marie and he had a hard time getting over to Mackinac where the Company had its head-quarters. Their sailboat got caught in the ice before the spring break-up where they were stuck without much to eat.

That was in early spring 1830. But since the business season at Mackinac didn't get going till sometime in June, there was no big hurry for me to get up there. So instead of going up Lake Huron by schooner I joined my father's fleet of canoes on its spring circuit to gather furs. I don't know about Dad. But as for me I never guessed this would be our last trip together. I remember he seemed to want to tell me something.

Before setting out, Dad had got together a five-man crew for each of his canoes. These were big 30-foot workboats able to float some very hefty loads. After leaving Detroit, we worked our way north and west across Michigan, following a route of rivers, lakes and portages that my father had blazed years before. Along the way we stopped at ten or twelve outposts collecting furs trapped during winter so that their pelts were in prime condition.

Along the way our canoes and portage loads were getting heavier after each stop. So according to the system Dad had worked out, we took an extra paddler at each of the last three posts. These extra hands would be dropped off again as the canoes came back loaded with freight and trade goods.

At night when we weren't stopping over at one of the posts, we'd usually quit paddling about twilight. After hauling the canoes ashore we'd get a couple of big fires going and cook up a kettle of dried peas and salt pork that had been soaking all day. When it was done the soup was so thick you could slice it with a knife. But it sure hit the spot after a long day on the water. With supper over and camp chores done, we'd smoke a pipe and then curl up under one of the overturned canoes.

One night after the rest were asleep, my father and I sat for a spell by the dying fire. And that night he told me something he thought I ought to know. As best I recollect, it went like this:

"I doubt I did you any favors getting you up at company headquarters. For young Sibley it's all right. He's white and also book smart. Besides there's a manner about him that makes me think he'll do real well with the company.

"But with you its different, not that you ain't smart. And it probably won't hurt none to learn something about that end of the business. But after that you'll probably do better out in the woods as a trader like me."

Except for teaching me things about the ways of the wilderness and the fur business, that's the most my father ever advised me. He was trying to tell me that a half-breed like me wasn't likely to get very far at company headquarters. Also he maybe saw something in Henry Sibley that even Henry didn't know about.

Our final run to Mackinac was up the Pigeon River and out onto the Strait. Our canoes were packed with pelfrey and riding low in the water. But with eight paddlers in each one, we moved along smartly and got there in early June, just as the big central depot was starting to get busy after its long winter sleep. Furs and hides were beginning to arrive in big freight canoes paddled by trading crews from all over the Northwest.

Dad went into the serious business of checking in furs, getting accounts credited and loading up his canoes with trade goods for the return trip. All that would take a month or more. Meanwhile, Henry Sibley had arrived and Mr. Stuart, who was in charge of that big headquarters, took us in hand. Being the start of their rush season, he right away put us to logging in furs and crediting accounts. Working mostly twelve hours a day except for Sundays, we hardly had a moment to ourselves.

Early in July, my father finished up his business and left with his canoes loaded with trade goods. He made it back all right. But next spring I got a letter from Mom telling me Dad had died after being sick all winter with the croup. Mom lived a long time after but except for letters I never got back to see her.

At Mackinac, I soon found Henry was better at clerking than me. Also, he had an easy way about him that people took to. Shortly after we got started Mr. Stuart invited Henry to board with them in their family quarters. I stayed sleeping in a loft with about ten other clerks and sorters. But that didn't make no matter to my friendship with Henry. During the rare moments we got some time off, we did things together. I mind we went fishing and hiking around the island a couple times.

Business slowed down in the fall but there was still work cutting wood for our fireplaces and storing hay for the livestock. Later in the fall and winter we got more free time. Once Henry and I rowed over to the mainland where I shot a deer. When we brought it back was the time I got to eat supper at Mr. Stuart's.

Henry spent part of the winter reading books in Mr. Stuart's library. But three or four times when the weather was right, we rowed across the Strait to the old mission village of St. Ignace, where we sparked a couple of pretty Chippewa girls. We could of gotten married but neither one of us was ready for that yet.

After I learned about Dad dying, I thought about going back and taking over his string of posts. But one of his old trading cronies offered Mom $3,000 to buy it out. I had no regrets. Mom needed the money and up at Mackinac I was learning a lot about the business end of things. It was a good company to work for. As a clerk, I was earning about $200 a year, most of which I kept because board in the big eating hall was free. And except for tobacco and a few clothes at the commissary, there wasn't *much need to spend anything else.*

Still, after two seasons I had enough. Henry tried to talk me into staying but I sore missed the outdoors and free ways of the trader. Compared to that, clerking in the big compound was pretty dull. Henry felt the same way but Mr. Stuart had promised him it would be worth his while to stick around.

Anyway, it didn't take much persuading when trader George Bonga asked me to come in with him. Of all the hundreds of voyageurs and traders working in the Northwest, Big George was maybe the most famous. Half Chippewa and half black, he was known for his courage and great strength. I myself have seen him tote six packs of furs over a slippery portage trail, which is twice as much as I ever managed.

George was a bluff, kind-hearted giant who had grown up in the trade. His Dad, like mine, had been a trader for the North West Company. Starting out as a canoe man, George had been in the business since he was sixteen. Now he was in his middle 30s and a successful trader in his own right. He told me he had a string of posts in the middle of what was to become Minnesota. But he needed help to open more.

"I knew your father from long ago," he told me. "So I know you been trained right. Up here you been learning about the business end of things and you can speak Chippewa which is real good."

What he had in mind was for me to build up trade at his posts at Lac Platte and Leech Lake while he went after new business working out of Otter Tail Lake. I'd be on my own and to start would keep half of what we made from my two posts.

Well, that was my great chance. And it was the start of a partnership that lasted till the fur business finally petered out more than thirty years later. In all that time George and I never had anything more than a handshake. Excepting my father, he was the most honest man I ever knew.

One thing about leaving Mackinac was that I missed being friends with Henry. But the change to the Minnesota region and learning my way around kept me so busy I didn't have time to think about it. In spring I took my furs down the Mississippi to the trading post at St. Paul. So I didn't get back to Mackinac.

Then, I think it was 1834, old John Jacob Astor saw things was starting to change and got out of the fur business. His company was bought by somebody else and Henry got jumped up to be supervisor in charge of its trade for all of the Upper Mississippi area and beyond. With 30 or more posts to manage along with hundreds of traders, voyageurs and Lord knows how many Indians to deal with, this was a big job for a 23-year-old. I know, because it was all I could do to keep up with the handful of posts I was running.

First I heard about it was a letter Henry sent me. He'd set up headquarters on the St. Peter's River, what they now call the Minnesota, across from Fort Snelling. He asked if I could come down and help him get started.

Since it was winter and things was slow, I went over to Otter Tail to see what George thought. Although we were independent we did a lot of business with American Fur, and George agreed we wanted to get along with them. It helped that I was friends with Henry and this would be a good chance to work things out. By then we were running a dozen posts between us and we'd stay out of Henry's way if he'd leave us alone.

So after leaving George I went over to the Mississippi and down to where Henry was. Although the place was nothing but the post and a few log huts, it was a good spot, being near the fort and close to St. Paul and all. Henry had already got started on the foundation of the big stone house he was building there.

After not setting eyes on each other for a couple of years, he greeted me real hospitable. What with catching up and going over to visit the Fort, we didn't get around to talking business right away. But the second night after roast beef and brandy, I agreed to help Henry meet some Chippewa chiefs up north. But at that time he was more concerned with getting to know the Sioux, who were closer.

So a couple days later we went by horseback south to

Lake Traverse. Trailing along behind was a pack mule loaded with blankets, hand mirrors and a few bolts of colorful cloth. It was a trademark with Henry that he never met with Indians without bringing along some sort of gifts.*

At the Lake Traverse stockade Henry got to talk to a couple Sioux chieftains. Besides that, it was a special pleasure for me to get to meet a couple old-time traders like Jean Faribault and Joe Renville, who they have since named places for. Renville recollected marching to my father's drumming during the Revolutionary War.

I expect I wasn't much help to Henry on that trip. The Indians we met were all Sioux and I wasn't great shakes in that tongue. Besides, once they learned I was part Chippewa they weren't very friendly. But they sure took to Henry. Even though his Sioux at the time was worse than mine, he hit it off with them something famous. And I think it was on that trip he got acquainted with a pretty Sioux girl he later took back with him to Mendota. Her name was Red Jacket Woman and all I know is the next time I saw Henry, she was living with him in the big stone house he built across the river from Fort Snelling.

That house had walls two feet thick made out of stones dug up and hauled there by Indians. They were stuck together by mud and clay from the riverbanks. Red Jacket Woman was still living there the next couple times I stopped by. I know they had a child, a little girl. But I don't know what became of them. They just weren't there no more after Henry got married to Sarah Steele. She was the sister of Franklin Steele, the biggest merchant in the territory, who started out as chief sutler at the fort but was soon into everything from steamboats to lumber mills. It was a big wedding and I got invited. But it was too early in the spring and I was busy taking in furs up at Leech Lake.

I don't fault Henry none about Red Jacket Woman. It's no secret that most traders and voyageurs took up with a pretty Indian girl. It wasn't hard. The girls were looking for a better

---

* Near present day St. Peter.

life and their fathers sold them cheap, for a horse or a rifle or maybe just a couple of blankets. Some like my Dad stayed hitched. Others moved on and left the squaw and any kids to fend for themselves. I heard Henry provided for the daughter. But after he got married to Sarah Steele you never heard any more about Red Jacket Woman.

Well, a lot of years went by and each time I went calling the settlement around Fort Snelling got bigger and bigger. Henry always seemed glad to have me stop by. Seemed like he was that way all the years I knew him. But as he got older he got to be a real charmer, handsome, and maybe helped by his wife, courteous and hospitable to everybody. I recollect staying at the big house while maybe twenty Indians would be sleeping up above in the loft. The Sioux he used to visit and hunt with respected him for dealing fair. They gave him a name that meant "Walker in the Woods."

When Henry was in his late 30s he got into politics and they somehow engineered a deal that got him appointed to the Congress as a delegate from "The Territory of Wisconsin." That one was pretty shaky. Wisconsin had become a state and wasn't a territory anymore. And even Henry didn't think this would hold up when he got to Washington. But somehow it did and Henry gets a lot of credit for his speeches in Congress that helped get Minnesota declared a territory in 1849.

Then, when Minnesota was close to becoming a state, he ran for governor. That election was in the fall of 1857, six months before we were even a state. Henry was a Democrat and he ran against Alexander Ramsey, who had earlier been Territorial Governor. The two of them were probably the best-known men in the territory and I doubt but that there was ever another election like it in Minnesota. The parties on both sides made up charges out of whole cloth. Republicans claimed that Sibley was English and if he got elected Minnesota would be under British control. Democrats went around telling newly arrived immigrants that if Ramsey was elected slaves and crooked politicians would run everything.

Charges like that were false. But when the votes were being counted each side hollered fraud and that was true. In some places both parties turned out more votes than there were people. In others they changed votes and even got unnaturalized immigrants to vote for their man.

As it happened, my partner George Bonga and I were in St. Paul after bringing down a late summer run of furs. We watched as the votes slowly came in from far-off places. One day Sibley would be ahead, the next day Ramsey. No one was sure who won until Joe Rolette finally arrived from up northwest with 317 votes for Sibley and none for Ramsey. This was the difference that put Sibley over the top by about 200 votes.

Jolly Joe Rolette ran a fur post up in Pembina from where he got elected to the Territorial legislature for three or four terms. Two years before, in his devil-may-care way, he had saved the capital for St. Paul by running off and hiding with the bill that would have moved it to St. Peter.

Every now and then, George and I had run across Joe on the trail or in St. Paul. We usually stayed at the Fuller House and one night after the election we walked into the saloon where he was drinking and joshing with friends. When he looked up and saw us, nothing would do but that we had to join them.

George, who was maybe 10 years older than Joe, took to teasing him about how it took three weeks to get to St. Paul with the votes from Pembina. Joe threw back his head laughing and hollered "I'd a got here sooner, 'ceptin I had to wait and see how many votes was needed."

Someone asked how he managed to squeeze 300 votes out of Pembina when there weren't that many whites there.

"Well," he grinned, "we got lots of Indians."

"How do you know they're eligible?"

"As long as they wear pants we let 'em vote."

"Yeah, Joe," one of his cronies put in, "we heard as soon as one of 'em votes, he takes off his pants and gives 'em to the next Indian in line."

"Now boys," Joe chortled, "do you think I'd tolerate

something like that?"

It turned out that was Joe's last act as a legislator because when Congress set the Red River as Minnesota's west boundary, Pembina was on the wrong side of the River. But Joe had the last laugh. The votes he delivered six months before Pembina got ruled out of the state gave his old friend Henry Sibley, the honor of being Minnesota's first elected governor.

Two years later it was Ramsey's turn. Henry didn't run that time and Ramsey beat Democrat George Becker by a slew of votes. It was kind of funny. Even though they were in different parties, Henry and Ramsey stayed good friends. Matter of fact, the last time I saw Henry was during a party at his new house in St. Paul, just after Ramsey won the second term as Governor. When I came in the two of them were joshing about the shenanigans during their race four years before.

Both men were important to Minnesota. They knew it and trusted each other. And when the uprising by the Sioux happened in 1862, Governor Ramsey turned to Henry. I don't know how good a General he was because I've heard good things and bad. But he rescued a lot of captured settlers and he did drive the Indians off. By the time Henry was done the Sioux were never again a threat in Minnesota.

What I do know is Henry Sibley is a man's man, a great hunter and fur trader. He's pretty famous now but he sticks by his friends. It's been a long time and now we're both old men. But I expect I could call at his house and still be welcome. Maybe some day I will before it's too late.

‡‡ ‡‡ ‡‡ ‡‡ ‡‡

In 1847, Kilbourne St. Onge married Hestor Briggs, the daughter of a Methodist preacher working with the Chippewa. They had three children. By the time he got out of the fur business in 1866, St. Onge was a prosperous man. After that, he moved to St. Peter where he ran a dry goods store for many years. Kilbourne St. Onge was in his late seventies when his niece began the series of visits that led to her compilation of his statement. He died in 1891, just two months after the passing of his boyhood friend, Henry Sibley.

- 30 -

"... LET THEM EAT GRASS"

Deceitful management of Indian affairs stands as a shabby chapter of 19th century U.S. history. Government treaties by which land was stripped from Indians amounted to little more than outright swindle. And nowhere were such deceptions conducted more brazenly than in Minnesota, the most tragic example being the cynical manipulations that were to lead to the Sioux uprising of 1862. This most violent of all Indian outbreaks was the almost predictable action of a people driven by white avarice to the point of desperation.

For the Sioux, the main provocation was long simmering discontent over land grabs that had snatched away their hunting grounds. For Governor Alexander Ramsey, the insurrection was the bitter harvest of shady land dealings he had helped promote. Of these, the most blatant were the treaties negotiated at Traverse des Sioux (near present day St. Peter) and Mendota during the summer of 1851.

In return for promises largely unfulfilled, Sioux chieftains gave up an empire of land to include virtually the lower half of what today is Minnesota. Worse, they were tricked into signing a second paper they assumed was a treaty extension but which was in reality an agreement to turn over such moneys as were to be paid to satisfy alleged debts owed to white fur traders.

Indian protests after learning how they had been duped were to no avail. For despite wrangling over their misunderstanding of the so-called "trader's paper," Governor Ramsey disbursed most of the cash payment to the traders.

Later, a Senatorial committee looking into charges of fraud concluded that Ramsey had been unwarranted in paying out money to the traders. Although he was later exonerated by vote of the full Senate, Ramsey stood in the opinion of historian Doane Robinson as "morally reprehensible in his conduct" (*A History of the Dakota or Sioux Indians*). Ramsey and Luke Lea, Superintendent of Indian Relations, had been loose and unbusinesslike throughout the treaty proceedings. "Their whole action looked to the protection of the traders at the Indian's expense. They must always bear a large share of the responsibility for the awful tragedy which followed" (*ibid.*).

Others were equally scathing in criticism. Meridel LeSueur described how Bishop Henry B. Whipple, writing to President Lincoln at a time when white outrage was at fever pitch, placed blame for "A border stained with blood" squarely on the shoulders of "greedy whites." Charging that the Indian Department was the most corrupt in our government, he asked: "Who is guilty of the causes which desolate our border? At whose door is the blood of these innocent victims? I believe God will hold the nation guilty" (*North Star Country*). Whipple, the Episcopal Bishop of Minnesota, was known to the Sioux as "Straight Tongue" for his advocacy in their behalf.

Deceitful as they were, the fact remains that the treaties at Traverse des Sioux and Mendota were to prove epochal in the life of the young state. After their signing in 1851, the frontier was open and the rush to claim free or cheap land was on.

First came lumbermen eager to slash into rich pine forests of what had been Indian country. They were followed by farmers and settlers. Towns and villages were springing up everywhere, some of which, like the dream city of Nininger, vanished into the mists of history during the national depression of 1857. On the banks of the Mississippi near Hastings, Nininger was the ill-fated vision of Minnesota politician and orator, Ignatius Donnelly. But optimism soon returned, bringing with it newcomers by the hundreds and thousands.

Land was the magnet, and as the demand for it became more urgent so did the plight of the Sioux. By the treaties of 1851, they had been squeezed into a narrow strip of land ten miles wide along either side of the Minnesota River. Now, as farmers advanced to the southwest with little regard for treaty boundaries, the Sioux were gripped in the tightening vice of Manifest Destiny.

With plows digging ever deeper into precious hunting grounds, the complaints ran two ways. White settlers, protesting harassment and the stealing of their livestock, sought protection by state militia against Indian incursions and plundering.

The Sioux, for their part, were embittered by encroachment on their lands. "The whites keep coming. We find them in the woods, by the lakes and rivers. They hunt and build on our land. They do not listen when we tell them to go away."

Their troubles were made even worse when by treaties of 1858, their 20-mile wide strip of land was cut down to ten. Then in 1862, blunders by U.S. agents resulted in delays and shortages of annuities due the Sioux each year by treaties of Traverse des Sioux and Mendota.

In August of 1862 some 5,000 Indians swarmed to the Agency at Yellow Medicine in the southwest corner of the state. Hungry and in some cases on the edge of starvation, they clamored for money to buy food and other provisions stored there. Matters came to a head when the agent refused to give out provisions until the delayed funds arrived from Washington. With a horde of hungry Indians outside a warehouse bulging with food, it was predictable that someone would break in. And when a mob of them did just that, the agent backed down and gave out food.

In mid-summer 1862, at a time when Minnesota was pressing to find volunteers to fight Civil War battles to the south, Indian troubles at home finally boiled over. Following years of meager subsistence on their shoestring tract, the Sioux had begun to dream of taking back the hunting and fishing domain from men they believed had robbed and cheated them. Knowing about the war going on between white men, they reasoned that the soldiers left behind were not in sufficient strength to resist them.

Primed by years of grumbling around the council fires, the time for torch and tomahawk needed only a spark to set things off. As it happened, two such flash points occurred within days of each other.

The first, in the form of a demeaning insult, took place at the Agency at Redwood. There, as at Yellow Medicine, provisions were stored while agents waited for the delayed arrival of annuity payments. Chief Little Crow, speaking for some hundreds of Indians assembled, appealed for an issue of rations. To which Andrew Myrick, one of the storekeepers, snarled, "If they are hungry, let them eat grass" (Bjornson, *The History of Minnesota*).

Little Crow later ascribed this heartless remark as one of his reasons for going to war. And three days later, on the morning of the outbreak, Myrick was killed and his mouth stuffed with grass.

- 31 -

"... THE INDIANS ARE RAISING HELL"

What finally touched off Little Crow's long smoldering resentment turned out to be a senseless act of random savagery. On Sunday, the 17th of August 1862, four young Sioux appeared at the cabin of a white farmer. Accounts differ as to their purpose or what happened to trigger the bloodletting. But what is agreed is that after some bickering, one of the youths, acting on a dare, suddenly raised his rifle and shot the farmer. He and his companions then murdered four others, including a woman and a young girl.

For Little Crow, encamped near the agency where two days before he had been sneeringly rebuffed, these killings were decisive. The whites, he reasoned, would seek terrible vengeance, at the very least cutting off annuity payments and supplies of food. Their recourse, he told a hastily assembled council, was either to turn the boys over to the whites for punishment, or to go to war. When the council shouted for war, Little Crow gave orders for attacking the agency at Redwood and for the killing of the traders and looting of their stores.

And so began a reign of horror, later to be described by historian Folwell as "The bloodiest Indian war of the American continent."

Within hours of the assault at Redwood, flames and

pillage had spread to the agency at Yellow Medicine and its settlements along the Minnesota River. All that terrible day, marauding parties raged up and down the valley, killing men, capturing women and sometimes butchering children.

Meantime a rescue party sent out from Fort Ridgely was caught in a deadly ambush near the Redwood Agency. Of 50 men sent out, only half lived to straggle back to the fort. Among the dead was the troop's leader, Capt. John Marsh. Fortunately before leaving the fort, he had dispatched a message to Lt. Timothy Sheehan, who with another 50 men had been earlier sent for duty at Fort Ripley. The message read: "It is absolutely necessary that you should return with your command immediately to this post. The Indians are raising hell at the Lower Agency. Return as soon as possible" (Folwell).

As the forays continued on the second day, thousands of frantic refugees were in flight, some so thoroughly frightened as to never return. At Fort Ridgely, where 19-year-old Lt. Thomas Gere had been left in charge, refugees were pouring in on foot or by the wagon load. Recognizing the enormity of the outbreak, Gere sent a courier galloping off to Fort Snelling, 165 miles away. The 18-hour ride of Pvt. William Sturgis lasted throughout the night and into the next afternoon. It has since been called "one of the epic rides of frontier history" (Oehler, *The Great Sioux Uprising*).

During two days of devastation, Sioux raiding parties had rampaged across a two hundred-mile frontier. On the third day, Little Crow began to assemble his scattered warriors for a crucial attack in force. Behind him was a valley ablaze with fire and destruction. Ahead, if he could seize Fort Ridgely, the way would be open for a sweep all the way down the valley to the Mississippi.

Little Crow's strategy and plan of attack was excellent. But his timing and sense of enemy strength were not. Had he struck the first day after the slaughter of the relief company sent out from the fort, the skeleton garrison left behind would almost certainly have been overrun. However, by the time of the Sioux attack on the third day, the fort's manpower had been considerably reinforced.

In command, after a 42-mile forced march back to the fort, was Lieutenant Sheehan. His total strength included 51 men he had brought back, plus a 50-man troop of half-breeds hastily recruited and sent there from the Indian agencies. Counting the remnants of the garrison and roughly 25 volunteers from the several hundred refugees crowded within, he was able to deploy some 180 armed defenders.

Little Crow's first bold attack was broken up by a surprise hail of canister. Sergeant John Jones, an expert gunner, had directed the fire of three field pieces, loaded and fired by a squad of infantry he had converted into cannoneers.

After two days of withering fire from concealed places surrounding the fort, Little Crow tried again, this time in strength estimated at nearly 800 warriors. Charging out of a nearby ravine, the attackers were once again repelled by a concentration of rifle and cannon fire.

Disheartened by the roar and sweep of cannon fire as well as by so unexpected a display of defensive manpower, Little Crow withdrew. At a cost of three defenders killed, Fort Ridgely had been saved and the cause of the Sioux lost.

Indian casualties have been estimated from being very light to Lt. Gere's after battle report of perhaps a hundred. Whatever the count, the real consequence was Little Crow's failure to reduce this roadblock in the way of his sweep down the valley.

The setback was later described by Chief Big Eagle, a leader in the final attack. "We thought the Fort was the door to the valley … and if we got through the door nothing would stop us this side of the Mississippi. But the defenders of the Fort were very brave and kept the door shut."

The surviving defenders were later awarded medals bearing Sioux words meaning, "They kept the door shut" (Oehler, *ibid.*)

With the situation in trouble, Little Crow's decision to

next attack New Ulm may have been designed for little more purpose than to salvage his leadership credibility. Whatever the reason, his assault there on August 23rd was all-out. And the remarkable defense put up by civilian volunteers against a horde of screaming attackers ranks with the battle of Fort Ridgely as a turning point in the Sioux War. It is a story best told by its leader, Charles C. Flandrau, who at the time of the uprising was a 35-year-old circuit-riding judge residing near St. Peter. A congenial jurist, Flandrau was a former Indian agent and Territorial delegate. As a member of the Minnesota constitutional convention in 1857, it was said he helped shape most of its provisions. He was also advocate general for the state militia, forerunner of today's Minnesota National Guard. In later life Flandrau became a chronicler of events, many of which he had experienced during the first half century of Minnesota's political existence. Flandrau State Park near New Ulm is named in his memory.

Here follows Flandrau's personal account of the battle at New Ulm, excerpted from his 1900 *History of Minnesota*.

- 32 -

STATEMENT OF JUDGE CHARLES E. FLANDRAU

" ... *The people at New Ulm dispatched a courier to St. Peter as soon as they became aware of the trouble. He arrived at 4 o'clock a.m. on the 19th, and came immediately to my house ... and informed me that the Indians were killing people all over the country. Having lived among them for several years, I thoroughly understood the danger of the situation, and knowing that ... the frontier was no place at such a time for women and children, I told him to wake up the people at St. Peter, and that I would be there quickly. I immediately placed my family in a wagon, and told them to flee down the river, and taking all the guns, powder and lead I could find in my house, I arrived at St. Peter about 6 a.m. The men of the town were soon assembled at the courthouse, and shortly a company was formed of 116 men, of which I was chosen captain.*

Great activity was displayed in equipping the main body of the company for service. All the guns of the place were seized, and put into the hands of the men. Rifles were scarce, but shotguns were abundant. All the blacksmith shops and gun shops were set at work moulding bullets, and we soon had a gun in every man's hand, and he was supplied with a powder horn or a whiskey flask full of powder, a box of caps and a pocketful of bullets. We impressed all the wagons we needed for transportation, and all the blankets and provisions that were necessary for subsistence and comfort.

Our advance guard reached New Ulm just in time to participate in its defense against an attack of about one hundred Indians who had been murdering the settlers on the West Side of the river between the town and Fort Ridgely. The inhabitants of New Ulm were almost exclusively German, there being only a few English-speaking citizens among them, and they were not familiar with the character of the Indians, but the instinct of self-preservation had impelled them to fortify the town with barricades to keep the enemy out. The town was built in the usual way of western towns, the principal settlement being along the main street, and the largest and best houses occupying a space of about three blocks. Some of these houses were of brick and stone so with a strong barricade around them, the town was quite defensible.

" ... The main body of my company, together with a squad from LeSeuer, reached the ferry about two miles below the settled part of New Ulm, about 8 p.m., having made thirty two miles in seven hours in a drenching rainstorm. The blazing houses in the distance gave a very threatening aspect to the situation, but we crossed on the ferry successfully, and made the town without incident."

[After detailing reinforcements that came in from nearby towns, Judge Flandrau numbered his forces at about three hundred men, most of them poorly armed.]

" ... We improved the barricades and sent out daily scouting parties who succeeded in bringing in many people who were hiding in the swamps, and who would undoubtedly have been lost without this succor. It soon became apparent that, to maintain any discipline or order in the town, some one man must be placed in command of the entire force ... and the selection fell to me. A provost guard was at once established, order inaugurated, and we awaited events.

I have been thus particular in my description of the

movements at this point because it gives an idea of the defense-less condition in which the outbreak found the people of the country, and also because it shows the intense energy with which the settlers met the emergency, at its very inception, from which I will deduce the conclusion at the proper time that this prompt initial action saved the state from a calamity, the magnitude of which is unrecorded in the history of Indian wars.

" ... Saturday, the 23rd of August, opened bright and beautiful, and early in the morning we saw column after column of smoke arise in the direction of the Fort, each smoke being nearer than the last. We knew to a certainty that the Indians were approaching in force, burning every building and grain or haystack that they passed. The settlers had either all been killed, or had taken refuge at the Fort or New Ulm, so we had no anxiety about them. About 9:30 a.m., the enemy appeared in great force on both sides of the river. ... Immediately, the enemy advanced, some six hundred strong, many mounted and the rest on foot. I had determined to meet them on the open prairie, and had formed my men by companies in a long line of battle. ... Down came the Indians in the bright sunlight, running, yelling and gesticulating in the most fiendish manner. If we had good rifles they never would have got near enough to do much harm, but as it was we could not check them before their fire began to tell on our line. ... My men appreciating the inferiority of their armament, after seeing several comrades fall, ... fell back on the town. ... I think if they had boldly charged into the town and set it on fire they would have won the fight; but, instead, they surrounded it on all sides, the main body taking possession of the lower end of the main street below the barricades, from which direction a strong wind was blowing towards the center of town, and the fighting became general on all sides.

" ... We held several outposts, being brick buildings outside the barricades, which we loopholed, and found very effective in holding the Indians aloof. The battle raged generally all around the town, every man doing his best in his own way. It was a very interesting fight on account of the stake we were

contending for. We had in place twelve or fifteen hundred women and children, the lives of all of whom, and of ourselves, depended on victory ... for in a fight like this, no quarter is asked or given. The desperation with which the conflict was conducted can be judged from the fact that I lost sixty men in the first hour, ten killed and fifty wounded.

" ... The enemy seeing his advantage in firing the buildings in the lower part of the main street, and thus gradually nearing our barricades with the intention of burning us out, kept up his work as continuously as he could with interruptions we made for him by occasionally driving him out; but his approach was constant and about 2 o'clock a roaring conflagration was raging on both sides of the street, and the prospect looked discouraging.

[It was at this critical juncture that Flandreau decided to go on the offensive and called for fifty volunteers.]

" ... In a short time we had a squad ready, and sallied out, cheering and yelling in a manner that would have done credit to the wildest Comanches. ... When the conformation of the ground disclosed their whereabouts we were within one hundred feet of them. They opened a rapid fire on us, which we returned, while keeping up our rushing advance. When we were within fifty feet of them, they turned and fled down the street. We followed them for at least half a mile, firing as well as we could.

" ... The next morning (Sunday) opened bright and beautiful, but scarcely an Indian was to be seen. They had given up the contest, and were rapidly retreating northward up the river. We got an occasional shot at one, but without effect except to hasten retreat. And so ended the second and decisive battle of New Ulm.

In this fight between ourselves and the enemy we burned one hundred ninety buildings, many of them substantial and valuable structures. The whites lost some fourteen killed and fifty or sixty wounded. The loss of the enemy is uncertain, ... but judging from the length and character of the engagement and the number of dead found, their casualties must have equaled, if not exceeded ours.

There were in the town at the time of the attack on the 23rd, as near as can be learned from 1,200 to 1,500 noncombatants, consisting of women and children, refugees and unarmed citizens, all of whose lives depended on our success. It is difficult to conceive a much more exciting stake to play for, and the men seemed to fully appreciate it and made no mistakes."

- 33 -

"... EXCLUSIVELY A MINNESOTA AFFAIR"

There being yet no telegraph wires stretching out into the Minnesota valley, word of the outbreak did not reach Governor Ramsey until a full day after the initial attacks. He at once hurried to Fort Snelling where he conferred with officers and asked Henry Sibley to accept command of such forces as could be mustered to check the advance.

On the next day, Colonel Sibley with four companies of volunteer infantry was on his way up the Minnesota by steamboat. Arriving at St. Peter August 22nd, their ranks were shortly bolstered by the addition of six more infantry companies along with a unit of several hundred mounted men. With these reinforcements, Sibley's force numbered around 1,400 men—most of them raw recruits, who had just signed on at Fort Snelling for Civil War service. Two days later, after doing what could be done to instill at least a shred of discipline, Sibley moved the force out to Fort Ridgely.

By then, although the uprising was not over, its threat to overrun the Minnesota valley had been checked. Sioux warriors continued their murderous raids on isolated farms and villages. And there were yet battles to be fought. But the war had entered a new and final phase with Sibley's arrival at Fort Ridgely.

Before taking to the field, Sibley struggled to train and

equip his green troops. On August 31st, he sent a reinforced company up river to bury the dead and reconnoiter the enemy position. Under command of Major Joseph R. Brown, the unit found and buried 54 massacred persons before making camp in the timber line above Birch Coulee, a ravine about three miles from the Redwood agency. Although Major Brown on personal reconnaissance found no sign of Indian presence, they were in fact there.

As it happened the presence of soldiers was discovered by a marauding band of several hundred warriors on their way to a surprise attack on the undefended settlements at St. Peter and Mankato. Sensing a chance for easy victory and plunder, they immediately gave up their plans for harassment of towns down the river in favor of an attack on the unsuspecting troops.

That night, under cover of darkness, they crept into concealed positions surrounding the camp. From there, just at daybreak, they opened up a murderous curtain of rifle fire. Caught off guard, many of the soldiers were killed before they were able even to reach for their own weapons. Somehow organizing a makeshift defense in which most of them fired back from the shelter of their dead horses, they managed to hold off what threatened to become a total massacre. As it was, fully a third of Brown's command were dead or wounded before Sibley, who had been alerted by the sound of distant small arms fire, arrived to drive the attackers away.

For the whites, the Battle of Birch Coulee was a disaster. In addition to their human casualties, they sustained the loss of all but one of their mounts, leaving Sibley with less than 20 horses with which to pursue the enemy.

However, as was later learned from interviews with Sioux warriors who had fought in that battle, their spur-of-the-moment decision to attack the troops at Birch Coulee very likely saved the defenseless towns of St. Peter and Mankato from even more fearsome slaughter.

For Sibley, advancing further up the Minnesota valley, the main concern was rescue of nearly 300 white captives Little

Crow was holding at a camp somewhere beyond Yellow Medicine. By means of a note attached to a stake and left at Birch Coulee, Sibley urged Little Crow to release the captives. But after two weeks of waiting, Sibley and his command again moved up river to the vicinity of Yellow Medicine. On September 22nd, the force pitched camp near a lake since known as Battle Lake.

Meanwhile, Little Crow's efforts to draw other Sioux tribes into the fray were not going well. In a great council called to discuss the matter, Sioux chiefs from reservations further up river told him bluntly that it had not been wise for him to make war against the whites. Their departure left him to carry on with about 800 warriors in the camp where he was holding the captives.

Prompted perhaps by frustration or sense of losing his followers, Little Crow summoned them to outline a bold plan of attack against a white force twice their size. Using their familiar ally of darkness as cover, he told them they would fall upon and massacre the sleeping soldiers. It would be easy, he assured them. And along with much plunder, they would once again be in command of the valley.

But this time Little Crow's fiery words fell short and his plan was dropped in favor of the kind of dawn attack so devastating at Birch Coulee.

At first light, the morning of September 23rd, the Indians stormed into the encampment howling and shooting, only to be driven back by a quick and determined counter attack. Sensing this to be the last throw of the dice, Little Crow sent his warriors back in to fight desperately before finally being driven off with heavy losses.

With Little Crow discredited and left with only a remnant of followers, the captives held at his encampment fell under the protection of Indians not disposed to war with the whites who had stayed out of the fight at Battle Lake. Following assurances from Sibley that he would come to them in friendship, they agreed to release the captives over whom they stood guard.

On September 25th, Sibley led a detachment of troops into the place henceforth to be known as "Camp Release." There, according to his report, the captives received them "with indescribable joy."

Little Crow had not awaited Sibley's arrival. In the wake of defeat, he and a handful of hostiles fled into the surrounding wilderness, hated by whites and held in contempt by Indians of their own tribe.

It remained now only to bring to a close this sorrowful chapter in Minnesota history. As straggling bands of warriors were rounded up or, facing starvation, came in to surrender, Sibley appointed a military court to try those braves accused of murdering settlers.

After being set up at Camp Release, the court acted promptly. Aided by self-confessing boastfulness of some of the Indians and the accusations of survivors and a few turncoat Sioux, it quickly convicted and sentenced to death 307 of the hostiles.

Passions were at fever pitch as survivors, generals, politicians and newspapers raised cry for immediate retribution. General John Pope, in command of the military in the Northwest, after wiring the names of the convicted to President Lincoln, urged his immediate authorization for their execution. Governor Ramsey added to the outcry, going so far as to suggest to the president the possibility of citizen revenge.

A lesser President might have crumbled. Lincoln did not. Instead, he ordered General Pope to send him the complete court proceedings so that he could make full and thorough determination of guilt. And it was only after toiling over the individual files for a month that he sent his hand-written warrant to Sibley, ordering the hanging of 39 of the leaders, whose crimes he painstakingly itemized by Indian name and case number. The warrant closed with instruction that other prisoners be held "subject to further orders, taking care they neither escape, nor are subject to any unlawful violence." That Lincoln, plagued by his over cautious generals and a series of defeats at the hands of

Confederate armies, could make time to so personally involve himself in the fate of Indian insurgents in far-off Minnesota, speaks more than words to his sense of justice.

On December 26, at Mendota, a cordon of troops stood by to restrain jeering citizens, as side-by-side on the same gallows, 38 Sioux were plunged to their death. The sentence of one Indian was later commuted to life imprisonment. The rest of the condemned Indians were shortly transferred to Davenport, Iowa from where, after some years, they were set free and sent to Nebraska.

By year-end 1862, all but a few hundred friendly Sioux had been driven from Minnesota. And a few months later, the U.S. Congress revoked all existing treaties with them. Payment of annuities was cut off, and the Sioux reservation along the Minnesota was opened to settlers for farming.

In 1863, Sibley, now a Brigadier General, continued at the head of Minnesota troops, helping drive the Sioux into and beyond Dakota Territory. As Flandrau describes it, "The troops marched nearly 1,200 miles. They fought three well-contested battles. They drove from eight to ten thousand Indians out of the state, and across the Missouri river. They lost only seven killed and three wounded, and inflicted upon the enemy so severe a loss that he never returned to his old haunts. For this meritorious service General Sibley was appointed a major general by brevet on November 29th, 1865."

Although conflict with the Sioux was to flame on for many years, its battles were removed to locales far west of Minnesota. Little Crow, whose venomous action had ignited the Sioux uprising, did not survive to play a part in the later conflicts.

In mid-summer 1863, after wintering near the Canadian border, Little Crow and a small party of followers sneaked back south, intent on stealing horses with which to flee far into British Canada and away from punishment. On July 3, after reaching a position near Hutchinson, Minnesota, the party scattered out to look for horses. Awaiting their return, Little Crow and his young son were picking berries to relieve their hunger, when they were fired on by a farmer, who then fled. The boy escaped injury but Little Crow soon died.

Thus, shot in the back during a petty act of filching berries, perished the war chief whose so recent dreams of conquest and glory had set off the appalling carnage of the Minnesota valley. In less than two months, nearly 500 white civilians and soldiers had been killed, with many others wounded or emotionally scarred. Farms, agencies and settlements were burnt out and plundered. And finally, this war-within-a-war added to the stress of a young state already taxed by the demands of a national crisis. Amid its intensive effort to recruit and equip troops to fight for the Union, Minnesota had been confronted with a desperate emergency at home. Savagery at the door had suddenly become more pressing than the needs of battlefields a thousand miles away.

Writing in his introduction for volume II of Folwell's *History of Minnesota*, Solon Buck summed up the conflict as follows:

> " ... In the history of the nation the Sioux outbreak is only an incident, while the Civil War is a major event. In the history of Minnesota, however, the relative importance of the two is reversed. The Indian War took place at home, it was almost exclusively a Minnesota affair, and until the savages were defeated or driven away the settlement and development of the state could not go on. In the Civil War, on the contrary, the action was far away. Minnesota was only one of many states involved and the immediate effects were less noticeable, however important the ultimate influence ... "

- 34 -

MINNESOTA AND THE CIVIL WAR

Almost the youngest of American states, Minnesota had been in the Union less than three years before the outbreak of the Civil War. As it happened, Governor Ramsey was in Washington seeking political favors when word of the attack on Fort Sumter arrived. The next morning, April 14, 1861, he hastened to offer a thousand men from Minnesota in defense of the Union.

Although this spontaneous gesture secured for Minnesota the distinction of being the first to offer troops, there has been speculation as to its prompting. At the Republican National Convention a few months earlier, Ramsey had supported William Seward over Lincoln. Now, after backing the wrong horse, his quest for patronage under the new administration found hard going. So Ramsey's offer may have been spurred by political rather than patriotic concerns.

Whatever the motivation, the actual recruiting of Minnesota troops went slowly. It was not until June that Ramsey was able to report a muster up to regimental strength. And most of these from militia companies around the state had signed up for just three months.

As the enlistees trickled in at Fort Snelling, they were assembled into companies of the First Minnesota Regiment of Volunteers, where Commanding Officer, Willis A. Gorman, set them to a rigorous course of drill and maneuver. For some months thereafter the First coped with a supply problem unique to the North Star State.

Unlike older and more prosperous states able to bear the initial cost of outfitting their troops, Minnesota lacked such means. Ramsey had expected the Federal government to pay for uniforms and other basic equipment. But when it didn't, he refused to obligate his state by issuing bonds. Without assurance of payment, suppliers refused delivery. It was not until after Bull Run that the Federal government assumed responsibility for troop supply. Up to then, First Minnesota with red shirts and baggy pantaloons had the motley look of a company of mummers. Although they at least had rifles, some of them were of a make and caliber for which they had no ammunition.

Upon being declared "Battle Ready" by Colonel Gorman, the First left Fort Snelling in June 1861. They were the vanguard of ten more infantry regiments, four artillery batteries and other special detachments Minnesota was to send out to fight in the Civil and Sioux Wars. In days to come, the young state was to contribute 22,000 officers and men, an outpouring amounting to one eighth of its population. Of these, 2,500 were killed or died from camp diseases. Parenthetically, a total of 200,000 troops, more than half of all Union deaths during the Civil War, died from diseases such as scurvy and chronic diarrhea.

In sum, Minnesota troops fought with distinction in most of the important battles of the Civil War. Tramping through heat and dust of summer, slogging in mud and chilling rain of winter, young men from the North Star State were to follow their regimental colors to places undreamed on the farms and in the villages they left behind.

First Minnesota was blooded July 21, 1861 at Bull Run, the first major engagement of the War. The regiment's three years with the Army of the Potomac are detailed in the manuscript to follow.

Here briefly are notable actions of other Minnesota regiments. On October 5, 1862 at Corinth, Mississippi, Fifth

Minnesota, led by Col. Lucius F. Hubbard, drove back a strong Rebel force that had broken through Union lines. Later to become a governor of Minnesota, Hubbard had risen from Private to command of the regiment. Commanding General William Rosecrans was later to cite the Fifth for its gallantry during that critical action.

Fourth Minnesota fought with Grant at the siege of Vicksburg. On July 4, 1863, its regimental band led Union forces into Vicksburg to cap the victory that gave the North control of the Mississippi.

Late that fall, Second Minnesota took part in the spectacular charge at Missionary Ridge from which position Confederate artillery had dominated rail and Tennessee River traffic around Chattanooga. Despite heavy losses, Second continued its advance to help carry the day against Rebel General Braxton Bragg.

In 1864, Second and Fourth Minnesota were with the Army of William Tecumseh Sherman based in Atlanta. They went with that army on its devastating "March to the Sea," across Georgia.

Eighth Minnesota took part in Sherman's Carolina campaign. It suffered heavy casualties while helping beat off a major attack by Nathan Bedford Forrest's Raiders at Murfreesboro, Tennessee.

In December 1864, in front of Nashville, Fifth, Seventh, Ninth and Tenth Minnesota took part in the grand assault that routed the Confederate Army of the Tennessee. Two future governors of Minnesota, Col. William R. Marshall and the aforementioned Lucius Hubbard took part in that battle.

The sole blot on Minnesota's Civil War record of valor occurred in mid-summer of 1862 at Murfreesboro, where Third Minnesota had been sent to guard an important supply point. On July 13, Rebel cavalry made a surprise attack on a small Michigan unit helping defend the town. Col. Henry C. Lester, commanding Third, did not respond to Michigan's call for help. Instead, without being himself seriously threatened, Lester abruptly surrendered his own regiment. It is believed he misjudged the size of the attacking force.

Captured enlisted men of the Third were later paroled and went on to fight bravely in the War with the Sioux. Colonel Lester and the officers who voted with him to surrender were dishonorably discharged from service.

If Third's surrender was the low point for Minnesota troops in the Civil War, First's magnificent charge at Gettysburg was the apex. In fact its entire wartime history is written in courage second to none.

- 35 -

"... IT JUST SEEMED THE RIGHT THING TO DO."

All kinds of records exist to describe the course and campaigns of Minnesota regiments during the Civil War. The Minnesota State Legislature in 1889 established a special commission to gather and publish such documents, and the multi-volume *Minnesota in the Civil and Indian Wars*, published between 1890 and 1893, was the result.

But rarely, even in soldiers' letters to family, is there to be found the day-to-day logging of a unit smaller than a regiment. A notable exception is the diary of Charles Porter Weldon,* which turned up in the archives of his *alma mater*, Hobart College. It was called to my attention as a surprise response to my request for information about that school's illustrious graduate, William Watts Folwell. Weldon, from St. Paul, interrupted his Hobart studies to enlist in First Minnesota. Here follow excerpts from the diary he kept during three years that brought great honor to that regiment and his home state.

---

* Charles Weldon and the enlisted men named in his journal are fictional characters created to chronicle life inside a company of the First Minnesota Regiment.

April 20th, Hobart College-News from Fort Sumter swirls about the campus like a whirly gust. In Chapel this a.m. Prexy Jackson urged us to stay till term's end. I doubt many will. 8 fellows from the South are gone already including my roommate Thad Stevens, gone home to Roanoke to join the militia. I rode with him to the station and almost cried when we said goodbye. After 3 years of playing baseball with Thad out back of Trinity, sure hope we don't wind up playing catch with bullets.

April 28th-I leave tomorrow. Army life can't be much worse than being clanged awake by the Chapel bell at the uncivilized hour of 5:30. Last week there were 60 of us here. Now there's hardly a baker's dozen. I'm all alone on this floor. I call down the hall and hear only echoes.

May 4th-Welcome home not effusive. Mom distraught. Dad furious I won't be reading law in his chambers this summer. Insists I sign up for 3 months only. Thinks war will be over by then and I can go back and finish up at Hobart. Not likely, methinks.

May 7th-Tried to enlist with St. Paul Volunteers but told all full. Last night called on Melissa Hunzinger. Pretty as ever. Upset with me but agreed to write. I love it when she pouts.

May 11th-I'm a soldier. But—they changed it to 3-year enlistments. Physical exam a laugh, couple of thumps on your chest and you're pronounced fit. Fellow ahead of me couldn't make out the letters on the eye chart. He passed anyway by telling him he didn't know how to read. A Sgt. swore us in and assigned us to different companies. Most went to G which lost a lot of 3-month recruits when they raised the term of service. As a favor, the Sgt. sent me to A Company, the old St. Paul Guards. Told me to go home for the night and report back in a.m. ... At home: The Last Supper. Mom tearful, Dad testy! He grumbled about 3 years and going to the Guards. Seems its Capt. is a

Democrat. Offered to get me transferred to the Volunteers, whose Capt. is a strong Republican. Told him I doubted Rebs would know the difference.

May 15th, Fort Snelling-I was wrong. Being jolted awake by a whistle is worse than the Chapel bell at Hobart. There you could steal a few more winks. Here you'd get dumped on the floor. ... Somebody mutters a malediction as to where the blower might care to situate his whistle. ... Reported here 4 days ago and was handed a red shirt and a blanket. No word on when we'll get real uniforms. On the drill field we look like a cavalcade of clowns, some with pants too long and baggy, others in billowing pantaloons, a few like me still wearing civilian trousers. It differs throughout the regiment. E Company's dandies are togged out in the scarlet and blue of French Zouaves. But you have to hand it to them. They're crackerjack marchers.

St. Paul the only town with 2 companies. The rest all come from different places. But now we go by alphabet:

A-St. Paul Pioneer Guards
B-Stillwater Guards
C-St. Paul Volunteers
D-Lincoln Guards
E-St. Anthony Zouaves
F-Goodhugh Volunteers
G-Faribault Volunteers
H-Dakota Volunteers
I-Wabasha Volunteers
K-Winona Volunteers

At full strength there should be 1,000 in the regiment with each company having 100 men divided into 4 squads. I'm in Co. A, 2nd squad. Sgt. George Sullivan is squad leader. Our barracks surprisingly cozy, plastered walls, neatly spaced double bunks and a fireplace to take off the night chill. We take turns being fire orderly. Nice, but they don't let us spend much time here.

May 16th-We may dress like comics but there's nothing funny about our day after they roust us out:

5:40 am-Roll call in pitch dark, some of us half dressed. After the Sgt. is satisfied no one has slipped off to join the Rebs, he does about face and hollers, "A Company present and accounted for SIR!" Similar shouts echo around the parade ground. A pause, presumably to digest this information, before out of the dark comes a bellow of dismissal. ... A cold splash of water at the Co. pump and then back for 20 minutes of pre-prandial exertion known as "quick time march." Still dark and nobody too happy.

6:15-Breakfast: oatmeal, sorghum, bread and coffee. Make up bunks and fall back out for drill.

7:30-9:30-Platoon and Company close order marching. "By the right flank, March!" "To the rear March!" "By the oblique! Etc." The command to march is given as the left foot hits the ground, so we're all together. That's the idea but this a.m. the Lieut. got a little too enthusiastic and we wound up in a muddle.

9:30-Half hour of bayonet drill. "Thrust-Swing up stock-Slash! Again! 1-2-3, Again! 1-2-3!" Until finally thrusting and slashing we jam bayonets into a straw dummy tied to a pole. The dummy accepts it in good grace. But I hope I never have to learn how somebody with a bayonet of his own responds to this curious exercise in mayhem.

10:15-After a short break it's dry fire rifle drill—prone, kneel and standing. Aim at target, tell Cpl. to mark, do it 3 times and Cpl. spots the size of triangulation. Poor Jenson, who did badly, compounded his woes by asking when we'd get to shoot real bullets. "Don't worry about it," the corporal snapped, "the way you aim, you'll do better to swing the damn thing like a club."

11:45-Wash up for dinner. After sausage and boiled potatoes most of us go back to barracks for a nap.

1:00-Afternoon formation and 2 mile hike outside Fort.

2:00-Regimental drill. Colonel Gorman cuts a dashing figure prancing back and forth on his spirited steed. But our drill master is Capt. Woodbury, former C.O. of the crack marching St. Anthony Zouaves. We're still ragged but getting better.

5:00-Dismiss and prepare for Retreat. Despite conglomeration of garb we try to present our best appearance. Company forms at Parade Rest. Bugle blows Retreat. Troops with rifles come to Present Arms. Flag is lowered. Civilians turn out for ceremony and Retreat parade. Band playing, colors flying, we pass in review. Felt a big lump rising in throat. A new experience, very stirring.

6:00-Supper: Beef, mashed potatoes, beans and bread. Hungry men wolf down everything in sight, then cuss the cooks.

7:30-Time to ourselves after supper? Hah! Assemble in Co. day room while 1st Sgt. rattles off who's on guard duty or kitchen detail for tomorrow. He reads sections from Articles of War dealing with discipline and court martial. Sass a non-com and I'll get to march around the parade ground with a log on my shoulder. Fall asleep on guard duty and I get shot.

8:30-Tattoo bugle call to quarters. Talk to my bunk mate Jasper Sproat about day's rumors. Write Melissa.

9:30-Taps. Lights out. A Co. barracks is given over to snuffles and snores. Even if we don't look the part they're trying hard to turn us into soldiers. Makes for a long day. But can't complain. After all they pay us nearly 40 cents a day!

May 17th-There's 30 of us on this floor. Most are workers or farm boys like Jasper Sproat, who made their living with their hands. At first, they didn't know what to make of someone who's been to college. But we get along fine, sing songs while marching, crack jokes and help each other out. They call me "Perfessor." ... Jasper is quite a young man. In order to enlist he walked all the way here from Willmar. When I asked him why, he said, "It just seemed the right thing to do." He's 18, with an easy smile, asks questions about everything. I can answer most of them and do useless things like read Greek. But I've never milked a cow, fixed a wagon wheel, shot a rabbit or done a lot of other things that are second nature to Jasper. He's had just enough school to read and write but I doubt not that before this is over, he'll be more of the teacher than me.

May 23rd-Today's rumor is we're headed for Fort Ripley to replace the regulars there now. This one sounds real. Nobody very happy about it. Food continues so so. Still no uniforms. If this keeps up I'll have to go home and get another pair of pants.

June 5th, Fort Ripley-Well, that's one rumor that came true. Capt. Wilkin led A Co. out of Fort Snelling 7 days ago. Marched north beside the Mississippi. Haversack felt like an anvil, weighted down with all our possessions, canteen on belt, musket over shoulder and tramping 20 to 25 miles each long day. At night after beans, it got quiet in a hurry. When we got here 2 days ago, the regulars were so happy they invited us to a beer party. Jasper and I went but were too tired to stay long. Regulars left yesterday, some of them still wobbling from the night before.

June 10th-Now I know why the regulars were so pleased to see us. Hard to imagine a more desolate place. So dull it's a relief to go on guard duty. One day on, three off. Rest of the time we drill, write letters or mend clothes. Mail once a week takes precedence over even mess call. For all the earthly use I am here, I might as well be back at Hobart. Managed to pick up a decent knapsack and a pair of uniform trousers from stores left behind by the regulars. No band or dress parade but we do have a drummer for drilling every morning and afternoon. "Left wheel march!—By the right oblique march!—Left shoulder arms!" and on and on. To the beat of that drum we're stepping out pretty lively.

June 18th-A courier from Fort Snelling brought mail and good news we're going to Washington. But A Company has to stay here till we're relieved by a new company of volunteers. E Company leaves in the morning for Fort Snelling.

Letter from Melissa full of cheerful prattle. She apparently not lacking for male attendance. Her envelope was scented and the men around me keep asking for a sniff. Dad writes that Governor Ramsey is doing his best to get us proper uniforms. Also a surprise note from Bishop Whipple, * *who so long ago sent me off to Hobart. He prays I'll soon go back there for my degree. Wonder if I ever will.*

June 21st-Fort Snelling-Back where I started. 3 days ago Capt. Wilkins sent me and Sgt. Sullivan to requisition supplies for our trip to Washington. Sgt. Sullivan knows what we need but is not very good at paperwork. Coming back on a pack mule is easier on the feet but harder in a certain other area.

June 22nd-Work done. Supplies piled up and loaded in quartermaster wagons. Got pass this afternoon to visit folks. Saw Melissa. She doesn't know what to make of us. Neither do I. Have to wait and see if it's true about absence and the heart.

---

* Henry B. Whipple, first Episcopal Bishop of Minnesota, was a friend of the Bishop who founded Hobart College.

June 29th-Washington-We're here at Camp Minnesota on Capitol Hill. At night across the river we can see the twinkling of Rebel campfires. Our Company rejoined the Regiment yesterday. It took us 4 days by steamboat to Prairie du Chien and the rest of the way by trains through Wisconsin, Illinois, Indiana, Ohio and Pennsylvania. After a great supper from citizens in Pittsburgh it was back on another train to Washington by way of Harrisburg and Baltimore. Got here yesterday afternoon just in time for a regimental review. They say there's 90,000 of us camped around Washington.

July 1st-Aside from drill and guard duty there's time to look around. Jasper and I went for a walk this afternoon. Saw the unfinished Capitol where Lincoln took his oath of office. Looking at it Jasper said, "I guess that's what we're fighting for." In the sense that building stands for the Union, I doubt if Abe Lincoln could put it any better. As for me, I have no use for the bondage of slavery. But on that issue alone I would not take up arms against old college classmates like Thad Stevens. But for defense of the Union I'm prepared to follow the flag and make any sacrifice.

July 3rd-Alexandria, Virginia—This a.m. we marched down to where a steamer took us across the Potomac. Set up camp a ten minute march west of Alexandria. Sgt. Sullivan says we're part of a perimeter defense of the Capitol.

July 10th-Been here a week. Co. had its turn guarding a nearby telegraph line. Subsistence poor. Salt pork like chewing on a razor strop. Hard tack comes in packages labeled BC, which the boys say was the time it was laid down.

July 16th-Orders come down to march. After breakfast we roll up coat and spare socks in a blanket, tie off the ends and throw over shoulder. Move out with 3 days rations and 40 rounds of ammunition. Marched 11 or 12 miles west. Camped by a stream with odd name of Pohick Creek. Heard musket fire just before dark.

July 19th-Northeast Virginia—Slow going yesterday. Trail through woods in wretched condition. To make it worse Rebs had chopped down trees to form crude barriers. Got here late this afternoon. Capt. Wilkin led a few of us out to look for the enemy. Signs they're around but keeping out of sight. This is poor country, scrubby growth, sun-blistered shacks, the people ill-clad and looking hungry.

July 24th-Washington—"We seen the elephant!" Just at dawn 3 days ago we broke camp and marched a few miles west down a turnpike. Forked off the turnpike and went down a rutted path where we forded a meandering creek called Bull Run. Sounds of cannon fire and muskets. Everybody excited and nervous. Jasper smiles at me and best I could manage was a sick grin. Terribly hot. Mouth so dry I can barely talk. Word comes down we've got the Rebs on the run. Somebody orders a cannon battery up to shell the Rebs at close quarters. A Company is sent along to cover them.*

Suddenly out of the woods bursts a mob of screaming Rebs. Cannon balls and grape shot sweep at us from hidden places in the woods. They had us sighted in before we ever got here. Men falling and crying for help. All afternoon we fought under a blazing sun. No food or water. The Rebs overrun our cannons. But lying on their flank we keep firing, in between ramming powder and reloading. A minie ball hits a rock in uncomfortable proximity to my head. Came bussing in like a hornet. Sgt. Sullivan shouts that the Reg't has fallen back. We're out here by ourselves. Finally, someone orders us to pull out. We move back firing as we go. Across the way I glimpse a mob of men,

* Phrase used by troops on both sides to explain the bedlam and horror of battle, a description for which no words exist.

horses and wagons in mass exodus. It's a rout. The Rebs have whipped us bad.

Catch up to the Reg't at stream we forded in the a.m. Back at Centreville at dark we flop down too spent to bother with food or shelter. At daylight Jasper tells me my forehead is caked with dry blood. Must have been a fragment off the rock the mini ball hit. Couple more inches and I might still be out there. We look around and know we lost some men. Sgt. Sullivan is missing and so is our mess mate Bill Becher. Wash down hard tack with muddy canteen water from creek. We move out and after two days straggle back to where we started from 3 weeks ago. Col. Miller, who was with us on the flank at Bull Run, comes by to tell us we fought well and helped cover the retreat. Not very consoling considering the Rebs have run us clear back to Washington. Reg't hard hit. H Co. had 5 killed and 20 wounded. G lost its Capt. and had about 20 other losses. K Co. about the same. Out on the flank, we got off easier with 2 killed, 6 wounded and 6 missing.

- 36 -

THE ROAD FROM BULL RUN

For the North, Bull Run was a harsh awakening. Instead of the three glorious months that everyone expected, it was going to take a lot longer to subdue a stubborn foe holding down its interior line of defense. As the Union licked its wounds, it stared at the cold reality that its war machine needed more of everything: more capable leaders, better trained troops and the industrial production of enormous stockpiles of armaments and other needs of battle.

President Lincoln reacted promptly, naming General George B. McClellan to head the Army of the Potomac and getting Congress to approve a loan for $250 million. At that time of crisis, the professional leadership of McClellan was exactly what the dejected army needed. He launched a vigorous program to train a huge new force of volunteers.

Northern industry cranked up to produce the needed tools of warfare. Political appointees unfit for battle command were weeded out and sent packing. And for the men of First Minnesota bivouacked in Washington, spirits began to lift with issue of back pay, regular army uniforms and brand new Springfield rifles.

The First also got a new leader. Col. Napoleon J. T. Dana replaced Col. Gorman, who had been promoted to command of a brigade. Dana set out at once to restore the regiment's fighting spirit. Training was stepped up and discipline tightened. Dana also went to bat to get his men better food and equipment.

In other organizational changes, A Company's Captain Wilkin was promoted and transferred to Second Minnesota. His successor, Lieut. Henry Coates, promptly offered Pvt. Weldon command of a platoon. When Weldon declined in order to stick with Jasper Sproat and his original mess mates, Coates summarily promoted him to First Sergeant, telling him, "You're the only one here smart enough to deal with the shit load of paper that piles up here everyday."

The "Perfessor's" appointment was confirmed by unanimous approval of A Company's men. His diary tells about "getting the hang" of drawing up training schedules, work details and the daily reports needed to draw rations and supplies.

In early August 1861, the regiment settled in for nearly six months at Camp Stone on the Maryland side of the Potomac. Sgt. Weldon records going up to the picket line where Yanks and Rebs posted to warn of any movement by either force shouted cheerful insults back and forth across the river.

As winter came on the men hauled logs to put up huts and tore down farm fences for firewood. Through Weldon's eyes we see them bored in camp, whittling, rereading crumpled letters from home, patching tattered garments, drilling and occasionally spit polishing for inspections or special reviews. In summer we plod with them along dusty roads, sweltering in woolen uniforms, tongues parched, dirty faces streaked with sweat, stumbling, cursing and foraging.

As one who had "seen the elephant," Weldon records the trembling anxiety of approaching battle along with its soul-numbing aftermath, untidy heaps of mangled human flesh carelessly strewn midst the litter of battle, the wail of the wounded echoing from crowded barns where surgeons without anesthetics sawed away at arms and legs.

By the end of its second year, the regiment had lost half of its original strength, some transferred or discharged from wounds, a few missing or taken prisoner. Many more were killed or dead from disease. Those left were lean, hard and no longer boys. When replacements came in old timers hollered, "Fresh Fish!"

In early 1862, Colonel Dana was promoted to brigade command. His successor, Col. Alfred Sully, led the First during McClellan's attempt to capture Richmond. The so-called Peninsula Campaign lasted through spring and into late summer. Finally, after months of desperate attacks through muddy swamps, higher command faced up to the futility of capturing the Confederate capital from this direction. The Army of the Potomac withdrew and the bitter lesson paid for in blood and anguish was that "Little Mac," so able in training and revered by his troops, turned out to be unequal to the cry for aggressive leadership in battle.

A Company came off the Peninsula with several killed and a dozen wounded, one of them being Corporal Sproat, grazed in the leg by canister. Helped back to a field hospital set up in a barn behind the line, Sproat gritted his teeth while an aid man put a rope around his thigh and twisted it with a stick to stop the bleeding. After a sleepless night amid the groans from the wounded and dying, he hobbled back for duty.

Events were to leave the First with little time to rest and refill its ranks. Within days of leaving the Peninsula, they were thrust back into spirit-sapping marches to help block a strong Confederate advance into northern Maryland. At less than half strength the regiment went into action about 20 miles south of Hagerstown. On September 17, 1862, First attacked across Antietam Creek to help drive General Lee back out of Maryland. The human toll for that fierce battle was staggering—more than 11,000 killed or wounded for each side. At that terrible cost, where the creek ran red with blood, Lee's Maryland campaign was put at end.

Antietam is generally thought of as a Union victory. In fact, it was more of a draw, because McClellan with a superior force ignored orders to press the pursuit and let the Rebels escape. Finally, after weeks during which Little Mac failed to move, Lincoln once again removed him from command of the Army of the Potomac.

Twice as many were killed or wounded at Antietam as occurred in the War of 1812 and the Spanish American War combined. In his diary entry the next day, Sergeant Weldon reflected on the horror of that bloodiest day in American military history.

- 37 -

AFTER ANTIETAM

Sept. 18th-Oh, to be away from this terrible place where the stench of death lays upon us like a ghastly miasma. Yesterday's battlefield is strewn with wreckage: dead horses in grotesque positions, sometimes still hitched to overturned wagons, trees splintered by canister shot, burning stores and worst of all, the bloated heaps of blue and gray that yesterday were men. Don't know who won. But a few more battles like this and there won't be enough of us left to keep the war going. The Reg't lost 100 men but other units near the center had it worse. A Co. lucky to get off with 5 men wounded.

Sept. 24th-Near Harpers Ferry—Two days ago we came to this God given escape from the horror of Antietam. We're on a bluff overlooking the Potomac. They call it Bolivar's Ridge.

Oct. 2nd-It's been a welcome change from marching and fighting. Our first rest since leaving Camp Stone 7 months ago. Except for a little drill they're letting us take it easy for awhile. President Lincoln here yesterday. Capt. Coates saw him ride by with Gen. McClellan. He said Lincoln on a horse is a curious sight. His feet hung almost to the ground and with his stove pipe hat he towered over "Little Mac."

Nov. 6th-Bivouac in Northern Virginia—On the march again, going south along the Blue Ridge. Moving easily, about 20 miles a day.

Nov. 9th-Near Warrenton, Virginia—Doing picket duty by the Rappahannock. Weather miserable, cold and rainy.

McClellan has been dismissed. News is a shock. "Little Mac" is real popular with the men. Whenever he'd dash by on his black horse we'd stand up and give him our hurrahs. Quite a sight with his yellow sash and twirling his cap on his sword. My feelings mixed. Maybe it's time for a change. No doubt "Little Mac" has our loyalty but somehow he keeps coming up short. All those grinding weeks on the Peninsula. And where did it get us? All those bodies heaped up at Antietam. For what? He had Lee on the run but let him go. Too cautious maybe. So afraid of losing he doesn't know how to win. So now we'll march with General Burnside.

Dec. 9th-Been camped here 3 weeks across the Rappahannock from Fredericksburg. Rebs dug in on high ground back of town, blocking the way to Richmond. Bridge builders have come up to lay a pontoon span across the river. Don't like the look of this. Rebs have full sweep over the country around here. And have had weeks to entrench and sight in their cannon. A direct attack up that hill would be madness.

Dec. 12th-Despite getting shot at, engineers somehow got their bridge up. We came across last night. After shelling by both sides and plunder by our troops there won't be much left for the citizens of Fredericksburg to come back to. Our men didn't do much looting but they did come up with a small keg of corn whisky. Capt. Coates ordered me to ration it out. Not a popular move but necessary to keep the whole Co. from getting drunk.

Dec. 14th-Yesterday witnessed the most tragically stupid battle of the War. From where we were, supporting a battery of *artillery, we watched in horror as one after another of our regt's stormed into that vortex of death only to be scythed down like fields of blue wheat. Rebel guns had the range and the slashing of their canister was devastating. When it came our turn, General Sully put his career on the line to save us.* He disobeyed orders to attack. Instead, he moved us back away from Rebel shelling.*

Slept last night wherever we could find some kind of shelter in the ruins of this forsaken town. This a.m. the Rebs granted a truce to let us bury our dead. It was horrible, most of them frozen to the ground. Buried them on that awful hill in unmarked graves.

Dec. 17th-Bivouacked at Falmouth, across the river from Fredericksburg. Came over last night. Nobody likes this place but all indications are that we'll be here for a spell. Meanwhile the mood is bad. Men blame Burnside for that insane butchery above Fredericksburg. But just now they're too fagged to even gripe. God, we're a sorry sight, uniforms ragged and filthy, unshaven faces streaked with grime. Glad Melissa can't see me like this—pants in tatters, coat caked with mud and ashes, shirt a ripe mix of smoke, sweat and grease. If I take it off it'll stand by itself. Wagons due to come with food and new clothes. Till then we'll get by with hard tack, potatoes and dried beans brought over from Fredericksburg. This afternoon Capt. got word for us to dig in here for winter.

Dec. 18th-Wagons finally arrive with mess supplies and winter canvas. Spent most of a.m. with Capt. writing up requisitions for practically everything. Co. strength down to 52. We need more men, reissue of uniforms and equipment, rations,

---

* According to "Narrative of the First Regiment," *Minnesota in the Civil and Indian Wars, Vol. 1*: "Sully, as judicious as brave, realizing the utter folly of also sacrificing his brigade … detained it in a place of safety, and his action which saved the First Minnesota was approved, or at least passed without question."

better rifles and ammunition. Raining this a.m. which isn't very helpful as we try to set up winter quarters.

Dec. 22nd-Will it ever stop raining? This camp is a quagmire. Wagons got here yesterday with quartermaster supplies. Mules needed a lift from the men in order to force the wagons through the mud of our camp street. Men ignore the rain to put up raised platforms covered by canvas. Each hut looks different, some built on stilts, other resting on logs, most sided with logs and chinks stuffed with mud (which is one thing in good supply.) I fuss around and try to help Jasper and Brandt set up ours. But mostly I'm just in the way. They're now working on a stone fireplace. Rain, cold or snow, this promises to be a snug hut.

Our mess group has 8 men. We have a cook chest with skillet, coffee boiler, pots, cups, axe and water buckets. Chests are heavy. When we move they're piled on Co. mess wagon. We boil soup and coffee in a pot suspended over the fire. This a.m. for breakfast Jasper mixed up flour and water for slap jacks. Fried them in the skillet. Spread with apple butter contributed by Adams, they tasted pretty good. There's a creek nearby where after dinner we'll fill the soup pot with water and try to boil the grit out of our shirts.

Dec. 26th-Didn't have the heart to write yesterday. Pretty glum around here recalling Yuletide at home. No doubt Rebs across the river feel the same way. River here shallow with sand bars. Couple days ago, Jasper on picket duty waded halfway across to swap some coffee for a sack of their tobacco. The Reb stuck out his hand and wished Jasper a Happy Christmas. Yesterday the two sides sang Silent Night in unison. Didn't hear as much as a musket shot all day.

Jan 5th, 1863-This is a gloomy place to be. Rain every day. Field too soggy for drill. Walking anywhere is like floundering through a swamp. Men while away the sluggish hours griping, writing letters or playing checkers. I used to be pretty good at chess. But I can't seem to beat that sly Jasper at checkers. Picket duty a welcome relief from camp tedium.

Jan 28th-Burnside is out and nobody is sorry. We hear the Army is now commanded by "Fighting Joe" Hooker.*

Feb 12th-A rare treat for supper last night thanks to a well lubricated Pvt. Wilbur Bottiford. It began when Sgt. Wright, out with a foraging detail, spotted a cow. Bottiford knows how to butcher but claims he needs liquid courage. Capt. Coates and Co. officers donated spirits which Bottiford drained before parting. An hour later Wright came back to report that while relocating the bovine Bottiford had sobered up. Capt. looked hard at Wright but finally sent him off with a fresh supply. Two hours later they came back with enough of Bossie's neatly sectioned remains to feed the whole Co. After gorging themselves at supper the men gave up three cheers for Bottiford. But by then he was snoring happily in his bunk.

March 15th-Ice and sometimes trace of snow. Chill digs into the bones but at least the frozen ground is better than slogging through a foot of muck. Picket duty last night in coldest rain I ever knew. Co. drill this a.m. followed by Regt'l review in p.m.

April 2nd-This p.m. we assembled in spit and polish order for a review by Alexander Ramsey, who's a U.S. Senator now. After belaboring our ear drums with 20 minutes of high blown rhetoric, he presented Col. Morgan with a new Regimental flag. Men still remember his delay in getting our uniforms and back

---

* Burnside, whose wooden-headed stubbornness at Fredericksburg sent thousands of young men to their graves, is best remembered for the curious mutton chop whiskers he wore and which have ever since been called "sideburns." Hooker turned out to be a poor battle leader. At Chancellorsville his blundering led to heavy casualties and another defeat by an enemy of lesser strength. Once again Lincoln was forced to make a change. Hooker was replaced on June 28, 1863 by Major General George Meade.

pay. They gave three weak cheers. By contrast, Gen. Sully, who saved our skins at Fredericksburg, got a rousing reception.

- 38 -

GETTYSBURG

After two years of war the North had yet to win a decisive battle. This changed in July 1863, beginning with Grant's capture of Vicksburg to open the length of the Mississippi to Union Army traffic.

Even as the guns grew silent at Vicksburg, a battle of equal importance was shaping up in the east where General Lee was once again on the prowl. His objective, along with gaining access to the lush farmlands of southern Pennsylvania, was to discourage the North from continuing the war.

As Lee moved into Pennsylvania, he was shadowed by the Army of the Potomac. On July 1, near the country town of Gettysburg, battle was joined. Its intensity gradually built as each side committed more and more of their forces. After two days of furious combat failed to produce a decision, Lee gambled on the frontal assault since described as "The most thrilling and tragic spectacle ever seen on the American continent" (Hansen, *The Civil War*). Spearheaded by Gen. George Pickett's three brigades, the Rebels stormed through shot and shell toward the Union center entrenched on a rise known as Cemetery Ridge. There, at the peak of the ridge, they were repelled in fierce hand-to-hand combat. When at last their shattered ranks broke, their magnificent failure was to be the final major offensive of a now doomed cause.

Although remnants of First Minnesota helped turn back that assault, later immortalized as "Pickett's Charge," that regiment's hour of glory had occurred the day before. During a heroic charge down the slope from Cemetery Ridge, the First delayed a force six times its size long enough for reinforcements to come up and prevent a Rebel breakthrough. The nearly 200 men First lost that day was the highest percentage of casualties in a single engagement of the Civil War. Among the most seriously wounded was the regiment's commander, Col. William Colvill, who had assumed command, May 6, 1863 after Colonel Morgan fell ill.

General Winfield Hancock, who ordered Colvill to charge at Gettysburg, was later to say, "There is no more gallant deed recorded in history." However, Sergeant Weldon in his diary entry for that day saw it in terms less exultant.

June 30th-Nr Pennsylvania border—Resting here after forced march yesterday. They pushed us hard. Must be something up. Tired but more concerned about blisters. Got one on both feet bigger than a silver dollar. God only knows how far we've traveled by shanks mare in this war. Must have come 140 miles or more since we left Falmouth 2 weeks ago. At least the grub wagon has kept up with us.

July 1st-Moved to a bivouac near a town called Gettysburg. Rumor is there's a fight brewing and we can hear cannon fire. Orders came down for no fires. So it's water and hard tack. Jasper nods off while chewing on his. We pitch our dog tent and pile up some hay for a mattress. There's a feeling about something big tomorrow.

July 2nd-Cemetery Ridge—Can't sleep. Never in my life felt so bad. I sit by flickering embers to write about this awful day. Down slope not very far are 9 from this Co. who were here a few hours ago. Now they're dead, just heaps of bloody rags. One of them is Jasper Sproat. He grabbed my shoulder when we got the order to attack. It was like he was saying goodbye. He's down there somewhere but we couldn't find him. Out of the black silence someone cries out, "Oh, sweet Jesus, help me!"

Before the mists cleared this a.m. we had already marched to this ridge a mile south of Gettysburg. We stayed most of the day atop this ridge near a farmhouse where they said Gen. Meade had his Hqs. Except for a few cannon shells not much happened where we were. About 4 p.m. we got orders to move south along the ridge to support a battery of artillery firing into a peach orchard down below.

A shambles down there, overturned guns, splintered trees, dead horses and shattered bodies. In late afternoon the line down there started to give away. A couple 1,000 Rebs charging and our people stumbling back. Just then a General galloped up and hollered to Col. Colvill to get down there and break up the Rebel advance. It was clear 300 of us couldn't drive off a whole brigade. Best we could do was stall them long enough for help to arrive. The General knew this was a suicide attack and so did we. But when the Col. shouted "Charge," we went with him to a man.

For a time we stayed in good order, trotting down the slope, bayonets fixed, Capt. shouting to hold our fire. Then their canister began ripping holes in our line. Someone near me goes down screaming. Col. Colvill, a head taller than most of us, was out in front with the colors waving his sword when I saw him go down, hurt bad. Running and jumping over a dry creek we charged into them firing, cursing, jabbing and clubbing. Their first line broke and their second faltered. But then they came screeching and driving us back. Took shelter in shallow bank of the creek. Kept up uneven fire fight as they start to get around us. Just when it looked hopeless help came charging in from the flank.

Finally, it got dark and Rebs back off. We had plugged the gap but I doubt a third of the Regiment is still standing. Besides Col. Colvill most of his staff is wounded or killed. In pitch dark we look for wounded. Corpses all around like dis-

carded bundles. We pass Rebs looking for theirs. Too shocked to say anything. Out of the darkness we hear agonized cries of the wounded. We find two of our people and get them carried up and back to a field hospital. Didn't find Jasper but Capt. said he saw him go down with a bullet in his head.

There's 18 of us left in A Co. Tonight we sleep with ghosts.

- 39 -

HAIL AND FAREWELL

The foregoing was the final entry in Sgt. Weldon's dairy. On July 5, with the remnants of First Minnesota helping pursue Lee's forces, he was shot dead by a Rebel sharpshooter. Captain Coates secured his knapsack and a few months later delivered it personally to Weldon's parents in St. Paul. In it, along with the diary, was a bundle of letters from Melissa Hunzinger.

The charge of First Minnesota at Gettysburg has been celebrated in historical retelling and in battle field monuments. When in February 1864 the First came home, schools in St. Paul were let out and the troops were greeted by a mammoth reception. Colonel Colvill, never to fully recover from his wounds, was carried by his men to a carriage for the Regiment's triumphal parade through town.

‡‡ ‡‡ ‡‡ ‡‡ ‡‡

In the rotunda of the Minnesota State Capitol there exists a striking bronze plaque:

IN MEMORY OF

The First Regiment Minnesota Volunteer Infantry. This Was The first Regiment Tendered To President Lincoln At The Outbreak Of The Civil War And It Served For Three Years In The Army Of The Potomac During Which Time It Engaged In The following Battles And Operations:

Bull Run ◆ Ball's Bluff ◆ Siege of Yorktown
Fair Oaks ◆ Peach Orchard ◆ Savage Station
White Oak Swamp ◆ Glendale ◆ Malvern Hill
Flint Hill ◆ Vienna ◆ South Mountain ◆ Antietam
Fredericksburg ◆ Chancellorsville ◆ Hay Market
Gettysburg ◆ Bristow Station ◆ Mine Run

AT GETTYSBURG

The Loss Of The Regiment On July 2nd, 1863 In The Charge Against The Confederate Brigades Of General Barksdale And General Wilcox, Was 82 Percent Of The Men Engaged. General Hancock Ordered The Men To Charge "Because I Saw I Must Gain Five Minutes Time. Reinforcements Were Coming On The Run, But I Knew Before They Could Reach The Threatened Point The Confederates Unless Checked Would Seize The Position. The Charge Was Necessary. I Was Glad To Find Such A Gallant Body Of Men Willing To Make The Terrible Sacrifice."

‡‡ ‡‡ ‡‡ ‡‡ ‡‡

On the second floor of the Capitol rotunda stands a larger-than-life statue of Col. William Colvill. With drawn sword, the figure faces toward the encased colors of the Regiment he commanded on its most valorous day. Although forced by his wounds to hobble with a cane, Colvill survived the War and managed to practice law and tend to his farm holdings. He died at St. Paul on June 13, 1905. As one of his many obituaries noted:

> " … The time, place and manner of the old veteran's death were at once appropriate and pathetic. Coming to the capitol of the Commonwealth which he had so well and nobly served to witness the transfer of … his regiment's battle flags to their magnificent new abode, upon the very eve of the ceremonies in which he was to be perhaps the most striking figure; in the home dedicated to his old comrades, he lay calmly down to sleep at the sounding of taps only to awaken at the reveille of the last trump." *The Daily Pioneer Press*, St. Paul, Minnesota, June 14, 1905.

Through four bitter years of the Civil War, Minnesota troops stayed the course, enduring steamy heat, bone-chilling cold, hunger, fatigue, sickness, and unutterable terrors of battle. From Bull Run to Appomattox, the histories of a dozen Minnesota regiments record their valiant action in almost all the important battles and campaigns of that long and harsh conflict.

Finally able to shed their uniforms, most who had fought and survived under Minnesota colors came home to take part in dynamic changes that reshaped state and nation in the aftermath of war. Many went back to farms or trade, others to law and politics. The list of distinguished public servants who saw service in the Civil War includes nine who were later to become governors of Minnesota.

‡‡ ‡‡ ‡‡ ‡‡ ‡‡

NEWSPAPER ITEM
June 27, 1911

Willmar—A prominent area farmer was one of the survivors of the First Minnesota Regiment of Volunteers honored last week at a reunion in St. Paul. The occasion was the 50th anniversary of the First's departure for the seat of war in Virginia.

Jasper Sproat, 68, from Kandiyohi township, was one of 58 veterans of that famous regiment, who stood on the steps of the old State capitol to review a remarkable parade in their honor.

Sproat, who was grazed in the head by grape shot at Gettysburg, lay unconscious on the battlefield for 24 hours. He was picked up by a Union burial party, who discovering he was alive carried him to a temporary field hospital. Later, he was taken to the Army general hospital near Gettysburg.

His parents, having heard their son was killed, were planning a memorial service when word came that he was alive. Corporal Sproat came home in December 1863 and was mustered out of service at Fort Snelling.

Sproat and his wife, the former Hannah Olsen of Kandiyohi, have reared two sons and three daughters. Charles, the oldest, is named for a wartime comrade buried at Gettysburg.

Besides farming Sproat has served for many years as a township supervisor and a deacon in his church.

Fifty years ago Sproat walked 83 miles to enlist as a private at Fort Snelling. It took him three and a half days. On last week's occasion it needed but three hours to get there in his 1910 Ford touring car.

- 40 -

AFTER THE WAR

The roaring vitality unleashed in America after the Civil War was nowhere better reflected than in Minnesota, where dynamic changes had begun with the driving out of the Sioux. Writing in 1867 to urge kinfolk to follow him, a young Norwegian gave assurance that the Indians "are now chased away." Regardless of justification, removal of the Sioux as a frontier threat had transformed the young state into a haven of settlement. As immigrants began to arrive, Minnesota grew steadily even during the closing years of the war in the South. After more than doubling its population during the years of that conflict, Minnesota jumped from a quarter of a million to nearly 800,000 by 1880. Roughly a third of the newcomers had come from Europe.

New towns were springing up across the state while older places like St. Paul were vaulting in size. The capital city had climbed to 20,000 souls by 1870 and to twice that many ten years later. Even so, and hurtful to St. Paul's civic pride, Minneapolis had caught up and gone a few thousand ahead. For forty years St. Paul had led in population, river trade and commerce. But the 1872 merger with St. Anthony, along with its harnessing of water power for lumber and flour milling, had nudged Minneapolis ahead.

Today, the once bitter rivalry between the two cities has more or less settled into a state of good humored banter. But in 1880, while it still waxed hot and heavy, St. Paul only grudgingly assented to a slim Minneapolis lead. Ten years later, sure that it had caught up or at least held its own, the town was aghast by U.S. census reports that its rival had further widened its lead.

As painstakingly described by Folwell, charges of fraud that followed turned up almost comical examples of padding on both sides. Families had been inflated by the addition of fictitious children, relatives and boarders. Factories reported imaginary employees and sometimes counted workers who had also been counted at home. In St. Paul a single house reported 79 residents. On another street, 78 persons were said to live in a house that was still under construction.

Finally, after months of bitter wrangling, the matter was settled by a recount supervised by agents of the census bureau. Although the result cut into the totals earlier announced, Minneapolis held onto a margin of more than 31,000. It was a lead that was to keep on growing in years ahead. At the time St. Paul took it hard; for days after, its newspapers referred to Minneapolis as "Pad City."

Overlooked in the census controversy was the booming growth of both cities. By 1890 Minneapolis and St. Paul had mushroomed into an urban center of 300,000 people, a leap of almost 1,500 percent in 25 years.

As for Minnesota at large, its post-Civil War growth was a reflection of across-the-state settlement, cultivation of thousands of acres of farmland and the opening of new industries. In order to help compete with other mid-west states for the manpower needed to exploit its resources, a state board was formed to promote immigration. Flyers were printed and agents dispatched to foreign countries to extol the good life of the North Star State. The resulting boost in population led to explosive economic growth.

In the closing decades of the 19th century, Minnesota after shedding its fur-trading legacy became a major supplier to the needs of national expansion. In years leading up to the 1900s, Minnesota grew more wheat, harvested more white pine, milled more flour and scooped up more iron ore than any place else on earth.

- 41 -

LUMBERING IN MINNESOTA

Lumbering first arrived in this area in the 1830s, logging the white pine stands along the St. Croix River. Sawmills were few and much of the lumber was floated down the St. Croix to the Mississippi River and on to the other states. ... By the 1880s the industry boomed with the influx of new wealth. ... Sawmills powered by steam engines ripped through millions of logs annually as lumberjacks spilled out into the forests of the north. In 1900, the peak year of the pine log harvests, the state produced over one billion feet of logs, enough timber to build a nine-foot-wide board walk around the earth at the equator.

Production began to decline after 1905, as pine timber was depleted and timber companies shifted their interest toward new pine stands in the Pacific Northwest and the South. By 1930, the pine sawmill industry died with the closing of the last sawmill near Virginia, Minnesota. After 100 years of logging most of the pine was gone.

— Plaque erected by Minnesota Historical Society, along Interstate Highway 35 in the Kettle River area.

It was not until after the Civil War that the lumber industry began its golden age in Minnesota. Nature had endowed the state with what at the time seemed an unlimited boon of white pine forests. In complement to this marvelous resource were great river highways to carry the lumber to far-off mills.

Much of the lumber produced went to meet needs of the treeless prairie states. Towns like Kansas City, Chicago and St. Louis, reachable either by the Mississippi or through a combination of river and rail, were largely built from lumber hewn in Minnesota.

During all those years of felling Minnesota pine, little thought was given to any notion of replacement. Concern was aroused only after the unthinkable was at hand. Minnesota was running out of white pine. By 1900, arrangements were already underway for moving the industry to other regions.

As one after another of the lumber camps and huge sawmills shut down, the ring of axes fell gradually silent. By the early 1920s the last logs had been cut. And for Minnesota, the colorful era of the lumberjack, a time personified in the legends of Paul Bunyan, was over. The big timber scene had moved on, leaving behind a waste land of stumps, scarred soil and tangled piles of brush.

Here arise questions of value that can neither be avoided nor adequately addressed in a course of this nature. In brief, should the titans of wealth, who led the way to Minnesota's—and by extension America's—phenomenal 19th century growth, be praised for their response to the needs of a lusty nation? Or, are they rather to be condemned as greedy exploiters of a public heritage?

There is no easy answer. For most of America's frontier history, the land and its resources were considered proper subjects for exploitation. Clearly there were abuses by fraudulent land grabbers and cut-and-run despoilers of forest lands. Timber men gobbled up vast tracts of forest in their relentless move westward. Weighed against this is the fact that in the 19th century conservation was a non-issue for most Americans. Lumber was needed for national expansion and it was sublimely believed our timberlands were an endless resource that would always be there. So long as negotiations were above board, lumbermen who sought and acquired cutting grounds as cheaply as possible were merely following the entrepreneurial practices of their times.

Congress, along with the public at large, was deaf to the cries of the few who, like Carl Schurz (Secretary of Interior under President Rutherford B. Hayes), pleaded for controlled cutting and crackdown on shady land deals. America in the closing years of the 19th century was a nation dependent on wood for every aspect of urban and rural life. The demand was insatiable, not only for homes, farms and factories, but also for thousands of miles of railroad track laid down on hundreds of millions of wooden ties. In the process of meeting such demands, Minnesota lumber barons were providing wages for countless lumberjacks, sawmill workers, carpenters and the like, who had come here in hopes of a better economic life.

In a classic case of locking the barn door too late, public anger over logging shenanigans was aroused only after the closing of the white pine era. In belated hue and cry, the entire industry was taken to task, in some cases unfairly. For while it is true that lumber empires such as the Weyerhaeuser companies were negligent about conservation, so too, it must be said, was the rest of the nation to whose wants they were so enormously contributing.

The debate continues today. Lumber interests speak proudly of their programs to regenerate new forests from cutover land. Tree farms, they argue, provide a renewable resource. As old timber is felled, they say it is being replenished by systematic planting.

Conservationists disagree, claiming that the half a century of growth projected before the harvest of newly planted trees is far less than the centuries required to replace the forests they are cutting down. They argue forcefully against what they consider the plunder of such of our national heritage as America's redwood forests.

The controversy, if anything, has grown even more heated and is far more complicated than can be resolved in our short time together. On one side is the economic fact of employment for millions while meeting a specific and urgent demand for building materials. On the other are moral and ecological concerns for protecting a precious natural resource. As always in a democracy, ultimate solutions rest with greater or lesser public mood for change.

Those who wish to look further into this debate are referred to several studies which, in espousing opposing views, offer bibliographic reference to support arguments on either side. *Defending the Environment,* by Joseph Sax (New York: Alfred A. Knopf, 1970), takes up the cause for conservation. *Timber and Men, a history of the Weyerhaeuser companies* (New York: MacMillan Company, 1963) speaks to the industry side.

- 42 -

HOW KALLE MAKKI BECAME A LUMBERJACK

There is no one still around who lived through the glory days of logging in Minnesota. However, one who was there as they ended was my Great-Uncle Kalle, who went into the woods at a time when the industry here was still in swing, even though past its peak. Hiring on with the Cloquet Lumber Company, 20-year-old Kalle Makki found himself working with grizzled oldsters, including some who had worked in the woods during the roaring days of Minnesota's logging boom.

Here follow excerpts from Kalle's story as told by his son, who is also my cousin once removed and is now a lumber executive in Everett, Washington: *Fifty Years A Lumberman*, unpublished manuscript, 1968, by Richard Makki. I include them in this course by way of bringing back to life what was perhaps Minnesota's most colorful era.

‡‡ ‡‡ ‡‡ ‡‡ ‡‡

Although he didn't know it, the day my father went to work for Cloquet Lumber was the start of a lifetime in the logging business. That was after he dropped out of the University of Minnesota in 1913.

During two and half years at the University, Dad earned more distinction on the gridiron than in the classroom. But his reasons for leaving were not academic. His transcript reveals nothing worse than a cluster of C's and a few B's. The simple fact was that after a knee injury, he lost his football scholarship. He went to work hoping to earn the means to come back and graduate.

Dad could have hired on with his father's carpenter crew back home in Hibbing, except at age 20, he wanted his independence. Also, he once told me, after a dozen Saturday afternoons hearing the roar of thousands jammed into college football stadiums, the sound of pounding nails struck him as pretty dull. Despite a slight limp, he still had strength and agility, and the lure of a season or two in a logging camp was a compelling challenge.

In those years, Cloquet, with a vast supply of pine floated down from nearby rivers, was an important center of the Weyerhaeuser logging empire. Milling operations had begun there some 20 years earlier when the place was still a rude village known as Knife Falls. Although the St. Louis River bordered it, the town had since been renamed for an upriver tributary, the Cloquet. By the time of my father's arrival, the place had grown to a full-sized town of more than nine thousand people, with Cloquet Lumber being but one of four mills operated there by Weyerhaeuser.

Each of these mills ran separate logging camps. And it was to Cloquet Lumber's Camp Two that Kalle Makki was assigned in early winter of 1913. If it was adventure he sought, Dad got all he wanted in short order. One glance around the bunkhouse told him he was the youngest, in some cases by 30 or 40 years, of Camp Two's 60-man crew. He was also the only one there to have set foot in a place of higher learning.

The one man there bigger than Dad was a hulking bully with a game leg and a layer of fat over his burly shoulders. Once "Frenchy" Bernier had been the ablest and most daring of all lumberjacks working for Cloquet Lumber. In winter the brutish son of a French Canadian trapper and an Ojibway mother was an axe-man renowned as the king of choppers. In spring, working with cant hook and peavey, he guided winter-cut logs down plunging rapids to the mill. In this risky work, as with axe and saw, he was the best, the boldest and most boastful.

But then, in a mammoth log jam still talked about years later, he was knocked into the frigid waters by a hurtling log. Somehow, despite the agony of a crushed leg, he managed to fight free of the maelstrom of swirling logs and rapids. Although he survived and gradually regained his strength, Frenchy's days as a lumberjack were over. Now, as the camp's "Bull Cook," he kept the kitchen and the mess hall clean, tended fires and hauled the men's lunch out to the cutting grounds. He was also the unofficial "Boss of the Bunkhouse," making bed assignments, toting wood for the stoves and rousting out the men in the morning while lashing them with bitter invective.

Though hobbled, Frenchy Bernier was still powerful and feared as the meanest man in camp. Never to recover from his lost eminence, he was a man driven by dark resentment and ever on the lookout for somebody to stomp in a knockdown bunkhouse brawl. One look at the new college kid and Frenchy reckoned he'd found just the scapegoat he needed for venting his sour spleen.

The goading began the first morning, when instead of standing at the end of the bunkhouse, Frenchy limped down to Dad's bunk in order to blast his wake-up horn directly into his ear. Jolted out of a deep sleep, my father stared dumb-faced as the snarling Bull Cook pulled him by his union suit and roared, "You collitch kid—Go fetch wood!"

On this, his first morning, Dad was the rawest of greenhorns. No one had told him about Frenchy, or what was his authority. But on a new job and anxious to oblige, Dad tugged on his boots and went out into the darkness to pick up an armload of wood. If Frenchy had been alert he might have noticed what Dad brought back was almost twice what most could tote. Instead, after sneering at the rest of the crew, he glared back at

Dad, "Next time you better move quicker"

At breakfast, where the rule was "eat fast and no talkin'," no one spoke to Dad. As a greenhorn, he was bottom man on the camp totem pole. On top was the foreman, a laconic type, who slept by himself in the camp office, and whose $150 a month pay depended on meeting his production quota. After laying out the cutting areas and assigning the workers, his only concern for the men was the number of logs they stacked up. Short of burning it down, what happened in the bunkhouse was not his problem.

Ranking just below the foreman in camp hierarchy, and the real "King Bee" of the camp, was the chief cook, who more than anyone was responsible for keeping the men happy. In a logging camp, where life boiled down to grinding toil and huge appetites, nothing could cause the crews to jump ship quicker than a "belly robber," who served bad food.

Next in camp importance followed a cluster of varying skills: sawyers and choppers, teamsters, blacksmiths, a saw filer, skidders, a barn boss and so on down to where my father toiled 12 hours a day cleaning out slash and other debris left after the stripping of felled lumber. Day after day, Dad dragged himself back to camp, aching in back, legs and arms, wryly recalling he had once thought football practice was tough. And morning after morning he was blasted out of his bunk by the blare of Frenchy's bullhorn. Each day the bully came up with a new goading demand. One time it would be cleaning out ashes, another it would be trimming lamp wicks or wiping soot out of the globes.

Dad wasn't intimidated by his bellicose tormentor. But with nobody to tell him different, he simply assumed his was standard hazing for greenhorns. Kind of like his days as a fraternity pledge.

Meanwhile, he was observing and learning. Days out in the woods, he watched the easy rhythm of the choppers swinging with precise strokes deep into their chopping wedge. At night, he looked on as the cutters honed and whetstoned their axes to a razor's edge. Their's was the job he wanted and knew he could do well. But first there was the problem of hazing. He'd put up with it without a whimper, but after a week, he'd had enough.

Dad had learned that while none of the jacks would volunteer information, they'd usually respond to a direct question. Alone one night with "Fullhouse Phil," who'd logged for the company since its earliest days, Dad asked him about camp rules.

"Whataya mean rules?"

"You know, the ones about how long a greenhorn has to put up with this crap I'm getting from Frenchy?"

"Oh, them rules," and Fullhouse Phil turned away as though to end the subject. But then he hesitated. "Look kid, there ain't no rules. That big slob'll keep after you just as long as you let him."

Dad winced as it sank in that what he had gone through wasn't hazing.

"What can I do about it?"

"You been to college, kid. Ya oughta be able to figger that out."

It was two nights later before Dad was able to corner Fullhouse Phil again. "I've been thinking about what you told me"

"Yeah, whataya gonna do about it?"

"Well, I just wanted to ask what happens if I get in it with Frenchy? Am I liable to get fired?"

"Only if you kill him. Nobody likes the sunava bitch. But he gets away with it cuz everybody's scared of him, even the boss."

Fullhouse looked at Dad. "You're big enough maybe to handle him. But you better get it done quick cuz he'll come at you kick'n, goug'n and bite'n."

The showdown came the next night, when Frenchy stormed into the bunkhouse to order Dad over to the cook shack to scour pots and kettles. This was clearly part of a bull cook's chores and as a quiet fell over the bunkhouse, Dad just smiled.

"Nah, Frenchy, that's a job for pigs like you."

Frenchy blinked, and then with a bellow like a wounded

moose, he charged. But to a young buck who four months before had gone head-to-head with a future Wisconsin Hall of Fame tackle, Frenchy was just a fat old man. Dad hit him with a flying tackle that slammed the old bull's head back onto the pinewood floor.

Groggy but snarling Frenchy struggled to sit up only to be poleaxed by a double-fisted, swung-from-the-floor rocket that caught him square under the chin. Then, to the incredulous eyes of 60 bunkmates, Dad hefted the old bull like a sack of potatoes, kicked open the door and threw him head first into a snow bank.

As Frenchy came around Dad grabbed him by the collar. "Listen to me good, Fatso. If you ever give me trouble again I'm gonna personally kick your sorry butt all the way up to Canada."

When Dad came back in, the bunkhouse had a new unofficial boss. Some worried that Frenchy might slip back with a knife. But the next morning, ten minutes late, one of the cook's assistants delivered the wake-up call. He reported that the bull cook had turned into a defeated old man moping in a corner of the kitchen. And that night when the men came in from the woods, Frenchy Bernier was gone, never to show his face around Camp Two again.

Two days later, Dad was assigned to Fullhouse Phil's felling crew.

- 43 -

LIFE IN THE WOODS

As a tree feller, Kalle Makki found life much more to his liking. Along with a pay jump to $45 a month went the satisfaction of work for which he was a natural. The day still began with a pre-dawn wakeup. But to Kalle, the call of "Coffee's bilin' ... Come and get it," was almost musical compared to the screech of Frenchy's bullhorn.

After a splash in the face with cold water, the men bundled up with layers of clothing. Like the rest of the jacks, Kalle wore a union suit which doubled as pajamas. Over this went a cotton parka topped by a plaid wool shirt and a double-breasted mackinaw. Crammed into the pockets were extra gloves and wool socks for changing after the first pairs, soaked by sweat and snow, began to freeze.

Breakfast was a gargantuan affair with mounds of flapjacks, slabs of ham, oatmeal, fried potatoes, biscuits, toast and jam, washed down with gallons of scalding coffee. This was "packing" for a long day's toil in the penetrating chill of a Minnesota winter. And no one stoked it down with more gusto than my Great-Uncle Kalle.

Out in the woods, still before daylight, the felling crew tramped through snow drifts and across frozen marshes to the chopping ground staked out by the foreman. Once there, they picked out trees earlier notched for cutting.

Fullhouse Phil had taken Kalle under his wing and in short order taught him the swinging arc that allowed the double-bitted axe to do the work instead of the muscles. Working in easy tandem, the two soon moved to the top of the camp's cutting crews. After picking a tree, the pair would first chop out a deep wedge on one side of the trunk. Then, picking up an eight-foot crosscut saw, they moved to the other side of the trunk and began to cut a few inches above the wedge. Pushing and pulling in steady rhythm, they most always brought down even the thickest of tall pines in five or six minutes.

After cleaning their resin-pitched saw blade with a kerosene-soaked rag, they moved on to the next tree. In that fashion, felling five or more trees an hour, they usually brought down fifty or more pines a day. Along with being the fastest cutting team, Kalle and Fullhouse several times won the "stake-driving pot."

This was a contest of felling accuracy in which each crew anted up fifty cents a week to see which one of them could drop a tree so precisely as to land on a stake partly driven into the ground. In case of a tie, the winner was determined by which stake was driven the deepest. As Kalle recalled, he and Fullhouse won it three or four times, usually for about five dollars. The only problem was, if they got to town Saturday night, the winners bought the first round.

Meanwhile, as the fellers moved on to another tree, a lot of action followed in their wake. Immediately behind came a team of sawyers to square off the butt of the trunk and section it into manageable logs. Next came strippers to cut off branches and remove bark for easier skidding along the frozen ground.

It being important to get the logs out before they were blanketed by snow, a skid team moved in quickly. Working with a horse, or in places less accessible, using sheer brawn, they muscled the logs to a collection point. From there, loaders used chains and levers to pile the big logs on horse-drawn sleds for hauling over icy skidways to a nearby float stream.

Long before the jacks had tumbled out of their bunks, road monkeys had been out icing tote roads. Inside a huge sprinkling tank mounted on a sled was a built-in stove to keep the water from freezing.

At the collection point, landing men used a heavy stamping maul to mark each end of the logs with the Camp Two brand. Then the logs were stacked up in huge banks at river's edge to await spring thaw.

For all hands, it was a daily routine broken up only by the clang of an iron triangle to signal the arrival of lunch. The men swarmed in to cluster around a slash fire. Except for Sundays, their noon meal was always served at the work site. The fare, brought in by sled in insulated boxes, consisted of hot soup, pork and beans, mashed potatoes, corn bread, cookies and hot tea. The men wolfed it down before the beans froze on their plates or the tea skimmed over with ice.

After a few pulls on their pipes it was back to work. Fullhouse Phil, who didn't smoke, carried a plug of chaw tobacco which he generously offered his young partner. But after almost losing his lunch over his first chomp, Kalle never tried a second.

Despite the harshness of winter in the north woods, sickness was rarely a problem. However, accidents were. And it was a rare camp where one or more jacks weren't maimed or killed on the job. If the injury was minor—a cut, scrape or even a chopped-off finger—a jack would shrug it off. The wound could be cauterized by a squirt of tobacco juice and sealed with pine pitch.

Really serious injuries most often occurred during the felling of a tall tree. Such accidents—the men called them "widow makers"—might happen when a big pine crashing down got tangled up with another tree to hurl shattered branches down on the less nimble of foot. If not fatal, accidents of this kind usually led to rude emergency aid—splinting, tourniquets, a sling or a crutch—followed by a painful siege of bunk house recuperation.

If the injury was beyond the rustic skills of a camp practitioner, there loomed the jolting agony of a sleigh ride back to proper medical treatment in Cloquet. On arrival, the driver sometimes skipped the clinic in order to go straight to the undertaker.

After charging at timber all day, the men came in from the woods red-faced with cold. Crowding around the giant cookhouse ranges, they dipped their cups into pots of boiling tea waiting for them. Then after a yell of "Soup's On," they fell to for a huge evening meal that might include roast pork, beef stew, baked beans, mashed potatoes, bread, tubs of rice pudding, platters of cookies and rows of apple pie.

At night in the bunkhouse where the men pulled off boots and hung wet clothes to dry, the pungence was a blend of steaming socks, sweat, tobacco and wood smoke. Years later Kalle claimed he could be taken blindfolded into a logging bunkhouse and know at the first whiff where he was.

For an hour or so before turning in, it was a time for mending socks, lighting up pipes and spinning yarns. Lumbering had gone through a number of changes during its colorful history in Minnesota. And Kalle, astride the long "deacon's seat," picked up much of its lore listening to old jacks talk about their experiences in earlier times. One of them, "Two Bit" Johansson, loved to tell about the days when the chopper was king. That was around 1880 when Cloquet was still known as Knife River Falls. The sawmill company of that name was taken over by Weyerhaeuser in 1883.

Two Bit, whose nickname attested to skill with a double-edged axe, was 16 when he hired on as a camp "cookie." For $15 a month plus room and board, he peeled potatoes, stoked fires, set tables and scrubbed pots and pans. By the time he was 18, he'd moved into the woods as an axe man at a dollar a day. This, before big-bladed crosscut saws bumped the chopper off this throne.

Two Bit insisted that jacking back when the axe men did it all was a lot tougher. Once the tree was down, they stripped it, sawed it into sections and used a crude sled called a "go-devil," to muscle the logs down to river's edge.

At night, they came back to a camp that was little more than a shanty, with a cook pit at one end and space to sleep on the floor at the other. A hole in the roof let the smoke out along with the shanty's heat. Chow was a familiar sequence of meals limited to dry stores. And a cook was known by his beans.

Cooked properly, beans were a work-of-art that began with an all-day soaking. Then they were scalded and put in a huge pot along with sliced onions, strips of white pork and molasses stirred-in to cook's taste. Finally, the pot would be sealed and buried in embers of the bean hole. By the next morning the mixture was a thick, golden dish served along with flapjacks at breakfast and again with other staples at lunch and supper.

Things changed as railroad spurs were extended into cutting areas. Fresh meat and other perishables were brought in from Cloquet or Duluth, dropped off at nearby collection points and hauled into camp by horse-drawn sled.

The ever-swelling demand for white pine led to mechanized improvements. Two-man saws speeded up the felling process. And the old go-devil disappeared into logging oblivion, replaced by horse or ox-drawn sledges able to carry much larger loads to water's edge. As more contrivances came along to speed up work, so did the need for special skills: saw men, strippers, teamsters, smithies, saw filers and the like. New and larger camps sprang up to handle crews that shortly doubled and tripled in size. By 1900, Minnesota was the biggest logging state in the Union with as many as 40,000 jacks in its forests.

Two Bit remembered a time when a 15 or 20 man crew slept on pine boughs at one end of the shanty under a blanket that stretched across them all. They woke to the clatter of pots and pans at the other end. Now the camps were like a compound, with separate quarters for cooking and sleeping, along with a company store, a barn, blacksmith forge and a shop for filing and grinding. The bunkhouse slept up to eighty hands with separate bunks and straw mattresses.

"You boys think you got it tough," Two Bit snorted. "How it was back then woulda sent you bawlin' for your mommies."

He paused while the men hooted. "When once a month or so, we'd get into town, all we could get was corn likker for a nickel a jar. 'Squirrel Whiskey' it was. Only a real man could drink that."

"Squirrel Whisky?"

"Yup. One drink of that and you'd run up a tree like a squirrel."

Although Kalle joined in the good-natured joshing, he reckoned those old boys really did have it tougher.

According to Two Bit, "What really separated out the ribbon clerks," was when the river drive got underway. That was when the ice began to melt and the tote roads became too mushy for skidding logs.

In mid-April the winter cutting ended and most of the jacks left to work on farms or sawmills, or sometimes just to carouse in a grand spree that might last till their money ran out. Only the nimble and the bold stayed over for the hard and dangerous work of driving logs. One of them from Camp Two, challenged by accounts of this most capricious aspect of logging, was Kalle Makki. Here, we return once more to his story as recorded by my cousin Richard Makki.

- 44 -

RIVER DRIVING

Each spring after the ice break-up, "river pigs" descended on the stream and river landings where thousands upon thousands of logs were stacked. First, they needed to topple the huge banks of logs into the waters below, a job that called for iron nerves and exceptional brawn.

To start a tumble-down, men with peaveys poked and pried to loosen key logs. Once something moved there was a shout and a mad scramble for safety. Rare was the season when death or serious injury did not occur for one or more unfortunates trapped by an avalanche of crashing logs.

Once the branded logs were rolled into waters swollen by rain and melting snow, the river drive was underway. My father, Kalle Makki, worked hard and at risk, helping get the logs into the river. But for all his strength and courage, he knew he was in over his head the first time he saw a white water man gracefully riding a log downstream. These were men who as kids had begun to master the art of balance on a spinning log by practice on a rolling barrel. To watch them now, with caulked boots and spiked soles, hopping nimbly from one log to another, herding them through seething rapids and around bends, was to witness grace and cool disdain for danger not unlike a Spanish bullfighter.

Without experience and with a trick knee, Dad knew this

was a craft in which he was never going to excel. But game to the core, he tried, and after repeated dunkings into the frigid waters, won the grudging respect of even the most arrogant of the live water men.

Fullhouse Phil, past his prime as a log rider, finally advised Dad to join him in working from a bateau. * *"You plainly got the guts, partner. You just ain't got the swagger. But you can do real good work in a bateau."*

And that is where Dad spent the Spring of 1914, following the main drive as part of a rowboat clean-up crew. Ahead of them the white water boys kept great masses of logs moving toward down-river sorting booms. The bateau crews bringing up the rear were like cowboys rounding up strays, jabbing at logs piled up on rocks or along the shoreline, sometimes wading in shallows to free up logs snagged on a sandbar.

And like cowboys, they sometimes had to deal with rustlers, who skulked along river's edge waiting for a chance to pirate off valuable logs hung up along the shoreline.

One day a straw boss detached Dad's bateau crew to clear out a small jam of logs pushed by quirk of current into a backwater of the St. Louis River. Camping along the shore that night, Dad woke up to the squeal of an ox cart moving away from where they had been working. Pulling on his boots and armed only with a logging pike, he followed the sound for a half mile or so into a moonlit clearing. He watched as two men unloaded the logs before retiring into a tumble-down shanty. Then he hunkered down until dawn crept up to reveal a stack of logs piled up by a crude sawing shed.

Thinking to himself that here was about as far down the entrepreneurial ladder as you could get, Dad set to work piling hay next to the shanty. Then he threw a rock at the door.

"Wake up in there! And just one of you come out with your hands up."

After a minute a scraggly oldster stepped out in his long

---

* A stout rowboat pointed on both ends.

johns. Crouching behind the ox cart, Dad hollered: "Here's the deal, old man. I got five men here ready to torch this place with you inside. Or you can haul this pile of logs back where they belong and nobody gets hurt."

"But them's our logs."

"That so? Then how come you put a Cloquet Lumber brand on 'em?"

When the old fellow hesitated, Dad prompted him. "I ain't gonna waste any more talk. Get your partner out here with his hands up. If he comes out with a gun, you're both dead men."

When the second man turned out to be a younger copy of the first, Dad reckoned he was dealing with a father and son business.

"If anybody else is in there, they better come out, cause we're fixin' to fire this place."

When nobody came, Dad yelled back to the woods. "O,K. fellas. Keep these two covered while I check the place out."

Then running up to the shack, he kicked the door open and charged in to find nobody. When he came out clutching a loaded shotgun, Dad was in total command.

By late afternoon and still clad in their long johns, the rustlers had made two trips to the river hauling back about fifty company logs. Dad, riding shotgun, decided on one more bluff.

"Now I'm gonna turn you over to the foreman." He paused. "He's a mean 'un. I guess you'd be better off if we hung you right here."

While the two miscreants howled for mercy, Dad pretended to think it over.

"All right," he finally nodded. "I'll give you one chance to vamoose. If you're around these parts in the morning, you'll be pushing up sod by noon."

Although timber rustling continued to be a problem along the St. Louis, nobody remembered coming across that pair again. Meanwhile, word of my father's remarkable recovery of half a hundred company logs spread quickly throughout the Cloquet logging community.

The drive foreman himself came by to pat Dad on the back and hand him the ten dollar gold piece he wore for the rest of his days on his watch fob. He called it his good-luck charm because after he got it, his life in the timber business got steadily better.

Just like in the woods, it took food and plenty of it to keep the river crews happy and working well. The only difference was that on the river the men did not swarm in to camp for supper. Instead it came to them in a kitchen scow called a "wanigan," that followed along behind the main drive.

The crew aboard a wanigan included a pair of brawny sweeps, who muscled stout oars to keep the scow on even keel through stretches of white water. The cook and helpers got up long before the drivers to make breakfast and mounds of sandwiches for the men to carry in their lunch "nosebags." Next, even before casting off to follow the drive, they peeled potatoes, soaked beans, and baked bread and pies to get supper underway.

One corner of the wanigan served as a company store, selling tobacco, snuff, spare socks and the like. The store keeper was a grizzled ex-jack known as "The Beaver," so named for the beaver-like chips he had once piled up during his tree chopping days. Although the Beaver couldn't read, he could count. And using his fingers like an abacus he easily kept track of his sales. After toting up the bill, he made his customers sign or make their mark next to the total he toted up in his ledger. At pay day the tab would be deducted from their wages.

The Beaver's days as a jack had ended years before during a massive log jam on the St. Croix River. As he told it, a snag at Taylor's Falls started a back-up from hundreds of camps. Before word got out to suspend further drives the jumble of tangled logs stretched upriver for miles. For six weeks, sawmills down river at Stillwater stood idle as 200 men worked round-the-clock to break it up.

Beaver was one of a dozen hands maimed in the process. While jabbing with his pike, he loosened a log that smashed down on his shoulder. After a long, painful recovery, he found himself no longer able to handle a pike or swing an axe. After that, he managed to hang on in the woods as saw filer, cook's helper and finally storekeeper. His retelling of the St. Croix log jam of 1886 made for a colorful campfire tale. The men, soaking it up, didn't know that they were shortly to be caught up in a jam of their own.

It happened after the main drive got snagged on a sand bar just past where the Whiteface River runs into the St. Louis. Though not as large as the great St. Croix jam, the choke-up of logs stopped traffic on both rivers. With no logs to saw, mills down river stood idle while river pigs poked and pried to break it up. Rudolph Weyerhaeuser, in charge of the company mills in Cloquet, came up to the site to see for himself the extent of the problem.

With their boats blocked by a heaving sea of jammed-up logs, the bateau crews came ashore to help wherever they could. My father inched his way across heaped-up tangles out to where the white water men took their lives in their hands probing to break up the jam. Crouched alongside a wall of piled up timber, they jabbed with peavies trying to locate and loosen key logs.

Whenever something started to move, everyone scrambled to get out of the way of a deadly tumble-down. Once one of the men slipped and was almost trapped between slowly twisting logs before Dad grabbed him by the back of his shirt and yanked him to safety.

When Rudolph Weyerhaeuser, standing on the shore, happened to see Dad's quick action, he asked the name of the rescuer. Upon learning it was the same man who had so recently recovered a pile of logs stolen from the company, he went up to shake Dad's hand. "Young man, after this drive is over, I'd like you to come and see me."

When, a week or so later, the jam was finally broken up, Dad stayed with the drive down to where boom masters shunted the logs into huge enclosures and sorted them out according to brand marks. The first drive was over. But before going back for another, the crews swarmed into town to blow off steam.

Much later that night, Dad and Fullhouse Phil sat nursing a final mug of watered-down rum. Fullhouse, after a polite hiccup, began what may have been the longest speech of his life.

"Well partner, I don't think we'll be seeing much of ya after ya talk to the old man. But I gotta tell ya kid. Ya got the stuff and here's wishing ya luck."

Dad grabbed the older man by his shoulders. "I don't know what's gonna happen, Phil. But I owe you more'n I can say. You're my friend and I ain't never gonna forget you."

‡‡ ‡‡ ‡‡ ‡‡ ‡‡

I have introduced Uncle Kalle Makki's year as a lumberjack to provide a glimpse into that life before human brawn gave way to mechanical contrivance. This, while there were still enough white pine stands to keep the industry going in Minnesota. Logging companies in Cloquet kept busy up to the end of World War I. But with dwindling supplies of white pine, the end was in sight.

Meanwhile, with sponsorship from Rudolph Weyerhaeuser, Kalle was learning the milling end of the business. By 1916, he was foreman for a company subsidiary that logged tamarack and cedar to make railroad ties and fence posts. In 1917, after being turned down for military service because of his football knee, Kalle was promoted to manage the company's planing mill.

In mid-October of 1918, he was one of a few dozen men to stay behind during the fire that ravaged Cloquet's mills and virtually wiped out the town. Using hoses and a bucket line down to the river, they were able to save the company's steam mill and part of the town's industrial section. Dawn found the cinder-coated fire fighters staring bleakly at smoldering ashes, charred stone foundations and twisted metal. Overnight a thriving center of the lumber industry had all but vanished.

In what has been called "The Miracle of Cloquet," only a

handful of people perished from the inferno that engulfed their city. Some had fled on foot, others by automobile. However, it was railroad trains and the heroic action of their crews that carried nearly 8,000 people to safety. Elsewhere in the area, the toll was much worse. The calamity has been judged the worst ever in Northern Minnesota.

Kalle Makki remained in Cloquet during much of the work of its rebuilding. But by 1920, with most of its virgin pine depleted, logging in Minnesota was almost over. Years before, as early as the 1890s, Midwest lumbermen had begun looking for new sources. By the turn of the century, Weyerhaeuser interests had bought up huge tracts of Douglas firs in the Pacific Northwest.

In 1920, following the recommendation of his mentor, Rudolph Weyerhaeuser, Kalle went west to manage a company milling unit in Everett, Washington. His only condition was to be allowed to take along Fullhouse Phil. His old friend adapted quickly to forests of towering fir and finished out his logging days as a timber cruiser.

It was in Everett that Kalle met Annabelle Cromer, the daughter of a local shopkeeper. They were married in 1923. And it was Richard, the oldest of their three children, who compiled the story of his father's half century in the timber business.

Kalle Makki retired in 1963 at age 70. Although he kept touch with kin in Buhl by occasional letter or phone call, he never came back. Dad and Uncle Ty Makki remember him from when they were boys, but I never set eyes on my Great-Uncle or Great-Aunt Annabelle. Now they are both gone.

- 45 -

A LETTER FROM CHRISTIE

Snowflakes falling softly transformed the Harwell campus into a Currier and Ives Christmas Scene. Christmas! It seemed barely yesterday I was saying hello to my class in Minnesota history. Now, with just seven lectures to go, I had to finish it off with a look at the state's transition from rural-agrarian to urban-cosmopolitan.

It was Saturday evening and I had spent the day in the library digging up information about Minnesota in the 20th century. Now as I trudged toward my bachelor digs, chimes from the chapel carillon somehow stirred an ache of longing. Fact is, I was damn lonely. My pal Sue Humboldt was off seeing her boyfriend that weekend, and I missed her. Worse, I still hadn't heard from Christie White. Even after all these years it was hard for me to think of her as Christie Cosgrove. A few weeks before in Duluth things had seemed so hopeful. I had even dreamed of somehow seeing her at Christmas. But there had been no word and I didn't know why or what to do about it. As it turned out, these questions were shortly to be answered.

The blue envelope with its distinctive handwriting fluttered out as I opened my mailbox. No return address. But I had no doubt who it was from. Dropping my book bag on the floor, I tore open the envelope. And there it was, my future with

Christie spelled out in one word: None!

Like a kid who'd just learned the truth about Santa Claus, I sat there crushed and confused. Finally, grasping for even a glimmer of hope, I slowly reread her letter.

December 12, 1972
Jim, Dearest Jim:

How do you tell someone you love that you are going to marry someone else? You see, Jim, I haven't been honest with you. My marriage to Buddy is over. I think you can guess why. He had moved out and I had filed for divorce even before I saw you last month. I couldn't bear to tell you because I was already engaged to another man. Then when you called I knew I simply had to see you. And I will cherish that night all my life.

Jim dearest, I am not the girl you think I am. The truth is I am selfish and spoiled rotten. My breakup with Buddy wasn't all his fault. I simply wanted more out of life than he was able to give me. And that, dearest, is my fear about us. I can't see myself as the wife of a college professor. Before long we'd both be unhappy. And you deserve better than that.

Don is older but very nice and able to give us the kind of life we both want. By the time you read this we'll be on our honeymoon. After that we'll live in San Francisco.

Jim, my knight in shining armor, please believe that you'll be in my heart for all of my days. I beg you not to think too badly of me.

Christie

It's not easy to live with bitterness. Did I hate her? Not really. I was more upset with myself for being so hopelessly moonstruck. How could I have been dopey enough to think Christie and I had a future? How could I have gone so long chasing a will-o-the-wisp?

Foolish or not, don't let anybody tell you a thing like that doesn't hurt. I know better. Because deep down inside, there was a ragged hole in my life. I ached for months. At night I tossed and groaned. Daytimes in the research stacks, I'd drift away to hear the huskiness of her voice or sense the touch of her fingers alongside my face.

During those months that I recall as my "wallow of despond," Sue Humboldt was a rock of support. But a busted romance is one of those things that only time can deal with. Gradually my unhappiness about Christie seeped away. Whatever was left seemed a vague sense of having lost something I'd never really had—in short, a fantasy.

- 46 -

A METROPOLIS IS BORN

As the glory years of fur trading came to a close, lumbering had come along to take its place as the state's top industry. Next, after the Civil War, circumstances arose that were to thrust Minnesota into world leadership in wheat and flour production.

The Homestead Act of 1862, in company with railroad land grants, made available vast acres of fertile soil. At the same time an extending network of railroads brought in European immigrants eager to acquire free or cheap farmland. Going the other way, the railroads carried out farm goods headed for distant markets. With wheat as the major crop, farming had blossomed into a major industry, its yields greatly increased by the invention of mechanical reapers and other labor-saving implements. And in Minneapolis, new grinding methods led to the milling of a superior flour.

The influx of immigrants propelled state population to 1.3 million by 1890, of which seventy percent was farm related. Farmers hauled their grain to towns that had sprung up alongside the railroads. There, the grain could be stored in elevators to await favorable prices before being shipped by rail to Minneapolis.

By 1875, two-thirds of Minnesota farmlands were planted in wheat and Minneapolis had become widely known as "Mill

City." The irony is that except for the Falls of St. Anthony, Minneapolis, if in fact a place of that name even existed, might today be little more than a suburb of St. Paul. Father Louis Hennepin could not have dreamed that the roaring cataract he had named would two centuries later bring about the birth of a great industrial metropolis.

For many years, visitors, including artists who came to view or sketch the Falls, were drawn solely by scenic beauty. The first to visualize use of its cascading power was Col. Joseph Snelling, who as commandant of the fort that bears his name erected both a saw and a grist mill on the west bank.

However, it took the entrepreneurial instincts of Henry Sibley and his always profit-seeking brother-in-law, Franklin Steele, to realize the value to be gained through private possession of the Falls. Folwell describes how Steele, who was post sutler at Fort Snelling, preempted the east bank of the Falls barely ahead of the fort's then commander, whose covetous eye had been beamed on the same property. It seems both Steele and Colonel Joseph Plympton got word of the land's availability at the same time. But in a classic example of the early bird getting the worm, Steele got there first.

As Folwell tells it, Steele " … With one or more assistants … immediately started along the east bank of the river for the falls. Working by moonlight they staked out a claim along a stretch of surging rapids."

Colonel Plympton was content to wait till morning before starting out with a small squad of soldiers. Proceeding along the west bank, he forded the river above the falls where he turned downstream to find the land he had hoped to claim already snapped up by the fort's storekeeper.

After much contention involving law suits and the selling off of properties to meet over-extended loans, Steele managed to raise the capital needed to develop the Fall's power-making capabilities.

In 1848, he and his associates dammed the river's eastern channel, constructed sluiceways to regulate water flow, and built mills to saw the logs as they were floated down the Mississippi. Then, as the area around the Falls blossomed into a community, Steele shortened its name to St. Anthony.

During the 1850s, with sawmilling developing as a prime industry, Steele helped establish booms above the Falls to catch and sort logs coming down from up-river lumber camps. Most of the logs dispatched through the St. Anthony booms were assembled into huge rafts and floated to mills as far south as St. Louis. But the St. Anthony mills also kept busy sawing lumber to meet expanding local needs including those of nearby St. Paul.

Side-by-side with sawing operations, there were shortly erected mills that soon began producing high quality flour for national and world markets. With lumber and flour mills humming on the east bank of the Falls, covetous eyes turned toward land across the river still lying within the boundaries of the Fort Snelling reservation. A first toehold on the west bank had already been wrested by means of trickery and political influence.

Illinois Congressman Robert Smith, pretending to live on nearby land, petitioned the War Department to let him use waterfront acreage for subsistence farming purposes. It seems inconceivable that a ruse so transparent could have been successful. Nevertheless, in 1849, Smith was granted a lease on the west bank where the Army's old grist and lumber mill stood.

That was the breakthrough, and in short order other land along the west bank was occupied. At Steele's suggestion, his associate, John Stevens, won a lease in return for operating a ferry at the Falls. There, where wigwams still stood, Stevens built the first permanent home on land that would one day be part of the city to be known as Minneapolis—a name derived from a combination of *Minnehaha*, the Sioux word for laughing waters, and *polis*, the Greek word for city.

Others, including officers from Fort Snelling, speculators, and settlers, also marked out claims they sought to reinforce by the building of crude shanties. For many of them this paid off in 1852 when Congress passed a bill that released more than three-quarters of Fort Snelling's 34,000 acres for public auction. However, actual sales were held up until further Congressional action gave the squatters already on the land first crack for $1.25 an acre.

Remember now that the gobbling up of this precious land took place while Minnesota was still a wilderness territory whose total white population was less than 8,000. But suddenly, lured by the chance to buy cheap land, there began an onrush of settlers, lumberman and land speculators. Among the latter was the ever-acquisitive Franklin Steele, eager to add west bank acreage to this choice holdings across the river.

His chance came in the late 1850s when the War Department, no longer fearing incursion by Indians or a foreign power, abandoned Fort Snelling. By maneuvers so dubious as to later be challenged by Congressional investigation, Steele got title to the fort and much of its adjacent land.

Fort Snelling was reactivated at the start of the Civil War. But in the war's aftermath, Steele billed the Government for the fort's wartime rental. When after a period of legal squabbles the matter was settled, the Government retained the fort while Steele came away with 6,000 acres of land that was to become a part of the future Minneapolis. By 1860, both banks of the river at St. Anthony Falls were lined with saw and flour mills. In 1872, the parent suddenly became the ward when St. Anthony merged into Minneapolis. Eight years later, as we have already seen, the "City of Laughing Waters" went ahead of St. Paul in the disputed census of 1880.

What might be considered the miracle of the Falls of St. Anthony is that by the turn of the century, Minneapolis, a place that 50 years earlier had not existed, had blossomed into the 18th largest city in America. Labels from its recycled flour bags hung from dish towel racks across the land, not to mention generations of farm kids who walked to school with "Gold Medal" stamped on the seat of their home-made under-drawers.

Today, anyone visiting restored St. Anthony should make it a point to walk out onto the Third Avenue Bridge stretching across the dams and spillways that gave rise to a great city. Nearby, looming in spectral silence, is the boarded-up structure of the Pillsbury "A" Mill, once the largest flour mill in the world. Further downstream is the picturesque Stone Arch Bridge, built by railroader James J. Hill in 1883. In its shadow once stood the first hydroelectric central station to begin operating in the United States. Built by the Minnesota Brush Electric Company in 1882, it lit up the nearby area and later became part of Northern States Power Company.

To the west, as described by Lucille Kane, " ... is the shimmering skyline of the new Minneapolis, no longer a water-power city but still a queen City of the Northwest." Meanwhile, St. Paul has stayed apace as a center of banking, insurance and printing.

It is beyond the scope of this survey course to detail the emergence of the Twin Cities as one of the nation's most important metropolitan areas. Together with their suburbs, they are home to nearly one and a half million inhabitants. They are the upper Midwest hub of a diversified manufacturing, technical and financial base that includes home offices of major corporations, as well as headquarters of the 9th Federal Reserve District.

Included in their strong cultural mix are a number of colleges, the University of Minnesota, museums, theaters, a symphony orchestra and numerous sporting venues. Minneapolis has become well known for its park system that includes the striking Mississippi River Parkway. Within sight of each other in St. Paul are the towering domes of the State Capitol designed by Cass Gilbert, and the Cathedral of St. Paul, the fourth-largest Roman Catholic cathedral in the country. The two structures erected on high ground near St. Paul's elegant Summit Avenue, are perhaps the most recognizable landmarks in Minnesota.

In brief, the Twin Cities have flowered well beyond the once dominant fur, lumber and grain industries that not so long ago fostered their birth.

- 47 -

"A BRIDGE OF GOLD"

" ... With nearly a billion acres of unsettled land on one side of the Atlantic and with many millions of poor and oppressed people on the other ... let us build a bridge of gold across the chasm ... "

Ignatius Donnelly

It was Theodore Blegen who pointed out that without flour milling, the drama of wheat would be like playing Hamlet without Hamlet. He might well have said the same about immigration, which was also part and parcel of Minnesota's era of world leadership in wheat production.

In some ways those who first left the woods and slopes above the Baltic had it tougher than those who came later. Heading toward unknown shores in sail-powered vessels, they faced weeks of pitching and rolling in the gray Atlantic. Crowded together and often seasick, they survived on hampers of hard tack, cheese and dried meats they brought with them. More than a few, especially children and the very old, died and were buried at sea along the way. Many who came had barely more than a few blankets and just enough money for passage.

On arrival, they were awed by the size and bustle of east coast ports and often confused about where to go next. For some, there were family and friends to join. For others, there was only the hope of settling someplace and finding work. But where and what kind? And what about different language and customs in this land so far away from all that was familiar and dear?

Along with their hopes for a better life, what must have carried them through was the powerful dream of being equal. Here, they had heard, a person could walk as upright as the nobility. What mattered was not who you were but what you could do that was useful, whether it be in farming, the trades, or in the case of a few, the professions.

During the half century that followed the Civil War, millions of Europeans left family and their old life to come to America. Regardless of nationality—German, Irish, Scandinavian or a score of other ethnic groups—what caused them to pull up stakes was the dream of a better life. In short, an uncertain future in the New World seemed more attractive than the bleak prospects of life at home.

Much has been written about the basic causes of emigration to America: the shortage of arable land, onerous taxation, religious intolerance, threats of military conscription, or as in the case of Ireland, famine and hunger. But what mainly set off the greatest movement of people in history was a yearning to escape a life of servitude as field hands or house maids.

Contrasted against an outlook so dismal was the siren call of opportunities across the sea. States anxious to attract settlers printed pamphlets extolling the good life to be had in their domains. So did shipping lines eager to fill their holds with emigrant passengers.

Even more persuasive was word from friends and relatives who had gone before. Letters from "Amerikka" glowing with accounts of free land and higher wages were handed around entire villages, where they were read and re-read countless times.

For all these reasons, emigration fever was contagious. As it spread, Minnesota, with an abundance of forest and prairie lands, attracted its full share. By 1870, several hundred thousand immigrants lured by the chance to claim free land of their own had boosted the state's population to nearly half a million.

Prior to the passing of the Homestead Act, land in Minnesota could be secured from the government by preemption, as was the case for most of the land claimed around the Falls of St. Anthony. Preemption required that settlers claim no more than 160 acres on which they must previously have erected a house. The cost was usually $1.25 per acre.

After 1862, homesteaders could get 160 acres of free land by building a house, cultivating their claim and proving residence for five years. Government land was surveyed and numbered by mile-square sections. Ideally, a square mile of land should contain 640 acres. However, the surveying was not always precise and some sections contained a few acres more or less. A homestead claim for 160 acres represented a quarter section. Claims were platted by local land agencies using 66-foot surveying chains. It required 40 chain lengths to measure each side of a square quarter-section.

Coming from rural backgrounds, most of the early immigrants claimed land for farming. However, this was not true for many Germans, who until the early 20th century made up the largest single foreign-born group in Minnesota. While some of them went into farming, many others were drawn to cities and towns clustered near the confluence of the Mississippi and Minnesota Rivers. There they engaged in trade as bakers, grocers, saloon-keepers and brewers.

The Germans, like other newcomers, gravitated to places where people spoke their language and shared their customs. New Ulm, for example, sprang up as a town that might have been transplanted from the old country. Other Germans who chose St. Paul or Minneapolis settled in neighborhoods where they could hear God's word preached in their native tongue. There they also established schools and newspapers to perpetuate their language and culture.

During successive waves of emigration from the Old World, many more ethnic communities emerged in Minnesota. Even before the Civil War, Swedish farmers were breaking soil and felling trees near farm towns like Red Wing and Willmar. Both Swedes and Norwegians chose settlements like the Twin Cities and Duluth along with smaller farming and lumbering towns like Cloquet. By the end of the 19th century, Minneapolis had added to its sobriquet of "Mill City" a reputation for being the second largest Scandinavian city in the world. The quarter of a million Norwegians living in Minnesota by 1900 was the largest number for any state. However, a turn-of-the-century boast that more Norwegians lived in Minnesota than in Norway was gross exaggeration. In that year, Norway's population was more than two million.

Finlanders, who came along later, wound up grubbing out homesteads on cut-over forest lands in St. Louis County. Others who followed to work on the Iron Range settled in towns like Biwabik, Eveleth and Chisholm.

Norwegian farmers, who started out along a belt south of the Minnesota River, gradually worked their way west toward the fertile soils of the Red River Valley. There they settled around towns like Moorhead and Crookston. By the 1880s, wheat being ground at St. Anthony had propelled Minnesota into world leadership in flour-milling. But the real heroes were Red River homesteaders, many of them Norwegians who endured the setbacks and hardships of pioneer farming and kept wheat pouring into Minneapolis granaries.

Life for the pioneers who turned Minnesota's unbroken soil into farms was never easy. Those toiling on treeless prairies lived in crude huts fashioned out of blocks of sod. Using primitive tools to attack never-before-turned earth, the men paid in sore muscles and backaches.

For the women, it was even worse. Besides tending to children, they cooked, washed clothes, patched pants, milked cows and took care of vegetable gardens. In harvest time they put up preserves and slaved over wood-burning cook stoves to feed the hungry crews bringing in the sheaves.

For years, until new inventions came along, most of the field work—scything, raking, bundling and binding—was done by hand. Although McCormick's reaper speeded things up, the drudgery for farmer and family continued.

Reaping began in mid-July, the hottest and driest part of summer. There followed three or four weeks with the men in the field from dawn to dusk. Even with the crops in and under cover, there was little to lighten the load of routine chores. Children, when they got old enough, hauled water from the well, split wood for the stove and fireplace, gathered eggs, fed the chickens and slopped the pigs.

Such realities of daily life on the frontier farm were compounded by vagaries of weather and other obstructions. Pioneers braved blizzards in winter, drought and prairie fires in summer. With no sprays to control insects, crops were often damaged by blight. And worst of all, in the 1870s came clouds of grasshoppers.

For four years beginning in 1873, farmers in the Red River Valley looked on helplessly as swarms of "hoppers," so thick as to blot out the sun, devoured their crops. It was only after a heartbreaking period of devastation and destitution that the plague finally ended. As suddenly as they had come the grasshoppers took flight for parts unknown.

More than a few homesteaders who had lost everything during that terrible ordeal were forced off their land. But the miracle is the number who somehow made it through. These, the survivors, were the real backbone of Minnesota's wheat era. And in time their grit and determination were rewarded by bumper crops and better living conditions. A stream of new inventions like McCormick's self-raker cut down the back-breaking process of harvesting by hand.

As railroads penetrated to bring farm produce close to markets, whole settlements sprang up along with shops, schools and churches. Primitive sod huts gave way to frame houses built by lumber brought in by rail.

By 1900, Minnesota farmers had learned the harsh consequences of single crop failure. If for example, drought, frost or locusts ruined a season's wheat growth, it was vital to have other crops to fall back on. There was also the problem of declining soil fertility from growing the same thing year after year. As wheat yields decreased, other crops such as flax, hay, corn, beans and peas received increased attention.

For roughly 25 years, "King Wheat" had ruled the roost in Minnesota agriculture. During that short but dynamic reign, railroads were extended to open the market from the farm to the world. Towns and grain elevators had sprung up alongside the railroads and Minneapolis had become a world center of flour milling. Finally, wheat farming had been a strong factor in Minnesota's frontier settlement while laying a base for its diversified farming, livestock and dairying economy. Although the state continued for some years as a leader in wheat growing, never again would a single crop obsession take over its farm land as it had during the years when Minnesota was "The Breadbasket of the World."

Besides farming, immigrants in their assimilation as laborers, tradesmen and shopkeepers contributed enormously to Minnesota's 19th and 20th century economic growth. Equally important was their infusion of a rich new vitality into the cultural mosaic that is Minnesota today. In this kind of introductory course there is time only to allude to the pouring of enormous energy and learning into religion, music, the arts and manifestly the state's political life.

Consider, for example, that four of its early governors were born in Europe and that a dozen who followed were of Nordic origin. One of them was the immensely popular John A. Johnson, who before his untimely death in 1909, had been considered by Democrats as a likely standard bearer in the run for the Oval Office.

But it was Norwegian-born Knute Nelson who made the historic break-through. In 1892, he became the first of Scandinavian birth to be elected Governor of this or any other American state.

- 48 -

A BRAVE SON OF NORWAY

It was snowing that blustery afternoon in December 1892, and outside the temperature had dropped. But neither snow nor chill were on the mind of the stocky figure standing by the window of his second floor law office in Alexandria.

Brushing back a lock of unruly gray hair, the Governor-elect of Minnesota reread the hand-written note with its distinctive flourish. Then he turned back to the special messenger, who had carried it all the way from St. Paul.

"You may tell Mr. Hill that it would be unwise for us to meet at this time. However, I will give every consideration to his recommendation."

He paused, "Can I get you anything before you start back?"

Upon being assured otherwise, he helped the messenger into his great-coat.

"Thank you for coming on this wintery day. And please convey my felicitations to Mr. Hill."

Then after warming his hands over the coal stove burning briskly in the center of the unpretentious office, he sat down to consider the unexpected but not surprising missive from his old employer, J.J. Hill.

"Recommendation, hell," he snorted. "It's a damn order."

Knute Nelson, 50 years old, Norwegian-born, American-educated and battle-hardened, had kicked around the rough and tumble of frontier politics long enough to sort through flattering pleasantries to the gist of a letter like this. Hill, the man who was pushing his Great Northern Railroad almost 2,000 miles to Seattle, was telling him to reappoint the man of his choice as State Commissioner of Railroads.

Wryly, Nelson reflected that Hill had wasted no time in calling in favors. Not favors exactly, but it was to the man they called "The Empire builder" that he owed his turn-around from being a lawyer struggling to make ends meet. Some years before, while working with Hill on railway cases, he had finally begun to prosper.

Now that was behind him. But sitting there as winter twilight slowly crept across the room, Nelson knew this was no idle suggestion. Hill wanted to hang onto a Commissioner who had not been averse to his bidding. Perhaps too, this was a not very subtle way of testing to see if he could still exert control over the man who was soon to be Governor.

Either way, Nelson knew this was a decision likely to alter his standing with one of the nation's great railroad lords. James J. Hill was not one to lightly suffer rebuff. To turn him down on so trifling a matter would be to risk a split with Minnesota's most powerful citizen.

Striking a match to one of his ever-present stogies, Governor-elect Nelson sat back. Here was a decision that needed some thinking. Puffing and thinking about what might lie ahead, he let his mind turn to where he had come from.

For a man who never knew the name of his real father, the path from rural Norway to the State Capitol had not been without its bumps and twists. How long ago it seemed, that Fourth of July in 1849, when the ship had nudged up to the pier at the tip of Manhattan. There at Castle Garden, Ingeborg Haldorsdatter, claiming to be a widow, entered America with her son after nearly two grueling months at sea. Seven-year-old Knute had quickly captured the excitement as New Yorkers celebrated

Independence Day with a display of fireworks.

In Chicago, a year or so later, Ingeborg married a man who hailed from the same valley in western Norway. Nils Grotland, an older man, had come to America a few years earlier. With his new wife and stepson, Nils moved to Skoponong, a farm area populated by Norwegians in southern Wisconsin.

Young Knute, pleased to have someone he could call father, changed his surname to Nelson, an Anglicized version of "Nil's son." In later years Knute often talked about his life and early education in Skoponong. He recalled with particular gratitude his three years in a log school house under the stern tutelage of a school marm who had taken special interest in the eager-to-learn promise of her favorite pupil.

In his teen years, Knute found the inner spunk to carry a heavy work load on the family farm while going to nearby Albion Academy. His course toward a degree at Albion was interrupted by the outbreak of the Civil War.

Less than a month after the firing on Fort Sumter, 19-year-old Knute along with a number of his classmates signed up with a local militia company. However, after six weeks of hazing by tough-swearing, hard-drinking townies who made up most of the company, the Albion boys were able to transfer to the Fourth Wisconsin Infantry Regiment.

By size alone, Private Nelson was not destined to stand out. But erect carriage, steely blue eyes and determined thrust of chin more than made up for lack of height. With quick intelligence and a lively sense of humor, Knute Nelson then and for all of his life was a person of attractive bearing.

During the more than three years of his wartime experience, Knute never wavered in his belief in the cause of the Union. His letters home expressed a hardening contempt for those Norwegians who refused to answer the colors of their adopted country.

In June 1863, during an attack on a Confederate fort near Baton Rouge, Nelson was wounded and taken prisoner. His captivity ended a few weeks later when the fort was captured.

Nelson rejoined his regiment and finished out his three-year hitch as a Corporal assigned to regimental headquarters.

Upon being mustered out in July 1864, he returned to complete his studies at Albion Academy. Hardened by battle and determined to earn his degree, Nelson finished first in his class before going on to read for the law. Then followed marriage to Nicholina Jacobsen, who was to become the steady anchor of his home life. After three years struggling as a lawyer in Wisconsin, Knute and Nicholina moved to the frontier village of Alexandria, Minnesota.

Try to imagine how that raw hamlet must have looked when they first arrived. Facing toward the vast prairie lands of western Minnesota, the place had no railroad tracks, not yet even a grain elevator. Its main street, a mud lane, ran past a sprinkling of frame houses, a few shops and a saloon. For some time Knute and Nicholina had to make do in a mean little shanty standing on their small sub-section just outside Alexandria. However, as fees from his law practice began to trickle in, Nelson built a two-story farmhouse in which to raise a family shortly to expand to seven.

Caring for his farm while practicing law, Nelson still found the time and energy to get elected and serve in the Minnesota Senate. But in 1877, just as his political star began to rise, the family was crushed by the disaster of diphtheria. Three daughters perished, leaving Nelson heartsick and further estranged from the religious tenets of most of his fellow Norwegian-Americans. Lesser men might have crumpled before so personal a tragedy. Nelson did not.

Instead, using work as an antidote, he threw himself into the legislative cause of winning a railroad for Alexandria. Nelson's political role in bringing about the extension of the St. Paul and Pacific Railroad to Alexandria brought him to the attention of James J. Hill, who at that time had gained control of the railroad.

With his driving zeal to make the railroad succeed, Hill involved himself in all aspects of its operation, including acquisition of right-of-way along the line, now renamed the St. Paul,

Minneapolis and Manitoba Railway (SPM&M). Impressed by Nelson's skill as mediator, as well as by a work compulsion to match his own, Hill engaged Nelson's legal services in land purchase negotiation.

After several years of work in behalf of the railroad, Nelson began to prosper while at the same time winning the regard of the people of upper Minnesota for his fairness in negotiation. His qualifications as a Norwegian-speaking lawyer were rare on the frontier and served both Hill and the Scandinavians along the line.

The new 5th Congressional District allocated to Minnesota as a result of the Census of 1880 embraced 28 counties. With more than half of its people being Swedish or Norwegian, Nelson was persuaded that the District deserved a Scandinavian representative. Nine others also threw their hat in the ring. But the real battle settled down between Nelson and Charles Kindred of Brainerd. Now, a decade later, Nelson smiled to himself as he recalled their no-holds-barred struggle to capture the Republican nomination for the new seat.

Kindred, who had acquired wealth "by railroad operations legitimate or as alleged, illegitimate," ran what was later described by Folwell as "the finest example of dirty politics." Spending more than a hundred thousand dollars for both subtle and outright bribery, Kindred secured control of county delegations by such means as putting their Republican leaders on his well-paid campaign staff.

For the July 1892 nominating convention at Detroit Lakes, the Chairman, who was on Kindred's payroll, hired the local opera house along with police who were instructed to admit only those delegates bearing Kindred credentials. When Nelson backers burst in anyway, they were refused recognition. Meanwhile, in the hubbub of two delegations shouting at each other, Kindred wandered around the hall dispensing handshakes and free booze.

Finally, after an hour of jostling and shouting, the Nelson delegation withdrew, leaving thc opera house free to nominate

Kindred. However, in a hastily-erected circus tent across the street, the Nelson delegates nominated their candidate.

In the campaign that followed, agents for Kindred spread false rumors about his opponent and arranged to rig ballot-counting in places favorable to their man. Nelson, meanwhile, relied on personal appearances all over the District along with strong support from Scandinavian language newspapers.

Election Day in November witnessed several versions of blatant fraud, including cash payment for Kindred votes and use of a train to enable a group of his backers to vote in two or more polling places. In addition, borrowing from long-dead Joe Rolette, Kindred had it set up to hold votes from a handful of counties until it could be determined how many he needed to beat Nelson. This plan fell through when it became clear Nelson's lead was too great to credibly overturn.

In the end, Nelson beat Kindred by an official 5,000 votes and his Democrat opponent by more than 10,000. Actually, his margin over both was about the same, since it was later discovered that Kindred's total had been puffed up by 3,000 fraudulent votes.

As America's first Norwegian-born Congressman, Knute Nelson went on to be twice reelected. Short but manly in appearance, in a suit usually rumpled, he became a familiar figure to the people of the District. Those for whom he worked tirelessly came to know well the "Little Norwegian" with the tousled hair, flashing blue eyes and curious thatch of chin whiskers.

For six years, Nelson attended the needs of his frontier district including its Indian population. In 1889 he gave up his Congressional seat and returned to Alexandria, where he combined a successful law practice and work on his nearby farm. Although insisting he was done with politics, it seems likely his eye was on higher elective office.

It was a time when simmering farm discontent had boiled over into a populist organization known as the Farmer's Alliance. In Minnesota, their protest was leveled at government, banks, railroads, business, and just about any other form of entrepreneurial success.

In 1890, flexing the muscle of hundreds of local groups, the Minnesota Alliance decided to run its own slate of candidates for office. Desirous of a strong standard bearer, the Alliance looked early at drafting Nelson as their nominee for Governor. However, for reasons that included Nelson's apparent lack of interest, they shortly turned to someone else.

In the November election, Republicans barely hung on to the Governor's Mansion. But the Alliance nearly overwhelmed them in the legislature and other state offices. Shaken by their setback, the Republicans turned to Nelson to help them reclaim voters lost to the Alliance. At their 1892 convention, Nelson was nominated by acclamation as their candidate for Governor. His opponents were Democrat Daniel Lawler, a St. Paul attorney, and the old warhorse and Populist crusader, Ignatius Donnelly, nominated by the short-lived Peoples Party.

In the campaign that followed, traveling often by horse and buggy, Nelson stumped cities and hamlets all over Minnesota, countering Donnelly's fiery railings with solid, matter-of-fact arguments. The result on Election Day was a runaway for Nelson, whose 110,000 votes beat the Democrat by some 15,000 votes and smashed Donnelly, whose mere 40,000 obliterated both Populist and his own future hopes.

Now, as darkness settled in his office, Nelson reflected on his oft-repeated campaign assertion that he was beholden to no man or special interest. He had been close to Hill and admired his achievements. But the very fact of his recommendation had sullied its worth. In order to be true to his word, he must reject it. His subsequent act of appointing someone else sent a clear message to the Empire Builder that their former relationship had ended.

Two years later, Nelson was reelected by a considerably larger margin. However, he shortly stepped down from the Governor's chair when the Republican-controlled legislature appointed him to serve as United States Senator from Minnesota.

Born in obscurity in far off Norway, Knute Nelson had

been awarded the highest office ever for a foreign-born American. The man who had been the first Scandinavian in the U.S. Congress and the first to be Governor of any American state, had now become the first to serve in the United States Senate.

Senator Nelson continued in office for 28 years. On April 28, 1923, while aboard a train carrying him home from Washington, he died of a heart attack. After lying in state at the St. Paul Capitol, "The Grand Old Man of Minnesota," was laid to rest in Alexandria.

Today, in front of the main entrance to the state capitol building, there stands a life-sized statue of Knute Nelson with the inscription:

"Three years a soldier in the Civil War
Three times a member of Congress
Twice Governor of Minnesota
Five Times our United States Senator
A Brave Son of Norway"

- 49 -

THE EMPIRE BUILDER

Well, the old man is dead and we won't see his like again. They say he was a bad man to cross, a fire breathing, copper-riveted sunuvabitch. And he was all of that. But by God he was also the best railroad man who ever lived. And the day'll come when Jim Hill is remembered as the man who did the most to make the Northwest what it is today.

At a time when the railroad business was full of get-rich-quick swindlers whose main idea was to get free land and peddle phony stock, James Jerome Hill wrote his name in big honest letters. First and last he was a business man whose way to make money was to earn it by building something useful that would last. And once he set his mind he was never stopped by the idea that something couldn't be done.

That stone arch bridge he built across the Mississippi is rock solid just like his railroads. And just like him. It took one hell of a man to even dream about laying down a track to the Pacific, let along have the gumption to push it through and keep it running.

Jim wasn't even there when they hammered down the last spike for his Great Northern Railway. But he damn well knew he'd opened up just about all of America's Northwest. From the Great Lakes across the Rockies to Puget Sound—that's one awful big chunk of real estate.

After that, people started calling him "The Empire Builder." And knowing Jim's feelings about his own greatness, that name probably tickled him more than anything else that came his way. He never doubted that getting that track through to the Pacific did more than anything else to settle that part of America. Love him or hate him, old Jim Hill made big things happen. Without him, the whole history of the Northwest would have been different.

If you're wondering how come I get to judge him, let me tell you we went back a long ways. Here's how it was.

THE ADVENTURE OF A LIFE

My name is Toby Christianson and I've been in the railroad business all my life. I used to think I'd grow up to be a farmer. But that changed the day they began to build a railroad from Minnesota to the west coast. The tracks started out about a mile from where we lived near what is now the town of Carlton. I know, because I was there to see them pound the first spikes. That was in 1870 when I was 13 years old.*

My father, Ingemar, had brought my mother and me from Sweden eleven years before. But all I know about that journey is what I heard from my mother. Coming across the Atlantic was rough and took more than a month. After that we went by train to Chicago and across the state to catch a Mississippi River paddle-wheeler up to St. Paul.

Mom used to say the trip across the ocean was bad but the last leg from St. Paul up Minnesota's Military Road was even worse. We came in a train of wagons that kept breaking down from hitting on rocks and stumps or getting stuck in mud up to their axles, all the time plagued by mosquitoes and sleeping at night around a campfire.

---

* Like many of the narrators who have preceded him in these pages, Toby Christianson is fictional. However, his memoir is a true-to-life account of J. J. Hill's life and achievements.

After eight days of this with Dad carrying me on his shoulders much of the way, we came to Oneota on the wide estuary of the St. Louis River where it runs into Lake Superior. You can't find Oneota on a map because it's been swallowed up by Duluth. But back then it was a fair-sized village with log cabins, frame houses and even a few Chippewa wigwams. It also had a sawmill, a dock for lake schooners, a general store and a schoolhouse.

The first thing I remember about Oneota is the bell ringing for that schoolhouse. It also rang on Sundays when the school doubled as a church. That's where I learned my "Three R's." At recess we played tag and in winter we used to have snowball fights. In summer we'd swim in the bay or sometimes go camping. Two or three times my Dad took me along on the Mackinaw sailboat to help him and the crew set fish nets on the big lake. Once in a while we'd go down to the docks and watch the big schooners come in to load up lumber stacked there from the sawmill.

Until I was about 12, we lived in a two-room cabin on the north bank of St. Louis Bay. But then Dad took a notion to quit fishing and go into farming. One of his Swedish friends had started to raise cattle on cut-over land at nearby Otter Creek. And it was next to him where Dad staked his claim. After that, with the help of six or so neighbors working side-by-side, he shortly had a house and a barn. That was pretty good farm land and it wasn't long before Dad was growing all kinds of things, potatoes, cabbages, carrots and the like. Some of it we stored in the root cellar back of the house. Some we took to market in Oneota. The land was also good for grazing and before long Dad was running a fair-sized herd of cattle. In winter he went into logging camp for three months, leaving me to tend the cows.

It was a cold February day in 1870, when a bunch of businessmen came over from Duluth to break ground for the Northern Pacific. There was considerable excitement about it and my friend, Wid Neibert and I, trudged through the snow to a place in the woods where we watched a gang of workmen lay down a rail. Then the businessmen, looking pretty funny in their city suits and overcoats, took turns pounding in the first spikes.

As soon as they were done posing for a man with a camera, the real workmen started clawing at the frozen earth and putting down rails. And it wasn't many days before those tracks went out of sight to the west. Toward the end of summer we began to hear trains running back and forth through a corridor the workmen had hacked out of the forest.

There was something about hearing those trains chug out toward the unknown that stirred my blood. Those rails went to places I could only dream about, across prairies, to mountains and maybe some day a great ocean. At night the whistle of an engine heading out would tug at me like an ache.

Before very long that spot in the forest where it had begun was turned from a bunch of work shacks into a small village. By the time I left, there was already a hotel, a couple of stores, a sawmill and a bank. At first they called it Northern Pacific Junction. But after ten years or so they started calling it Carlton.

So as to handle the car loads of lumber coming in from Cloquet for transfer to big cities, they built switching yards and a depot. By the time they got around to incorporating it, Carlton was laid out with streets and frame houses, four hotels and a bunch of shops and stores. But by then I was gone and in the railroad business myself.

It was during the summer of 1872 that I made up my mind to follow those tracks out west. Dad wasn't very happy about it. He had been counting on me to help run the farm. But finally, with the help of some cajoling from Mom, he agreed.

I was a few days shy of 16 when, with his half-hearted blessing and ten dollars in my pocket, I climbed aboard a train out of the Junction hoping to find a job with the railroad somewhere in the west. I never did find where that might be, because I went broke in Grand Forks. The only work I could find was either a job cleaning out stables or as a roustabout on a Red River freight boat. I took the job on the boat mostly because it came with grub and a place to bunk.

Anyway, that's where I met Jim Hill, who was captain of the boat. At first sight he was a pretty ordinary looking guy, short and stocky with scraggly chin whiskers. But as soon as he spoke, you saw the inner force of the man. It was a sureness of purpose most men don't have. He was in his 30s then, but he seemed older with his gruff voice and sharp glance to size you up under bushy brows.

I didn't know it then but Hill had started out as a farm boy in Ontario. However, after his Dad died when he was 14, Jim gave up the plow in order to take a job clerking in a store. That's where he began to learn about business.

Even then, Jim Hill had a feeling he was born to do something important. But he didn't know what, and after a couple years clerking he took off to try and find the chance he was looking for. For maybe six months or so he poked around New York and other east coast towns before he took a notion to come west. Once he arrived in St. Paul, he quickly found work as a shipping clerk for a Mississippi steam boat line.

St. Paul in the 1850s was not much more than a rough frontier village. But Hill, with his knack for looking ahead, saw its future promise. At the northern hub of the Mississippi, it was the gateway to the Northwest. By the time he was thirty, Jim Hill was married and making a good living as a freight transfer agent. But being someone of affairs in St. Paul was just a beginning for a man who was always sifting ideas and looking for big opportunity.

The Red River was his next stepping stone. And by the time I came aboard, Jim was partners in the Red River Transportation Company, the first to run packet boats up to Fort Garry, the Hudson's Bay fur post that was to become Winnipeg. On a boat like this, mainly hauling furs and freight for independent traders, there wasn't a lot of bowing and scraping. Most often when we were putting on cargo, there'd be Jim pushing and lifting alongside us. But you always knew who the boss was, as I found out one day when we were getting set to leave port. Going over the manifest just before we pushed off, the old man was quick to spot a shortage. He fired the clerk on the spot and ordered him off the boat.

By chance I was nearby lashing down a crate when Jim hollered at me, "Can you do ciphers?"

When I said "Yes," he handed me the manifest. "You're the clerk for the rest of this trip. After that we'll talk."

That's how I got started with the only boss I ever had for 46 years. For all that time, I was just one of a bunch of people around him. But somehow he took a shine to me and every now and then he'd stop by or call me in to talk something over. Once in a while when he didn't like what I said he'd stalk off in a huff.

Jim Hill wasn't one to say he was sorry. But if he trusted you he had his own way of making amends. Once when he heard I was stumped about where to put some money I had managed to tuck away, he offered to take care of it for me. When a couple years later I got married and needed it to help buy a house, he gave me back a check worth three times what I had given him. He had invested it in a special fund along with his own money.

As a kid, Jim had lost an eye in an accident. But he still saw clearer than most people with two eyes. And for some time he'd set sight on getting hold of a railroad. Those were years when America was beginning to grow beyond the Mississippi and Jim had big dreams about the part railroads could play in its future.

His chance came with the St. Paul and Pacific, which had been the first railroad in the Upper Midwest. In spite of its grand name, the road never got closer to the Pacific than St. Cloud, where it ran out of money. In 1878, Hill and his partners were able to buy it for a lot less than its worth. After that, what Jim was to make of that railroad was like what he'd spent his whole life getting ready for. I doubt any American business man ever put more of himself into making a go of things. What he did was pick that dead line up by the scruff of its neck and shake it back to life.

Taking personal charge he set out to push his tracks west to the Red River and then on up to Canada. Up to then that huge territory had been used for not much more than fur trading. But way ahead of most, the old man saw the possibilities for settlement on the prime growing soil stretching out on both sides of the Red River. For frontier villages like Barnesville or Crookston leading up to Canada, a railway link to far-away markets could change everything.

Years before Hill had made a solo trip by dog sled up the Red River Valley all the way to Fort Garry. There, he bumped into Donald Smith, head of the Hudson's Bay Fur Company. The two got to be friends in a way that later led to Smith's helping finance the takeover of the St. Paul and Pacific Railroad.

As first order of business with that railroad, Hill drove his crews into laying a mile of steel a day on their way west and north to the Canadian border. The ultimate tie-in with the Canadian Pacific provided a continuous rail link between St. Paul and Winnipeg.

That was a time when thousands of Swedes and Norwegians were coming to America. And pretty soon Jim's SP&P was carrying them out to the Red River Valley and coming back with bumper crops of grain. The road was born again and Jim even gave it a new name, The St. Paul, Minneapolis and Manitoba.

Next he pushed the road up to the fast growing towns of Duluth and Superior. And never one to miss a trick, he shortly had a fleet of lake boats carrying wheat to Buffalo and coming back with coal.

An ordinary man would have been willing to rest on his oars. Instead Jim made his stockholders groan when he told 'em he aimed to push the railroad west to the Pacific coast. More'n a few of them jumped ship. But Jim wasn't one to give a hoot about doubters so long as they stayed out of his way.

He wasn't the first to dream about carving out a railroad to the west. But Jim Hill was the first to dare to do it without help from Uncle Sam. The Union, Southern and Northern Pacific roads all got big land grants and other subsidies. But to Jim this was simply a problem to be solved some other way. Once he set his mind to something he never worried about failure. His only thinking was about how to get it done.

His enemies, mostly people that feared him, called him ruthless. No question he was willful. But think what it took to follow through on a dream like that: raising millions of dollars, setting routes over rivers, gorges and mountains, solving the problems of grading, tunneling, and blasting trackways out of cliffs of sheer rock, building bridges, trestles, depots and railroad yards, looking after the needs of what amounted to an army of track layers toiling through the blizzards and bitter cold of the Northwest, getting hold of steam engines and rolling stock, and finally when the job was done, running and keeping up the completed road.

If ruthless means daring to tackle problems like that and being driven to succeed, well that's what Jim was. Because that's what it took to push a railroad across country so rugged not even ox carts had crossed it.

Sometimes working out of a private car hitched to a work train, sometimes by handcar or dog sled, Jim was everywhere goading his work crews. In 1889, helped by 3,300 teams of horses, they laid down 640 miles of rail across North Dakota and Montana wilderness.

Meanwhile, in order for his line to stay on its feet it needed to carry freight and passengers. And since he was driving his tracks through places where only Indians lived, he had to attract settlers. To do this he kept his rates low and gave all kinds of help to immigrant families willing to grow wheat on land alongside his railroad.

There's more than a few towns along the line where the tracks run right through the middle. That's because the tracks came first and houses and shops got built up around them. All in all, Jim Hill probably helped more immigrants put down roots in the Northwest than any one else.

In 1890, Jim gave his railroad a new name. Its words, "Great Northern," spelled out in a circle around a picture of a mountain goat are printed on company letterhead and stenciled on its rolling stock. Some reckon that Jim himself was the model for the goat. Lord knows he was stubborn enough.

After a year of being prodded by the old fire-breather, his crews had made it all the way to the Rockies. It had been one thing to lay track on flat country where the major engineering problem was leveling the grade. The Rockies, with deep gorges and streams, embankments to be blasted out of mountain sides and tunnels to be bored, were a different proposition.

To support the many trestles needed, they had to erect a cross-patch of stout timbers sometimes a hundred feet high. The workers, starting from the bottom of steep gorges, had to haul themselves up rope ladders that swayed in the wind. I used to get dizzy just watching them climb.

Jim knew the mountains would be tough but even he didn't reckon how much tougher. He had earlier sent John Stevens, a locating engineer, to find a straight, low altitude pass. Easier said than done. Up there with snow covered peaks, sliced up by chasms and streams, a man could wander around for hundreds of miles and still never find a suitable way across.

But Stevens, like Hill, was a man who wouldn't be stopped. He'd heard from Flathead Indians about a fabled pass they'd never actually seen. With one of them as a guide, Stevens scrambled up the eastern slope of the Rockies determined they'd find it. However, as the snow and freezing weather came, he crawled out of his tent one morning to find his guide had pulled up stakes.

After that Stevens pushed on by himself following down-flowing streams. Finally, late one day, he struggled through snow drifts right into what they now call Maria's River pass. It's the highest point on the Great Northern line and the lowest point along the whole Continental Divide. Nowadays there's a town there name of Summit, about a mile above sea level.

Once across the Rockies, the track pressed on through places so wild not even Indians lived there. Hill fumed over the slow going and kept checking every aspect of the engineering. No doubt he was a hard man to get on with, rushing back and forth, sometimes carping, other times trying to help, but keeping everybody on edge. The winter going was fierce for his thousands of workers slaving away in blizzards and freezing cold. There must be half a hundred of them up there, buried near the tracks.

They ran into a different kind of problem once they got to the Cascade Mountains. Since they couldn't find a pass they had to blast out a series of switchbacks. Up where human sounds had never been heard there suddenly echoed the shouts of men and the rumble of high explosives.

Finally, in 1893 The Great Northern reached Puget Sound, binding the Northwest to the rest of America with rails of iron. Jim Hill's tracks opened up the region to wheat and apple growing. Along with his branch lines they turned lumbering and Montana copper mining into big business. That's how he got to be called "The Empire Builder."

When in January 1893 the east and west sections of his track came together up in the Cascades, Jim was home recovering from rheumatism. But he was on hand five months later for the mammoth celebration back in St. Paul. The mayor called the Great Northern the biggest thing to ever happen in the Northwest and it seemed the whole town shut down at noon the day of the huge parade.

Along with his friend Fred Weyerhaeuser and a bunch of politicians, Jim watched from a special reviewing stand put up at Smith Park. It lasted two hours and had everything from mounted police to fire wagons and Indians. There were soldiers from Fort Snelling and even a log so big they had to ship it in two sections from Seattle. Besides that there must have been 20 marching bands and a hundred floats. I never saw anything like it before or since.

Meanwhile, the Northern Pacific that had started out from Carlton 23 years before went broke. It had been a shaky proposition ever since Jay Cooke, its chief money man, went under during the financial panic of 1873. Then, after a long stall, it was picked up by a group that barely managed to get it to the west coast before going bust.

Jim Hill seemed to be the only man able to run a major railroad in the black. And it wasn't long before he and his associates took over the all-but-defunct Northern Pacific. Now with two lines to the Northwest under his control, Hill set eye on a cross-country link-up with America's east coast.

But first, in order to get trackage into the Midwest, he needed to get control of the Chicago, Burlington and Quincy Railroad. And that's what touched off his famous takeover fight with Ed Harriman, head of the Union Pacific. Although maybe not as smart as old Jim, Harriman was just as tough. Both men wanted the CB&Q. And what they did to try to get control set off the worst stock market panic anybody ever saw.

Hill won the first round. With big banker J.P. Morgan in his corner, he began quietly buying into the Burlington. Before Harriman woke up to what was happening, the CB&Q had been snatched out from under his nose. But then Harriman came back with a surprise move of his own. If he couldn't have the Burlington, he'd quietly buy up enough Northern Pacific stock to steal the line away from Hill. He very nearly brought it off. Before Hill tumbled to what was happening, Harriman and his backers had snapped up enough of Northern's preferred to almost, but not quite, take over the line.

When Jim and Morgan finally woke up to what was going on, they were lucky there was still enough of Northern Pacific's common out there to tip the balance. Immediately putting up $15 million, their plan was to buy enough of the line's common to be able to retire the preferred and leave Harriman out in the cold.

Now, with both sides in a fierce bidding war, Northern's price per share exploded upward. Short sellers, betting it would come down, began to peddle stock they didn't own. Their idea was to buy it back at a cheaper price before the actual delivery date. But the price kept rising and speculators who had guessed wrong couldn't find enough shares of Northern Pacific to cover their shorts. In a frantic effort to stay out of jail, they sold off other stocks to try to meet Northern's ever-rising costs.

The result was a complete blow-up in the market place. As Northern's price skyrocketed up to a $1,000 a share, other stocks like U.S. Steel were falling like rocks. The panic lasted nearly a week before the two sides called a truce. In order to save Wall Street, they quit buying Northern Pacific common and allowed the shorts to settle at a fixed price.

Hill and Harriman had fought to a stand-still. Terms of the truce helped meet some of Harriman's concerns including use of CB&Q trackage. But it left Hill in control of a railroad system that stretched across the whole country.

Finally, the old man was ready to follow through on his dream of a trade route to the Orient. Cotton growing in the South, flour ground in Minnesota and clothing milled in New England were just a few of the goods carried by Hill's railroads and steamships to Japan and China.

Having accomplished all this, it would be nice to say Jim mellowed with age. But it wouldn't be true. As the years went by he got more and more prickly. For even a simple mistake he would bite the head off an employee. Once he fired a man because he didn't like the sound of his name. Another time, I saw him rip a phone off the wall when the operator didn't put the call through fast enough. Even with old friends he sometimes got testy. And with old enemies like Harriman he kept up a running battle for routes out west.

The funny thing is that despite being cantankerous, the old man did a lot of generous things. I recall once he got a telegram from Sauk Rapids where they'd been hard hit by a tornado and needed help. Jim sent me to round up half a dozen doctors that he sent out there along with a check for $5,000 to help out. And there was a black day when fire wiped out Fargo. He dropped everything in order to rush over there and take personal charge of relief efforts.

Jim gave a lot of money to the St. Paul library as well as other places. I even heard there's a statue of him out at the University in Seattle. Probably shows him chewing somebody out.

When Jim Hill worked, which was practically always, including Sundays and holidays, he put more into it than anybody I ever saw. It was only after he let go a bit that he began to enjoy more time with his family and his hobbies. Some times he'd take Mary with him on a business trip. What I think he loved most was to get together with a flock of kids and grandkids at their North Oaks farm.

Daytimes he'd be out tramping his acres, checking on livestock or talking to farmhands. At night the family would sit around telling stories, playing games or sometimes singing. One night when I had to take a business file out there, I found him by the piano bellowing out some kind of Scottish ballad. They say he knew a couple dozen of those that he'd sing at the drop of a hat.

Despite having only one eye, the old man was a crack shot in the field and at least once every fall he'd get away to hunt for pheasant or partridge. But he looked forward even more to his annual salmon fishing trip up in Quebec where he had built a big log-sided lodge on the bank of the St. John River. He had a steam yacht, the Wacouta, but all he ever used it for was to haul family and guests up the St. Lawrence between Montreal and his landing just where the St. John flows into the big river.

Besides family he'd invite old cronies up there for a few days fishing. After a day on the river, they'd sit around smoking or trading fish yarns. I had to go up there a couple times with important mail or reports he wanted. One time the only other person on the Wacouta was ex-President Grover Cleveland.

Going back, I was in charge of half a dozen ice-packed salmon for delivery to some of Jim's friends. One of them, I took to his long-time friend, the old Doctor Mayo down in Rochester.

I was there when the old man finally quit working. He gave a heck of a speech saying how the Great Northern was the adventure of his life. I never thought of it that way but I guess it was mine too. I've been with that railroad for all of its years.

The Great Northern is probably the best railroad ever built. But as proud as Jim was about it, he was even more proud of what it had made possible. Leastwise, that's what he told me a short time before he died.

The voice on the phone was weak but I'd of known it anywhere. He got right to the point. "Toby," he said. "If you've got time, stop by the house after work. I've got something to show you."

It maybe sounded like a request, but we both knew it was a summons, my first ever to his big sandstone mansion on Summit Avenue. When I got there, I was surprised to see him propped up in bed and looking pretty bad. The nurse, who asked me not to stay long, said they'd sent for Doctor Mayo down in Rochester.

It was pretty clear Jim Hill's life-fires were burning out. But there was still spark in his one eye as he ordered the nurse to quit fussing and leave us alone.

Once she was gone he pushed himself up. I forget the exact words. But what he said was that I was the one who'd been with him the longest. I had to lean down close because his voice wasn't much more than a hoarse whisper.

"We gave the Country four new states. All that land," he had to catch his breath, "it wasn't worth ten cents till we put that railroad through."

Then he started to cough and the nurse scurried back in. I turned to leave but he grabbed my arm. "Toby," he gasped. "Take this. You earned it."

It was one of the gilded spikes they'd driven in years before to complete the Great Northern's run to the west. Two days later, on May 29, 1916, the man who hitched together so much of America was gone.

During his time, the country saw some mighty big millionaires. Andrew Carnegie was one. So were Morgan and Rockefeller. But there was only one Empire Builder, only one Jim Hill, who built for the people as much as for himself. "When we're all dead and gone," he once said, "this railroad will run as usual."

The old man had a flaming temper and some said he was a bully. But the fact is, the ones who felt his lash had usually done something careless. What Jim valued most was loyalty and serious purpose. Once you got his confidence, you had a friend for life. Just ask the gray-bearded engineers, switchmen and the like, the "Old Timers," who came to pay their last respects. They'll tell you Jim Hill was maybe the only railroad owner that his workers cried for.

After the old man died, papers here and across the land sang his praises. One of them compared his work as a great builder with the schemes and greed of other business giants, whose main purpose was to line their own pockets. Another said, whenever Jim Hill invested money, the whole country benefited.

Of all the newspaper tributes, the one I thought came closest to the mark was the New York Times, which wrote, "Whatever he touched, it had been done greatly."

On the afternoon of his funeral something happened that Jim never would have stood for in life. At a given signal, every train in his system no matter where, stopped for five minutes in his honor. I have a pretty good notion what the old man would have said about that.

- 50 -

THE GREAT HINCKLEY FIRE

"ON THE FIRST DAY OF SEPTEMBER A.D. 1894 BETWEEN THE HOURS OF THREE AND FIVE O'CLOCK IN THE AFTERNOON A FOREST FIRE SWEPT OVER CENTRAL PINE COUNTY DEVASTATING FOUR HUNDRED SQUARE MILES OF THE COUNTY CONSUMING THE VILLAGES OF HINCKLEY, SANDSTONE, MISSION CREEK AND BROOK PARK, AND DESTROYING MORE THAN FOUR HUNDRED AND EIGHTEEN HUMAN LIVES."

— Monument erected
in 1899 at Hinckley

Forest fires had sometimes raged through Minnesota woodlands long before the coming of settlers. In the 19th century, however, the debris of logging operations ignited by sparks from passing railroad engines increased both the frequency and intensity of such fires.

For people living in northern Minnesota during its logging heyday, smoky overcast from nearby fires was commonplace during late summer and fall. What was uncommon was the pluck with which they faced up to times when such fires got out of control. Some, at risk of life, led people to safety. Others offered aid and shelter or stood tall in the work of rebuilding. Such was the case during the 1894 inferno since known as "The Great Hinckley Fire."

Situated in Pine County—named for its wealth of white pine forests—Hinckley was a lumbering town connected to the outside world by two railroads. It was also a town with a split personality, most of its people being respectable citizens whose livelihood derived from sawmilling, shopkeeping or the trades. But the town also catered to the lusty wants of lumberjacks who on weekends stormed in from nearby forest camps. As a result, Hinckley's three churches were counter balanced by a half a dozen saloons and an establishment just beyond town limits known as "Mrs. Garrity's."

During most of the hot, dry summer of 1894, fires burning in the region blanketed Hinckley with clouds of acrid smoke and falling ash. Accepting sore throats and runny eyes as a condition of life in timber country, its people were not particularly worried about a possible threat to life and property. There was also the reassurance of their well-drilled volunteer fire department along with its brand new fire engine.

Saturday, September 1, was another hot, parched day in Hinckley. Overhead the sky was smudged with a dirty haze from fires burning alongside the railroad tracks a few miles southwest. Nothing unusual about that until about noon when the wind suddenly picked up, cascading the town with a shower of sparks. In a twinkling, piles of seasoning wood stacked up in the yards of the Brennan Lumber Company were ablaze.

As firemen joined mill hands to fight those flames, winds that had increased to gale force hurled a fiery column into the heart of town. Suddenly, as though sprayed with coal oil, its streets burst into corridors of flame. Windows exploded like gunfire while a shower of firebrands poured down on people running frantically through dirt streets. Many were quickly overtaken by streaking flames. Others, crazed by fear, plunged into the

Grindstone River and were drowned.

One large group, directed by a Catholic priest, fled to a gravel pit, where shallow waters provided a haven against sheets of flame rolling overhead. Others crowded into railroad cars hastily strung together from two trains. One was a freight train. The other, with passengers, had stopped in Hinckley on its way to St. Paul. Now both train crews had decided to go back north.

Watching with alarm as flames flickered across the roof of the depot, Edward Barry, engineer of the freight train, signaled for immediate departure. But William Best, in the cabin of the passenger train, set his air brakes and clanged his engine bell to summon more townspeople aboard. It was only when the flames surged toward the train that Best released the brakes.

The train left Hinckley with more than 350 refugees crowded into its coaches and boxcars. It stopped again just past the bridge over the Grindstone to pick up one more group of people fleeing north along the tracks. Then, with wheels churning and still hearing the roar of flames behind them, Best and Barry pulled their trains backward through smoke and searing heat.

The train stopped briefly at Sandstone to warn its people before moving on through a curtain of blazing cinders. Only minutes later the firestorm struck Sandstone, killing 45 people. Coming up to the already flaming Kettle River Bridge, the train moved slowly across bare moments before the span collapsed. When finally it broke away from the firestorm, the smoldering caravan continued backing all the way to the train yard in Superior, Wisconsin.

Best's unassuming heroism was summed up in his official report, where sharing credit with the train crew who had loaded people into cars, he wrote, "We had done all we could, all that mortals could do under the circumstances." Somewhat less gracious was Engineer Barry, who wound up his accident report with the tart remark, "I think I am deserving of the credit rather than Best (Minnesota Historical Society, Original Documents)."

Death came in many ways that fiery afternoon of disaster. Some drowned. Other died screaming when set ablaze by overtaking flames. Many perished from suffocation while desperately cringing in culverts or water wells.

The worst of the day's horror occurred just beyond the Grindstone River, where 127 men, women and children sought refuge in a swamp alongside the railroad tracks. Believed to have suffocated from flames rolling overhead, all of them died almost instantly. Holbrook quotes Allen Fraser, a survivor who was near enough to hear their last terrible wail: "When the fire wave hit the swamp," he said, "there was one piercing cry of mortal anguish; then everything was still, except for the howling of the wind."

Fraser and his family survived by huddling in barrels filled with water. The miracle of their rescue has long been part of the folklore of the Hinckley fire.

The appalling toll in Hinckley would have been worse except for the providential arrival on another track of a passenger train from Duluth. Engineer Jim Root, hauling a five-car train, had probed through increasing clouds of smoke on his way to St. Paul. But a few miles north of Hinckley the smoke burst into flames on both sides of the track. Then as the train crept toward the outskirts of town, Root saw a horde of screaming people fleeing toward him barely ahead of a red sea of flame.

As 150 or more refugees crowded aboard, Root realized he could not make it through the advancing wall of flame. Climbing back into the cab, he reversed throttle and began backing toward Skunk Lake, a fetid swamp, six miles north.

Trees on both sides of the track were blazing as Root fought intolerable heat inside the cab. Twice he fainted, to be revived by his fireman, Jack McGowan, whose heroics that day may well have exceeded those of Root. Somehow during that run through hell, McGowan managed to heave enough coal into the fire pit to keep engine steam up while every few minutes throwing down his shovel to pour water on Root or douse fires breaking out in the cab.

Inside the burning cars they were pushing, John Blair, the porter, helped quiet frantic passengers by his calm actions. He passed out water and wet towels and pumped squirts from a fire extinguisher to put out flames. When at last the train backed up to Skunk Lake, Blair and McGowan assisted people off and got them moving toward the swamp. Then McGowan ran back through the flames to carry his unconscious engineer to safety in the water.

With fire bursting all around them, 300 people, more than half refugees from Hinckley, huddled in the muck and slimy water of Skunk Lake. Tearing off items of wet clothing, they protected their heads from falling cinders. Meanwhile, Blair waded among them squirting out cinders with the extinguisher he had carried from the train.

Earlier, as soon as the train had reached Skunk Lake, Conductor Thomas Sullivan risked his life in a run for help. Hurrying north along the track, gasping and half blinded from smoke, he somehow managed to stay ahead of the flames until stumbling into the station at Miller.*

The telegrapher at Miller wired a plea for relief of the survivors at Skunk Lake. It was to be the last message sent from that station which moments later was engulfed by wind-blown sheets of flame. Sullivan, along with the Miller station crew, survived by running further north, keeping ahead of the flames until being rescued by a freight train which had come down from Willow River.

Meanwhile, after the fires around Skunk Lake burned out, the survivors crawled to the edge of the swamp to await rescue. Crouching there on the banks, they gazed around at a scene of smoldering desolation, of blackened trunks and burnt-out tangles of ragged and fallen timber. There, through a seemingly endless night they huddled, moaning from chill, burns and unutterable distress.

First help came around midnight with the arrival of a handcar carrying two doctors. Hours later, separate trains got

---

* Some ten miles north of Hinckley, the small railroad community of Miller was wiped out by the fire.

through to carry the survivors to safety and succor. Thanks to the heroism of their train crew, all but three of them had made it through their hellish ordeal of dread, pain and discomfort.

Survivors trickling back into what had been Hinckley were able to recognize only a still-standing railroad roundhouse and water tank. Elsewhere, they stared dully at piles of ashes that scant hours before had been their homes and shops. Hinckley was destroyed and 250 of its people had perished. It would have been worse except for the actions of a few who, ignoring personal danger, had run through the streets shouting for people to flee to Engineer Best's train clanging its bell at the Eastern Minnesota depot.

One of them, Dr. Ernest Stephan, helped people aboard before climbing on himself. Arriving in Superior, he stocked up on bandages and burn-relief balm before returning on a rescue train to give aid to the injured—his but one of many such selfless acts. Everywhere during and after that time of fiery travail there were acts of courage, sharing and giving.

A Catholic priest, after alerting people to leave, ran through flaming streets to the Grindstone River, where he ripped his coat into shreds to cover others from searing embers. A Protestant minister and his wife shepherded people aboard Engineer Best's train but refused to leave themselves. Instead, they went to the aid of survivors in the gravel pit.

Black Feather, an Ojibwe woman, hearing cries for help from a woman and two children stranded in Grindstone Lake, paddled out in her canoe to bring them to safety. For several days after, she gave them food and shelter in her unburned cabin.

Immediately after the fire, a Pine City doctor went first to Skunk Lake and then to Hinckley to give medical aid. In tending to the suffering, he went without sleep for 72 hours.

Even as refugees huddled in the mud of Skunk Lake, relief parties were being sent out. As the extent of the tragedy became known, people near and far rallied to send aid and give shelter. Others flocked in to work on the scene, including the grim task of burying hundreds who had perished throughout the region.

The people of Duluth gave exceptionally of time, money, food and clothing to the multitudes who had fled there by train. That city's mobilization of hospitals and churches to provide medical care, shelter and meals was a magnificent example of civic compassion.

Elsewhere, prompt response from local groups in Superior, St. Paul, Minneapolis and other places large and small helped fill the breech until a State Commission arrived to coordinate relief efforts and to disburse meal tickets, money and clothing.

Reconstruction began at once with the work of railroad crews to clear the tracks from burnt-out rolling stock, repair bridges and railroad facilities. With even the high bridge of the Kettle River rebuilt in three weeks, both railroads were shortly up and running.

Hinckley was starting to look like a town again before the end of September. Homes were being rebuilt, two saloons were open for business and school children were back chanting their multiplication tables in a temporary building. By May 1, 1895, precisely eight months after its destruction, Hinckley dedicated a new town hall. An exultant editorial in the *Hinckley Enterprise* proclaimed the town's pride and determination: " ... Our town will stand though a thousand destructions come upon us. ... God made the world, but we rebuilt Hinckley."

The Great Hinckley Fire was one of many conflagrations that have ravaged Minnesota forests. Baudette, Spooner, Moose Lake and Cloquet are among others. But it is Hinckley, perhaps because of so many from one town who perished, that has come to symbolize the danger of life in the timberlands of Minnesota.

In Lutheran Memorial Cemetery, just east of that reborn village, are buried 248 men, women and children who died on that terrible day in 1894. They lie in the shadow of the tall, granite obelisk dedicated to "The Pioneers of Civilization in the Forests of Minnesota."

- 51 -

EL DORADO OF THE NORTH

Anyone who has ever camped in the Superior Forest of northern Minnesota has probably stumbled across some of the oldest rocks on the face of the earth. These are the nub of ancient mountains worn down by the erosion of 30 million centuries. By comparison the 60-million year old Rockies are rank beginners.

The volcanic forces that created these now extinct ranges subsided a billion years ago. More recently, towering sheets of ice coming down from Northern Canada further altered Minnesota's landscape, gouging out hollows for lakes and sweeping away massive layers of surface crust. The result was that iron ore, where it existed, could be found beneath only a thin layer of glacial drift.

Minnesota is heir to three great iron ranges, one of which was to produce more ore than the output of any other range before or since. "Mesabi," a Chippewa word meaning giant, is just that in every sense of the word. Stretching 100 miles diagonally across northeastern Minnesota, its deposits, molded by chemical action and prehistoric oceans, go back to dim recesses of geologic time.

The Hull-Rust-Mahoning open pit mines near Hibbing, now some 600 feet deep, are several miles wide and three miles long. For many years before mining ended there in 1973,

Mahoning was the world's largest producer of iron ore. Now, this man-made "Grand Canyon of the North" is a vast pit of silence.

Huge as it was, the Mahoning complex is but one of many iron mines to be discovered and worked on Minnesota ranges. At one time they provided more than half the world's supply of iron ore.

Surveyors trying to plat townships on the Mesabi during the 1840s scorned iron rock as a meaningless nuisance that threw off their compass needles. However, by the 1880s America's burgeoning steel industry demanded new sources of iron. The search spread from Michigan across to Wisconsin and finally to Minnesota. In St. Louis County, where two of the ranges were located, the effect on its population was without precedent in state history. From less than 5,000 in 1880, population soared to over 100,000 by 1900.

Suddenly on what had been trackless waste, iron mines were sprouting up everywhere. The first big find at Mountain Iron was made in 1890 when an equipment wagon broke through surface crust into a rich bed of iron powder. Two years later, loggers at Frank Hibbing's lumber camp hit iron ore while digging for drinking water.

Out of swampy bogs and pine forests there shortly emerged a network of railroads and raw mining villages such as Virginia, Eveleth, Hibbing and Biwabik. By 1900 hundreds of mines were being worked on the Mesabi. And by 1916 that range alone was producing more ore than the rest of America's iron ranges combined.

Backed by the capital of eastern tycoons like Rockefeller and Carnegie, giant steam shovels were scooping ore into specially built side-loading cars. At Duluth and Superior, docks a half-mile long thrust into harbors to serve a fleet of cigar-shaped vessels known as "whalebacks." The invention of a Duluth man, these freighters were built to carry iron ore eastward to ports on Lakes Michigan and Erie.

As it happened, the early development of the Iron Range coincided with the exodus from Europe of wave after wave of emigrants. The mines opening in Minnesota were eager to hire young, strong workers willing to toil long hours for low pay. For the immigrants who flocked in by the hundreds and thousands, it was not necessary to have a skill nor even to speak the language. Orders were passed along by a rude jargon called "Mine English."

Earlier immigrants to Minnesota came mostly from England, Ireland, Germany, Sweden and Norway. In 1891, when my Great-Grandfather Reino claimed land in St. Louis County, not many Finns had come before him. This changed with the opening of the Mesabi. By the turn of the century, St. Louis County was home for nearly 12,000 transplanted Finlanders, more than for any other county in Minnesota.

Of the many ethnic groups who fled Europe's poverty for a new chance on the Iron Range, the Finns were the largest. Others who put down roots on the Iron Range came largely from Southern and Eastern Europe. Among them were Italians, Hungarians, Bulgarians, Slovenians, Croatians, Serbs and Poles. With 40 or more different nationalities, the Range became a place unique for its blending of Old and New World cultures.

Encrusted tombstones in the shadow of the Hull-Rust-Mahoning mine are mute testimony to a diverse ethnic mix. Alongside McGuires and Bradys lie Makis and Kuusistos, Santinis and Propotniks. Some of their time-worn epitaphs are etched in English, some in Italian and others in the Cyrillic alphabet of Slavic peoples.

Used up by toil, killed in mining accidents, victims of disease or harsh winter, most of them died young. Had there been Social Security back then, few who rest in that all but forgotten cemetery would have lived long enough to cash a single check.

Ill-paid, with fingers stiff and gnarled, aching knees and crooked spines, they had labored hard all their lives and accumulated little. Instead they placed their hopes on education as the path to a better life for their children. In this they found vindication for the meagerness of their existence.

Even though tight-fisted mine owners paid wages of two

dollars or less for a long workday, they were reluctantly forced by taxation to contribute toward community improvement. So-called *ad valorem* taxes imposed on the assessed value of mine properties were a boon to the coffers of young iron range towns.

Communities like Virginia, Hibbing and Babbitt were quick to apply copious tax revenues to the very best in parks, streets, schools, libraries and other public buildings. Especially significant was the blossoming of Range schools with structure and facilities more lavish than their counterparts in other Minnesota cities. In 1913, my old high school back in Buhl was the first of the extravagant schools to be built on the Mesabi. And old timers will tell you they paid extra well to attract sixty of the best teachers. That was before my time, but the ones we had were also excellent.

Granted that Range schools in general were excellent, it was left to Hibbing High School to outdo them all. Completed in 1923, it is perhaps the most elaborate public school in the land. For years, visitors have come to see its classrooms and science labs as well as to admire its 1,800-seat auditorium lit by awesome chandeliers, with a stage to rival that of a Broadway theater and boasting a magnificent pipe organ.

Tax limitations that came along later cut into the funds that could be spent locally. But these were enacted only after immigrant forebears had seen realization of their dream of the best possible education for their children.

As a fourth generation Iron Ranger, I confess to bias. But to me the epic of discovering and exploiting the largest iron ore deposit the world has ever known stands as the most arresting of Minnesota's many dramatic chapters.

Because of the Mesabi, America became the world's leading producer of steel. And because of the Mesabi, it won the two great conflicts of the 20th Century. When America rolled up her sleeves in World Wars I and II, she did not have to melt down her plow shares. Instead she called upon her "Iron Spine" for the raw materials that built mighty armadas and weaponry to serve her fighting forces as well as those of her Allies.

Minnesota's iron has been called the greatest natural resource ever bestowed upon a commonwealth. The saga of its discovery and exploitation is an almost Homeric composite of tenacious questing, ruthless management, incredible engineering, grueling toil, danger and violence. Finally, it is the conglomerate experience of immigrant “Men of Steel,” who did the work while absorbing themselves into a Range civilization perhaps more tolerant of ethnic differences than any other so-called melting pot.

There never was another story like it, and in order better to tell it I have called upon the recollections of several who lived or saw it first hand. One of these was my Great-Aunt Johanna’s husband, Henry Eschweiler, a high school history teacher, who spent his retirement days looking into the early days of mining on the Range.

- 52 -

PATHFINDERS

Reflections On The Early Days
Of Minnesota's Iron Ranges

When I was very small, my father took me to see the open pit mine he was helping develop at Mountain Iron. All I remember about that was the four-mile wagon trip from Virginia. Over that bumpy trail, through the piney woods and jouncing over corduroy logs covering swampy ground, it seemed to take forever.

When we got there, someone took a picture of me standing between Dad and Leonidas Merritt, who owned the mine along with his brothers. Dad with his handle-bar mustache and derby hat was a big man, almost six feet. But burly Leonidas with his beard and busher's headgear seemed even taller. At age four, I came up to about where his pants tucked into his boots. For me, that old photo is a cherished reminder of my father's part in the start-up of iron mining in Minnesota.

It is hard to believe that scarcely a lifetime ago the Mesabi was sheer wilderness. In 1889, when I was born, there was no Virginia and except for the emerging mine village of Tower, no other settlement of consequence north of Duluth. Hibbing, Chisholm and Kinney, for example, were mining explorers who roamed the range looking for iron ore. Babbitt was a mining company attorney. The towns now named for them did not yet exist.

Mesaba Station seventy miles north of Two Harbors on the Duluth & Iron Range Railroad was a rude jumping-off place for ore prospectors. The railroad ended some twenty miles farther north at Tower. Elsewhere, except for scattered logging camps, there were only vast reaches of forest and muskeg.

My father, Robert F. "Spunky" Eschweiler, was born in Albany, New York in 1860. Once, when he was about ten, Dad stood up to a class bully. After that his classmates started calling him "Spunky" and the nickname stuck.

At age 15, Dad graduated from Schuyler Academy and went over to Troy to study earth sciences at Rensselaer Polytechnic. In 1878, diploma in hand, he went to work as a field geologist for a small mining company near Teel Lake on Michigan's Upper Peninsula. That at a time when iron deposits on the Marquette Range were starting to peter out.

As a mining engineer, Dad's job was cruising for possible new iron ore sites. The routine included long days in the wilderness drilling and testing core samples. It was a quest that carried him into Wisconsin with no avail. After that it wasn't long before the company failed and Dad struck out on his own.

Early in 1880, following the south shore of Lake Superior, he made his way into Duluth. There, in the taproom of the Jefferson House, Dad shared an occasional pint with a gregarious old timer, said to be the city's first permanent settler. George Stuntz had come to the area years before as a federal surveyor. And to Dad's mind he was to become the most heroic and least rewarded of all the men of steel who helped break through to the treasures of the Iron Range.

Just after the Civil War, while operating a store and dock business at Duluth's Minnesota Point, Stuntz had got caught up in the short-lived frenzy known as the "Vermilion Lake Gold Rush." Word from the state geologist in 1865 of discovery of quartz rock bearing gold set off a stampede of prospectors along with a diverse company of camp followers. In the vanguard were such worthies as the state's then governor, Stephen Miller, in partnership with former governor Henry Sibley.

To get up there, the hopefuls had first to hack out a passable road through the wilderness. A town named Winston sprang up and a hotel, shops, saloons and other "places of entertainment" were opened. And for a spell the place flourished. But after a year or so, the craze died down, not so much because of a complete absence of gold but because of the extreme difficulty of digging down through rock-hard quartz to extract anything of value. By late fall of 1866, many miners had moved on with no gold to show for their efforts, and by the decade's end, Winston was out of business, with only tumble-down shacks and rusting equipment as reminders of its once high hopes.

For Stuntz at least, the episode wasn't a total loss. Going back to Duluth he toted a sack of iron ore picked up from the pit of an uprooted spruce. For years after, he would sit around the Jefferson House tap room raving to anybody who would listen, about "red gold" that would some day be worth far more than the real thing. But no one took him seriously enough to put up financial backing. And the matter was all but forgotten until George Stone came along.

Stone had arrived in Duluth in 1869 as an agent for Philadelphia banker Jay Cooke, who had acquired a huge tract of land in that area. But during the so-called Panic of 1873, Cooke's financial empire collapsed and Stone went bankrupt. After that, recalling Stuntz's stories about "red gold," Stone seized upon the idea of restoring his fortunes through speculation in iron ore land.

As it happened, Charlemagne Tower, a wealthy owner of coal mines in Pennsylvania, had been a backer of Jay Cooke's effort to extend the Northern Pacific Railroad to the west coast. Somehow Tower had managed to get out before that dream collapsed in the panic of '73. And it was to him that Stone went in 1875, carrying samples of ore borrowed from Stuntz.

Although Tower warmed up to the idea, he wanted to know more about the potential value locked up in the rocks at Lake Vermilion. In July of that year Stuntz was hired to guide geologist Albert Chester out for field testing. Stuntz, who had earlier been in charge of improving the 70-mile trail up from Duluth, led Chester to the east end of Vermilion, near where the Soudan mine was later developed.

There, drilling and blasting, Chester gathered samples that he assayed as warranting further exploration. Despite these findings and Stone's urgings, Tower was not to be rushed. It was not until five years later, after word of a promising survey by a Minnesota geologist, that Tower decided to make his move.*

*In 1880, acting through Stone, Tower began quietly buying Vermilion ore-bearing lands as cheaply as possible. A silent but very important figure in these negotiations was George Stuntz. In his role as government surveyor at Duluth, it was his classification of land as swamp, farming or mineral that determined both the means and the price of sale. Using alleged homesteading** or preemption claims, methods that would not meet today's standards of ethical purpose, Tower shortly acquired 20,000 acres at a cost of around two dollars an acre.*

Next Stuntz lugged his transit and chains up to plat the newly acquired holdings into town sites. Impressed by 20-year-old "Spunky" Eschweiler, Stuntz took him along to help stake out promising ore sites. For shelter and storage purposes, the two built a small log cabin that Dad always claimed was the first ever erected on the shores of Lake Vermilion.

Meanwhile Stone, the inveterate manipulator, had managed to get himself elected to the state senate. In St. Paul, he went about seeing what he could do to relieve Tower's fears of burdensome taxes. Button-holing colleagues, twisting arms or whatever else it took, he pushed through a bill to limit mining

---

** Chester also concluded that ore samples he had examined at the east end of the Mesabi were low grade. He was unaware of the rich deposits a little further south and west.*

*** This on rock-strewn land clearly unsuited to farming. A government inspector looking into the so-called "ethics of the border," later testified he hadn't found a single shack on a dozen sites sold as homestead..*

*taxes to a penny a ton.**

Now there was only one more hurdle. But it was the tallest one of them all.

For a mine 70 miles from Lake Superior to be successful, it had to have access to a railroad. Charlemagne Tower planned to get this by building a single track from Duluth to his Vermilion mines. He proposed to call it the Duluth and Vermilion and in a wire to Stone instructed him to spell "Vermilion with one L according to the dictionaries."

In November 1881, George Stuntz and my Dad were out surveying the proposed line when they got word to call a halt. Minnesota voters had elected to do away with the granting of free land to railroad companies. With the Duluth and Vermilion dead aborning, it was up to Stone to once again come to the rescue.

In 1874, he and a group of associates had won approval to build a railroad from Duluth to the Mesabi. Their purpose at the time was mainly to grab miles of free right-of-way across land rumored to be rich in iron ore. However, after eight years, not a single track had been laid for the proposed Duluth and Iron Range Railroad.

*It is unclear to this writer how, in 1882, a route originally approved to run mostly northwest from Duluth wound up headed due north from Two Harbors, still carrying with it a land grant. But thanks to "delicate handling" by Stone, it did.** And Stuntz and Dad went out once again to survey a route for the Duluth and Iron Range, only this time in a new direction.*

During the road's right-of-way survey, carried out during the summer of 1883, my father bossed a field crew working out of Two Harbors. Later when construction started, his team helped unload tons of equipment and building materials brought there by lake boats.

Dad was there on that momentous day they unloaded the

---

* *The law was overturned in 1896, but only after Tower and his successors had enjoyed 15 years of virtual tax exemption.*

** *During the so-called "Gilded Age," such practices were considered smart business.*

D&IR's first locomotive. "Three Spot," an old time wood burner, was brought gingerly ashore after being tugged from Duluth lashed to a specially-built scow. It had come close to foundering during a flash squall that blew up a few miles short of Two Harbors.

When work on the railroad was halted during the winter months, Dad helped Stuntz lay out a town site at the east end of Vermilion. Mine workers being brought over from northern Michigan needed lodging. And in short order a cluster of frame houses and a company store appeared above the shoreline. Curiously, Charlemagne Tower, Sr., never set foot in the state, much less walked the muddy streets of the town named in his honor.

The mine at nearby Soudan started out as an open pit operation. Workers using sledge hammers and hand drills bored holes for dynamite. Then they blasted out a series of open pits from which they started stock piling iron ore.

Meanwhile, the track up to the mine was completed. And on July 31, 1884, after a roaring celebration, the miners began loading a string of ten wooden ore cars. As the train pulled out, Dad joined a line of miners and their families throwing in a chunk of ore for good luck. Eight hours later the train pulled by "Three Spot," finished the run to Two Harbors. It was the first ever shipment of iron ore in Minnesota.

Two Harbors, named for its pair of adjoining bays, became the main shipping port for Vermilion ore. Where before only railroad shacks had existed, there quickly arose a self-contained town with ore docks jutting out a quarter of a mile into the bay.

It is a reflection of the dog-eat-dog nature of 19th Century industrialism that most of Minnesota's pioneer mining operations were shortly swallowed up by titans of capital able to bring much larger financial means to bear. Charlemagne Tower was no exception. The tremendous needs of America's steel industry shortly marked the rich ore at Soudan as a target for seizure. And in 1887, only three years after the first shipment of ore down from Vermilion, Tower was forced to sell out to a syndicate backed by the financial power of such giants as Rockefeller, Marshall Field and Cyrus McCormick.

Although Tower claimed he hadn't wanted to sell, the eight million dollars he received presumably softened the blow. However, enjoyment of the wealth he had created was short lived. Two years later, the man who had brought Minnesota's first iron range into being was gone. His son and heir, Charlemagne, Jr., went back to business ventures in Pennsylvania and later to a career as ambassador to European courts.

George Stone, whose artful maneuvers had been crucial to the development of the Vermilion Range, came away a wealthy man. He continued to be involved in various ventures until his accidental death from leaking gas fumes in 1900.

And what of George Stuntz, who had stirred the whole thing up? It is an irony of Vermilion mining history that the man who captured the attention of both Stone and Tower, who pinpointed dig locations, surveyed the mine properties and laid out the route for the railroad, did not share in the pie. For all his years of service to Tower, Stuntz worked for eight dollars a day. In 1902, he died a poor man, leaving behind only his name to a bay in Lake Vermilion.

In years ahead, mining on the Vermilion Range grew by leaps and bounds. During Tower's stewardship, Soudan had been strictly an open-air operation with miners working from pits up to a hundred feet down. But after he sold, the Minnesota Mining Company went underground.

Shafts sunk into the earth at Soudan were progressively lowered to deeper levels of ore strata. Corridors running sometimes a mile out from these shafts were blasted out to provide space for miners to hack away at exposed veins. By 1894, ore was being hoisted from eight different shafts sunk from 400 to 800 feet down.

Miners, packed a dozen at a time into unlighted steel cages, would be lowered into the inky darkness of underground tunnels. There, stooped in the damp and chill, they toiled for hard, long hours, their work illuminated only by the wan glow of candles or carbide lamps.

Work crews, directed by a foreman, consisted of a few skilled miners who did the drilling and blasting, and general laborers, sometimes called "muckers," who removed blasted material from the work-ways. There were also men who tended the pumps needed to clear out surface waters that drained continuously into the mines. After sorting out ore from blasted rubble, workers shoveled it into trams which at first they had to hand-push to the shaft.

This changed in the 90s with the introduction of mules able to pull four cars loaded with ten tons of ore. Every working level had a barn tended by a mule skinner. In order to lower them into the mine, the animals were blind-folded and suspended from a sling underneath the elevator cage.

Dad used to tell us stories about the quirks of individual mules. They all had names and some were known as contrary, others quite docile or sensitive. Old timers claimed they were so smart they could understand five languages.

By 1902, more than 1,600 miners at Soudan were working at depths of nearly a fifth of a mile. Average wages in those days were around two dollars for a ten-hour shift. Taken together, Soudan and a number of other Vermilion Range mines were shipping out more than a million tons of ore each year.

By then Stuntz was dead and Dad had made his own name as a surveyor and ore cruiser. Shortly before the turn of the century, he was working as a test driller for the Chandler Mining Company. After that he helped plat Ely's town site. That's where he met Priscilla Buchman, daughter of the D&IR station master at Ely. They were married in 1888 and I came along a year later.

The raw mining and lumber town of Virginia was starting to boom in 1892 and Dad was hired by the Virginia Improvement Company to help lay out its street plan. The town is named for the owner of the company, who came from the Commonwealth of Virginia. With mines springing up all around, Dad decided to go into business there as an independent cruiser, surveyor and field engineer.

In 1901, he built the brick house on 11th Street South where my brother and I were raised. Mom and Dad entertained a lot of guests in that house, including such well-known Range pioneers as Leonidas Merritt, Frank Hibbing and Archie Chisholm.

Lon Merritt was the leader of the "Seven Iron Men," who were the first to unearth the barely concealed treasures of the Mesabi. Dad claimed to have drilled more than 300 test holes for the Merritts at Mountain Iron and Biwabik before those mines were taken over by Rockefeller.*

Frank Hibbing was a German immigrant and an early explorer of ore fields southwest of Virginia. Dad worked with both Hibbing and Canadian Archie Chisholm in test drilling and helping plat the towns named in their honor.

He also sometimes teamed up with Ed Longyear, whose invention of a diamond drill enabled Range explorers to bore down through the hardest rock. Their friendship stemmed from apprentice days cruising on Michigan's Upper Peninsula. During two decades that Longyear worked on the Mesabi, he is said to have bored more than 7,000 test holes.

Probably Dad's most rewarding friendship was one he shared with Cuyler Adams, the discoverer of Minnesota's third great iron range. The presence of a large bed of ore roughly 60 miles southwest of the Mesabi had long been suspected. But nothing happened until Adams, a former surveyer and land speculator, began to stir things up.

In the early 1890s Adams was roaming the woods with his dog Una when he noticed erratic deflections on his compass. Aware of the magnetic attraction of iron, he began a systematic effort to plot the boundaries of what he hoped might be a rich body of iron ore. The project went slowly and was only completed after Adams hired Ed Longyear and my Dad to help out.

As finally platted, the Cuyuna turned out to be a narrow

---

* *So named by Paul de Kruif in his book of that title published in 1929.*

strip of iron beginning at Brainerd in the west and running northeast across Crow Wing and Aitkin Counties. With backing from friends, including Dad, who put up $2,000, Adams incorporated a company that began drilling along the Range in 1903. But it was not until 1911, nearly two decades after the development of the Vermilion and Mesabi ranges, that the first trainload of ore from the Cuyuna Range was hauled down to Superior Harbor. In the years ahead, most of the manganese ore needed for the smelting of special alloy steels was to come from the Cuyuna.

If you think "Cuyuna" is an Indian name like Mesabi, you're wrong. It is a word made up by Mrs. Cuyler Adams to combine the first syllable of her husband's given name with the name of his St. Bernard dog that was with him on the day of his discovery.

Once it got going, the Cuyuna flourished with some 30 mines, many of them small, independent operations. Unlike Minnesota's other two ranges that had been carved out of wilderness, Cuyuna came into being after such towns along its path as Brainerd, Aitkin and Deerwood were well established. This relieved the need for some but by no means all of the capital investment that had been required for Mesabi and Vermilion.

By 1915, Minnesota's three great ranges were shipping out more ore to U.S. and overseas markets than any other mining center in the world. And my father, Robert "Spunky" Eschweiler, had been part and parcel of that mining history since its beginning.

During his years in the business, Dad had lugged his pack the length and breadth of all three ranges. He had come to know well the cruisers and prospectors, the railroad men and the miners, who did the work. He was as much at ease bending over a drill steadied by an immigrant worker as he was drinking beer and trading yarns with the likes of Cuy Adams, George Stuntz or pretty well most all of the "Men of Steel," who opened up these world famous ranges.

Arthritic joints finally forced my father to give up field work in 1920. A year later he sold his business to the Longyear

Company, which by then was test drilling all over the world.

Dad's final years were spent serving as a member of the Virginia school board. He is remembered for helping establish night school teaching programs for Range immigrant workers.

"Spunky" Eschweiler died in 1931, followed by my mother a year later. Johanna Makki and I were married in that same year and live now in the house my father built on 11th Street. Johanna retired from teaching shortly after we were married in order to raise our two adopted sons. And I retired in 1954 after 44 years teaching history at Roosevelt High School.

— Henry Eschweiler
Virginia, Minnesota, 1955

- 53 -

SLEEPING GIANT

Although iron mining boomed on the Vermilion Range during the 1880s, it was not until ten years later that the secrets hidden beneath the red earth of the Mesabi Range were exposed. The delay, due initially to the panic of 1873, was further extended by the unfavorable report of geologist Albert Chester.

As it turned out, Chester had examined only the eastern fringe of what was to become the world's greatest source of iron ore. Had he looked a little further to the southwest, the history of the Mesabi would have been considerably different.

Among the few who refused to be turned away by Chester's gloomy assessment were the Merritt brothers of Duluth. Long on grit but short of capital, their saga is akin to that of a poker player who holds the strongest cards but somehow manages to lose the pot. One account of their downfall depicts them as heroic innocents duped by masters of financial intrigue. Another version suggests they were victims of their own avarice. Although the truth likely rests somewhere in the middle, one thing is clear. The impetus that was to propel the Mesabi into its eminence in iron mining was set in motion by the Merritts.

That range as they worked it in 1890 was a dreary mix of forest and swampland, in which vast wilderness there existed not a single permanent settlement. Less than ten years later it had seen the development of twenty flourishing towns served by eight railroads. By 1912, the Mesabi was producing more than half of all the iron mined in the U.S. and had placed on the Great Lakes the largest commercial ore fleet in the world.

Someone has figured out that by 1920, more earth had been removed from northern Minnesota mines than in all the work of the Panama Canal. Edmund Longyear, who sank the first diamond drill hole on the Mesabi, lived to see its raw prospector camps transformed into thriving towns and to help the Range emerge as the world's leading source of iron ore. This, along the trail he had once described as "the most execrable imaginable."

- 54 -

RECOLLECTIONS OF AN INK-STAINED WRETCH

Here is the story of the Mesabi as seen through the eyes of a veteran Iron Range newsman. During nearly 60 years in the business, Pete Trobaugh* reported on just about every Mesabi happening from the day of the first shipment of ore from Mountain Iron to the early stirrings of the taconite industry.

I started to write this story as a history of the Mesabi's great mining era as I watched it unfold during my 60 years of huntin' and peckin' across the Iron Range. But somehow in an old man's recall of things it got all jumbled up with my life and happenings.

You hear how newspaper men are born with ink in their veins. Well, it wasn't like that for me. I just needed a job. That was in 1886, the year my father, a railroad brakeman, got himself crushed underneath a freight car at the switching yard over at Superior. I have no memory of my mother, who died when I was very little.

My Dad had done his best, keeping a roof over our heads and making sure I went to school. If he sometimes got drunk on payday he never got mean and we always had food on our table.

* Fictional character created to bring us the story of the Mesabi Iron Range.

But suddenly he was gone and at age 15, still without a trace of a beard, I was on my own.

The day of Dad's accident, they called me out of school. I never went back. Instead, a couple days later on a chilly March afternoon, I answered an ad in the Duluth Weekly Advertizer.

Most newspaper men learn their trade from the ground up. But I started out even lower, in the bowels of a one-room operation run out of the basement of the County Land Office. To get in you had to go through a trap door from an alley in back of the building.

Downstairs, I found a little old man picking letters out of a chest-high type case. To my surprise, he turned out to be the Advertizer's one-armed publisher, Ernie Burke. After losing his other appendage at Bull Run, Ernie had been mustered out and come home to work for the St. Peter Advertizer. In 1880, he had come north to start his own weekly in Duluth.

Two weeks before, the paper's staff had been cut in half by the abrupt loss of its itinerant pressman, whose departure for a better world came about during a disagreement in a nearby saloon. In order to get his paper out, Ernie was back to setting type.

Ernie's scrutiny of my qualifications consisted of asking me to recite the alphabet. When I got it right, he hired me on the spot as a printer's devil, with "portfolio," as he put it, shortly to expand. My wages, a dollar and a quarter a day for a six-day week, were supplemented by Ernie's offer to let me sleep on the battered sofa stuck in a corner of the room. There was a sink inside and a tin contraption back of the wood stove that I could use for my Saturday night bath. For the privy you had to go outside.

Under Ernie's watchful eye I quickly picked up the knack of arranging little print blocks into the heavy iron form which held a page of type. It took muscle to heft a frame of type over to the press bed. But for me the hardest part of the job was trying to decipher Ernie's handwritten scrawl. Originally he'd been right-handed, which was the arm he'd left behind at Bull Run.

The scribble he had reworked from his port side was barely a notch above illegible. It took a few weeks to get the hang of it.

Ernie's was the kind of a shop where Johann Gutenberg would have felt at home. And so did I before very long. For me the job was a totally new experience and kind of fun. The only part I didn't like was washing the ink off the type with coal oil after printing.

In order to be as up to the minute as possible, we waited till Tuesday before locking the forms. That way if somebody took a notion to shoot the mayor before noon Tuesday, we could reset the front page. Any later and His Honor would have to wait till the following week.

Once the type was locked in and inked, I would crank the Washington handpress to roll a sheet of paper over the flat bed of type. The end result was a four-page hodgepodge of ads and notices offset by a sprinkling of news items. The ads, which mostly sold for $10 a year, were mainly the business cards of Duluth shopkeepers, professional people or real estate dealers.

Our masthead called for a price of two cents a copy or a dollar a year. But Ernie had guaranteed his advertizers a circulation of 3,000. To achieve that he gave the paper away free. Beside ad revenue, he helped make ends meet by a fairly steady flow of small job printing wedding announcements, business cards, auction posters and the like.

Promotion unaccompanied by wage increment came fast on the Advertizer. By the end of the second week Ernie turned the responsibility for circulation over to me. This put me in a managerial position over three 12-year-old boys, who for fifty cents each were willing to pull a little wagon up and down Duluth streets dropping off free copies at homes, shops and saloons along the way.

My introduction to the editorial side of the business came a month later when Ernie didn't show up for work. Instead, he sent his wife to tell me to put out the paper while he fought off the bed-riding miseries of lumbago.

Since the ads rarely changed, all I had to do was glean

something to pass for news. The process, as I had watched Ernie do it, called for a round of visits to the police and fire station along with a hopeful stop at the undertaker's. Memory tells me that our lead story for that issue reported a fire at a nearby pickling plant—not exactly the stuff of Pulitzer prizes.

Along with learning every phase of its operation, a special benefit of my two years with the Advertizer was getting to know the people who made Duluth run, from politicians to business and church leaders. By the time I was 17, I was on a first name basis with most of them. That's how I had come to know Alfred Merritt. And that's why we pulled off our big scoop over the town's dailies.

During the summer of 1887, while covering a meeting of the St. Louis County Commission, I went over to say hello to Alf, who was telling one of the other Commissioners about a piece of high grade ore one of his brothers had stumbled over somewhere up in the northern woods. When I asked him about that, he told me his brothers had decided to attempt a systematic survey of the Mesabi's ore content.

Almost always it was either the Duluth Tribune or the News to hit the street with any story of consequence. But this time the Advertizer's front page story about the Merritt's plans caught both dailies napping. It was the biggest scoop our little old weekly ever had.

A week later, Bob Mitchell over at the Tribune offered me a job as a city reporter at $18 a week. Bob was a colorful, sometimes crusty publisher, who had actually started the paper as a weekly over in Superior. But in 1870, after several years of taking potshots at Duluth, he abruptly jumped over to the rival camp. His editorial explaining that he was moving the paper to Duluth in order to carry on business in a flourishing city rather than a dead one infuriated his Superior readers. In order to avoid being ridden out of town astride a rail, Bob loaded his press, type and everything else that was movable onto a tug and escaped over to Duluth under cover of darkness. A couple of years later he turned his weekly into a daily evening paper.

The offer to go to work for the Tribune was a welcome surprise. But I held off accepting till after I talked to Ernie, who was real nice about it.

"I hate to see you go, kid," he told me. "But this old ship is about to sink. And there's no use both of us going down with it."

For a minute he looked sad. But then he started to cackle. "The old girl's still got a few runs left. And by God, didn't she show 'em something last week!"

Ernie somehow kept the paper afloat a year or so longer. After that he got by doing small job printing. The last time I saw him was in 1892 just before I came up to Virginia to be the Tribune's first Iron Range correspondent.

Sometimes I wonder how my life might have turned if I hadn't come across Ernie Burke or the Merritts. Ernie got me started in the newspaper business. And it was owing to the Merritts that I stayed in it.

I first got acquainted with that family back in Duluth. Believe me there was a slew of them, including the brothers and a flock of cousins. They had come to Minnesota a few years before the Civil War when their father came there to build Duluth's first sawmill.

*Adventuresome like his sons to follow, Lewis Merritt got caught up in the 1865 Lake Vermilion gold rush that turned out to be a false alarm. But he did come back toting a chunk of iron ore that he told his sons was the indication of the real wealth yet to be uncovered up in St. Louis County.**

The boys listened with interest as they passed the sample back and forth. But it was 22-year-old Leonidas, known to all as Lon, who never forgot and kept coming back to his father's prediction. The old man died in 1880. However, his dream of iron ore riches, always a glow in Lon's mind, flared up again a few years later.

---

* Minnesota's largest county extends from Duluth all the way north to Canada. Named for the river flowing through its southern parts, it is roughly five times larger than Rhode Island.

It happened after Cassius, the second youngest brother, literally tripped over an outcropping of iron ore while cruising for pine near what was to become the town of Virginia. When the chunk he brought back was assayed as high grade ore, Lon persuaded the family to back a survey of the Mesabi. That was the 1887 story that led to my job with the Tribune. And it was two years later, after talking with another brother, that I went up to the Range to see for myself.

The Merritts' search, which began in the spring of 1888, was ambitious. Working with a crew of miners, they went out for weeks at a time into Mesabi wilderness. There they plotted quarter-sections, hacking through scrub growth, wading across swamps, fighting off mosquitoes and camping out after long wearying days. In teams of two they would pace off a section. Then using a dip needle, which reacted like a compass to magnetic attraction, they would trudge back and forth, stopping to chart wherever there was needle indication of underlying ore.

Whenever the reaction was particularly strong they would follow up by "test-pitting." Using pick and shovel, sometimes blasting through rock and cranking up loose dirt by a hoisting rig, the crews bored into Mesabi crust looking for verification of underlying deposits. Unhappily, this back-breaking toil failed to unearth the quality of ore so confidently indicated by the earlier needle findings.

As test pit after pit turned up empty, it was Lon who kept them going. As Andrus once told me, "That was hard expensive work and whenever we ran out of money, Lon simply went back to Duluth to hunt down more investors. He never let up."

It wasn't till 1889, when Alf Merritt and a crew of six set up a camp they called Mountain Iron, that the Merritt's long quest began to show signs of pay dirt. By then, like most of us, I was pretty sure they were chasing a will-o-the-wisp. But then Andy came in from the field with exciting word that they were close to hitting a big deposit of high grade ore.

It seemed every time one of the brothers showed up with promising news, Lon would set out to get control of the area involved. Back then because of Minnesota's effort to stimulate mining, he was able to pick up Mesabi land cheaply. At their peak, the Merritts held 121 quarter sections leased for fifty years at one hundred dollars each.

It was while listening to Andy that I began to wonder. Sure, the Merritts were dreamers. But they were also realists who had put a heap of time and money into this. And if they were right, this could turn into something very big.

Andy told me I'd be welcome to come and see for myself. But my boss at the Tribune wasn't much taken with idea of sending me off on a goose chase.

"Everybody knows there's nothing up there but trees and Indians."

"Well, the Merritts think there is."

"Don't tell me about the Merritts. They've been chasing that dream since Hector was a pup."

"What if they turn out to be right?"

That last "what if" must have got to him. Because after mulling it over, Bob Mitchell gave me a grudging okay to go up there for a week or so. I think it was his idea to shoot down once and for all the myth of hidden Mesabi riches.

What I didn't reckon on was how hard it was to get up there. I left Duluth during October Indian summer, riding the Iron Range Railroad up to Mesaba Station. The problem was how to get from there across a 30-mile tote road to Mountain Iron.

Lucky for me, at dinner that night in a Mesaba boarding house, I met Jim Foley, a wagoner who was to leave shortly with a load of supplies for the Merritts' drilling camp at Mountain Iron. He agreed to take me along.

"You can help push the wagon when we get stuck. But first," as he glanced at my city-cut high buttons, "we better get you proper shod."

Later, when I complained the new boots pinched my toes, he told me not to worry. "They'll get soaked through soon as we hit the swamps. After that they'll fit."

At daybreak two days later we pulled out with our big wagon loaded with vittles and mining gear. It was trial enough jouncing over corduroy sections, skirting around muskegs and swatting mosquitoes. But then we got mired down crossing a swamp and had to hand-carry most of our cargo across in order to lighten the wagon. Even then it took me pushing and Jim tugging at the horses before we got it unstuck.

Jim was right about the boots. Once they got wet they quit hurting. But by then my hind quarters were plumb frazzled from the jolting over rocks, roots and stumps.

Jim, ever cheerful, assured me things could be worse. "This time of year the skeeters ain't in full bloom."

It was pitch dark when, after 15 hours of that torturous passage, we pulled into a rough settlement about four miles east of Mountain Iron. The place had an inn of sorts, a sawmill and a stable. But it didn't have a name. That was my first sight of what was shortly to be named Virginia. I wasn't much impressed.

As a matter of fact I was beginning to think the idea to come up here was a bad mistake. Try to imagine the Mesabi as I first saw it in 1890. Everywhere was only a desolate mix of forest, swamp, bogs, and cut-over stump land. There were no real settlements, not a single one of the Range towns that were so soon to spring up like dragon's teeth. On the trail between this place and Mesaba Station we hadn't seen another human, not even a sign of habitation except for a lone abandoned logging camp.

My first glimpse of Mountain Iron the next day didn't do much to lift my spirits. We came there up a muck road, past a half dozen drill pits full of water, and finally to a crude shed that served as store room, cook shed and bunk house. The crews were out in the field drilling and the cook left behind to tend camp was not sure what to make of me. It didn't help when I told him I was a reporter.

"Um, well ... hmmn. The boys'll be in for supper pretty soon. Why don't you set a spell till they come?"

Perched on a log in the autumn sun, I amused myself

swishing at flies till the men came in shouting and laughing. Cass Merritt, who was leading the way, came over as soon as he spotted me. His face lit up with a huge grin when I told him why I'd come.

"Well, Mister Reporter, you picked a great time. Stick around a few days and I doubt not you'll get a bigger story than you ever dreamed."

At supper, between bites from a slab of corned beef, Cass told me the reason for the hoopin' and hollerin'. "There's bound to be iron here. We can almost smell it. And today we saw how it may be so close to the surface that we can almost dig it out by hand."

The next day he took me out to the test pit where Jim Nichols and his crew were finding promising traces just below the top crust. Nichols, an experienced ore assayer from Germany, told me in broken English how these deposits were different than anything he'd ever seen. Instead of being embedded in rock, they were in powdered form. And unlike mines such as at Vermilion where veins of ore extended downward, these deposits appeared to lie in horizontal tiers close to the surface.

Cass showed me his plot chart. "See how it's getting better all the time as we move southwest. Nichols thinks when we find the right place, we can scoop the stuff out with a shovel."

From up there, the only way to get in touch with the Tribune was by railroad telegraph from Mesaba Station. The next day I rode back there with Jim Foley and sent a message to Bob Mitchell that the Merritts looked to be within a few days of a major strike. The next morning he sent back word to stick around till they hit. So that's how I was nearby a week later when Jim Nichols accidentally found the first big body of ore ever discovered on the Mesabi.

On November 16, 1890, Nichols had been moving to a new test pit when one of his equipment wagons broke through the surface crust into a bed of powder that he knew by instinct to be high grade hematite. Not wasting any time, he gathered up a sack of the red earth and headed back to Duluth with me in tow.

I was with the Merritts a day later when the assay report confirmed the sample's high quality. And I'll never forget their excitement, especially Lon's, after all the time and money they had poured into this, and all the jeers and scoffing.

My story describing the find at Mountain Iron was a Tribune exclusive that was picked up by the Associated Press and sent to newspapers across the country. It created a sensation, kind of like if Old Mother Hubbard looked in her cupboard and discovered a big apple pie. Nobody expected it. But as soon as the word got out everybody wanted a slice. Even though someone bigger came along and grabbed it away, nobody can take away the fact that the Merritts were first. And everything that has happened since on the world's biggest iron range began with them.

For me, getting back to Duluth meant warm water and a decent bed. Other than that, except for a two dollar raise, it was back to the old news beat. Nothing much changed until, a year or so later, Bob Mitchell called me into his office. Sitting at his battered rolltop, paper cuffs on his sleeves, he stared at me from under a green eye shade. It turned out he had been thinking about the Mesabi.

"That Range," he opined, "is starting to boom. It's bound to be the biggest thing ever for this state. And it's right here in our own backyard."

Quite a switch from the boss who not so long ago opined there was nothing up there but trees and Indians. But I was smart enough not to gloat.

Bob had decided the Tribune needed a fulltime man on the scene, someone to go up there and open a news bureau. "If you want it," he wound up, "the job's yours."

His offer included a salary jump to $25 a week, an expense account and the opportunity to choose where I wanted to set up shop.

I accepted on the spot, partly because I was ready for a change, but mostly because I knew he was right. Big things were going to happen on the Range and I wanted to be part of it.

My only problem was to decide where on the Range to locate. The Merritts were already mining at Biwabik as well as Mountain Iron. And it seemed a good idea to seek their advice. Sometime during the last week in 1891, I think it was the day after Christmas, I went to see Lon Merritt in his Duluth office.

In his late 40s, Lon was a good-natured bear of a man, whose outward exuberance concealed the driving will that spurred the family on during the lean years of their search. His enthusiastic greeting was typical.

"Damn, son, that's a helluva opportunity you got there!" Then shrugging off other matters calling for his attention, he took time to give me his best opinion. Their operation in Biwabik, he was pretty sure, was about as far east as the good ore extended. The Mesabi's future he predicted would be to the south and west where prospectors like Frank Hibbing and Archie Chisholm were just getting started.

Unrolling a Range chart, Lon jabbed a finger at a spot just east of where he'd circled Mountain Iron. "That's where you should go. They already got a couple hotels and a sawmill there. Pretty soon we'll get our railroad through to Mountain Iron. And once we run a spur over there, that place is gonna be smack dab in the middle of some mighty important real estate."

I couldn't have paid for better advice. Within two years "that place," incorporated and named Virginia, was to become a rollicking center of Iron Range mining and sawmilling. Even by the time I went up there in the spring of 1892, it had changed from the drab collection of shacks I remembered from 18 months before.

Word of the Merritt's strike had brought all kinds of people flocking: immigrants looking for work in the mines, lumbermen, shop keepers, land speculators, saloon owners, bartenders, a Chinaman to run the laundry and a couple dozen ladies referred to politely as demimondes.

The young town's main thoroughfare, a crude path hacked through tall pines, was bordered on each side by a row of frame-built shops and a dozen saloons. There were two hotels, a barber shop, a dentist's office and a hostler's stable. On one corner there was a large hall for town meetings, traveling shows and the like. On Sundays it doubled as a church. At night, kerosene lamps lit the streets downtown. But there was talk of building an electric generating plant.

For me, however, the really important additions were the railroads. The Duluth, Missabe and Northern coming over from Wolf Junction in 1892 was shortly followed by an extension of the Duluth and Iron Range road from Mountain Iron. After that, Virginia was in touch with the rest of the world by railroad and telegraph. Instead of a mean day's run over the tote road to Mesaba Station, I simply had to walk down to the railroad station to send my stories to the Tribune.

As it turned out, 1893 was to be a memorable year in Virgina's life. Thanks to the DM&N link to Duluth, it was no longer necessary to haul heavy mining equipment and supplies across that swamp-ridden trail from Mesaba Junction. But just as the town blossomed as the center of Range mining and lumber milling, came disaster.

On June 18, 1893, Virginia was virtually wiped out by forest fire. It had been an exceptionally dry spring and on that hot day with everything dry and parched, bush fires were raging southwest of the village. And then, just as people were sitting down to Sunday noon dinner, a strong southwest wind began whipping the flames into town. First to sound the alarm was the Finlayson sawmill, which moments later erupted into a torch of flame. Next, ignited by fireballs exploding out from the sawmill, the hellish inferno blasted into Virginia.

Alerted by the Finlayson siren, townspeople began fleeing to the DM&N depot, where jumping aboard box cars, the caboose, or anything that was handy, they were shipped off to Duluth. Thanks to Tom Hurley, the railroad's telegraph man, I was able to get off a bulletin to the Tribune moments before the wires went out. By then the train had left, and we ran with others toward Silver Lake where we spent the next few hours crouched in its waters.

Up to his neck next to me was a six-year-old boy, so far as I know, the only one his age in town. When the siren sounded he was in the lobby of Pat McGarry's hotel waiting for his Dad to come back from an errand. Rushing out to see what the noise was he saw a wall of flame shooting toward him from down the street. With his eyes smarting and half-blinded by smoke, he ran screaming the other way. Happily he was caught by his Dad, who picked up the boy and ran with him to the lake.

There in the muck and water we rode out the cyclone of flame that leaped and roared around us. I don't know how long we huddled there, our faces scorched and dousing our hair with water to avoid igniting from the fiery rain of embers. And then it was over, leaving us staring at each other bedraggled and black with soot, not daring for a while to leave the water. Finally, hardly believing we had survived this fiery baptism, we began to stumble back toward a scene of smoldering ruins. It was a sight I never forgot.

Except for a few buildings near the DM&N depot, everything around the center of town was bare, blackened waste. Here and there a few people poked through smoking ashes, hoping to save something from a lost home or shop.

On Chestnut Street, the main business section no longer existed. Not a single building was standing. Gone were a dozen shops, the post office, school house, 30 saloons and four hotels. The oddest sight was the burnt-down ice house, whose fireproof contents sparkled like crystals out of the blackened ash.

Lucky for me, Mary Garrison's Virginia House, where I boarded, was one of the few places left standing. Mrs. Garrison was off in Duluth that day but her ten-year-old daughter, with the help of staff, threw open the door for homeless wanderers.

Although the hundreds who came back after that day of devastation found mostly heaps of ashes, by some miracle not a soul had perished. As in all mining towns, the homes and most of the buildings were wood frames that touched off like tinder boxes. And now in the midst of charred ruins with families wandering without shelter, their children crying from hunger, there came forward a company of heroes, a few of them most unlikely.

One of the first was banker O.D. Kinney, who recognized the immediate urgency for food. Ignoring his personal loss of home and business structure, Kinney organized a station where he and other volunteers handed out sandwiches and coffee. He is also said to have physically run off a bully who tried to crash the line of women and children. His was the selfless spirit displayed by a number of business and civic leaders in the wake of disaster.

Much more unexpected was the generosity of Mike Keaough, whose conduct of a so-called "dance house" at the east end of Chestnut Street was a subject not to be discussed within circles where decorum prevailed. By quirk of chance, the fire had not extended up the street to Mike's. And no sooner was it out before he flung open his doors for the hungry and homeless. The first night alone he fed 300 people and bedded down a hundred women and children.

When his cook rebelled at so much extra work, Mike threw him out and enlisted three of his female "wards" to take over in the kitchen. Shortly they were joined by several matrons who had come for shelter. Talk about strange bed fellows—there endures the memory of a well-endowed woman in black stockings and sheer negligee, wiping pots and pans handed to her by the calico-clad wife of a church deacon.

As always in times of disaster, outside help was quickly on the way. By the day after, citizens' relief committees had formed in Duluth and St. Paul to collect and send up food. Other donations, including cash and clothing, were collected from individuals, companies and social organizations. A D&IR train packed with food, clothes, blankets and tents was soon on the way, with the president of the line sometimes at the throttle while the regular engineer ate or rested.

Some of the 700 people who had fled to Duluth never came back. But many more did and rebuilding began immediately. Once again it was O.D. Kinney to the fore. First and last, that big man was an entrepreneur. But he was a large-hearted one and a born leader. With a rallying cry of "We'll be back," he organized a group of business associates to lead the way in the town's reconstruction. Considering that O.D.'s stamp is indelible in Virginia's history, it seems an oddity that his memory is perpetuated only in the name of the nearby town of Kinney.

All through the busy weeks of summer, the town echoed with the shriek of sawmills and the ring of hammers. By the time the leaves began to fall in autumn, I was able to send down the story of Virginia's gritty recovery. A new and better village had risen out of the ashes of the old.

In platting the town grid, the Virginia Improvement Company named north-south avenues after places, while the east-west cross streets were named for trees and fruits. Thus, we had an Orange and a Lemon at the north of town and a Hickory and a Sage to the south. Since then, for reasons obscure, most of these thoroughfares have been renamed by number.

But the main business street is still Chestnut and it was a great night in 1894 when it was first lit up by electric lights. And it wasn't much later before I was able to send down news about the installing of a telephone switchboard at the Central Hotel. After that I made it a point to stay on good terms with Molly Bassett, the operator. Along with putting through my calls to the Tribune, she usually knew what was happening in town before I did.

Even after the system was extended and we got our own phone in the office I shared with lawyer Jasper Hook, I kept in touch with Molly. Unless I was off somewhere else on the Range, my morning round usually began with calls to City Hall, the police and fire stations, the hospital and undertakers. It ended over a cup of coffee with Molly.

By 1900, Virginia, with 8,000 people, two railroads, four sawmills and surrounded by 15 mines, had become the hub of the Iron Range. Then somebody got careless while burning shavings at the Moon and Kerr sawmill, and sparks carried by the wind to dry roof shingles set off a fire that razed most of the business district a second time.

This time Virginia came back stronger than ever. And with its new ordinance that all downtown structures must be built of brick or stone, Virginia was shortly basking in its reputation as "Queen City of the Range."

On Christmas Eve 1912, most of the town's 12,000 citizens turned out to see the maiden run of the Electric Interurban passenger train, which in time was to hook Virginia up with most of the other important Range cities. Within a matter of months the Interurban put our horse stables out of business. The line was a welcome boon to my coverage of Range events. For example, during the great mining walkout of 1916, I was able to cover a strike meeting in Chisholm one morning and a picket line brawl in Biwabik that afternoon. The line stayed in business until 1927, when it in turn fell victim to the automobile.

During the long years of my beat on the Range, I was the Tribune's eyewitness to everything from cornerstone layings to such serious problems as mine cave-ins and barroom violence. It was a rare week when someone on the Range wasn't victim of a mine accident or done in during a saloon fracas. It was my 1906 series on violent death on the Range that earned my one Pulitzer nomination.

For a number of years, taxes on mining property enabled towns up here to build exceptionally fine schools, parks and other public facilities. And I was on hand with notebook and pencil for the opening of such opulent buildings as Roosevelt High and the new public library in Virginia. At least once a year I put on my drama critic hat to review one of the great stage productions in the magnificent auditorium at Hibbing High.

Over the years I was sometimes upset about the treatment the Tribune chose to give to stories I sent in. But my biggest disappointment was the editing given my stories during the great mining strikes of 1907 and 1916. As a reporter, I resented that my efforts to account fairly of those conflicts seemed always to get twisted around so as to put the miners in a bad light. The fact is that most papers, including those up here on the Range, pretty much went along with management's side of the story.

In their early days, towns like Virginia and Hibbing catered to a lusty crowd of lumberjacks and miners, most of them single. In Virginia alone we had forty saloons and half a dozen gambling and "sporting" houses. Respectable townsfolk made it a point to stay off the streets after dark. On weekends and especially on pay day, shots often rang out. And barroom brawls and killings were so common as to be all but ignored by Duluth papers.

It was almost the same for mining accidents. Once I sent down what I thought was a particularly touching story about a fatal mine cave-in near Biwabik. The Tribune buried it at the bottom of my weekly roundup of Range news, saying only that two miners were injured and one, a Serb named Alex Vujovich, was killed. The part about his having been a lay preacher in his church, a husband and the father of three children was left out.

In fairness to the Tribune, the demise of another immigrant miner was of about as much concern to the average Duluth reader as news of a Yak shortage in Outer Mongolia. On the other hand, I was sometimes surprised by the puff-up of an item sent down as little more than a filler on a no-news day.

One example was when the paper asked for more details about a prize fight in Virginia back in 1903. As a result, the three lines I had included in one of my weekly roundups were blown up into a full column on the paper's sporting page.

For several years, Billy Rhoads, a saloon brawler of local note, had supported himself rather handsomely by punching out a string of area toughs for $25 a fight plus side bets. Unhappily for Billie's pocketbook, he had run out of opponents. With no one willing to go up against his wild-swinging, head-butting charges, Bully Boy Billy was hard-put to meet expenses. After threats of eviction by his landlord and with his credit drying up in area saloons, Billy set out to rectify the situation.

His quest for an opponent ended at the Johnny-On-The-Spot Tavern, where he spotted one Wilhelm Haenke, a German miner peacefully quaffing his evening pint. Haenke took no offense when Billy jostled his drinking arm. But the second time got his attention. As he turned angrily to face Billy, the bartender by pre-arrangement interceded. A prize fight was suggested, to which Haenke agreed as soon as he understood the nature of the challenge.

Promoter that he was, Billy needed time to drum up both a crowd and the all-important betting action. And it wasn't until two nights later that several hundred men crowded into a nearby theatre to see what Billy had billed as a grudge match even though the smiling German didn't seem to be mad at anybody.

Most of those who had plunked down their bets on Billy looked for their man to give them a quick return on their investment. Only it didn't work out that way. After a minute or so of easily countering Billy's bull-like rushes, Haenke wrote "30" to the encounter with one tremendous roundhouse to Billy's chin. By the time he came around, Haenke had picked up the winner's purse and gone home.

That, along with being the end of the German's brief stint as a prize fighter, was Billy's farewell appearance in Virginia. One step ahead of his howling creditors, the bully boy skipped town, never again to be seen on the Range.

Hand-in-hand with Virginia's burgeoning growth in mining went its development as a lumber center. The Virginia and Rainy Lake Lumber Company was for years the largest white pine mill in the world. And the Rouchleau group of mines at the east edge of town were for a long time one of the world's top producers of iron ore. Visitors sometimes come here just to gape down into the awesome chasms of the mine's open pits.

Neither the financial depression of 1893 nor two forest fires were able to do more than temporarily slow down Virginia's growth. As for all the Range towns, the arrival of business people with their families, along with the establishment of churches, parks, lecture and concert halls, not to mention a police force, gradually brought about a refinement of Virginia's entertainment and social life.

Not so resilient were my friends the Merritts, whose fortunes were undone by the depression that gripped the country beginning in 1893. In other circumstances, the gritty enterprise spurred by Lon Merritt might have survived. But a mountain of debt built up by their capital requirements came crashing down, down on their heads with the sharp drop in ore demand during the financial panic of 1893.

- 55 -

HIGH HOPES AND RECKLESS FAILURE

There is much to be admired about pioneers like Thomas Edison and Alexander Bell, who after inventing something, managed to keep control of its industrial development. To their misfortune, the Merritts were not of that stamp. In their element as explorers, the brothers were over their heads in the world of capital finance.

In order to cash in on their rich discovery the Merritts had first to extract it and then get it to market. The essential requirements for earth moving equipment, an army of workers and the means of transportation, called for a financial base far beyond their personal means. Things might have turned out better had they been willing to move ahead more prudently. However, hard on the heels of their discovery at Mountain Iron they also found ore at Biwabik and Virginia. One can only speculate how it might have gone had the brothers been willing to concentrate at Mountain Iron while leasing out their other holdings. Instead, with visions of a fabulous mining empire, they plunged ahead on all fronts.

Before they could start digging it was necessary to haul heavy equipment and other supplies over difficult trails to their mining sites. Next came the problem of moving tons of ore to the nearest railroad. When other lines refused to extend trackage to their holdings, the Merritts built a railroad of their own.

The capital expense to equip their Duluth, Messabe and Northern RR along with extending its tracks to Biwabik and Mountain Iron sent the brothers into heavy debt. But with buoyant hopes of shortly marketing enough ore to pay off all their creditors, they pressed on. And in November 1892, they were able to celebrate sending down the first train load of ore from Mountain Iron. That shipment, bound for a foundry in Cleveland, was an historic day for the Age of Steel. It was also the crowning moment for the Merritts' star-crossed enterprise.

Within the year, triggered by the financial crisis of 1893, it all came crashing down. As stocks of iron ore gathered rust on Duluth docks, its price per ton plummeted. The Merritts, unable to meet even such basic obligations as their payroll, turned in desperation to America's richest man. Little did they expect that their financial rescue by John D. Rockefeller was to cost them control of all their holdings, including the DM&N railroad.

Despite bitter charges of fraud and years of litigation, the Merritts were shortly out of business on the Mesabi. So far as I know not one of them ever visited Mountain Iron again. Lon, Alfred and Andrus, hoping for one more big strike, went back to their basic calling as explorers. Although they roamed the west for years in search of copper or silver, they never again hit it big.

Lon continued to keep his home in Duluth where I interviewed him in 1926, a year or so before his death. The old Tiger was adamant that Rockefeller's agent, Frederick Gates, had hoodwinked them into believing the Merritts would keep control.

Gates, the former Baptist cleric who had negotiated the deal, saw it quite differently. During an interview he granted me in 1895, shortly after he took charge of the DM&N, Gates insisted the matter had been a straight forward business arrangement. With an amused twitch of patrician eyebrows, this vicar-turned-high-priest of finance patiently explained how Rockefeller dollars had bailed out the Merritts. It was they who had come hat-in-hand to plead for help. The barely concealed implication was that the brothers were bumpkins in the world of high finance, who according to Gates were victims of their own avarice. A harsh judgment, but one perhaps closer to the mark than charges of fraud.

My only problem with the good Reverend's argument was that it did not look past hard, cold cash. Nowhere during our discussion did he acknowledge the toil and sometimes anguish, the grit and the sweat that had made it all possible. For less than a song, Rockefeller had acquired a bonanza of mining and railroad properties. In the circumstances, one might have hoped negotiator Gates could have found it in his Christian heart to treat more kindly the lambs he had helped fleece.

It is such sentiments, I suppose, that have bestowed upon me the meager fruits of a lifetime in the newspaper business while as I understand it, the good Reverend appeared before his Maker as a personage of means. Should we perchance meet in the hereafter I must congratulate him on his perspicacity.

‡‡ ‡‡ ‡‡ ‡‡ ‡‡

Old reporter Pete Trobaugh never got to file his last story. On a June day in 1955, he was found slumped over his battered Underwood. It seems fitting that his unfinished copy had to do with a rumor about large scale taconite operations to be started at nearby Silver Bay.

- 56 -

CHANGING OF THE GUARD

As demonstrated by the Merritts, the operation of an iron mine was no place for owners of limited means. Out west, a grizzled old prospector with little more than his pick and a mule might hit a gold seam and walk away a rich man.

Not so for the producer of iron ore, who had to think of expensive equipment, large work crews and how to get the ore to market. Little wonder that big corporations shortly became the way of business on the Range. Of hundreds of independent mines begun during the early 1890s, only a handful were around by the century's end.

One of the first to understand the need for big corporate dollars was Henry Oliver, the owner of a small manufacturing firm in Pittsburgh. More promoter than business man, Oliver, a boyhood friend of Andrew Carnegie, was always on the lookout for the main chance. In 1892, during a visit to the Mesabi, he found it.

Excited by the possibilities, he talked the Merritts into giving him a lease on one of their unworked mine properties. Then, after giving them a check for $75,000, he scurried back to Pittsburgh to borrow funds to cover it. Next, in a truly masterful stroke, he engineered a merger by which Oliver Mining Company, backed by Carnegie money, dug ore from properties taken over from the Merritts, leaving Rockefeller railroads and lake steamers to carry it to market.

With the financial power of this consolidation behind him, Oliver, who had come on the Mesabi scene with a kited check, began gobbling up leases from independent mine owners. This, during the throes of economic depression when a buyer with means could snap up properties at fire sale prices. In short order, the Oliver Mining Company controlled an iron mining empire stretching from the Mesabi to Vermilion and over to Michigan's Upper Peninsula.

By the turn of the century Minnesota's iron ranges were pretty much the private preserve of three of America's richest men: Carnegie, Rockefeller and railroader James J. Hill, who got into the mix somewhat by accident. Hill's 1898 purchase of the Duluth and Winnipeg railroad carried with it a huge hunk of Mesabi right of way along with an ore dock in Superior. It was kind of like buying a house and finding an oil well in the backyard. A year later, Hill beat Rockefeller to the punch by buying up a block of logging and mining property which included the Mahoning mine at Hibbing.

Last to put his hand into the Iron Range capital mix was banker J.P. Morgan, the supreme deity of industrial consolidation. In 1901, following masterful negotiations with a group of competing iron and steel moguls, he put together the gigantic U.S. Steel Corporation. In a single stroke he had brought under one management roof an immense combination of everything from the mining of iron ore to its transportation and conversion into steel. Included in the merger were Carnegie Steel, its Oliver Mining division, Rockefeller's railroads, Great Lakes ore carriers and a host of smaller companies.

A joke at the time maintained that the world created by God in 4004 B.C. was reorganized by J.P. Morgan in 1901. U.S. Steel, America's first billion dollar corporation, was for years to take over the lion's share of America's iron and steel industry. Although J.J. Hill stayed outside, it was not long before he leased his ore properties to the new conglomerate.

It is an ironic twist that Rockefeller, who had acquired the Merritts' holdings for less than half a million, merged them into U.S. Steel for a reported eighty million dollars of its stock. According to the ethics of that financial era, it seems that few were scrupulous as to their methods if a great end was in view.

- 57 -

DOWN WHERE THE WORK IS DONE

"Why is a Ranger? I can't never know.
Some say we're different and others, 'Aint't so.'
Why does the pack sacker think we're so strange?
Soon he's like us, as he melts to the Range.

Was it the people from many lands arrive?
Working and helping so all could survive.
The ore knew no different which man used a spade.
Learning together is how Rangers were made.

Our music, our talking, our mixture of kin.
We argue with laughter, a strong love within.
Why is a Ranger? I just can't decide.
Maybe it's our history, maybe it's pride."
Finny Lager*

Although the Merritts are honored as discoverers of Mesabi's iron ore potential, neither they nor others who helped develop it can be thought of as true settlers of the Iron Range. In almost every case, these men—explorers, owners or tycoons—

* From *Happy Depression On The Iron Range*, H.E. Lager, D.D.S. Virginia, MN: Range Printing Company, 1979. *[N.B. from Jim Makki: Having discovered this poem in 1980, I have used it ever since.]*

were outsiders. Charlemagne Tower never even set foot in Minnesota. The Merritts lived in Duluth, Henry Oliver worked out of Pittsburgh and prospectors like Frank Hibbing and Archie Chisholm moved on.

The true settlers of the Mesabi were its miners, most of them immigrants, who provided the sweat and muscle. Coming into a land of cut-over forests, dirt streets and crude hovels, they endured harsh conditions to somehow survive and make of the Range a place to live. Much has been made of the ethnic mix of these peoples and of a solidarity that goes beyond cultural restraints to their spirit of a shared lot as Iron Rangers. It is a bonding tempered by a longstanding legacy of resentment towards management. These were people who had fled European tyranny only to fall under the oppressions of America's early industrial age.

The stern reality was that the mining companies were run to make money. To do it, they needed the kind of unskilled labor that immigrants provided so cheaply. Beyond that, absentee owners had little concern for their workers' existence as human beings.

In deep shafts below ground or open pits above, miners blasted, drilled and shoveled, stooped over from dawn to dusk. The work was so exhausting as to make them old before their time—and always there was the danger of explosion or cave-in. If the Mesabi was a place for the unskilled to eke out a living, it was also a place for them to die young. From 1905 to 1910 nearly 400 of them were killed in Iron Range mining accidents, while many more were injured or maimed.

In years since, many things have happened to improve the lot of the miner. Along with better wages, shorter hours, safer conditions, health and retirement benefits, there has occurred a humanizing of relations. Today, rather than going at each other with brickbats, labor and management are most often able to iron out their differences across a negotiating table.

Even so, Range kids, especially those of Finnish descent, are nurtured from childhood on a bile of management distrust. It was their grandfathers who, following the bitter mine strikes of 1907 and 1916, were blacklisted as trouble-makers. The result is a lingering cloud of ill-will that overshadows almost any discussion of the very corporations that provide their livelihood.

The last time I talked to my cousin Bob Makki, his union was threatening to strike the taconite plant where he works. Over a beer, I asked him about the wisdom of doing that while the economy on the Range was in the dumps. "The company is making noise about going out of business," I said. "You could lose it all."

"Whose fault is that?" he shot back. "If things are so tough, let 'em cut some of the fat out of their big salaries and bonuses."

God knows he has a point. But what if the company really did close up? It's like the crew of a sinking ship standing around arguing about who's to blame when they should be manning the pumps.

It is hard for people who've never set foot on the Range to appreciate this sort of us-against-them reasoning. To begin to understand you have to go back to its roots. There aren't many still around to tell us first-hand about those early days. But there are descriptions that have come down in the form of letters and other written accounts. One of these is the memoir of a second generation Finnish American who took an active part in the long battle for a miner's life better than bare existence.

Anders Korvala was born in 1900 and grew up on a shack on the edge of the Range town of Aurora. After his father was killed in a mine accident, 14-year-old Anders went down into the deep shaft of the St. James mine as the main support of his family of four. Here follow excerpts from his unpublished account of working conditions in the underground shafts of Minnesota's Iron Range during the early years of the 20th century. He writes also of his years in the front lines during labor's long struggle for better working conditions.

- 58 -

MEMOIRS OF A BLACK FINN

These observations are written as a narrative of things lived through or seen during the long, sometimes bloody struggle of immigrant iron miners to secure for themselves and their families a life better than stark subsistence. Without undue vanity, I think I can claim that not many who are still alive have more first hand knowledge of the events to be discussed.

Other than a bias toward aggressive unionism to which I frankly confess, the truth, even back to long years where memory dims, will be recorded as honestly as I recall it. No attempt will be made at misrepresentation.

Accordingly, I submit this statement as my personal witness to two generations of struggle against the iron yoke of primitive capitalism. It is offered as a tribute to the sacrifice and determination of immigrant miners as well as a reminder to present and future iron and steel workers, that benefits they now take for granted did not come without price.

— *Anders Korvala**
Duluth, Minnesota, 1967

---

* A fictional character but a true-to-life union man.

" ... If the sheep would escape the wolves they must unite in measures for their own defense. It would be madness for them to wait in hope that the wolves would someday in mass convention adopt resolutions of justice, mercy and generosity. ..."

— Ignatius Donnelly, 1873

In 1900, John Pierpont Morgan, the most powerful man in American business, began his U.S. Steel negotiations with Andrew Carnegie, whose personal income for that year exceeded $23 million, with no income tax to pay. This, at a time when my father, who dug the ore that fed the steel maker's foundries, was earning less than $3 for a 12-hour work day. That added up to barely $500 a year while most immigrant miners scrabbled for even less.

It was a year later on January 1, 1901, that death stilled the voice of Ignatius Donnelly, the Minnesota populist, whose cries for social justice rang like a lyric soloist in the rising chorus of protest against the evils of industrial tyranny. Coincidentally, but of considerably less importance, that was also the day of my birth, which earthly introduction attended only by my mother and a Finnish neighbor lady, took place in a two-room hutch on the outskirts of Aurora, Minnesota.

That's when I was born. But what you might call my real life began a little more than 14 years later. Up to then my boyhood had consisted of school, house chores like tending garden and chopping wood, fishing, hunting and growing up more or less happy in a family of five.

All that ended on a blustery day in 1915, when my father was one of three miners killed in a cave-in at the St. James mine. Since I was the oldest of three brothers, there was no help for it but that I take my place as the family breadwinner. Although I was tall for my age, the contract captain must have looked the other way when he hired me. But if he was sympathetic to our plight, he concealed it remarkably well by consigning me to the deepest recesses of the mine. There, working as a "trammer," the lowest paying job in the mine, I helped load ore cars which we pushed by hand to where a string of four of them were hitched up to a mule.

No one who has not done it can begin to understand the shock of my first day in the damp cold and blackness of an underground mine. It was still dark at six that morning when I crammed into the elevator cage to clank down hundreds of feet below the earth's crust. And it was dark again when almost 12 hours later we came back to the surface.

During the torturous hours in between I had worked half bent over, shoveling chunks of blasted-out ore into ten-ton trams. I lost track of how many we loaded and pushed up the spur to where the mule skinner took over. My partner, a recent Croat immigrant, was maybe five years older than me. So far as I know, his English consisted of five words: "Yes," "No," "Eat" and "Quit Time." But jabbing a finger in his chest, he made me to understand his name was something that sounded like Bozidar. I called him "Bozey." I never did figure out his last name.

Bozey had started in the mine just a few weeks ahead of me. But he knew the ropes and using his few words of English along with sign language and occasional grunts, he guided me through that terrible first day. Once, sensing my near exhaustion, he took the shovel out of my hands and pushed me down for a short rest.

When from somewhere a siren sounded, Bozey herded me over to sit down on a pair of nearby boulders. There, lighted only by the little carbon lamps in our hats, we dipped into our lunch pails. Mine was Dad's old dented bucket, stuffed by my mother with two cabbage rolls still slightly warm and a fruit jar full of coffee that wasn't. At home I would normally gulp down two or three of those "galumpkies." But that first day after barely getting through one, I gave the other to Bozey.

Then it was back to work and trying to ignore blisters forming on my hands. Sometime during that seemingly endless afternoon, I must have slipped into a trance, kind of like sleep-

walking, shoveling mechanically but with my mind off in another world. I was not even aware when the quitting time siren shrieked. And it was only when Bozey poked me in the ribs that I snapped out of it. The long day was over and I had earned $2. But I had lost a small piece of my soul.

When I shuffled home that night, exhausted and covered with dark, red iron dust, my mother took one look at me and started to cry. I put my arms around her feeling the hot tears on my cheeks. A little later, I fell asleep over my plate of stew and was only half aware when my brother, Esko, guided me to bed.

Morning, which came all too soon, found me aching with every bone in my body. It helped a little when Mom rubbed me with that smelly arnica she used to use on Dad. Then, bolstered by a mug of coffee and a bowl of oatmeal and molasses, I picked up my lunch pail and limped off to work.

So began a bleak procession of days broken only by supper and ten hours of sleep. After a while things got not so much better, but at least more bearable. By comparison, helping with chores around the house on Sundays seemed almost restful.

Along with what Mom took in doing washing and my $12 or so a week we were managing. My brothers put up wood for our stove and tended our garden. Esko ran a trap-line snaring rabbits for stew and in fall gathered nuts and berries after school. Weekends, he sometimes went with friends to net whitefish which Mom smoked and put up for winter. We were getting by as a family. And then one day, after a year or so, everything changed.

It came without warning, a strike which shut down most of the iron mining in northern Minnesota during the summer of 1916. Management was quick to accuse the International Workers of the World (I.W.W.) of stirring up the strike. But the fact is that "Wobbly" organizers came in only after the miners had acted on their own. I know, because it all began in the St. James mine where I was working.

The spark that touched off the strike was the dashing of our hopes for a wage increase. Costs of living on the Range were going way up and somehow after a specially productive May, the word had gotten around that we would be rewarded by a boost in our month-ending pay checks. When it didn't come, the miners took matters into their own hands. On the morning of June 2, after a hasty confab, a group of Italian miners decided to walk out. Others were quick to follow.

It took a while for the word to filter down to those of us who were already at work. But as soon as we heard we threw down our picks and shovels and headed for the elevator. At that time it seemed kind of a lark, like skipping school or getting a day off at Christmas. As we stood in line waiting for the cage to take us up, there was laughter and joking. It was a mood that was quick to wear off once we learned what it was really like to defy management.

Walking home, I was whistling with the pleasure of being outside on a warm summer morning. Except for Sundays when it wasn't raining, I hadn't seen much sunlight for a long time. But when I got home, my mother didn't see any reason to whistle. She'd been through the disastrous strike of 1907 when 10,000 miners, most of them Finns, had walked off their jobs.

"This is bad," she told me. "You can't win. They'll bring in stooges with guns to break up your meetings. And just like last time they'll find scabs to take your jobs."

When I protested, she snapped back. "You're too young to remember what it was like. It went on for weeks till they starved us out. A lot of men got beat up. Some got killed. And for what? They didn't get nothin.' And when it was over the owners took it out on the Finns who led it. They called them trouble makers and wouldn't let them have their jobs back. In order to eat they had to get off the Range and look somewhere else for work."

From my father and others, I heard many times how the owners had shipped up trainloads of Greeks, Italians and Slavs who broke up that strike in a matter of weeks. However, despite Mom's sobering prediction, our walk-out got off to a great start. Leaders of the day shift, who had set it off, came back that evening and quickly talked the night crew out, bringing work at St. James to a complete stop. All of us on both shifts met that night in the Aurora meeting hall.

That was quite a scene. Nearly half those present were recent immigrants, who with little English barely understood what was going on. Finally, after a half hour of babble and confusion, Joe Greeni, the Italian firebrand who had set us off, got the floor. We didn't know it then, but Greeni was very likely a labor agitator who had come to Aurora to stir up trouble.

This was before any I.W.W. people showed up and we were never sure just where Greeni fit in. All I know is that he turned what started out as not much more than a wildcat show of protest into a full-fledged strike. He did this by shouting out the terms he said management had to meet.

Without guidance from any visible labor organizer we voted our roaring approval to stay out till the owners agreed to a minimum wage of $3 a day. We also wanted to do away with the hated contract system whereby a mine foreman set wages on quality of ore dug rather than quantity or number of hours worked.

This system was a bone that stuck deep in the throat of the miners at the lowest end of the wage scale. In return for bribes of gifts, outright cash and even sexual favors from family members, a few miners were given the most productive locations. The rest, unable or unwilling to pay such bribes, were forced to labor long hours for wages so skimpy as to provide for little more than subsistence. Abuse of this sort by the foremen who assigned work locations was flagrant and widespread in the face of occasional mild reproof from management.

That first meeting in Aurora established a cross ethnic solidarity that up to then was largely missing among the people of the Iron Range. In short order St. James miners—Italians, Finns, Serbs and Croats—along with their wives and children began marching to other Range towns to enlist more and more miners to the cause. It wasn't more than a week or so before ten thousand Oliver Mining Company employees had joined in.

The strike leadership, realizing they needed guidance and support from organized labor, turned first to the American Federation of Labor. But that elitist union with its emphasis on the crafts—carpentry, brick laying and the like—turned a deaf ear to the petitioning of mainly unskilled, immigrant workers.

The A.F.L.'s rebuff opened the door for the I.W.W. to move in. The Wobblies had a history of concern for workers who had escaped European tyranny only to find themselves victims of a new kind of oppression. Without special skills and limited ability to speak the language of the country, they were little more than prisoners of industrial circumstance. Despite low wages and miserable working conditions, they could not afford to look for work somewhere else. Literally, they were at the mercy of owners, who except for paying a meager wage, felt little concern for their working conditions in the mines or their welfare outside. It was to these, the peasants of early 20th century capitalism, that the militant I.W.W. held out its arms.

From the miners' perspective, their grievance was with Oliver Mining, the company that controlled most of the Range's ore lands. But in fact they were up against the monolithic opposition of the world's mightiest trust. United States Steel, of which Oliver was a subsidiary, was the holding company for the mining and steel-making interests of such financial titans as Rockefeller, Carnegie and banker J.P. Morgan.

The Trust's reaction to the walk-out was in keeping with its standing resolve to give a cold shoulder to any attempt by labor to win bargaining power. Except for sending in hundreds of armed "deputies" to intimidate picket lines, it did nothing. As for the miners' demands, Big Steel's response was simply to ignore them. There would be no arbitration, no negotiations, no concessions whatsoever.

Against this corporate intransigence, the I.W.W. organizers who arrived to take control counseled non-violence. "It will only work against you," they told us. One of them was Sam Scarlett, who looked only a few years older than me but was a seasoned veteran of labor wars. During a rally in Virginia, he cautioned us not to stir up trouble. "Keep your hands in your pockets," he urged.

Unhappily, in this kind of face-off there was bound to be violence. Tempers flared and clashes occurred, especially on picket lines or during marches.

Once during a march through Biwabik, somebody grabbed at a the sign I was carrying. When I tried to snatch it away, I was jabbed in the side by a mine "guard's" billy-club. Except that my ribs hurt for a month, that one didn't start anything. But a few days later, a similar incident in Hibbing set off a brawl during which an Oliver mine guard was stabbed.

As in most finger-pointing situations, there were different versions as to who started it. More than a few bystanders insisted that the miners were behaving peacefully and that it was the company guards who started the melee. But according to the newspapers, it was the strikers, goaded by Wobbly rabble-rousers, who were to blame.

Along with police and most politicians, press coverage was most always favorable to management and particularly critical of the I.W.W. Here from the archives is a sampling of area newspaper headlines:

"Wobblies Preach Doctrine of Sabotage"
— Biwabik Times

"I.W.W. Follows Trail of Blood"
— Tower News

"Outside Agitators Are Disturbing Element"
— Eveleth News

"No Cause For Workers' Grievance"
— Daily Virginian

Things really heated up after that brawl in Hibbing. Citing the stabbing of their guard, Oliver Mining appealed to

Governor Joseph Burnquist for help in restoring order. In reply, Burnquist wired orders to the St. Louis County sheriff to organize a posse and arrest any striker creating a disturbance. In turn Sheriff John Meining recruited an army of gunmen, many of whom according to a later government report were thugs "from the slums of Duluth and other cities."

On July 3, four of these deputies, led by one Nick Dillon, on leave from his regular duties as a bouncer for an "assignation house," acting without a warrant, broke into the house of a striking miner in Biwabik. A fight broke out and a deputy and a bystander were killed by shots that all evidence indicated were fired by one of Dillon's henchmen from outside the house.

Regardless, all those living in the house, including the wife of the striker, were arrested, charged with murder and sent to Duluth. So were seven I.W.W. leaders, who despite being miles away from the scene, were charged with inciting the violence.

By any measure of justice, this sordid affair should have ended in speedy court dismissal. Instead, in the climate of outrage whipped up by vicious newspaper attacks, the case dragged on for months after the strike was over. Given the flimsy evidence against them, the I.W.W. leaders were shortly released. But eight other defendants remained in jail until the case was finally settled six months after their arrest. Three of those charged went to prison on three year sentences. The rest went free.

All through that summer of tension and violence, the mining companies continued obstinate in their refusal to negotiate or even to meet with strike leaders. After three months of sacrifice and bloodshed we had gained nothing except beatings from hired thugs. With no sign of concession and the chill of autumn in the air, our will began to crumble. Management's strategy of waiting for hunger to send the men back to the mines was working, as across the Range strikers began to trickle back.

By September, such strike benefits as were available to us through the I.W.W. had run out. When later that month our final appeal to negotiate went unanswered, the strike was called off. It was scant solace that two independent post strike investigations later placed blame for the strike squarely on the shoulders of the mine owners.

One report, after citing repressive company practices, went further to castigate Governor Burnquist and Sheriff Meining for actions that led to a reign of persecution of workmen and their families.

The second report was filed by investigators from Minnesota's Department of Labor. While it found that I.W.W. rhetoric had helped inflame the summer's tension, it concluded that the strike had been the consequence of justifiable grievance against deplorable working conditions. It further charged that the countless incidents of violence were mainly prompted by mine guards and police, rather than strikers.

If, as it appears, the miners had suffered through that harsh summer to no effect, it is ironic that within a month of its ending, Oliver Mining announced a round of wage increases to go along with changes aimed at protecting against abuse of the contract system. The implicit message was that these concessions would have come about without need for a strike or interference by an outside union. The more believable likelihood is that without the strike of 1916, none of the changes would have been made.

In whatever spirit the concessions were granted, the company took immediate steps to reinforce its rigid opposition to any form of unionism. As I was shortly to learn, it had bolstered its spy network by paying stool pigeons to inform on fellow workers. Anyone expressing criticism of the company or showing the least interest in labor organization was liable to be black-listed as a trouble maker.

I never found out the Judas who sold me out. But on the first day back to work a pair of company guards stopped me at the mine entrance. Somebody had reported me for carrying an anti-company banner during one of the strike marches. Along with about ten others from the St. James mine, I had been denounced as a Black Finn and barred from ever again setting foot in that or any other Range mine.

Desperate to find work, I turned for help to Local 490 in Virginia. That office had been I.W.W. headquarters during the strike. Now it was about to shut down. I got there just in time to catch Elizabeth Gurley Flynn, the radical unionist, who had tried so hard to prop us up during the strike's final days.

In this, my only meeting with Miss Flynn, I was surprised to find a much different person than the arm-waving firebrand we had seen and heard during her platform harangues. Here, she was a calm and sympathetic listener, who after hearing my situation stared at me with an almost mother-like expression. Hers, I believe, was a deep compassion, not just for me, but for all of us everywhere under the heel of corporate oppression.

"There's not much I can do for you, son," she sighed. "They've beat us this time. But our day will come and you'll live to see it."

Then, digging into her pocketbook, she pulled out a ten dollar bill that I needed too badly not to take.

She told me to go to Duluth and look for a job on one of the ore docks. "The dockworkers there have a union that don't back down from nobody. Tell 'em I sent you."

It was advice that changed my life. Two weeks later, as a loader on the docks, I was able to start sending money home to my mother. Elizabeth Flynn had been right. The dock workers union was strong and active. It was while I was attending a regular meeting of the local that Peter Lahte, its sergeant-at-arms, talked me into enrolling for night classes at Work Peoples College, a school run by Finnish Americans.

The College had begun as a place to train clergy. But by the time I started in 1917, it was mainly a breeding ground for labor leaders. At least half of the faculty were I.W.W. members looking for recruits to grasp hands on their battle-scarred standard.

After the collapse of the 1916 iron mine strike, the Wobblies had made one final effort in Minnesota. Early in 1917 they sent teams out to logging camps to whip up support for a strike underway against the huge Virginia and Rainy Lake

Lumber Company. Although they were initially able to shut down the logging camps of northern Minnesota, the strike was quickly broken up by a strong force of sheriff's deputies and lumber company security guards. Within two weeks, Wobbly leaders were either in jail or on the run.

That second failure within a year amounted to the I.W.W.'s last gasp in Minnesota, if not nationally. Leadership disunity and growing public distaste for radical agitation worked against the Wobblies. But even more, it was America's entry into the first World War that finished them off. As someone put it, "The blare of the bugle drowned out the voice of the reformer."

By 1919, with the country in the grip of anti-red hysteria, labor's extreme left wing was for all practical purposes out of business. Eugene Debs, who had been its spiritual leader, was in prison on trumped up charges under the wartime Espionage Act. "Big Bill" Haywood, the Union's president, awaiting conviction on similar charges, was making plans to flee the country. The I.W.W.'s once piercing cry against abuses of the capital system had faded to little more than a bleat.

Meanwhile, about a year after I started at Work Peoples College, one of the faculty asked me to speak to his class about the Range strike of 1916. For me, this was a new experience and I was surprised to find myself able to talk easily in front of an audience, most of them a lot older than me.

By then I had made up my mind to join the fight against industry's refusal to accept labor organization. However, my ideas about the nature of the battle had changed. I had decided that the way of the Wobblies was not for me. Although they were never the wild-eyed, bomb-throwing anarchists, the image so firmly stamped in the public mind, the fact is that their vision of social justice seemed always to be clouded by over zealous hatred of capitalism. This, I believe, reflects the I.W.W.'s embrace of so many immigrants from an east European tradition of radical overthrow.

As a second generation Finn, I had also come from a legacy of social protest. But it seemed to me that corrections of industry abuse must be made within the system, rather than by its overthrow. What was needed was a disciplined labor alliance with the muscle to beat down industry's overbearing resolve to resist it. By the end of the first World War, it had become apparent that at least some members of the body politic were starting to take notice of such glaring industrial problems as meager pay, long hours, work safety, injury compensation and child labor.

President Wilson, for one, had declared such questions to be paramount among all social issues. And at least a handful of Senators and Congressmen were in agreement that their resolution was of primary economic importance.

Talk was one thing. But in order to prompt them to set standards and establish regulations, labor needed to build a solid base of political power. To get it we needed organization for without it there is no power. This was the goal I was to spend my life working for.

‡‡ ‡‡ ‡‡ ‡‡ ‡‡

Anders Korvala's chance came in 1919, when Work Peoples College sent him to Chicago to observe a conference called to help promote a sense of solidarity among a diverse and often at odds group of unions. It was there during one of the sessions that his youthful zeal and quick intelligence caught the eye of John L. Lewis. The crusty head of the powerful United Mine Workers Union recruited Korvala on the spot and after a short training period sent him to see what he could do to help build up union sentiment in the coal mines of the South.

From then on through the 1920s, Anders spent most of his time traveling, recruiting and organizing. Years later, after Lewis helped found the Congress for Industrial Organizations (C.I.O.), Korvala was a key field director in setting up a number of the sit-down strikes that swept factories and mines during the latter days of the Depression.

Regarding their years of association, Korvala once wrote that he could sum up all that he had learned from Lewis in four sentences: "You can't get better work conditions unless you're willing to fight for them. ... Employers are powerful because they're organized. ... But labor holds the power of production. ... And whatever the situation, people can get things done together they can't get done themselves."

Anders Korvala usually made light of the worst of times during his 45 years of rallies, marches and tense hours on picket lines. Of half a dozen times he was jailed on charges of public disturbance, he said little except to joke about the food. Almost never did he talk about the broken nose or other facial evidence of scraps with company goons in long forgotten towns.

The bad times, he claimed, were offset by occasional moments of triumph for labor. One of these was the day in 1937, when the Supreme Court upheld the National Labor Relations Act—the act that legitimized the right of labor to organize and bargain through agents chosen by the majority. But his greatest personal satisfaction came in 1943, 27 years after his exile from the Iron Range, when he was there to see the Oliver Mining Company sign a labor contract with the C.I.O.

Probably because of his nomadic career, Anders Korvala never married. His only kin were the families of the younger brothers for whose support he had given up his boyhood. He died in 1967 and is buried beside his mother and father in Aurora, Minnesota.

- 59 -

MINNESOTA MISCELLANY

History 240—Lecture 32
J. R. Makki

Unfortunately our 16 weeks together have not been long enough to do justice to everything that sets Minnesota apart from anywhere else on earth. Take, for instance, our lakes and rivers:

Sky Blue Waters. State boosters have long beat the drums for our "Ten Thousand Lakes." But how many visitors realize that the true count is closer to 15,000. ... or that Minnesota lakes and rivers hold more water than any other state ... and can boast total shorelines longer than California, Hawaii and Florida combined?

The existence of these waters and their connecting portages was of enormous importance to the opening and developing of the wilderness that was to become America's thirty-second state. Waterways like the St. Louis and St. Croix, whose names reflect their French heritage, made possible the passage of 17th century explorers, missionaries and fur traders. Later they were to become floatways for a burgeoning lumber industry. But it was three much larger rivers, each of their waters flowing in different directions, that were to link Minnesota with the rest of the world.

Mississippi. We all know about Henry Schoolcraft and his discovery of Lake Itasca as the “true source” of the greatest river in North America. And how he chopped off the first and last syllables of two Latin words (*veritas* and *caput*) to form the hybrid name Itasca. But did he have it right?

Well, the evidence indicates he was pretty close. However, since all the waters near that lake are connected by springs and streams, it really isn’t correct to pinpoint a single lake as the sole source of that mighty waterway. Rangers in Itasca Park will tell you that the best bet is to say that the magnificent river, whose twisting course flows from Minnesota through the nation’s heart, begins in the Itasca basin.

During the steamboat era that lasted till after the Civil War, a huge fleet of packet steamers linked the output of Minnesota farms to the markets and industrial output of the eastern seaboard. In 1823, the *Virginia* became the first steamboat to come up river as far as Fort Snelling. From St. Louis it took 20 days. After that, until its eclipse by railroads, St. Paul became the big river’s northern terminus. Any traffic further up was blocked by the Falls of St. Anthony.

With the coming of the railroads, it seemed time had passed the Mississippi by. But then after a long hiatus, transportation needs of World War II restored its place as a major artery for heavy goods such as the Minnesota iron ore that fueled the Allies’ armament. After that came recognition that bulk goods like ore, coal and grain could be carried more cheaply by water. Today, for all but the few months when its northern reaches are ice-bound, the bluffs that frame the big river resound to the throb of powerful tugboat engines driving strings of barges.

Minnesota. Just beneath the citadel of old Fort Snelling, the Mississippi is joined by the longest American river wholly in one state. Starting from our western border, the Minnesota follows a curlicue course southeast to Mankato where it arcs north toward its confluence with the Mississippi. The Minnesota's water distance of 475 miles is about three times longer than a direct line between these two points.

In earlier times the domain of the Sioux, the river was later claimed by Spain, France, England and finally America. Reflecting those regimes, the river's name has been successively changed from St. Pierre to St. Peter and finally to Minnesota after we became a territory. Until the mid-1800s, trade on the narrow, winding Minnesota was by canoe or keelboat rowed or sometimes towed from its banks by long ropes. In time, steamboat pilots became adept at negotiating the river's myriad of twists and turns. Specially built shallow-draft boats soon turned it into a highway for settlement of its fertile valley. For a graphic description of steamboat traffic on the Minnesota, see the 1861 letter of Henry Thoreau cited by Evan Jones in *The Minnesota: Forgotten River.*

Next came the challenge to cross the divide that separated the Minnesota from its north-flowing counterpart, the Red River. Though named for its color under late afternoon sun, the river is actually brown from its muddy banks. When several tries to bridge the gap failed, steamboat traffic on the Red finally opened up after an enterprising captain and his crew hauled machinery overland to the river. There they cut timber, sawed lumber, built a boat and after installing machinery, sailed it to Canada.

During years to follow, whenever the water was high enough, Red River boats carried freight and passengers the length of the river up to Lake Winnipeg. As immigrants poured in to farm the rich soil of the valley, villages like East Grand Forks and Moorhead grew rapidly. And in the late 1800s with the coming of the railroads, towns along the river began to sprout grain elevators. Once serving as pathways into unexplored wilderness, Minnesota rivers continue today as important routes of trade and commerce.

Here are a few other items you won't be tested on but which are also important aspects of our Minnesota heritage:

The Great Seal. The evolution of Minnesota's state seal bears a confusing twist for the Indian brave seen in its background. The original version was designed to show a settler breaking sod while behind an Indian rides into the sunset. Somehow in the seal's stamping, the sun got placed in the east, creating the impression of an Indian cantering off for an early morning visit to Wisconsin.

In the next version after Minnesota became a state, Old Sol and the Indian were set back on course to the west. This was the edition that introduced the phrase E'toile du Nord, to recognize the French trail blazers who first ventured into our wilderness.

More recently, reflecting sensitivity to changing social opinion, the Indian has been moved to a new position, where trotting to the south he appears to be exchanging pleasantries with the settler who has been the one constant in all versions of the seal. With unerring instinct the settler has managed to plow a straight furrow to the east while looking over his shoulder to the north.

Of Great and Near Great. Minnesota has had its share of leaders in all walks of American life. There have been candidates for the Oval office, vice presidents, supreme court justices, cabinet members, war heroes, Nobel Laureates, physicians, surgeons, scientists, educators, authors, journalists, agronomists, sports figures, entertainers and captains of industry. But no other Minnesotan, nor for that matter few people anywhere, have ever been caught up in the worldwide adulation once accorded a young aviator from Little Falls, Minnesota.

In this country, 1927 is recalled as a year of celebrated events. George Herman (Babe) Ruth hit 60 homeruns, Jack Dempsey lost the famous "long count" fight and Al Jolson starred in the first successful talking picture. But none of these singly or together, came close to the electrifying response to the first solo flight across the Atlantic.

May 21, 1927, when Charles Lindbergh landed his *Spirit of St. Louis* at Le Bourget Airport outside Paris, has been called a signature moment of the 20th century. Heralding as it did the modern age of air travel, that nonstop flight across the Atlantic may have been the most important long-distance flight ever. A few months later, the "Lone Eagle" detoured from his triumphal national tour in order to fly to Little Falls for a homecoming celebration. The house in which he grew up was built by his father, Congressman Charles A. Lindbergh. It is now kept up as a state historical site.

Of course, with roots on the Iron Range, I can't leave out another baseball great—Hibbing native Roger Maris, who 34 years later hit 61 homers to shatter the Babe's record.

Minerals and Rocks. Geologists inform us that during eons beyond recall, Minnesota was submerged under ancient seas. That, followed by volcanic action and glacial erosion, has helped expose coarse-grained outcrops as old as any rocks ever discovered on earth. Among these, or beneath surface crust, have been embedded an immeasurable wealth of minerals.

When we think of Minnesota natural resources, iron ore comes quickly to mind. But long before ore was being mined on the ranges of northern Minnesota, Indians of the vanished Laurel culture were picking up copper nuggets and fashioning them into ornaments and tools such as awls, knives and fish hooks.

In southwest Minnesota, tribes throughout the region came to dig soft calumet-making stone from the site now known as Pipestone National Monument.

Even before the Civil War, Minnesota quarries had begun producing structural and decorative stone for building purposes. Over the years more than 50 kinds of architectural slabs have been cut, shaped and polished for monuments and buildings all over America. Granite quarried from around St. Cloud has been favored by architects for state capitol buildings, famous hotels and landmark structures like the Tribune Tower on Chicago's Michigan Avenue, sometimes called "a symphony in stone." In

New York City, it required 1,100 carloads of St. Cloud stone to finish the outside of the Federal Courthouse.

In St. Paul, the State Capitol combines European marble with Minnesota limestone. A few blocks to the south, the Cathedral of St. Paul is another fine example of the use of St. Cloud granite.

Minnesota stones used in a quite different way may be seen at Blue Mound State park in the southwest corner of the state. There, in what has been compared to England's Stonehenge, lies prehistoric evidence of advanced human intelligence. Somebody, no one knows who, set up a row of rocks a quarter mile long and aligned in an east-west direction so as to line up with sunrise and sunset on the first days of spring and fall.

A Tale of the Tape. Although no one seems to remember how the name came about, Minnesota is the birthplace of one of the world's most famous brand names. Developed by the Minnesota Mining and Manufacturing Company in 1930, "Scotch Tape" in short order became a home and office staple used for a myriad of sealing and mending problems all around the globe.

Scotch tape may have thrust 3M into the international marketing arena, but it is today only one of thousands of products developed by the Company's research laboratories. This, from an enterprise that began on a false premise and all but foundered as a result. 3M launched operations in Two Harbors in 1902 to mine what it believed was corundum, a natural abrasive in great demand by American industry. Sadly, its ore output turned out to be something other than corundum and virtually useless as an abrasive. Somehow surviving by making sand paper, the Company struggled along, always on the verge of going under until taken in hand by a shy young man who knew how to get things done. No one could have predicted that the 19-year old assistant bookkeeper 3M had hired in 1907 would shortly become the key player in the little company's rise to world eminence.

William L. McKnight, born in a sod hut on a windswept South Dakota prairie, was quick to catch the attention of his hard-pressed employers, who moved him steadily up to the position of general manager while he was still in his mid-20s. It was under McKnight's direction that basic policies, production standards and selling techniques were set in motion to gradually boost the Company onto the black side of the ledger and to its eventual role as one of America's most successful and diversified ventures.

Different opinions have been set forth as the reason behind the name of the Scotch Brand series of products. My own guess is that it reflects the Scottish heritage of the South Dakota farm boy who was to guide 3M during four critical decades of its emergence as a worldwide leader of industrial, consumer and medical products.

Prohibition. The 1919 bill known as the Volstead Act paved the way for the 18th Amendment which outlawed the manufacture, transportation and sale of alcoholic beverages. This action, which someone commented did not appear to "represent the settled conviction of society," bore the stamp of Minnesota Congressman Andrew Volstead, whose legal spadework helped ram it through.

As it turned out, policing of the Act by a small force of agents proved virtually impossible. Millions of Americans who wanted to drink either made their own brews at home, or more often bought their beer or spirits from hundreds of "bootleggers," who earned an illegal but well-paying living providing it. "Rumrunners" smuggled whiskey in from Canada and other countries. And in the Twin Cities, as in most of America's larger cities, illegal "speakeasies," did a flourishing business. When in 1933 the 18th Amendment was finally judged a failure, it was repealed.

Peace Pact. History has not embraced Congressman Volstead with the mantle of statesmanship accorded his Minnesota contemporary, Frank B. Kellogg. A native of New

York State, Kellogg came with his family to Minnesota at age nine. Although his formal education ended with grade school, he later studied law in Rochester. In 1916, he was elected a U.S. Senator from Minnesota. And in 1925, he was appointed Secretary of State by President Coolidge.

Three years later Kellogg won the Nobel Peace Prize for his part in negotiating a treaty to outlaw war. Although 64 nations were to sign the Kellogg-Briand pact, it, like Prohibition, turned out to be little more than an expression of hope. By the time of his death in 1937, Kellogg's once acclaimed pact had been consigned to history's dust-bin by the Japanese, Italian and German aggression that preceded World War II.

Population. When in 1849 Minnesota became a territory, less than 5,000 settlers lived within limits of what later became its state boundaries. Today, Minnesota is twelfth largest among U.S. states in land area. But its population remains under two percent of the nation's people.

In all, Minnesota has 87 counties. But well over half its 3.8 million people* live and work in a seven-county area around the Twin Cities. St. Louis County with Duluth, Olmsted with Rochester and Stearns with St. Cloud are the next most populated counties, with over a hundred thousand each. The rest of Minnesota's people are spread out in greater or less measure across the state. Lake of the Woods County, up north, has barely four thousand, and only a few more live in Traverse and Red Lake Counties in the Red River Valley.

Legends and Monuments. The bigger-than-life myth of Paul Bunyan is celebrated in small towns all over the state. Monuments to the legendary giant's storied possessions are to be found even in such unlikely places as Ortonville that may have never even seen a lumberjack. Tourists are lured to that town

---

* Based on estimates for 1972, when lectures were given. The total in 2001 is over 4.6 million.

near the source of the Minnesota River to see a 125-ton anchor supposedly left behind by Paul—skipping lightly over the question of whether the big fellow, off in his north woods domain, even knew what an anchor was.

In Brainerd, a 26-foot high talking statue is a prime attraction for that city's Paul Bunyan Amusement Center. Further north, the gentle giant and his faithful ox companion, Babe, are much photographed fixtures along the shores of Lake Bemidji.

Although Bemidji claims Bunyan as a native son, the evidence for nearby Akeley is more compelling. That tiny hamlet displays a mammoth cradle as well as a kneeling 42-foot high statue said to be the world's tallest Paul Bunyan. It was in fact at Akeley that Minnesota additions to the Bunyan legend first appeared in the writings of a lumber company journal.

Among Bunyan tales with a Minnesota twist is one about a hole he scooped out that later filled with water to become Lake Superior. Another yarn holds that our ten thousand lakes are the result of hoof prints stamped by Babe, the great blue ox. But these were tales spun at the end of Minnesota's logging era. And it is clear that stories about the giant's incredible feats were first hatched years before in the lumber camps of America's northeast. As cited earlier, historian Theodore Blegen doubted that lumberjacks who worked during Minnesota's logging heyday ever heard of Paul Bunyan.

Minnesota's penchant for the outsized extends across the state, where numerous small town booster groups promote an assortment of avian specimens including a duck, turkey, loon and even a blue-eyed chicken, all billed as "The World's Largest." There is also a 107-foot hockey stick, a monstrous walleye, the world's tallest Canadian Voyageur, "Big Ole the Viking," the Jolly Green Giant and a ball of twine 12 feet in diameter.

In more practical manner, Duluth is home to the world's largest aerial lift bridge, while at Hibbing can be seen the awesome canyon from whence came a third of the iron ore produced during World War II. For a natural marvel, consider the 60-foot underground waterfall at the Niagara Cave in Fillmore County, or the ten miles of caverns and passageways at nearby Mystery Cave.

But why go underground when beneath skies of "Minnesota Blue" are to be seen rolling hills and sparkling lakes, fertile river valleys and rockbound bluffs—a landscape so diverse as to let anyone with a sense of place know it could only be Minnesota.

North Star State. For many years Minnesota was known as the nation's most northerly-reaching state, a distinction it had to yield after Alaska came into the Union. However, the curious projection of land known as the "Northwest Angle" still remains the northern apex of the Lower 48.

Someone has figured out that the Twin Cities are exactly halfway between the Equator and the North Pole. Astride the 45th parallel of latitude, they are the most northerly center of major population. And so the words of our official state song: "Minnesota, hail to thee! ... Thou shalt be their Northern Star."

- 60 -

ONLY IN MINNESOTA

Our last regular class met the second week in January, with finals two days later. They'd been a good group, attentive and with lots of questions. But they looked a trifle nervous when I handed out a chronology of historical events. I told them to relax. The final exam would be a measure of what they had learned in general about Minnesota, and not a test of short-term recall for names and dates.

Ours had been an all-too-brief survey of Minnesota's formative years. Whenever possible, I had tried to tell it through the eyes of people who had been part of it. Too much that was important had been skimmed over or left out entirely. For more about the founding of a great university system, the 20th century growth of the Twin Cities into a commercial and industrial metropolis, of Duluth as a hub of international shipping, and of Rochester as a capital city of world medicine, I could only urge further study, perhaps using the chronology and attached reading list* as a starting point.

The final, two days later, consisted of one essay question in which I asked them to explain why the history we had spent 16

---

* NB from Jim Makki: Writing as I am after the turn of the 21st century, I've added more recent resources to the bibliography I handed out in 1972 to my first class of Minnesota History students.

weeks discussing could have happened only in Minnesota. Although I can't imagine what it would take to flunk something so simple, that wasn't the point. The aim had been to help the kids carry away a lasting impression of Minnesota's one-of-a-kind individuality. And in this, judging from the response, I had been successful.

After laying a base of the state's geological and topographical legacy—mineral deposits, the surface wrought by glaciers, the waterways, great forests and fertile soils, all 44 students spoke in greater or lesser extent of the spectrum of people and events that had shaped our rich history.

Where else, they asked, could a passing parade that had begun with prehistoric mammoth hunters have continued on as a cavalcade of mighty Indian tribes, bold explorers under the banners of three European countries, fur traders, voyageurs, missionaries, soldiers, river men, wheat farmers, flour millers, lumberjacks, sawmillers, railroad builders, prospectors, iron miners, titans of industry and workers and settlers from half a hundred foreign lands?

Many states could lay claim to some from so colorful a procession. But only one place had seen them all. Given what we've been and become, it could have happened only in Minnesota.

- 61 -

HARWELL COLLEGE

September 2001

I should tell you that not long after its inception, our course in Minnesota history was expanded to a full-year elective. The extra term details the state's 20th century economic and cultural growth. Today, Minnesota stands among America's leaders in farming, business, industry, technology and medicine as well as in public education and the arts.

It's been years since I've taught the course. But the young people who do teach it sometimes ask me back for a lecture on immigration. The kids look at me with the kind of awe associated with gazing upon an ancient ruin. Hard to believe its been almost 30 years since I first set foot on this campus.

Judson Leonard, who brought me to Harwell in 1972, stepped down as department chairman in the early 80s. He was succeeded by Walton Alexander, who had the original notion to bring me here. Jud is now gone and Walt retired in 1995. Both were exceptional scholars and I was humbled to be named in their line of succession as department chairman.

As Professor of Immigration, I've acquired a modest reputation for research and writings into the cause and effects of the 19th and 20th century waves that brought the forebears of nearly half of all living Americans to our shores. Away from the classroom, I've doubled as sprint and hurdles coach for the men's and women's track teams. Last spring I had the thrill of watching my youngest daughter, Sari, win the league championship in the 120-yard hurdles.

My stepson, Tim, also ran track at Harwell. He graduated in 1990 and is now Associate Professor of Literature at Hobart and William Smith Colleges. Our middle child, Lori, kicked over the traces and went to UM. She's now married to a Mayo doctor and does social work.

All of which brings me back to the gal with the freckled nose and impish grin who's been my best friend for 30 years. You'll remember it was Sue Humboldt who saw me through my slough of despond after the collapse of my affair that never was, with Christie White.

Sue retired a few years back from the job in the library. Now, by way of fulfilling her ambition, she is a feature writer and co-editor of the Harwell College *Literary Survey*.

In case you're wondering, Sue and I were married in 1973. Here's how that came about.

It was an early Saturday afternoon in February and we were finishing up a picnic lunch on a rocky bluff looming over the big river a hundred yards below. We had clomped up here on skis from the parking lot a couple miles down.

Brushing off a crumb from my sandwich, I looked at my buddy Sue. Flush with cold and a hint of smile setting off her dimples, she looked even prettier than usual. "So what's with you and Dave? You haven't said much about him lately."

Setting down her thermos mug, she stared at it for a moment as if searching for an answer. "You ninny, that's been over for months."

"But I thought —"

"I know what you thought." She cut me off. "I told you he's a nice guy, and he is. But the last time we got together, he started in again about setting a date. And when I told him I still wasn't ready, he asked me why."

Sue hesitated and seemed pensive. "Dave is a wonderful

man. But there has to be more. It's not enough to spend your life with someone just because he's nice. It came to me that Dave wasn't who I wanted to be the father of the little boy I'm about to take back from my folks."

"Well, that's just great!" I was little miffed. "Why'd you take so long to tell me?"

"Because I've been waiting for you to let go that baggage of feeling sorry for yourself about Christie White."

"What's that got to do with anything?"

"Everything, you idiot." And now tears were running down her cheek. "But if you're too dense to figure that out, I'm not going to tell you." And then she got up and stumbled away in the snow.

Too surprised to react, I looked after this girl, my best friend. There was nobody, including the ghost of Christabel White, I cared for more. Christie had been a mirage while Sue was the flesh and blood, warm-hearted woman who had helped me through my worst time ever. There was nobody I'd rather be with. It was Sue all the time and I'd been too blind to see it.

She tried to break away when I caught her. But I kissed her and just like that, clinging to each other in snow up to our knees, she became more than my best friend.

"Sue," I said, "I've been a total jerk mooning over Christie when all the time I've been in love with you."

I took her wet snuffle in my ear to mean agreement. "But about you and Dave, I just always thought that was settled. I was maybe even a bit jealous. I just wish you'd told me sooner."

Sue and I were married in the Harwell Chapel just after school let out in May. Both our parents were there along with Sue's young son Tim—now my son, too. After that we took off for our honeymoon at Lake Vermilion, surrounded perhaps by the ghosts of departed Makkis, who had lived and enjoyed their time in that precious old cabin.

My Dad fell in love with Sue almost as much as I, one reason being that she taught herself to be nearly as good as he was at catching walleye. Mom loved her too, partly because of

Sue's down-to-earth ways and probably also for ending her worries about me growing old without a wife.

Well, all that was a long time ago. And there isn't much else to say except I never saw Christie White again. Through the mists of time she comes to me only as a tender memory. I have no idea how life turned out for her. But I know now that she made the right decision. And I'm just glad she did.

- APPENDIX -

SOME LEADING EVENTS IN MINNESOTA HISTORY

1659	French traders Pierre Radisson and Sieur des Groseilliers are probably the first Europeans to enter Minnesota during an expedition west from Quebec.
1679-80	Daniel Greysolon, Sieur du Luth lands near site of present day Duluth ... Travels inland to hold peace conference with the Sioux on the shores of Mille Lacs ... Reaches the Mississippi via St. Croix ... Frees Father Louis Hennepin from Sioux captivity ... Shortly thereafter Hennepin sees the Falls of St. Anthony, which he names for his patron saint.
1689	Nicholas Perrot erects a fort on west shore of Lake Pepin and claims surrounding country for France.
1695	At what is now called Prairie Island, Pierre Le Sueur builds first of a series of French forts and trading posts within present day Minnesota.

1762	France cedes part of future Minnesota to Spain. A year later, after losing the French and Indian War, France cedes land east of Mississippi to England.
1803	Three years after Spain ceded land west of Mississippi back to France, U.S. gains control by means of the Louisiana Purchase.
1805	Lieut. Zebulon Pike leads expedition up Mississippi to explore lands acquired by Louisiana Purchase ... Makes treaty with Sioux to obtain rights to land on which Fort Snelling is later erected.
1819-20	Fort St. Anthony is established. Col. Josiah Snelling, its Second Commandant, begins construction program for the fort later named in his honor.
1823	The *Virginia* is first steamboat to ascend the upper Mississippi, landing at Fort Snelling following a 20-day trip from St. Louis.
1832	Explorer-writer Henry Rowe Schoolcraft determines Elk Lake to be the true source of the Mississippi. Renames it Lake Itasca.
1834	Henry Hastings Sibley settles at Mendota as regional supervisor for the American Fur Company.
1838	Franklin Steele, sutler at Fort Snelling, lays claim to land alongside Falls of St. Anthony. Later builds a dam which leads to start of the lumber industry at the Falls. French-Canadian Pierre Parrant builds a whiskey-selling shanty at site of

present-day St. Paul. Squatters settling nearby call it "Pig's Eye," after Parrant's nickname. The name of the future state capital changes after a rude chapel dedicated to St. Paul is built there.

1849 Territory of Minnesota is established. President Zachary Taylor, who had once been Commandant at Fort Snelling, appoints Alexander Ramsey as the new territory's first governor.

1851 Through treaties at Traverse des Sioux and Mendota, Minnesota gains nearly 20 million acres. The way is opened for large scale immigration and settlement of land west of the Mississippi.

1854 Commercial flour milling begins at what is later to become Minneapolis.

1858 On May 11, Minnesota is admitted to the Union as its thirty-second state. Henry Hastings Sibley is elected its first governor.

1860 Alexander Ramsey elected to succeed Sibley as governor. State population reaches 172,000.

1861 Civil War begins. Governor Ramsey promises a thousand volunteers, giving Minnesota the honor of being the first state to offer troops.

1862 In late summer, Sioux attacks on Minnesota Valley forts and towns result in massacre of about 800 settlers. By end of September, troops under command of Sibley put insurrection down. On December 26, thirty-eight Indians charged with murder or other crimes of violence are hanged at Mankato. This black chapter in Minnesota history was the result of shoddy and often fraudulent administration of Indian affairs.

1863 On July 2, First Minnesota Regiment saves the day at Gettysburg. While stemming a breakthrough by a much larger Rebel force, two thirds of the First's 262 men were killed or wounded.

1865 Civil War ends. From 1861 to 1865, Minnesota sent out 22,000 officers and men to fight in Civil and Sioux Wars—a total amounting to around nine percent of its population of 250,000. Of these, nearly 2,600 were killed in action or died from disease or accidents.

1869 The University of Minnesota opens its doors under leadership of Regent John Pillsbury and its first President, William Watts Folwell.

1884 First iron ore is shipped from the Soudan Mine on the Vermilion Range.

1890 Merritt Brothers discover ore at Mountain Iron on the Mesabi Range.

1893 James J. Hill, "The Empire Builder," completes his Great Northern Railway link to Puget Sound.

1894 Forest fires wipe out Hinckley and other nearby towns. More than 400 men, women and children perish. Over the years, other disastrous fires ravage Virginia, Baudette, Spooner, Moose Lake and Chisholm.

1898 Alexander Ramsey lays cornerstone for the present Minnesota State Capitol. The building was designed by Cass Gilbert, architect for the U.S. Supreme Court Building and New York's Woolworth Building, and was completed in January, 1905. Spanish American War starts. State supplies four regiments for service during that conflict.

1917-18 Fort Snelling reactivated as a reception center and officer training school. More than 126,000 Minnesotans see service during World War I. Nearly 3,500 killed or die in service while 5,000 others are wounded.

1941-45 More than 300,000 Minnesota soldiers, sailors and airmen fight in every theater of World War II. Our iron ranges produce most of the ore for America's "Arsenal of Democracy."

1956 Reserve Mining Company begins large-scale production of taconite at Silver Bay, Minnesota.

1959 The St. Lawrence Seaway is opened to make Duluth a leading world port.

1960 Following its final service in World War II, old Fort Snelling is designated a national historic landmark.

- END NOTES -

Source documents and additional materials
in support of historical facts

Chapter 5: The Recallings of an Old Ox Cart Driver

LeSueur, Meridel. *North Star Country*. New York: Duell, Sloan & Pearce, 1945.

Flandrau, Charles E. *The History of Minnesota and Tales of the Frontier*. St. Paul, MN: Porter, 1910.

Chapter 7: Way Up North

Havighurst, Walter. *Voices on the River*. New York: MacMillan Company, 1964.

Severin, Timothy. *Explorers of the Mississippi*. New York: Alfred A. Knopf, 1968.

Silverberg, Robert. *Mound Builders of Ancient America*. Greenwich, CT: New York Graphic Society, 1968.

Chapter 16: Supplement for Lectures 3 to 6

Adams, Arther T., Editor. *The Explorations of Pierre Esprit Radisson*, from original manuscript in the Bodleian Library; Loren Kellsen, Modernizer. Minneapolis, MN: Ross & Haines, Inc. 1961.

Hennepin, Father Louis. *Description of Louisiana*, translated by Marion E. Cross. St. Paul, MN: University of Minnesota Press, 1938.

Jones, Rev. Peter. *History of the Ojebway Indians*. Freeport, NY: Books For Libraries Press, 1861.

Neill, Rev. Edward D. *History of the Minnesota Valley*. Minneapolis, MN: North Star Publishing Company, 1882.

Nute, Grace Lee. *Caesars Of The Wilderness*. St. Paul, MN: Minnesota Historical Society Press, 1978.

Parkman, Francis. *France and England in North America*. Boston, MA: Little, Brown & Co, 1865-1892. Reprint: New York: Viking Press, 1983.

Robinson, Doane. *A History of the Dakota or Sioux Indians*. Aberdeen, SD: State of South Dakota, 1904. Reprint: Minneapolis, MN: Ross & Haines, Inc., 1956.

Severin, Timothy. *Explorers of the Mississippi*. New York: Alfred A. Knopf, 1968.

Chapter 17: Black Robes in the Wilderness

Parkman, Francis. *France and England in North America*. Boston, MA: Little, Brown & Co, 1865-1892. Reprint: New York: Viking Press, 1983.

Chapter 19: The Battle of Sandy Lake

Jones, Rev. Peter. *History of the Ojebway Indians*. Freeport, NY: Books For Libraries Press, 1861.

Pike, Zebulon. *The Journals of Zebulon Montgomery Pike*, edited and annotated by Donald Jackson. Norman, OK: University of Oklahoma Press, 1966.

Warren, William W. *History of the Ojibway People*. Reprint: St. Paul, MN: Minnesota Historical Society Press, 1984. Originally Published by Minnesota Historical Society, 1885.

Chapter 21: Beacon in the Wilderness

Blegen, Theodore C. *The Land Lies Open*. Minneapolis, MN: University of Minnesota Press, 1949.

Hansen, Marcus L. *Old Fort Snelling, 1819-1858*. Iowa City, IA: State Historical Society of Iowa, 1918.

Chapter 23: King Beaver

Morison, Samuel Eliot. *The Oxford History of the American People*. New York: Oxford University Press, 1965.

Chapter 28: Sibley and Ramsey Come to Minnesota

West, Nathaniel. *The Ancestry, Life and Times of Hon. Henry Hastings Sibley, LL.D*. St. Paul, MN: Pioneer Press Co., 1889.

Chapter 30: "... Let Them Eat Grass"

Bjornson, Val. *The History of Minnesota, Vol. I*. West Palm Beach, FL: Lewis Publishing Company, 1969.

LeSueur, Meridel. *North Star Country*. New York: Duell, Sloan & Pearce, 1945.

Robinson, Doane. *A History of the Dakota or Sioux Indians*. Aberdeen, SD: State of South Dakota, 1904. Reprint: Minneapolis, MN: Ross & Haines, Inc., 1956.

Tolzmann, Don. H., Editor. *Memories of the Battle of New Ulm*. Bowie, MD: Heritage Books Inc, 2001.

Chapter 31: "The Indians are Raising Hell"

Bjornson, Val. *The History of Minnesota, Vol. I.* West Palm Beach, FL: Lewis Publishing Company, 1969.

Flandrau, Charles E. *The History of Minnesota and Tales of the Frontier*. St. Paul, MN: Porter, 1910.

Folwell, William Watts. *Minnesota, The North Star State*. Boston, MA: Houghton Mifflin Company, 1908.

Oehler, C. M. *The Great Sioux Uprising*. New York: Oxford University Press, 1959.

Chapter 34: Minnesota and the Civil War

Minnesota Board of Commissioners on the Publication of History of Minnesota in the Civil and Indian Wars. *Minnesota in the Civil and Indian Wars, Vol. 1*. St. Paul, MN: Pioneer Press, 1890.

Chapter 38: Gettysburg

Hansen, Harry, *The Civil War*. New York: Duell, Sloan and Pearce, 1961.

Chapter 40: After the War

Folwell, William Watts. *A History of Minnesota, in Four Volumes*. St. Paul, MN: Minnesota Historical Society, 1921-1926. Reprint: St. Paul, MN: Minnesota Historical Society Press, 1956. Vol. III.

Gjerde, Jon and Carlton C. Qualey *Norwegians in America*. St. Paul, MN: Minnesota Historical Society Press, 2002.

Chapter 41: Lumbering in Minnesota

The special qualities of white pine were recently described as follows: "Of all woods, the straightest, the most desirable, the best for building homes, churches and barns, [white pine] was ... abundant and in great demand." Minnesota Department of Natural Resources: *Minnesota White Pine*. St. Paul, MN: Minnesota Department of Natural Resources, 1996.

Chapter 46: A Metropolis is Born

Folwell, William Watts. *A History of Minnesota, in Four Volumes*. St. Paul, MN: Minnesota Historical Society Press, 1921-26. Reprint: St. Paul, MN: Minnesota Historical Society Press, 1956.

Kane, Lucile M. *The Waterfall That Built A City*. St. Paul, MN: Minnesota Historical Society Press, 1966.

Gjerde, Jon and Carlton C. Qualey. *Norwegians in America*. St. Paul, MN: Minnesota Historical Society Press, 2002.

Jarchow, Merrill E. *The Earth Brought Forth: A History of Minnesota Agriculture to 1885*. St. Paul, MN: Minnesota Historical Society Press, 1949.

Chapter 47: " ... A Bridge of Gold"

Fish, Everett W. *Donnelliana; Excerpts from the wit, wisdom, poetry and eloquence of Ignatius Donnelly*. Chicago, IL: F. J. Schulte & Company, 1892.

Chapter 50: The Great Hinckley Fire

Minnesota Historical Society. *Great Northern Railway Co., Eastern Railway Co. of Minnesota, Samuel Hill File 94*. Original Documents. St. Paul, MN: Minnesota Historical Society.

Holbrook, Stewart H. *Burning An Empire*. New York: The Macmillan Company, 1943.

Swenson, Grace Stageberg. *From the Ashes*. Stillwater, MN: Croixside Press, 1979.

Chapter 51: "... The Greatest Natural Resource Ever Bestowed"

Holmquist, June Drenning, Editor. *They Chose Minnesota*. St. Paul, MN: Minnesota Historical Society Press, 1981.

Chapter 52: Pathfinders

DeKruif, Paul. *Seven Iron Men*. New York: Harcourt, Brace, 1929.

Chapter 53: Sleeping Giant

Longyear, Edmund J. *Mesabi Pioneer*. Edited by Grace Lee Nute. St. Paul, MN: Minnesota Historical Society Press, 1951.

Chapter 59: Minnesota Miscellany

Huck, Virginia. *Brand of the Tartan: The 3M Story*. New York: Appleton-Century-Crofts, Inc., 1955.

Jones, Evan. *The Minnesota—Forgotten River*. New York: Holt, Rinehart and Winston, 1962.

Appendix: Some Leading Events In Minnesota History

Bjornson, Val. *The History of Minnesota*. West Palm Beach, FL: Lewis Historical Publishing Company, 1969.

Castle, Henry A. *Minnesota: Its Story and Biography*. Chicago, IL: The Lewis Publishing Co., 1915.

Minnesota Secretary of State: *Minnesota Legislative Manual*, 2001-2002. St. Paul, MN: Minnesota Secretary of State, 2001.

Kunz, Virginia Brainard. *Muskets to Missiles*. St. Paul, MN: Minnesota Statehood Centennial Commission, 1958.

BIBLIOGRAPHY

In writing this fictional but factual account of Minnesota history I have drawn heavily on the scholarly efforts of others. Here follows what is at best a partial list of works to which I am indebted. I must also pay respects for the innumerable newspaper articles gleaned from microfilm collections in the libraries of the Minnesota Historical Society and the Iron Range Research Center as well as for yellowing manuscripts and tattered city directories available at libraries in Rochester, Duluth, Virginia, Hibbing and Buhl, Minnesota.

GENERAL HISTORY:

Anderson, David, Editor. *A History of Downtown Minneapolis and St. Paul.* Minneapolis, MN: Nodin Press, 2000.

Billington, Ray Allen and Martin Ridge. *Westward Expansion: A History of the American Frontier, 5th edition.* New York: Macmillan Publishing Co., Inc., 1982.

Bjornson, Val. *The History of Minnesota.* West Palm Beach, FL: Lewis Historical Publishing Company, 1969.

Blegen, Theodore C. *Minnesota: A History of the State.* Minneapolis, MN: University of Minnesota Press, 1963.

________. *The Land Lies Open*. Minneapolis, MN: University of Minnesota Press, 1949.

________. *Building Minnesota*. New York: D.C. Heath and Co. 1938.

________, and Philip D. Jordan. *With Various Voices*. St. Paul, MN: Itasca Press, 1949.

Borchert, John R. "The Network of Urban Centers," from *Minnesota in a Century of Change*. St. Paul, MN: Minnesota Historical Society Press, 1989.

Burnquist, Joseph A. A. *Minnesota and its People*, Vol. I. Chicago, IL: The S. J. Clarke Publishing Company, 1924.

Castle, Henry A. *Minnesota: Its Story and Biography*. Chicago, IL: The Lewis Publishing Co., 1915.

Clark, Clifford E., Jr. Editor. *Minnesota in a Century of Change*. St. Paul, MN: Minnesota Historical Society Press, 1989.

Felton, Harold W. *Legends of Paul Bunyan*. New York: A.A. Knopf, 1947.

Folwell, William Watts. *A History of Minnesota, in Four Volumes*. St. Paul, MN: Minnesota Historical Society, 1921-1926. Reprint: St. Paul, MN: Minnesota Historical Society Press, 1956.

Gelbach, Deborah. *From This Land: A History of Minnesota's Empires, Enterprises, and Entrepreneurs*. Northridge, CA: Windsor Publications, Inc., 1988.

Gilman, Rhoda. *The Story of Minnesota's Past*. St. Paul, MN: Minnesota Historical Society Press, 1989.

Holmquist, June Drenning and Jean A. Brookins. *Minnesota's Major Historical Sites*. St. Paul, MN: Minnesota Historical Society Press, 1972.

Johnson, Frederick. *Goodhue County, Minnesota*. Redwing, MN: Goodhue County Historical Society, 2000.

Lass, William E. *Minnesota: A History*. New York: W.W. Norton & Company, 1977.

Oliphant, Laurence. *Minnesota and the Far West*. Edinburgh and London: William Blackwood and Sons, 1855.

Pike, Zebulon. *The Journals of Zebulon Montgomery Pike*, edited and annotated by Donald Jackson. Norman, OK: University of Oklahoma Press, 1966.

Szarkowski, John. *The Face of Minnesota*. Minneapolis, MN: University Of Minnesota Press, 1958.

Willard, D.E. *The Story of the North Star State*. St. Paul, MN: Webb Publishing Company, 1922.

MINNESOTA GEOLOGY AND PREHISTORY:

Bray, Edmund C. *Billions of Years in Minnesota*. St. Paul, MN: Science Museum of Minnesota, 1985.

Ojakangas, Richard W. and Charles L. Matsch. *Minnesota's Geology*. Minneapolis, MN: University of Minnesota Press, 1982.

Sansome, Constance Jefferson. *Minnesota Underfoot: A Field Guide to the State's Outstanding Geologic Features*. Stillwater, MN: Voyageur Press, 1983.

Silverberg, Robert. *Mound Builders of Ancient America.* Greenwich, CT: New York Graphic Society, 1968.

Willard, Daniel E. *The Story of the North Star State*. St. Paul, MN: Webb Publishing Company, 1922.

Winchell, Newton H. *A Report: On the Geological and Natural History of Minnesota.* Vol. 3, Part 2. St. Paul, MN: State of Minnesota, 1897.

RIVERS AND WATERWAYS:

Botkin, Benjamin Albert. *A Treasury of Mississippi Folklore.* New York: Crown Publishers, 1965.

Havighurst, Walter. *Upper Mississippi: A Wilderness Saga.* New York: Farrar & Rinehart, 1937.

_______. *Voices on the River*. New York: MacMillan Company, 1964.

Jones, Evan. T*he Minnesota—Forgotten River*. New York: Holt, Rinehart and Winston, 1962.

Kane, Lucille. *The Waterfall That Built a City*. St. Paul, MN: Minnesota Historical Society Press, 1966.

Lund, Duane R. *Lake of the Woods*. Staples, MN: Nordell Graphic Communications, 1975.

_______. *Lake of the Woods: Earliest Accounts*. Staples, MN: Adventure Publications, 1984.

_______. *Leech Lake Yesterday and Today*. Cambridge, MN: Adventure Publications, 1998.

Price, Willard. *The Amazing Mississippi.* New York: The John Day Company, 1963.

Waters, Thomas F. *The Streams and Rivers of Minnesota.* Minneapolis, MN: University of Minnesota Press, 1977.

________. *The Superior North Shore.* Minneapolis, MN: University of Minnesota Press, 1987.

EUROPEAN EXPLORERS:

Adams, Arther T., Editor. *The Explorations of Pierre Esprit Radisson,* from original manuscript in the Bodleian Library; Loren Kellsen, Modernizer. Minneapolis, MN: Ross & Haines, Inc. 1961.

Neill, Rev. Edward D. *History of the Minnesota Valley.* Minneapolis, MN: North Star Publishing Company, 1882.

Nute, Grace Lee. *Caesars of the Wilderness.* St. Paul, MN: Minnesota Historical Society Press, 1978.

Parkman, Francis. *France and England in North America.* Boston, MA: Little, Brown & Co, 1865-1892. Reprint: New York: Viking Press, 1983.

Severin, Timothy. *Explorers of the Mississippi.* New York: Alfred A. Knopf, 1968.

Syme, Ronald. *Bay of the North: The Story of Pierre Radisson.* New York: William Morrow and Company, 1950.

FUR TRADE:

Gebhard, Elizabeth L. *The Life and Ventures of the Original John Jacob Astor*. Hudson, NY: Bryan Printing Co., 1915.

Madsen, Axel. J*ohn Jacob Astor: America's First Multimillionaire*. New York: John Wiley & Sons, Inc., 2001.

Morison, Samuel Eliot. *The Oxford History of the American People*. New York: Oxford University Press, 1965.

Nute, Grace Lee. *The Voyageur—Reprint edition.* St. Paul, MN: Minnesota Historical Society Press, 1955.

Parkman, Francis. *France and England in North America.* Boston, MA: Little, Brown & Co, 1865-1892. Reprint: New York: Viking Press, 1983.

Stuart, Robert. "How the American Fur Trade Conducted its Affairs." Testament before a Congressional Committee, from *With Various Voices*, T.C. Blegen. St. Paul, MN: Itasca Press, 1949.

Terrell, John Upton. *Furs by Astor*. New York: Morrow & Co., 1963.

Trevor, Robert. *Voyageur Country*. Minneapolis, MN: University of Minnesota Press, 1979.

FRENCH AND INDIAN WARS:

Blegen, Theodore C. *Minnesota: A History of the State*. Minneapolis, MN: University of Minnesota press, 1963.

Folwell, William Watts. *A History of Minnesota, in Four Volumes*. St. Paul, MN: Minnesota Historical Society, 1921-1926. Reprint: St. Paul, MN: Minnesota Historical Society Press, 1956.

Havighurst, Walter. *Three Flags at the Straits: The Forts of Mackinac*. Englewood Cliffs, NJ: Prentice-Hall, Inc., 1966.

Parkman, Francis. *France and England in North America*. Boston, MA: Little, Brown & Co, 1865-1892. Reprint: New York: Viking Press, 1983.

INDIANS IN MINNESOTA:

Berg, Lillie Clara. *Early Pioneers and Indians of Minnesota and Rice County*. San Leandro, CA: Lillie Clara Berg, 1959.

Danziger, Edmund Jefferson, Jr. *The Chippewas of Lake Superior*. Norman, OK: University of Oklahoma Press, 1979.

Densmore, Frances. *Chippewa Customs*. St. Paul, MN: Minnesota Historical Society Press, 1979.

Eastman, Mary Henderson. *Dahcotah or, Life and Legend of the Sioux*. Afton, MN: Afton Historical Press, 1995.

Ebbott, Elizabeth. *Indians in Minnesota*. Minneapolis, MN: University of Minnesota Press, 1985.

Hassrick, Royal B. *The Sioux: Life and Customs of a Warrior Society*. Norman, OK: University of Oklahoma Press, 1964.

Jones, Rev. Peter. *History of the Ojebway Indians*. Freeport, NY: Books For Libraries Press, 1861.

Kohl, Johann Georg. *Kitchi Gami: Life Among the Lake Superior Ojibway*. St. Paul, MN: Minnesota Historical Society Press, 1985.

Meyer, Roy. *History of the Santee Sioux*. Lincoln, NE: University of Nebraska press, 1968.

Nelson, Bruce. *Land of the Dacotahs*. Minneapolis, MN: University of Minnesota Press, 1946.

Robinson, Doane. *A History of the Dakota or Sioux Indians*. Aberdeen, SD: State of South Dakota, 1904. Reprint: Minneapolis, MN: Ross & Haines, Inc., 1956.

Utley, Robert M. *Frontiersmen In Blue: The United States Army And the Indians, 1848-1865*. New York: Macmillan, 1967.

Warren, William W. *History of the Ojibway People*. Reprint: St. Paul, MN: Minnesota Historical Society Press, 1984. Originally Published by Minnesota Historical Society, 1885.

TERRITORY AND STATEHOOD:

Hall, H. P. *H. P. Hall's Observations: Being More or Less a History of Political Contests In Minnesota from 1849 to 1904*. St. Paul, MN: H.P. Hall, 1904.

Hall, Steve. *Fort Snelling: Colossus of the Wilderness*. St. Paul, MN: Minnesota Historical Society Press, 1987.

Hansen, Marcus L. *Old Fort Snelling, 1819-1858*. Iowa City, IA: State Historical Society of Iowa, 1918.

Sibley, Henry Hastings. *The Unfinished Autobiography*. Minneapolis, MN: The Voyageur Press, 1932.

Swanholm, Marx. *Alexander Ramsey and the Politics of Survival*. St. Paul, MN: Minnesota Historical Society Press, 1977.

West, Nathaniel. *The Ancestry, Life and Times of Hon. Henry Hastings Sibley, LL.D.* St. Paul, MN: Pioneer Press Co., 1889.

Ziebarth, Marilyn and Ominski, Alan. *Fort Snelling: Anchor Post of the Northwest*. St. Paul, MN: Minnesota Historical Society Press, 1970.

CIVIL WAR:

Bassett, M.H. *From Bull Run to Bristow Station*. St. Paul, MN: North Central Publishing Company, 1962.

Bellard, Alfred. *Gone for a Soldier*. Boston, MA: Little, Brown and Company, 1975.

Botkin, Benjamin Albert. *A Civil War Treasury of Tales, Legends and Folklore*. New York: Random House, 1960.

Carley, Kenneth. *Minnesota in the Civil War*. Minneapolis, MN: Ross & Haines Inc., 1961.

Catton, Bruce. *Gettysburg: The Final Fury*. Garden City, NY: Doubleday & Company, Inc., 1974.

Folwell, William Watts. *A History of Minnesota, in Four Volumes*. St. Paul, MN: Minnesota Historical Society, 1921-1926. Reprint: St. Paul, MN: Minnesota Historical Society Press, 1956. Vol. II.

Hansen, Harry. *The Civil War*. New York: Duell, Sloan and Pearce, 1961.

Imholte, John Quinn. *The First Volunteers*. Minneapolis, MN: Ross & Haines, Inc., 1963.

Johnson, Robert Underwood. *Battles and Leaders of the Civil War. Vol III*. Edison, NJ: Castle Books, 1995.

Kunz, Virginia. *Muskets to Missiles: A Military History of Minnesota.* St. Paul, MN: Minnesota Statehood Centennial Commission, 1958.

Minnesota Board of Commissioners on the Publication of History of Minnesota in the Civil and Indian Wars. *Minnesota in the Civil and Indian Wars, Vol. 1*. St. Paul, MN: Pioneer Press, 1890.

SIOUX UPRISING OF 1862:

Carley, Kenneth. *The Sioux Uprising of 1862*. St. Paul, MN: Minnesota Historical Society Press, 1976.

Flandrau, Charles E. *The History of Minnesota and Tales of the Frontier*. St. Paul, MN: Porter, 1910.

Folwell, William Watts. *The North Star State*. Boston, MA: Houghton Mifflin Company, 1908.

LeSueur, Meridel. *North Star Country*. New York: Duell, Sloan & Pearce, 1945.

Tolzmann, Don H., Editor. *Memories of the Battle of New Ulm*. Bowie, MD: Heritage Books, Inc., 2001.

POST CIVIL WAR:

Blegen, Theodore C. *Minnesota: A History of the State*. Minneapolis, MN: University of Minnesota press, 1963.

Blum, John M. *The National Experience*. New York: Harcourt, Brace & World, Inc., 1963.

Folwell, William Watts. *A History of Minnesota, in Four Volumes*. St. Paul, MN: Minnesota Historical Society, 1921-1926. Reprint: St. Paul, MN: Minnesota Historical Society Press, 1956.

Gelbach, Deborah. *From This Land: A History of Minnesota's Empires, Enterprises, and Entrepreneurs*. Northridge, CA: Windsor Publications, Inc., 1988.

Morison, Samuel Eliot and Henry Steele Commager. *The Growth Of the American Republic, Vol II*. New York: Oxford University Press, 1950.

RAILROADS AND J.J. HILL:

Martin, Albro. *James J. Hill and the Opening of the Northwest*. New York: Oxford University Press, 1976.

Holbrook, Stewart H. *The Age of Moguls*. Garden City, NY: Doubleday & Company, 1953.

_________. *The Story of American Railroads*. New York: Crown Publishing Company, 1947.

Jensen, Oliver. *Railroads in America*. New York: American Heritage Publishing Company, Inc., 1975.

Whitehouse, P.B. *Great Trains of North America.* New York: Crescent Books, 1974.

Yenne, Bill. *Railroads of North America.* New York: Barnes & Noble Books, 1992.

IMMIGRATION:

Ager, Waldemar. *Sons of the Old Country.* Lincoln, NE: University of Nebraska Press, 1983.

Blegen, Theodore C. *Minnesota: A History of the State.* Minneapolis, MN: University of Minnesota press, 1963.

Flom, George T. *A History of Norwegian Immigration.* Bowie, MD: Heritage Books, Inc., 1992.

Friberg, Eino. *The Kalevala: Epic of the Finnish People.* Helsinki, Finland: Finnish-North American Literature Society, 1988.

Geiske, Millard L. and Steven J. Keillor. *Norwegian Yankee.* Northfield, MN: Norwegian-American Historical Association, 1995.

Gudmandson, Wayne. *Testaments in Wood: Finnish Log Structures At Embarrass, Minnesota.* St. Paul, MN: Minnesota Historical Society Press, 1972.

Holmquist, June Drenning, Editor. *They Chose Minnesota.* St. Paul, MN: Minnesota Historical Society Press, 1981.

FARMING:

Letterman, Edward J. *Farming in Minnesota.* St. Paul, MN: Ramsey County Historical Society, 1966.

Jarchow, Merrill E. *The Earth Brought Forth: A History of Minnesota Agriculture to 1885.* St. Paul, MN: Minnesota Historical Society Press, 1949.

FIRES:

Carroll, Francis M. and Franklin R. Raiter. *The Fires of Autumn.* St. Paul, MN: Minnesota Historical Society Press, 1990.

Holbrook, Stewart H. *Burning an Empire.* New York: Macmillan Company, 1943.

Swenson, Grace Stageberg. *From the Ashes.* Stillwater, MN: Croixside Press, 1979.

LUMBER INDUSTRY:

Andrews, Ralph W. *Timber.* Seattle, WA: Superior Publishing Co., 1968.

__________. *This Was Sawmilling.* Seattle, WA: Superior Publishing Co., 1957.

Hidy, Ralph, Frank Hill and Allan Nevins. *Timber and Men.* New York: Macmillan Company, 1963.

Kohlmeyer, Fred W. *Timber Roots.* Winona, MN: Winona Historical Society, 1972.

Larson, Agnes. *History of the White Pine Industry in Minnesota*. Minneapolis, MN: University of Minnesota Press, 1949.

Minnesota Department of Natural Resources Report. *Minnesota White Pine*. St. Paul, MN: 1996

Salmi, John. *Minnesota Lumberjack*. Detroit, MI: Harlo Press, 1971.

IRON MINING:

Bayless, Willard. *The Discovery of Iron Ore and Development of the Mining Industry at Chisholm, Minnesota*. Unpublished, undated manuscript. Duluth, MN: St. Louis County Historical Library.

DeKruif, Paul. *Seven Iron Men*. New York: Harcourt, Brace, 1929.

Gelbach, Deborah. *From This Land: A History of Minnesota's Empires, Enterprises, and Entrepreneurs*. Northridge, CA: Windsor Publications, Inc., 1988.

Lager, H. E. *Happy Depression on the Range*. Virginia, MN: Range Printing Company, 1979.

Longyear, Edmund J. *Mesabi Pioneer*. Edited by Grace Lee Nute. St. Paul, MN: Minnesota Historical Society Press, 1951.

Nute, Grace Lee, Editor. *Longyear: The Mesabi and Beyond*. Gilbert, MN: Iron Range Historical Society, 1984.

Sloane, Howard and Lucille L. Sloane. *A Pictorial History of American Mining*. New York: Crown Publishing, Inc., 1970.

Walker, David A. *Iron Frontier: The Discovery and Development of Minnesota's Three Ranges*. St. Paul, MN: Minnesota Historical Society Press, 1979.

Wall, Joseph Frazier. *Andrew Carnegie*. New York: Oxford University Press, 1970.

NORTHERN MINNESOTA CITIES AND TOWNS:

Blacklock, Craig and Nadine Blacklock. *The Duluth Portfolio*. Duluth, MN: Pfiefer-Hamilton, 1995.

Carey, John R. *History of Duluth and Northern Minnesota*. Duluth, MN: Duluth News Tribune, 1898.

Cooley, Jerome. *Recollections of Early Days in Duluth*. Duluth, MN: 1895.

Hecimovich, Stephen. *A Town Is Born: The History of Buhl*. Buhl, MN: 100th Year Anniversary Publication, 2000.

Karni, Michael, Editor. *Life on the Industrial Frontier of Northeastern Minnesota*. Chisholm, MN: Iron Range Research Center, 1991.

Krier, John G., Compiler. *Hibbing: The Richest Little Village*. Hibbing, MN: Hibbing Historical Society, Inc., 1981.

Sandvik, Glenn N. *Duluth: An Illustrated History of the Zenith City*. Woodland Hills, CA: Windsor Publications, Inc. 1983.

Skaurud, Marvin. *A History of Virginia, Minnesota*. Thesis. University of Minnesota, Minneapolis, MN: 1941.

Van Brunt. *Duluth and St. Louis County, Minnesota*. Chicago, IL: The American Historical Society, 1921.

Woodbridge, Dwight E. and John S. Pardee, Editors. *History of Duluth and St. Louis County*. Chicago, IL: C.F. Cooper and Co., 1910.

Works Progress Administration. *The W.P.A. Guide to the Minnesota Arrowhead Country*. St. Paul, MN: Minnesota Historical Society Press, 1941.

IRON RANGE LABOR STRIFE:

Berman, Hyman. *Education for Work and Labor Solidarity: The Immigrant Miners and Radicalism on the Mesabi*. St. Paul, MN: Unpublished Study in Minnesota Historical Society Press.

Bernstein, Irving. *Turbulent Years: A History of the American Worker*. Boston, MA: Houghton Mifflin Company, 1970.

Dubofsky, Melvyn. *We Shall Be All*. Chicago, IL: Quadrangle Books, 1969.

Eleff, Robert M. "The 1916 Minnesota Miner's Strike Against U.S. Steel." *Minnesota History* 51(2): 63-74, 1988.

Fraser, Steven. *Labor Will Rule*. New York: The Free Press, 1991.

Lens, Sidney. *The Labor Wars*. Garden City, NY: Doubleday & Company, Inc., 1973.

Lillie, Ronald George. *The International Workers of the World and the Strike of the Iron Ore Miners of Minnesota in 1916.* Graduate Research Paper. Bemidji State University, Bemidji, MN: 1979. On file at the Iron Range Research Center, Chisholm, MN.

Millikin, William. *A Union Against Unions.* St. Paul, MN: Minnesota Historical Society Press, 2001.

Roedinger, Dave. *Fellow Workers: The Life of Fred Thompson.* Chicago, IL: Charles Kern Publishing Company, 1993.

West, George P. "The Mesaba Range Strike," *New Republic*, September 2, 1916.